i'm glad about you

i'm glad about you

THERESA REBECK

G. P. Putnam's Sons
New York

PUTNAM

G. P. PUTNAM'S SONS
Publishers since 1838
An imprint of Penguin Random House LLC
375 Hudson Street
New York, New York 10014

Library of Congress Cataloging-in-Publication Data

Rebeck, Theresa.
I'm glad about you / Theresa Rebeck.
p. cm.
ISBN 978-0-399-17288-5 (hardcover)
1. First loves—Fiction. 2. Man-woman relationships—Fiction. I. Title.
PS3568.E2697I47 2016 2015025079
813'.54—dc23

Printed in the United States of America
10 9 8 7 6 5 4 3 2 1

Book design by Jennifer Daddio / Bookmark Design & Media Inc.

For Rima Horton
A great reader
And a great friend

i’m glad about you

part one

one

"BUT WHAT IS a *demimonde*, anyway?" said Alison.

The guy she was talking to, someone named Seth, smiled like he knew the secret answer to that. He wrote a column about celebrity bedside reading for *Vanity Fair* and his name had shown up once even as a byline on a feature for that esteemed publication. Alison did not fully realize the import of this accomplishment but he did.

"*The* demimonde, actually," he told her. "There's only one of them, grammatically speaking."

"What?" said Alison, confused.

"The demimonde. It's called *the* demimonde. Not like *a* demimonde, not a demimonde like there's a lot of demimondes and this might be one of them. There's only one to begin with, so it's *the*."

"Is there only one of them if you're speaking any other way?" Alison asked.

"Apparently not; it's all the same demimonde, no matter where you find it," he noted, pleased with the inane complication that had grown like a flower out of his correction of her grammar. "It's okay," he told her kindly.

"What's okay?"

"That you didn't know."

"That I didn't know that people call it *the* demimonde?" she asked.

"I just mean, you don't have to be embarrassed," he said.

"I'm not," she replied, unembarrassed. The pleasure he had been taking in the grammatical discussion was fleeing quickly, and in fact it was occurring to him that the young woman was not quite as attractive as she had seemed mere moments before. She smiled at him with that sort of absurd warmth that transplanted Midwesterners tossed about New York like an unappreciated breeze. Because of that *Vanity Fair* byline, in addition to his rangy height, he was used to having a different effect on the women upon whom he bestowed his attention in social situations. Usually they sparkled more, with a charming willingness to acknowledge the sexual undertones of any discussion and the innate superiority of his position in the demimonde. He had often mocked them, frankly, to his male comrades, for that very thing—their eagerness to attract was, finally, a bit of a bore, he thought. But this girl, who was clearly some sort of nobody, didn't get any points for avoiding all that. She was unsettling. Attractive, but not attractive enough to get over that bump of her own sense of equality.

"Should I be embarrassed?" she asked. She sipped one of those relentless glasses of white wine and grinned slightly while tilting her head, so that she had to glance up at him under long dark bangs. Her eyes were a startling green and they looked like they were laughing at him, but not unpleasantly. This was actually better flirting than he'd had in months. Why didn't he like it more?

"No, no," he said, but a whisper of polite dismissal had snuck into his tone. It smacked her enough for a crinkle of worry to appear between her eyes, and he felt bad. He felt bad! This girl was really no fun at all.

"Oh, well. Oh! Okay," she said, recovering from the startling appearance of male aggression over what to her, frankly, seemed like a nearly nonsensical discussion. Her friend Lisa had invited her over just a few hours ago for drinks in her loft, which wasn't actually a loft; it was more like sixteen square feet and a skylight. And now a total stranger was clearly miffed with her because of some weird obsession he had with the demimonde, and whether or not it was "a" demimonde or "the" demimonde. *This isn't eighteenth-century France,* she thought. *Who gives a shit?*

"Well," she laughed, opting for good humor, "I did know generally more or less *about* the demimonde. I was an English major in college and we tossed the whole thing about during one *endless* class on Trollope and I finally figured it out, that there really is only one in general, that it's a general sort of thing. But it's not a bad question, 'the' versus 'a.' I just never quite put it all together so specifically. Until tonight! Thank you so much for clearing that up."

This was, of course, both completely true and utterly sardonic, but the wry amusement of her tone didn't win her any points. These seemingly simple situations were frankly problematic for Alison, whose untamed heart and effortless intelligence combined to create an unfortunately toxic cocktail for a certain breed of male ego. An ex-friend of her ex-boyfriend Kyle once told her that he got sick of how she had to show off how smart she was all the time. It was an irrational misreading of her character—Alison wasn't particularly interested in showing off; she just was not a fool and felt no need to pretend to be one, under any circumstances or for any reason. Unfortunately, her ex-boyfriend's ex-friend was not the only male creature who had ever mistaken this trait for something less defined and more blameworthy.

"Where was that?" Seth the OCD word fanatic asked.

"Where was what?" Alison asked, confused again.

"Where'd you do your undergrad?"

"Undergrad?" she repeated. "Oh, I went to Notre Dame."

As soon as she had admitted this, she wished she hadn't. Having arrived in New York only five months before, she was already acquainted with the eagerness with which those interminable Ivy Leaguers pried into the facts around your college education just so they had an excuse to bludgeon you with their own. And she had stepped into his trap! "Let me guess. You went to Harvard," she said, beating him to the punch line. She tilted her chin at him, aiming for charming defiance.

"Well, yes, actually," Seth admitted with a nod. Unfortunately, the charming defiance didn't manage to outshine the leaden fact of Notre Dame. He glanced over her shoulder, to see if anyone more worthy of his attention had drifted into view behind her. She hated New York at times like this, so full of intellectual phonies desperate to take any opportunity to assert their superiority in ways that, honestly, would have been considered just rude in the Midwest. "Guess they weren't supposed to let girls from Ohio into this particular corner of the demimonde," she told him tartly. "A Harvard boy who writes for *Vanity Fair*, how on earth did you get stuck talking to a loser like me?"

"Just lucky, I guess." He shrugged, playing the double negative now. "And what do you do, Alison?"

She looked him straight in the face. "I'm, actually, I'm an actress." She tried to keep her confidence up but she knew how idiotic this would sound to him, or anyone, in point of fact.

"So how is that going for you?" he asked, with deliberate disinterest. *Too bad*, she thought. *I thought he was kind of cute.* He was already someone she had known in the past. "I'm going to get another glass of wine," she told him.

"Terrific," he noted flatly. It was so dismissive she blinked a little, and took a step back. He had turned away, and was saying hello to some other loser friend of Lisa's, a girl with an eager smile and enormous breasts. Alison felt her heart constrict with a tinge of fear and disappointment. *Whatever, he's a creep,* she told herself. Then she pushed through the bitter little crowd of young professionals who had gathered for a fun evening in Lisa's ugly and overpriced apartment, trying to get to that table in the corner where people had dumped the wine bottles they'd delivered as party gifts.

"You met Seth!" Lisa exclaimed, sticking her head out of the closet-sized kitchen and raising her eyebrows with smug, conspiratorial glee. "He's so fabulous. Really it is ridiculous how successful he is, he has his own column for *Vanity Fair* and he's had pieces everywhere, I think he's doing something for *Vogue* right now. Maybe GQ. Or that piece maybe already came out, I can't remember. He's very prolific and he knows a ton of people plus *I* think he's really hot, he's so *tall.* His family has buckets of money, his father is something huge at Goldman Sachs and you should *see* where he lives in Tribeca."

"Goldman Sachs is like the institutional version of the anti-Christ, Lisa," Alison reported with an air of sincere regret that this fact had somehow escaped her friend's notice.

"I'd put up with people calling me the anti-Christ if I had money like that," Lisa tossed back at her.

"Yeah, well, I think your friend mostly wanted to get laid, so it's fine. I'm from the Midwest, we don't do that on a first date," Alison reported. "Plus he's an asshole."

"No, he's great!" Lisa insisted, pretending that Alison's position on sex with strangers was so outdated and ludicrous she didn't even have to acknowledge it. "He's juggling a lot of different commitments, magazine people have to have so many things going on that sometimes it takes them a little time to unwind and just be themselves. Plus he told me he just got here from a big meeting with the *Times* Sunday magazine, which he's been really worried about . . . So he's probably still just thinking about that; he's under a lot of pressure because so much is happening for him right now. And tomorrow he's running out to the Hamptons, his parents have a place in Amagansett and there's some big family party he has to go to."

Alison could not for the life of her understand why going to a party in the Hamptons tomorrow might be considered an excuse for lousy behavior today, and she sincerely wished that she might be asked to care more about the young man's character than his résumé. But Lisa's attention had moved on to other subjects. Alison watched as her friend found herself caught in a web of arms and hands reaching desperately for the half-empty bottles of cheap wine, which cluttered the table behind her. Lisa was an elegant, slender blonde who moved with an amused grace through the center of it all. The apparently ravenous young professionals who surrounded her were consuming a simple tray of grapes and cheeses in mere seconds in a piranha-like frenzy. Blonde Lisa laughed with delight and threw her hands up in a gesture of mock despair. "I never get enough food," she admitted happily.

In the Midwest, there's always enough food, Alison thought. She thought of her mother's housewarming parties, where neighbors who had known one another for thirty years would gather on the back porch and talk about golf scores and school functions and the weather. Her mother would serve hot hors d'oeuvres, sesame chicken with a honey-mayonnaise dressing, toasted cheese rounds, and everyone's favorite, sausage balls, a spectacular concoction made of grated cheddar, Jimmy Dean sausage, and Bisquick all mashed together and cooked in the broiler. Then Mom would load the dining room table with platters heaped with sliced ham and turkey and roast beef, alongside a breadbasket filled with miniature sandwich rolls, around which she had curled lovely little dishes of ketchup and mustard and even more mayonnaise. And down there at the far end of the table, a big bowl of salad for anyone who was maybe thinking of trying to eat healthy. After everyone had gorged themselves on sandwiches and finger food and a few bites of salad, there would be plates of cookies and brownies and, if Aunt Sis was coming, a chocolate sheet cake, or an extra plate of those crazy peanut butter cookies with an entire Hershey's Kiss shoved into the middle of each.

Beside the memory of this plenty, the one platter of Brie, Swiss, crackers, and seedless grapes that Lisa had bought at a deli two blocks away looked exactly like what it was—lame. It was already finished off a mere thirty-five minutes after the first guests had arrived; the piranhas had swept it clean and moved on to the consumption of more wine and booze, of which there was a river.

Lisa picked up the empty platter and held it over her head. "Go back and talk to Seth," she ordered Alison.

"We didn't like each other, Lisa," Alison said clearly, hoping this would put an end to the discussion.

"You talked to him for three minutes! You have to try harder, I mean it. I've been in New York a lot longer than you and I know what's out there. Trust me. He's the only guy in the room smarter than you." Having delivered this pronouncement with definitive finality, she sailed off into her minuscule kitchen.

He's not smarter than me, Alison said to herself. Which, she admitted in her proud and lonely heart, was the problem.

two

"NO, HE *DOESN'T* have a temperature but he's been extremely fussy for five days, it's been five days and his nose is running non*stop*," the determined woman announced. She clutched a miserable two-year-old on her knee and talked over the kid's head impatiently, like he was some kind of unmanageable ventriloquist's dummy, although he was really quite patient, Kyle noticed. Not listless, just tired. Slightly heightened color in the cheeks but no tears or frustration, no fussiness whatsoever. "I saw Dr. Grisholm last week and *he* said that it was a virus and there's nothing anyone can do for a virus but this has been going on much too long and he needs an anti*bio*tic. I don't know why you people can't just prescribe that stuff over the phone, it's not going to hurt *anybody* and we *need* it and I'll tell you I know you make us come down here to pick up the prescription just so you can charge us for the office visit and it's ridiculous, the way you are *gouging* us when all we need is an antibiotic! He's sick! He's really sick! And I'm tired of all this messing around with the insurance company. If there was someone to complain to I would, I would really complain but, well, you've fixed that, haven't you, no one is even allowed to have an *opinion* without being *charged* for it."

Kyle reached out his hands with a gentle confidence, holding them open toward the child with a simple gesture. "May I?" The bottle-blonde mother was only too willing to get the kid off her lap. She handed him over abruptly. The baby looked up with mournful brown eyes as Kyle swung him through the air with a breezy lift—that always made them grin or giggle, no matter how bad they felt—and set him on the edge of the stainless steel counter, rather than the examining table. They liked that too.

"Is that safe?" the dreary mother asked.

"It is when you have a big boy, like Joseph, who's not reeeeally sick," Kyle observed, ruffling the kid's curls easily, like he was some kind of pet dog. He floated his fingers under both sides of the boy's jaw, palpating the glands so gently the kid thought he was being petted. The little boy looked up at Kyle with contented adoration while Kyle carefully wiped his nose with a Kleenex. "Let's just take a peek into your brain here, Joseph, just for the heck of it," he said.

"I don't care what you do 'just for the heck of it,'" the mother snapped, refusing to fall for the young doctor's charms. "As long as I get a prescription."

Kyle cupped his left hand around the child's chin, to hold his head steady, while he gently inserted the otoscope into the tiny ear. It took only seconds to record the tinge of pink around the drum and the suggestion of a clear discharge; it wasn't much but it did put forward the possibility that the cold might be moving into the ears, and he might in fact assuage the woman with a scrip for Zithromax without completely compromising his principles. Even as the thought passed through his consciousness, he regretted the impulse. There was no question that antibiotics were still rampantly overprescribed in children, they rarely did any good, and the consequences both immediately, in terms of diarrhea and other digestive disorders, and in the long run—ever more refined strains of bacterial infection which increasingly resisted these previously effective treatments—were not insubstantial.

"Has he been pulling at his ears?" Kyle asked, hoping the hideous mother might provide him with more reason to just do what she wanted, so that he could be done with this.

"I don't know. Maybe. Why can't you tell if he even has an ear infection? Isn't that what that thing is for?"

The woman was awful, no question. That didn't mean he could do something his medical training warned him would be potentially damaging to her child.

"There's some indication of a slight infection but honestly I'm not convinced this is bacterial," he started, cautious. "Unless it develops further there's really no indication that an antibiotic is going to do anything more than give him a stomachache, on top of the cold. I'm inclined to agree with Dr. Grisholm; it's probably viral. In a couple of days I think you'll start to see some improvement."

The horrible mother didn't go for it. He had known she wouldn't. "I came *down* here," she informed him, her voice rising. "I came all the way down here and all you can do is tell me he's sick? That's ludicrous. And you know I'm going to be charged for this, there will be a *co*pay, or a de*duc*tible, and I didn't want to come *anyway*, I *said*, 'Just give me the prescription!' And your nurse—whatever her name is, on the phone, she was the one who in*sis*ted he had to be seen by a doctor and now I came all the way *down* here to be charged for *nothing*? Are you kidding me? I mean, seriously, are you kidding me?"

"I'm giving you my best advice," Kyle began again.

"Your best advice is not what I want," she informed him. She took a step forward, reaching out to snatch her child back from Kyle's now-suspect care. Startled by the suddenness of her move, he took a step backward and relinquished the boy without argument. "I want to see another doctor," the woman announced. "I want another doctor!"

She had not yet made it out the door, but her voice was loud and had already breached the privacy of the examination room. Kyle knew that she was well within her rights to ask for a third or even fourth opinion on this matter, and that as soon as she had stepped out into the hallway with her impatience and her complaints, the nurses and aides on shift would scurry about and do her bidding, avoiding his gaze as they bowed to the patient's right to usurp his authority. He also knew there were two other doctors present in the building who would have little trouble issuing a scrip for Zithromax, which is the easiest thing in the world, without even examining the child.

"Could someone help me here?" she yelled. It was excruciating, watching her swing that kid to her shoulder just roughly enough to startle tears and a wail of anxiety out of him. She tossed a contemptuous gaze back at Kyle, as if to accuse him of making her child cry, and turned the doorknob uselessly, while she struggled to bend over and pick up her purse, a brown-and-black designer sack which clearly cost a fortune while simultaneously looking like knocked-off sophomoric junk. He had known girls in college who carried bags like that, from which experience he also knew that women who carried designer bags were not to be messed with. In addition, he was aware that if he didn't issue the prescription and someone else did, the office manager, Linda, would make note of it in the daily report she emailed to the local headquarters of the HMO which administrated their practice. And then that report would worm its way through seventeen levels of health care bureaucracy, before winding up as a reprimand in the file they kept on him and examined every six months when his performance came up for review.

The kid was wailing. The horrible mother was hissing a long string of complaints under her breath as she struggled with the kid, the designer bag, and the doorknob. It wasn't worth the headache. "I'm happy to give you a prescription, if that's what you want," Kyle said, without inflection. He reached into his jacket and pulled out a pen. "I just wanted to make sure you understood the drawbacks."

"I understand the drawbacks for you, if I don't get that prescription," she snapped back. He stopped, pen in midair, and stared at her. If he was going to be bullied into writing a scrip against his better judgment, he was not going to let her be hateful about it. They stared at each other for the briefest of instants before she smiled tightly and nodded. "Sorry. I am just really on my last nerve. You know how it is when your kid is sick! Just everything wears you out."

"Of course," he said, pulling out the prescription pad and scribbling silently. He ripped the top page off and handed it to her. She took it with little grace, but then, he offered it with none. With his left hand he reached behind him and opened the door for her with the careless ease of a magician. The casual gesture revealed her wild struggle with the doorknob for what it was: cheap drama.

Completely fried, and it was only two o'clock. His shift went until seven. Most of the young patients of Pediatrics West were brought in by women like this one, upper-middle-class suburbanites who didn't have the good grace to be thankful for the money and the schools and the parks and the half-acre lots every single house stood on, much less the immediate access to health care anytime some kid looked sideways, or sneezed. The whole northwestern suburban sprawl around Cincinnati was a veritable slap in the face to Betty Friedan and the seminal revelations of *The Feminine Mystique.* It was 2012, and these women were perfectly happy to have their husbands run off to high-paying jobs halfway across town, leaving them bored and alone with children whom they didn't like and who didn't particularly like them back. As long as the money came in and they didn't have to do anything for it aside from wiping noses and making lunch, they were content in a kind of nasty, she-devil way. Again Kyle felt a pang of guilt as soon as the snarling judgment flitted through his consciousness—there were plenty of women whom he knew personally who were vastly more caring than this harridan—but he had little time with which to berate himself for the quick spite of his exhausted brain. In the waiting room, the bedraggled crowd of infected kids was stacking up. He had to stop thinking and move on.

"Kyle?" A voice behind him shook him out of his tailspin and he turned, the gentle, practiced smile which was his physician's calling card at the ready. The woman who stood before him returned it with a good-natured sincerity which shamed him in its innocence. "I thought that was you! Do you work here?"

"Mrs. Moore, hello!" Kyle felt a fast and fierce jolt in his heart, which he quickly moved past as he shook her hand with his best presentation of calm competence. "Yes, I'm doing my pediatrics residency here. What, what are you doing here?" He looked around quickly to see if she was somehow attached to any of the sick children—or the young mothers—in the waiting room but she laughed and shook her head. "Howard has been having some trouble with kidney stones, and he is really in a lot of pain; it's been horrible, he can't keep the painkillers down, he just vomits up everything," she said, assuming like everyone that any doctor must be interested in the most intimate facts of even a near-stranger's health. "He's been seeing Dr. Drake, in the urologist's office down the hall, but he couldn't even get out of bed this morning, so I had to bring in the urine sample."

"Oh, I'm sorry to hear that," Kyle told her, sounding sorry.

"My daughter Megan—do you remember Megan?—she's due with twins in two months and she's been looking into different pediatricians and I thought I'd just stop by here. I told her that there's a big pediatrics office right down the hall from your father's urologist, you should look into that too because that's so close! I didn't know you were here, I'll tell her I saw you."

"Please do." Kyle both wanted to flee and couldn't bring himself to move. Just standing there and listening to Mrs. Moore's chatter brought back for him a rush of affection for this woman, who had fed him dinner, served him tea, listened to his dreams, and kicked him out of her house more than once during four long, tumultuous years of his youth. "It must be so nice for your parents to have you right in the neighborhood!" Mrs. Moore continued. "Your sister is still here as well, isn't she? I think I heard from Louise Breslin that she saw your sister, she's living in Clifton!"

"Susan is a nurse, she's over at Good Sam," he reported.

"Your parents must be so proud," Mrs. Moore noted. Then, quickly, a shadow of some grief passed over her face; she was not the kind of woman who knew how to hide feelings; she never had been. "You know, until Megan moved back, not one of my children stayed in Cincinnati. Not one! Last year, I was so mad at all of them!" She laughed self-consciously, as if to let him know that this wasn't the life-crushing disappointment she had just admitted it was. "The Dilmeyers, did you go to school with any of them? Ten children and *all* of them stayed here! Margaret Dilmeyer can't stop bragging about it, she has twelve grandchildren already, I hear about it *all* the time. I don't mean to complain; I'm not complaining! Well, I'm glad that Megan's here, at any rate. She just moved back! So that's nice. Your parents must be so happy, to have you both living in the same city."

"I think they enjoy it, yes," Kyle acknowledged. He was touched by her confession and leaned back on his left foot, acknowledging with that simple gesture that he didn't really have to run off; he had a few minutes to chat. "But everyone's well?" He wanted to suck the words back into his soul as soon as he had uttered them.

"Oh, they're all great. Just great!" she bubbled, a conscious brittleness entering her tone. "Jeff is in Germany, of all places, on a Fulbright. He's got all this research with DNA. Nobody knows what he's talking about half the time but he's successful. He's always being published in big science magazines. *Nature.* He's got an article in that one, coming out, he's really proud."

"Well, I don't actually know a lot about research publications but I know that a Fulbright is a big deal," Kyle said, grateful that she had had the good grace to pretend that he actually cared about Jeff, her patently favorite son. Both of them knew there was really only one of her eight children in whom he had any interest at all. But he really had to get out of these waters before they got any more perilous. The nurse at the desk had raised her eyes impatiently more than once, and he could tell from her familiar tics that she was about to butt in and embarrass him for taking five minutes off to chat with an old friend, when the waiting room was turning into a veritable petri dish of infected toddlers. "It's great to see you," he told her. "Please tell Mr. Moore I hope he feels better. Kidney stones are no fun."

"Alison's still in New York!" she announced. He wished he could have kept his heart from hammering in his chest, but barring that, he could at least control any sign of interest in this line of discussion. He had known as soon as he saw Alison's mother that he would not get out of this conversation without hearing about her, but that didn't make it any easier when it finally happened. He forced a nod which he hoped carried with it an air of professional disinterest.

"Yes, I had heard that," he said politely.

"She's still crazy about this acting thing, but she hasn't had much luck yet," Mrs. Moore continued. "A couple of *auditions.* It's a big deal, apparently, even getting into the hallway out*side* the auditions. She has lots of stories, it's a big adventure, I understand that, but I finally said to her, don't you have to actually get *in* something, a television show, or something that pays you something, isn't that the point? Well, that wasn't the right thing to say, obviously. But I'm worried. You can't blame me for worrying. She has no money. She was working in an office for a while but she didn't like that, I guess there were a lot of people there who were really unethical and they expected her to do things that just bothered her too much. She wouldn't tell me anything specific. Anyway, she finally quit that and now she's waitressing for some company that does private events. So she makes a lot of money when they call her but they only call her once in a while and I think she should get a real job, something with health insurance, but she says she went to New York to act. But she's not doing that either! At least in Seattle, she wasn't making any money but she was *acting*, which I thought you won't get anywhere by acting in Seattle, but in New York she's not even doing that much." All of this information was excruciating to Kyle. He stared at the floor and nodded diligently, hoping that she would somehow understand that she was making him miserable, and do the decent thing and shut up. She did not. "She hasn't asked for money," the woman continued, again offering up the most private details imaginable, at the top of her lungs, in the middle of a waiting room full of strangers. "She's too proud for that! She was always too proud, no one could tell her anything. Her father says she's going to have to come to us sooner or later. I wanted her to fly home for the weekend a couple months ago, just to get out of that *city*, and she said she couldn't afford the plane fare! And fares are low now. But she doesn't have any extra money at all. She just can't keep going on with nothing! Her father is really disappointed. She did so well in school, he really thought she might go on and do something with herself. He said to me, it just seems like a waste, a total waste of her time and her twenties. I don't know, maybe she'll get tired of it and come home."

He knew she was offering this possibility to him as a hope. Kyle thought about what to say, as he looked at the floor. There he found something resembling courage and raised his eyes. "I don't," he said. "I hope she finds everything she wants there. Okay, where's Heather?" he asked, glancing at the name on the file in his hand and tossing his question confidently back toward the nurse at the desk.

"She's in four," the nurse replied, sour. Kyle tipped his head toward Mrs. Moore with a quiet nod of respect and left. *If you gave that woman any more leeway*, he thought, *she'd keep talking about nothing for the rest of the afternoon.*

three

"GUESS WHO I saw yesterday!" Rose asserted cheerfully, holding the telephone with one hand while stirring the spaghetti sauce with the other. The pot had been on the stove for two days and the whole house smelled like tomatoes and garlic. There was a pleasant steam floating over the burners.

"I don't know, who?" said Alison. She tried not to sound too much like she couldn't give a shit, but her mother frankly did not make it easy. Rose seemingly could call only when she had some bit of news to report about bumping into some girl whom Alison had gone to high school with, and how well that person was doing, how many children she had or the nice car she was driving. Buried not too deeply in the conversation would be cautious questions about how things were going for Alison in her newly adopted city, Gomorrah.

"I was at the urologist," Rose told her, suddenly feeling the need to draw this out a little. "Because your father was really feeling bad, and they needed a urine sample and he couldn't even keep the pain medication down, he could hardly get out of bed, he was feeling just awful. So I had to take in the urine sample for him. I said, if you're in this much pain you need to go in and see him, but you know your father, he won't be told anything."

"So you saw someone I knew at the urologist's office?" Alison prodded her, trying to get this story back on course.

"Kyle," Rose said.

Really, it felt like a slap, only inside her chest somewhere, an abrupt physical moment of something very much resembling violation. She made note of it in her head: *Someday I might be able to use that somewhere.* She had been to so many acting classes over the past five years, it was ingrained in her thinking now, a sort of double consciousness. Record your emotions. They are your tools. "Kyle," she noted lightly, recovering with a practiced sardonic edge. "What was Kyle doing at Dad's urologist?"

"Well, he wasn't at the urologist," Rose said, stirring the pot both literally and figuratively. "He was at the pediatrics office, down the hall."

"You just happened to stick your head into the pediatrics office, while you were running around Cincinnati with Dad's urine sample?" Alison asked. "This story is starting to sound a bit improbable, Mom."

"Well, it's what happened," Rose informed her, with a slightly superior tone. Alison really did always sound like she thought she was smarter than you, and this time she wasn't. "Your sister Megan is looking into pediatricians and I told her that I'd stop in for a brochure, and there was Kyle. He looks great. He was wearing one of those white doctor coats."

"Wow, he was wearing a white doctor coat! Maybe that's because he's a doctor."

"Well, I thought he looked handsome. And the office was crowded, I think they do well over there."

"Did you ask him what he was doing in a suburban doctor's office outside Cincinnati? I thought he was going to go to South America and work with war victims in refugee camps, that was always his plan,"

Alison noted dryly. She hated the sound of her own voice making fun of Kyle's passionate beliefs, which were beautiful and, she knew, deeply held. But she was also angry with him. She had not seen or spoken to him for almost a year, and the anger had not abated. "What happened to going to the Navajo nation to take care of dying beggars with a bunch of nuns?"

"I didn't ask," Rose said. "Mostly we talked about you." Alison felt her heart start up again. *Honestly*, she thought, *if this phone call goes on much longer I'm going to die from it.* "Look, Mom, I have to go, I have a big audition tomorrow and I have to prepare," she announced. No matter how much she wanted to hear about the man who had completely unmoored her for years, she simply could not let this go on.

"Well, he was interested in hearing about you," Rose continued. "I told him what you were doing up there in New York and I could see how much he wanted to hear about it. You were so foolish to let him go. That boy loved you. I think he still does."

"That boy is married, Mom," Alison snapped. "Did he mention that, while you were chatting him up in the waiting room of his pediatrics practice?"

On the other end of the line, Rose fell silent. "No—why, no he didn't," she said. She was mortified. And heartbroken. "Is that true?"

"He got married last month. Next time, check for the ring."

"Oh, sweetheart," Rose said. "I'm so sorry."

"I can't— Seriously, Mom? I just cannot, I cannot talk about this."

"Oh, Alison," her mother said, honestly woeful.

Alison wanted to slam down the phone and break her mother's unthinking eardrum. This was going to take hours to get over and she really did have a big audition tomorrow and she had not prepared for it yet because she'd had three catering shifts back to back, none of which she had the luxury of passing on at this financially precarious moment in time. "Look, I have to go," she finally said. "I really do, I have to go."

"Okay! Well, maybe we'll talk next week," Rose replied, careening instantaneously into an attitude of maternal good cheer. It was one of her most inexplicable tricks but she used it often, when caught in a bind with one of her children: Just pretend that nothing upsetting was happening at all. Be positive. That was all anyone could do. "You should see Megan!" she announced, falling into the second default position: Change the subject and talk about one of the other kids. "She's really showing now. Those babies are on their way!"

"Yes. Yes, they are." Alison sighed. "Bye, Mom. Bye. Tell Dad I said hi." Panicked now, she felt terrible for having been mean to Mom. It wasn't her fault, she knew. *This is all your fault, and you know it.* "Tell Megan I can't wait to meet the twins!" She wanted her mother to know she cared, she really did. "Another baby, that is going to be so fun. See you later, Mom. Bye. Bye." She hung up.

She glanced back to the hallway, hoping that neither of her largely invisible roommates were in the apartment and listening to her pathetic phone call. There was unfortunately no actual door in the doorway to her room—some previous tenant had made off with it two years ago, for unknown reasons—so the empty door frame stood open to the hall and the small kitchen and living room as well. Which meant, among other things, that you had to keep your voice down if you didn't want anyone overhearing your calls. Unfortunately, Mom was already losing her hearing and when you tried to talk softly she would just say, "I can't hear you!" or "These cell phones are terrible! Can you not afford a real phone?" and then Alison would have to repeat everything extra loudly anyway. Sometimes it bothered her, and sometimes it didn't. Tonight, even though the apartment was practically ringing with its own emptiness, it bothered her a lot.

It was all context. The previous weekend, Lisa's parents had come into town from Philadelphia; they had an extra ticket to a Broadway play and

Lisa had invited Alison along. It was a startling gesture of generosity—Alison was well aware that those tickets were worth more than a hundred dollars apiece, which was why she could never afford to go see a Broadway play on her own nickel. But Lisa's date had fallen through at the last minute and they couldn't return the ticket and, Alison realized, she had somehow become Lisa's pet project, her neophyte friend who needed help adjusting to the trials of a famously difficult city. The invitations from Lisa always came with little lessons about what this event or that gesture meant, in the social fabric of New York. A free ticket to a Broadway play, which would have seemed excessively generous, even unacceptably so, in Ohio, was nothing here. Everybody of a certain class tossed Broadway theater tickets about willy-nilly. To offer to pay for it would be not so much an insult as a faux pas.

So Alison had, after some coaching from Lisa, accepted the extra ticket with good grace and found herself treated to dinner as well, at a rustic and expensive restaurant on a seemingly shitty block of Forty-sixth Street. The decor was unprepossessing but the food was spectacular, and Lisa's father, a tall man with a full head of steel-gray hair, ordered a bottle of Barolo which cost more than eighty bucks. Her mother, who insisted that Alison call her Sally instead of Mrs. Hastings (making Alison feel briefly like the rube she was), wore a sea-green raw silk suit which managed to look both casual and chic. There were no matching shoes or excessive strings of pearls, and her easy grace made her seem almost a regal presence in that crowded eatery. The waitstaff allowed her to change her order four times, one waiter even laughing as he trotted back to the kitchen to stop the chef from tossing her salmon on the grill because she had changed her mind yet again, finally settling on the halibut. Her husband, Alan, was clearly annoyed but he did nothing more than gently chide her by sighing her name, "Sally!" on the fourth go-round.

In between discussions about the wine and the penne arrabiata and the salmon and the halibut, Alan and Sally chatted energetically about art and politics and the foibles of the money market and the disasters emanating from Washington in the name of public policy. They inquired about Lisa's boyfriend, who was in a permanent state of evaporation by that point, which Lisa didn't bother to lie about. Both Alan and Sally expressed complete support for her. They asked about the rounds of auditions Lisa had made in the past few weeks, which were significantly more numerous than Alison's. They expressed more interest in the theater auditions than the television ones, because those were more serious, although even if Lisa landed one of those parts it wouldn't pay her a penny, really. Sally was reading a new novel which had gotten a terrific review in the *New York Times*. She frankly found the book disappointing but wanted Lisa to look at it, to find out if she just wasn't getting something. They talked about the play they were going to see, and how they preferred straight plays to musicals, because the musicals were all so banal and geared too blatantly to the tourist trade.

Next to these people, her own parents were, Alison knew, unsophisticated and boorish. She had never thought of them that way—they were from Cincinnati, for crying out loud, not some hick town in Nebraska—but their suburban manners and Catholic values marked them as surely as one of those Cockney accents leaping like a curse out of the pages of a Dickens novel. She felt mean and disloyal even acknowledging it to herself in her secret heart, but in the circles to which she aspired in New York, her parents were an embarrassment.

It was a horrible thought, but not an inaccurate one. During one of those interminable phone calls from her mom shortly after she had moved to New York, Alison had allowed herself a moment to wander down the hallway, only to catch her two roommates rolling their eyes at each other in comic dismay. Alison might not have put it together even at that point, but when she hung up the phone, Roger the gay chorus boy who had the biggest bedroom actually laughed out loud. "Who was that, your mother?" he said. "She sounds like a nightmare."

"Oh! No, she's all right," Alison said, startled at his assessment. Ginger, also a chorus animal albeit of the busty slutty type, snickered and tossed her gorgeous red-blonde mane about like a pony. Nothing more was said, but Alison tried to keep phone calls from Cincinnati out of the living room after that. She didn't care if they made fun of her mom behind her back, but she didn't want to have to watch it.

They were never there anyway. "We're musical theater gypsies; we're never home," Ginger reassured her. "You'll get tons of privacy." This turned out to be essentially true. The place was small and the public spaces of the building were dirty and ill-maintained but her share of rent and expenses usually didn't top $950, so the room actually was a good deal. Plus, even though it was way over on the west side, it was still in Manhattan. So many of her equally desperate peers had to schlep in from Brooklyn and Queens, which clearly made a schedule of running from one dispiriting audition to another even more exhausting and hopeless. Consequently, until the road tour of *A Chorus Line* burned itself out and their real roommate wanted his shitty little room back, she was one of the lucky ones.

And she did, as it turned out, really have the whole apartment to herself, as Ginger had promised. There was no telling when she or Roger might show up for a few days, gossiping incessantly about what new musical got creamed in San Francisco, and who was having a boob job, and what talent-free television hack had most recently snuck into town and stolen what part from what long-suffering New York actress. They arrived without notice and then disappeared as quickly, leaving leftover macrobiotic takeout, dirty dishes, and quite a bit of smelly laundry in their wake. The first few times it happened Alison was bemused at their careless assumption that she would clean up their abandoned messes, but then she realized they didn't actually make those assumptions because they didn't bother to think about things that deeply. They came and they went. If they arrived home to find mold growing in the sink they would be pissed off, but they never put two and two together in terms of the causal effect of their own inability to clean up after themselves. But the fact was, neither one of them ever missed a rent check. So after they breezed through, Alison cleaned up the kitchen, lugged their sweat-stained leotards and yoga pants down to the laundry room, and, like them, didn't think much more about it.

Truth be told, even though they had virtually nothing in common, Alison came to enjoy the chaotic interludes when her wayward roommates managed to show up. Ginger was correct when she told her that she would have a "ton of privacy"; she had not told her how lonely she would be. Especially now that she didn't have any place she really needed to be, first thing in the morning. Once she had dumped her horrible job answering phones for a bunch of crooks masquerading as real estate agents, she took Lisa's advice and signed with Ponce Gourmet, a specialty gourmet food shop that also booked semi-swank catering gigs in the financial district. Lisa had explained how advantageous such jobs could be for a New York actor, since they booked you only for late afternoon or evening events, leaving the better part of the day available for auditions. Plus you didn't even have to agree to the shifts they offered you—the arrangement was more or less built on your availability.

The downside being, of course, that when they didn't call, Alison had nothing to do all day. More drastically, she also had no income. She had been too shy to mention this concern to Lisa, or the weirdly cheerful booking agent at Ponce Gourmet, because she had already figured out that people in New York actually didn't want to know how poor you were. Being poor was dreary and problematic in this expensive city; you simply had to have money. Everyone was so stressed out by the noise and the crowds and the cars and the enormous buildings and the anonymity of it all that whenever you landed in a restaurant or a store you had to buy something, just to calm your nerves. And there were so many wonderful overpriced dresses and shoes and cocktails and meals to buy. The times she had gone shopping or had a drink with Lisa and her New York posse she was truly alarmed at how casually everyone flashed their credit cards about; most of these women were actresses like herself but they behaved as if they all had trust funds that would never run dry. Occasionally she'd hear one of them worry about cash flow but no one seemed to be constantly reworking the numbers in their heads the way Alison was, wondering if she was going to be able to have enough to pay for her cell phone, apartment, and grocery bills at the end of the month. She couldn't even let herself wander down to a bar for a drink when she had no catering gig, no roommates, and nothing to do on a Thursday night. Her pragmatic brain and what it knew about the basics of economics—do not run up those credit cards—wouldn't let her.

There was of course that scene to prepare. That might take four minutes. She had exaggerated—or, in other words, blatantly lied—to her mother when she called it a "big scene." It was a little scene, a scene so small any bonehead you picked out of a crowd on the street could feasibly do it. It didn't even take up a whole page:

```
EXT. STOOP—CRIME SCENE—DAY

Small groups of bystanders, milling about.
McMurtry wanders through, looking for his
witness.
Spots the Uniform holding her to one side.
He gestures them over.

                    McMURTRY
          She saw something?
```

UNIFORM

That's what she says.

WITNESS

It was just people running.
There were so many people.

McMURTRY

You see a gun?

WITNESS

(scared)

No. Just everybody running, and yelling.
Can I go? My boyfriend's waiting.

McMURTRY

Sure.

She ducks away. A street tough in a sweatshirt waits for her, puts his arm around her, and walks her off. McMurtry looks to Ramirez, who has approached.

McMURTRY

She saw something but she's not talking.

RAMIREZ

No one is.

Alison was auditioning for the part of the witness, a character so unimportant it didn't even have a name. And yet it was a big deal that they had agreed to see her for it. She didn't yet have an agent and no one—not even the girl who sits at the desk outside—would talk to you unless they could see on the list in front of them that you had been submitted by Abrams, or Innovative, or Paradigm, or Writers & Artists. The fact that she was being seen for this lousy two-line part was all due, again, to Lisa, who had called her agent and asked him to get Alison an audition, as a personal favor.

"It was just people running. There were so many people," Alison murmured to herself, to see if there was a rhythm to the language that she might exploit. There was something there, she thought, something deceptively simple but humming with fear. "It was just people running, there were so many people," she said, louder. The grammatical inaccuracy of "it was," the image of the spilling, panicked crowd, then the repetition of that simple word "people." When she tried it a third time, "It was just people—running. There were so many *people*," she felt the whisper of this girl's fear start to curl around her brain. Her eyes drifted down to her next line. "No. Just everybody running and yelling." A breath, a shift. "Can I go? My boyfriend's waiting." Was he really her boyfriend? He was the source of her fear, that's for sure. But that "no" was important; it was the place where she shut down. It stopped her, turned her in a different direction. She was scared of one thing on the first line, and something else on the second. The fear on that second line was a different kind of fear, something more personal and threatening. "NO," she repeated, abrupt, a bit too forceful. Then, with an edge of defiance, "Can I go? My boyfriend's waiting." Alison thought this chick was stupid talking to the cops like that. She toned it down to something more approximating a whine. "Can I go? My boyfriend's waiting." Made her sound like a moron. Alison hated playing scenes like that. Plus it honestly didn't feel right. This girl was scared, first of what she saw, then of something worse. She didn't have the self-control to try to manipulate the cops. "Can I go? My boyfriend's waiting," she insisted, out loud. Forceful was better. She really shouldn't talk to the cops like that, but the fear was fueling it.

Was she making this all up? The scene really seemed like nothing when you just looked at it as a whole. But then when she considered her little piece of it, those few words and what she felt when she said them, it seemed clear there was more there. All those coaches and teachers and directors and acting classes told her the same thing over and over: *Let the words do the work.* Whether it's Shakespeare or *Law & Order*, the words are going to teach you everything you need to know about what to do. That wasn't always true—back in Seattle she had slogged her way through dozens of bad new plays by half-baked young writers who thought they were deconstructing reality when really all they were doing was writing incomprehensible bullshit. In those cases you couldn't let the words do the work because they were never doing anything but floating around the page. But this really did seem like it presented her with something to play. Not much, but something.

She thought she might actually have a shot at landing this one. There were only two lines, and she had heard through Lisa that usually in these situations they let the casting agent just hire a friend, that's how insignificant these throwaway parts were, just a step up from extra work. If they were going to go through casting on a two-line part, they certainly weren't going to waste a ton of time on it. They couldn't possibly see more than three or four girls for something this minor. She might actually get it.

Alison took great comfort in this rigorously argued line of thinking while she channel flipped between news stations (the apartment came with basic cable, and nothing more), then went to bed. She woke early, went for a 7 a.m. run up the West Side Highway and back down Riverside, went home, took a cold shower, ran over the lines again, blew her hair dry, chose a sexy little camisole top to wear over jeans and heels—completely inappropriate for a street kid who maybe witnessed a murder, but she knew not to be stupid and to just wear the sexy outfit—went over her lines again, put her makeup on, and went over the lines again. By that time she was practically chanting them: "It was just people running, there was so many people. It was just people running, there was so many people." It seemed an appropriate mantra for the three blocks she had to walk to the subway, where everybody was, in fact, running, and there were so many people.

When she walked into the holding area for the auditions—a long hallway, Formica floors, plasterboard walls, fluorescent lights, metal folding chairs—her heart sank. So much for her theory that they wouldn't spend an unnecessary amount of time auditioning twenty-something actresses for a two-line part about people running. The hall was lousy with girls of every stripe and color. Tall, short, black, white, Asian, Hispanic, Indian, redheads, blondes, brunettes, a couple with crazy pink and blue streaks in their hair and pierced tongues and noses. As a white girl standing five foot ten, with long shaggy brown hair and a camisole top over jeans and heels, Alison was most definitely among the more conservative choices in this group. She felt her palms start to sweat. *Oh well*, she thought, *just get it out of your head that you could land this. Just do a good audition. Just get them to remember you.* It was pathetic making yourself feel better before you haven't gotten the job, but at the same time it helped. Her brother Andrew was obsessed with basketball, and there was a period of time when he just kept lecturing everybody on the fact that the journey was the goal, and the goal was the journey.

Megan and Jeff finally got sick of hearing about it and yelled at Andrew anytime he brought it up, but that deceptively simple idea had entered Alison's spirit and at times it peeked its head out, when she really needed it. *The journey is the goal, and the goal is the journey*, she told herself. It did; it made her feel better.

She went up to the exhausted metal desk which had been shoved up against the wall at the end of the hallway and leaned in politely to make sure the girl sitting there saw her. The girl was wearing a pink sweater and had loads of Hello Kitty paraphernalia cluttering the corners of her desk. She was all impatience, and elbows.

"Hi," Alison started.

"Just a minute," said the girl, who held up a finger as she made notations down the side of a page filled with names. Alison did as she was told and waited patiently until the girl looked up, sudden. "What's the name?" the girl asked.

"Alison Moore," Alison told her politely.

"We have you down for eleven," the girl reported, reading off the page. She glanced up at the industrial wall clock bolted to the wall right above their heads, which reported that it was only 10:50. The girl at the desk looked at Alison with a raised eyebrow.

"Oh!" said Alison, startled at the accusatory nature of the glance. "Yes, I realize I'm early."

"We're backed up as it is," the girl at the desk reported, as if this fact were also Alison's fault. She ran her pen down the second page of appointments until she found Alison's name somewhere near the middle. "There's no contact information. Who made the appointment?"

"Ryan Jones, from Abrams," Alison stated with brightness and confidence. She was just repeating what Lisa had told her to say.

"Is he representing you?"

"He's hip-pocketing me right now," Alison stated. She barely knew what that meant, but the girl at the desk accepted it and wrote it down. "You have a head shot?" she asked.

Alison dutifully handed over her head shot. It was easily the most beautiful picture that had ever been taken of her. Her long bangs hung perfectly over the startling intelligence of her green eyes, and the way her cheekbones tilted toward the light made her look like she might carry some sort of Cherokee blood in there with all the Irish-English-German–Eastern European mutt that the rest of her was. Her smile was wide and joyful for once, rather than cocky. She looked like a movie star; it was the smartest $1,500 she had ever spent. The girl at the desk didn't even glance at it. "They'll call you when they're ready," she informed Alison. "But like I said, they're already way behind."

Alison nodded politely at this and scooted herself down the hall, to the first open chair that she spotted. She ended up sitting between an ill-tempered Hispanic girl and one of the Goth chicks, the one with blue streaks in her hair. Hispanic girl in a bad mood wouldn't even look at her. Goth chick grinned, hapless, and stuck out her hand.

"Hi, I'm Rae," she informed Alison. "Are you reading for the witness?"

"Yeah," said Alison, appreciating the gesture of camaraderie. "There are a lot of people here."

"For a fucking two-line part! Like, how much are they going to pay if you get it, even, seven hundred bucks? Bite me with your seven hundred bucks."

"Well, I'm just glad they'll see me," Alison admitted. "I'm pretty new here."

"Oh no, totally, you *got* to do it. Got to be *seen*. Those fucking agents, they'll drop you like you got the plague or something, if you can't even get *seen* for this shit. It is such a cataclysmically shitty time. They keep using this shitty economy as an excuse to drop people, my agency, they just let half their client list go. I'm, like, fuck, what the fuck! I don't know why I'm still on the rosters. Last year I had a good year, I ended up with a four-show arc on *Blood Brothers*, that might be why they haven't axed me yet. Who knows. I hope this Goth thing works. It's a totally retarded look I'm well aware but I had to give it a shot. I have *got* to land something."

It was a lot of people running, there was so many people, Alison thought. She watched the far end of the hallway, where a tall skinny blonde in six-inch platform heels swung out of the doorway, looking like she was trying to not look unhappy, while behind her some guy in jeans and a crummy blue windbreaker, wearing a baseball cap, leaned over the girl at the desk to see who was his next victim. "Maria Isabella Rodriguez!" called the Hello Kitty assistant. The Hispanic girl to Alison's left stood slowly, stretched, took a piece of gum out of her mouth, and deliberately stuck it to the bottom of the folding chair she had been sitting on, before strutting down to the waiting auditioners.

"She's going to get it," Rae informed Alison under her breath. "Everybody wants Hispanic right now. Nobody wants a white girl. You would not *believe* how many times my agent told me, you had that except they wanted to go Hispanic. That's why I went for this Goth thing. It doesn't matter how good you are, you got to have a look or thing, something they can buy. You can't just be white. I mean, I'm sure you're good? But you got to know what you're up against."

"Thanks," Alison said. She had been glad enough when she first sat down that this person seemed like a friendly chatter, but now she wished Goth Girl would just shut up. For an instant Goth Girl oddly reminded Alison of her mother, who, the one time she had visited New York, had talked to absolutely everyone she sat down next to on the subway. Rose even showed photographs of all her children to the elderly black woman seated across from her.

"I'm just telling you don't take it personally if you don't get it. That's what I learned from experience, don't take it personally," Rae continued, biting her thumbnail with a worried glance down the hall. The door swung open and the Hispanic girl swished out, moving quickly past them with that continued sour look on her face. "Well, guess that didn't go so good," Goth Girl muttered, clearly pleased. "They don't *always* go for the Hispanic thing. I mean, it's not like you can *count* on that. You have to be *good*. As long as you have a look, something that pops you out, and you're *good*, you got a shot." She was clearly talking to herself now, and had been all along. *It was a lot of people running, there were so many people*, Alison thought. *The journey is the goal, and the goal is the journey.*

"Rae Leavitt," called Hello Kitty assistant girl. Rae stood up and straightened out her skirt, revealing a massive hole in her black wool stockings. She was wearing worn-out red Converse sneakers as well. The Goth thing she had going was a whole look, top to bottom.

"Wow, look at you," said Hello Kitty. "Rich said you were going for something different but he didn't say what."

"Yeah, I thought it might be kind of fun to just switch things up," Rae told her.

"Absolutely," Kitty girl agreed. There was an easy familiarity between them which Alison envied. Goth Girl wasn't, as it turned out, some kind of nut; she was an old hand, just as she had intimated. Alison felt her confidence in her own ability to at least make an impression seep away. *The goal is the journey*, she told herself, but the mantra was wearing thin, a magical spell that was losing its potency through overuse. She looked up at the clock. It was only 10:57.

Even though her appointment was for 11 a.m., they still had not called her name at 12:13. By then the hallway had been drained of its myriad bouquet of female witnesses, and had refilled itself with potential uniformed officers. There was apparently no age or weight restriction involved in the casting of this part—Alison couldn't help but notice that all the actresses who were up for the part of the witness were young and pretty, and all the actors who were up for the uniform were not necessarily either. She knew very well that a television production office was no place to ponder the unfairness of gender politics, but you couldn't help it when the thought wafted through your head, *How come the girls have to be pretty and the guys can look like gargoyles?* One of the gargoyles caught her glancing over at him and he smiled at her, shy and nervous, and she felt a pang of guilt for envying him his bulbous features. He was just another dumb actor who somehow thought that hanging around in a dirty hallway all morning in the hopes of landing a two-line part on a cop show would somehow eventually add up to a life. In other words, he was just like her, only with a big nose.

"Alison Moore." Alison jumped, feeling both frightened and oddly reassured by the sound of her own name floating down the hallway.

"Oh yes, that's me!" she called back, immediately feeling like an idiot. Hello Kitty assistant didn't help matters any by raising her eyebrows in a gesture of obvious sardonic ridicule at how eager this girl without an agent was willing to let herself look. But there was no time, frankly, to worry about whatever the casting assistant might or might not think. The guy in the jeans and baseball cap was hanging in the doorway again, smiling at her. "Hi, Alison," he said, as if there was no one on earth he would rather see. "I'm John Maynard, I'm directing this week's episode. Thanks for coming in."

"Oh, thank you! I mean, thanks for seeing me," Alison replied, fighting her Midwestern impulse to seem overly grateful for absolutely everything. It didn't matter; no one was really looking at her anyway. "This is our producer, Dan Chapek, the writer of the episode, Bill Wheedon, and our casting director, Leslie Frishberg." John the director rattled off the names quickly, as if he assumed she would have no need to remember any of them, but Alison glued the names into her memory nonetheless, nodding quickly to each face at the table with what she hoped was professional charm. The casting director, the only other woman in the room, glanced up from the sheets in front of her.

"Ryan Jones from Abrams is representing you?" she asked, blunt.

"He's hip-pocketing me for now."

"I just saw him yesterday, and he didn't mention you were coming in."

"You'll be reading with Michael," the director noted, uninterested in the casting director's clear if unspoken suspicions. Whether or not Alison and her friend had figured out a clever way to sneak her past the gatekeepers of the casting office to get her a reading for this unbelievably minor part, it wasn't worth the time it would take to call her out on the lie. The crowd of actors waiting in the hallway was, in fact, enormous, and growing by the second. They had to move this ship along.

"Great," Alison nodded, turning her attention to Michael in the corner. He was sitting next to a camera on a tripod, and he looked bored out of his mind.

"Can you slate yourself?" he asked rhetorically. She nodded. "Good. Whenever you're ready." There was no friendly eye contact or extraneous banter. He tapped a button on the camera and flicked his gaze at her, impatient before she had given any cause for it.

"Alison Moore," Alison stated clearly for the camera. Bored Michael looked down at the half page of type in front of him.

"She saw something? That's what she says," he read, and then he glanced up at her, expectant. After all the waiting and hours of obsessive preparation Alison was not, in fact, ready. The stupid jerk had read the two lines together, as if it were one person's line instead of two lines, from two different characters. It threw her for a moment, and she paused, trying to figure out why her cue wasn't the same line she had had memorized. Then when she realized what he had done she had to take a moment to reconfigure how she was going to respond and just say the first line. *It was just some people, people were running*, she thought, but that wasn't it, she knew the rhythms better than the words themselves by this point and those were off; she had momentarily forgotten the lines. And now the whole thing was going too fast. It was only two lines. How could she make two lines work? *How on earth can you be an actress,* she thought, *when you only have two lines?* No wonder her mother thought she was a moron. She was living like a hermit, or a rodent, in a hellish little apartment and spending her whole life worrying about two mediocre lines for an audition for a bad scene in a mediocre cop show. At least in Seattle she was actually acting. Shakespeare and Tennessee Williams and even some Molière, plus all those bad readings by hapless playwrights, which were actually about something even if they were unintelligible. She hadn't been making enough money to feed herself in Seattle, but she was getting out there and putting some art into the world, even if it was bad art. Now she was doing—what was this, anyway? She felt a tremor run through her body. She had given up everything for this, and this was truly idiotic, New York City was filthy and the people rude and spiritless and this whole enterprise was just fucking stupid from start to finish.

"It was just people running," she said. Her own terror and disappointment at the mess she had made out of her young life mysteriously entered the room and hung there. Her weariness was tangible. "There were so many people."

"You see a gun?" Michael asked, completely uninterested.

"No. Just everybody running, and yelling." She felt the tears rise to her face. Why was she crying, why now, why did this have to happen right now? She wanted to scratch her own eyes out but instead she just blurted out the rest of the line. "Can I go? My boyfriend's waiting," she informed the camera, defiant now. She really did; she just wanted to get out of there.

There was a moment of silence. "Thank you," said Leslie the suspicious casting director, dismissing her. Two fucking lines and she hadn't even watched, Alison felt sure.

"That was really great," piped up the writer. "Seriously, that was fantastic." He turned to the director. "That's what I'm talking about," he informed him, firm. "It's only two lines but there has to be *stakes*."

"No, I get that," said the director.

"You can't just throw some Goth girl in this, just so you have something to point the camera at," the writer continued, as if he were in the middle of a private discussion with the whole room. "She's the first indication we get, the way she is acting is the first time McMurtry gets the scent of what might be going on here."

"If it's that big, then *everybody* gets the scent," the director said, annoyed to be having this conversation at all, much less in public.

"What would be wrong with that?" asked the writer. "It's a triple homicide, hello, it's going to make the *Daily News*. There's a whole crowd watching, we're supposed to have something like twenty extras that day." This was important to that guy. Those two lines were everything.

"I just don't see the point of giving the whole show away in the teaser," the director announced. He turned back to Alison, pointed. "Thank you, that really was terrific."

"I'm not saying—that's not what I'm saying," said the writer, frustrated.

"Thanks," said the casting director, as she stood. Alison was clearly being dismissed. She turned, relieved, ready to bolt out of there.

"No, that's—could you wait?" said the writer. Alison looked back, confused. She looked around at the others. Was he talking to her? "Yes, you, I mean you, you should wait. Just wait outside the door for a moment, please," he ordered her. He stood himself, heading toward the closed door with a purposeful authority. "That was terrific, really just wonderful, Alison. I want you to wait right here." He waved his hand vaguely as he opened the door. The gesture would have been dismissive if what he was saying wasn't so pointedly not. As she stepped outside he continued to talk. "The last three episodes came in short, and we're getting hammered by the studio, they want us to come up with scripts that are closer to sixty pages and I think that to do that we have to bite the bullet and . . ." The door slammed shut behind him. Alison stared at it, wondering how they were going to bite the bullet. Hello Kitty girl looked up at her.

"He asked me to wait," she told her.

"Yeah, fine," she said, impatient again. Two looming potential cops hovered over them both, trying to sign in. "I don't know where you're going to sit, though. There's some room down there, you can stand down there." Alison glanced to where she was pointing; it looked like it was in Siberia, it was so far down the hallway. There were at least twenty-five actors in folding chairs, leaning against doorways, a couple sitting on the floor. The place was starting to smell a little too strongly of human sweat.

"She can sit here," said the guy with the big nose, standing politely and offering her his folding chair. Hello Kitty girl shot him a glance.

"Great," she said, although she didn't seem to think so.

"I can stand," Alison informed the guy. Why was he being so polite? She wasn't an invalid.

"No, please," he said, bashfully. Then he shrugged. "I'm from the Midwest. It's what we do."

four

"ALISON MOORE IS going to be on television tonight, did you hear? I saw Eleanor Dilmeyer at Kroger's this afternoon, she heard about it from her mother. They're real excited about it. Alison's hit the big time I guess."

Kyle listened silently as his sister, Susan, puttered around their mother's kitchen, gossiping about his least favorite subject in the world.

"Be careful with that, Kyle, you don't need to *murder* it," Van chided. "My doctor husband doesn't always know his own strength!" She turned to the room with an adorable smile. "Dad, can you do it?" She had recently taken to calling his father "Dad." Kyle found it affected but how would you tell her to stop? His father nodded politely and took the bottle without comment, completing the final two turns of the screw and easing the cork out with a quiet pop. Then he picked up the bottle, leaned over to the counter, and gave it back to Kyle. It was a small, easy gesture but there was no mistaking its intent—*don't embarrass Kyle in front of his folks, now*—and Van didn't mistake it, as a sudden blush rose up her neck. It was a delicate moment, as at times Van's insecurities could be volatile. Before he could reassure her, she went code red, latching on to Susan's news with an excruciating brightness.

"Well, that is exciting, that Alison is going to be on television!" she announced. "I haven't met her yet, but Kyle has told me all about her. The love of his life!"

"You are the love of my life, Van," he laughed, pretending this was easy. "Which would be why I married you."

"Awwwww," said Susan, making an annoying but playful face. "Here, let's drink to that." She grabbed two of the glasses Kyle had already poured, a decent inexpensive merlot, and passed them around. "Here's to Kyle and Evangeline, how many months is it already, Van?" Susan had been the one person who questioned the speed of the engagement and the marriage, and she did so with so much heat that Kyle had actually told her he'd never speak to her again. But when you have only one sister and your parents are in their seventies, forgiveness is more easily accomplished than otherwise. They weren't like some Catholic families, so many kids across so many years that half of them didn't even know all their siblings' names. In a family that size you had the option of letting things fester—Alison had an older sister she hadn't spoken to in years, and when the subject was touched on she could go on for hours; the history of betrayal and mutual dislike was as long and complicated as some bitter Sicilian feud. Kyle and Susan didn't have that choice. She had quickly moved past her objections to the suddenness of her little brother's marriage, and now she was the picture of sisterly acceptance. She went out of her way to tell Van how pretty she looked. She asked Van about her work at the law office. She made approving comments about Van's clothes. Susan's interest in Van's life was terrible in its perfection, but there was no question that she was trying.

Kyle felt deeply the achievement of his parents in these quiet, steady dinners. His father worked full-time well into his sixties as a senior managing officer at a medium-sized firm which made cooling towers. His mother was a cheerful and steady woman who never wavered in her housekeeping or her cooking or her gardening, and all with a perfect hairdo, it was true. The popular media had left these people behind, or somehow managed to make them all look like crazy Republican cranks, an attitude which Kyle found offensive in its carelessness. His father worked hard his whole life, paid his taxes, attended church, and gave money to the poor. That didn't mean he only watched Fox News.

And Van had appreciated them both from the start. Which was, truth be told, not that long ago. Shortly after his last and clearly final breakup with Alison, Kyle had had no plans to pick up a new girlfriend anytime soon. If anything, he was annoyed by the entire gender; all the too-smart girls in his class at med school frankly put his teeth on edge. So when someone calling herself "Evangeline Shelly" texted him out of the blue to ask if he'd like to see a movie with her, it took him a moment to remember who she was. He finally placed her—a dinner party at a friend's apartment, apparently he'd been too stupid to realize he was being set up—but before he could get out of it she had more or less arranged the entire date. The movie was fine, but when he finished the glass of wine she had insisted on after, he assumed he would never see her again. That was when she invited him to spend the weekend at a hotel located on some island in the middle of Lake Erie.

It was such a bold suggestion Kyle had actually laughed at it.

"Why are you laughing?" she asked, tilting her head with a gesture that was both knowing and innocent. "Have you ever done it? You can take a ferry out to Middle Bass Island for seven dollars, there's a terrific old Victorian inn that's walking distance from the pier. I've never been there but it sounds so easy to do, and then you're just out there, in the middle of Lake Erie. Take a couple bottles of wine. I think it sounds fantastic."

Kyle looked at her, aghast, and almost started laughing again. He was used to the boldness of his female contemporaries, and until Alison had completely stomped on his heart he had even enjoyed it. But this invitation was in a league of its own. He thought for a minute that maybe he misunderstood her intentions.

"What would we do out there?" he asked.

"Well," she said, "I think we would go to the inn, drink one of the bottles of wine, and see what happens next."

"Well," he said. "That is a—remarkable proposition."

"Is that a yes?" she asked him, allowing her eyes to stay on his face, unwavering.

"I think I maybe need to think about it," he told her. Which was completely ridiculous, of course, as his erection, fortunately hidden by the tablecloth, was straining at the front of his trousers. This young blonde's direct gaze was proving a welcome assault on his untended manhood; he wanted to have sex with her right then and there. He almost shuddered as her hand crept up his leg and fingered the taut fabric with a light, feathery touch.

"I don't think you should think about it, actually," she told him. "I think you should just say yes."

The fact that there was no romance in this was what, finally, landed him. If this young woman had even once leaned forward, breathless, looking for a kiss, his sore heart would have revolted. But she didn't go looking for kisses, not in the restaurant, and not at the door of her apartment, when he walked her home. She smiled at him mysteriously and shut the door in his face, but by then he had agreed to join her on her proposed expedition Saturday at noon. And while he was more on his guard as they greeted each other on the windy pier, the weekend moved forward as smoothly as anyone might have hoped had they bothered to think about it. Kyle's reluctance was seemingly narcotized by Van's blonde femininity, as well as her unapologetic sexual assurance. She chatted carelessly on the ferry ride and allowed herself to be charmed by the starkly uninteresting resort town. She located the inn quickly and picked up the key to their room without letting the clerk involve them in any needless conversation. And then she didn't bother with the wine. Once in the room, she approached Kyle with that direct gaze, laid her hand on his crotch, and smiled. He hesitated, but only long enough for her to undo the top button of his jeans.

Kyle considered himself a moral person, but as this educated young woman whom he barely knew twisted her fingers into the waistband of his pants he allowed his mind to go completely blank with desire. Acting on an animal instinct which consumed him with alarming speed, he shoved her into the room and pulled her convenient skirt up past her panties, which he forced off her barely in time to push his erection into her vagina. The sex was violent and thrilling, and left both of them exhausted, embarrassed, and hungry to do it again.

By Sunday at 10:30, Kyle and Van had had sex four times, and were trying to figure out if they could go one more round before the inn's stated checkout of 11 a.m. There was no question of love between them, from Kyle's point of view, but if he was not besotted, he was at the very least drunk on sex. He had been living the last year of his life as a monk in a cell, and this blonde stranger had somehow understood how to turn the key. This considerable accomplishment was made easier by one noteworthy fact, of which the blonde stranger was completely unaware: Up until this moment, Kyle had been a virgin.

The fact of Kyle's virginity was neither careless nor accidental. His physical appeal was considerable—many nubile young things had been attracted to him over the years, not to mention Alison, whose passion for him had been consistent, overwhelming, and doomed, in spite of the fact that he returned it. His parents had taught him to respect the church; his teachers had taught him that his destiny was to become a man of God. This he believed not as a simplistic call to vocation, which he had rejected in childhood, but as an overarching commitment to his life's journey. He was no prude, as Rose Moore—who had caught him far too often entwined beyond the place of reason in the arms of her daughter—could attest. But he believed what he was told: Sex is a sacrament, which belongs in marriage. He loved Alison and he refused to have sex with her. For the six years on and off of their volatile courtship, they had explored every possible way to satisfy and frustrate themselves sexually, short of actual intercourse.

Evangeline Shelly's assault on this young idealist's sturdy vow of celibacy would perhaps have been even more assured if she had known all the facts; his hesitancy and confusion were charming enough on their own merits, as was his gratitude when she finally and simply took charge. She moved ahead solely on what she knew, which was that she was lonely, and that men like sex. Her instinctive seduction—so wildly and instantaneously successful compared to the years of Alison's frustration—was as much a matter of timing as it was of approach. Kyle was exhausted, Van was a stranger, he was attractive, she was willing, and he wanted to fuck somebody. While he would never admit it to himself, the level of hostility he bore toward all women at that particular moment was not insignificant. She and Kyle managed to fuck each other one last time before the maid knocked on the door to remind them about checkout, and both of them were so racked with the passion of it that they almost forgot to call out and stop her from letting herself in.

SIX MONTHS LATER they were engaged. It wasn't a shotgun situation; the weekend of fucking out in the middle of Lake Erie had passed by without sexually transmitted diseases or pregnancy, but what it had set in motion was irrevocable nonetheless.

The passing months had only proven to Van what she had sensed from the beginning—that Kyle was one man among millions and she would never find another to match him for intelligence, grace, and steadiness. With him in the palm of her hand she felt herself balanced uncertainly on a tightrope. She actually *didn't* want to be some liberated feminist who insisted on having a career in addition to marriage and children, that sounded like a lot of work and for what? The *law*? She didn't have any passion for the law, finally; the only thing in her life, she felt, that she had ever had a passion for was Kyle. And now she was running around to one interview after another fiercely explaining to everyone why they should hire her for jobs that were boring and didn't pay enough. For months she and Kyle carefully discussed what her options were, what offer was the one she was most passionate about, which might lead to the ideal job, how long they might have to be separated if she took the children's advocate position she had been offered in Pittsburgh, how much commuting would be possible on weekends between Cleveland and Pittsburgh or maybe Cincinnati, if that was where she ended up. She tried to stay focused and discuss these choices rationally but there were so many levels of internal deception involved she couldn't keep track of who should or did care about what. She became dull and evasive. Finally when he asked her what was wrong she burst into tears. The make-up sex was mind-blowing.

And so they decided to move to Cincinnati, where she could become a junior associate litigator and he could do his residency in a major pediatrics partnership in an affluent suburb. Once they had untangled the solution from the endless parade of questions, their sense of relief carried them giddily through planning the wedding, buying dresses, introducing families to each other, and dreaming about their future together. They drove back and forth between Cincinnati and Cleveland dozens of times, looking for the right apartment which would be both cozy and affordable—although both of them would be making a decent wage, they both had substantial student loans to manage. In no time the marriage and the move were accomplished, the apartment was furnished, and the new jobs begun. In spite of obstacles others might have considered significant, Kyle and Van had gotten themselves transitioned into a whole new life without so much as a significant pause.

The one fly in the ointment, of course, was Alison. Kyle would have loved to rub it in her face how effectively he had moved on, but she had made no effort to contact him and he would not be the one to break the silence between them. He suspected that the few friends who were still in touch with her would be filling her in on every detail of his whirlwind marriage and that suspicion provided his heart with the occasional stab of glee. Unfortunately, this was not quite as true for Van. With her easy blonde grace and charm, she was used to having the field to herself without acknowledging even the breath of competition from other women. So no matter how distant her rival was in this situation, the mere fact of Alison's presence—*her significant presence*—in Kyle's past was an unacceptable irritant.

"So Alison Moore is on television tonight," she noted to Susan, pretending to be cheerfully interested and uninterested at the same time. They had moved past the wine pouring and on to the serving of dinner, a lovely pecan-crusted chicken cutlet with a humble mustard-and-mayonnaise sauce. "Can we watch it? Everybody says she's terrific and I've never seen her!" Susan didn't immediately respond. She seemed absorbed by the culinary necessity of moving the chicken onto the plates and then doling out portions of the sauce fairly. So Van's cheery question hung in the air a second longer than it should have done.

"What show is it? *Law and Order*?" his father asked Kyle, as if he were the one who had mentioned it in the first place.

"I don't know," Kyle shrugged. "Susan was the one who heard about it, not me."

"It's one of those crime shows, I can't remember the title," Susan admitted with a sudden unwillingness to share the rest of the details. "Eleanor just said her mom said they were real excited. She thought I maybe had heard about it already."

"Why would you hear about it?" asked Van, a little arch, like this was a stupid thing for other people to assume.

"Cincinnati is still kind of a small town. A local actress on a big network television show, people get excited, although you're right, it's not that big a deal."

"Well, is it a *big* part?" Van asked. Her brittle tone had gone on for really too long now. She was, after all, the one who was keeping this horrific subject alive; it seemed unfair that she would also be so patently annoyed by it.

"Apparently it is a pretty big part, that's what I'm told," Susan responded, the breath of annoyance entering from her side now. Van's bright femininity most definitely had an edge, which someone like Susan was never going to particularly forgive. A nurse, she dealt daily with people who were in a lot of pain, and she didn't like a lot of foolish small talk. Not that Van was a fool. But she was, to Susan, an exquisite annoyance. Susan had a long plain face and a sturdy build, and she worried about being left alone in the world. It galled her that her handsome brother, who could have had his pick of any girl out there, went for this, whatever she was. It also galled her that this Van had clearly gotten Kyle to have sex with her and that his idiotic dedication to their parents' mid-fifties version of Catholicism had doomed him. Susan felt her life moving through her like a curse.

Kyle knew he had to step in and smooth the waters before they got any more roiled in these mysterious female ways. "I talked to Dennis, he talked to Alison last week, and he said that apparently you never really know what's going to happen until it airs." The room fell silent at this, as if he were imparting news of great import. Dennis Fitzpatrick had been one of Kyle's best friends for sixteen years, and he was a great favorite with all the Wallaces. Dennis also had known Alison since the first day Kyle laid eyes on her, and it was to be expected that Dennis would still have some loyalty to her. There was nothing incriminating about Kyle getting information through Dennis. The most natural thing in the world.

"Oh, *Dennis* talked to her?" Kyle's father noted. "And she told him about it?"

"He talks to her all the time." Kyle nodded, trying to match his father's politely disinterested tone. Once again he was embroiled in the last thing he ever wanted to do again, as long as he lived, which was talk about Alison. But this whole sorry conversation was seemingly unstoppable.

"What I don't understand is why all those shows have to be so violent," his mother sighed, shaking her head with a quiet but decisive disapproval which Kyle had learned to dread in his childhood. "Everyone acts like there's nothing you can do about it but I say turn it off! They'll just keep putting that garbage on television unless we stop watching it. There didn't used to be shows like this on all the channels. Now it seems like no matter when I turn it on, it's all killing and shooting and sex. I'm sorry that Alison thought it was a good idea to get involved in something like that. I thought she had more sense than that, I really did." Kyle's mother had never forgiven Alison for breaking her son's heart not once but four or five or six or seven times—who could keep count how long those two made each other miserable? She was a smart girl and pretty and she had had every chance in the world. But there was clearly something wrong with her character.

"Well, we don't actually know if she's shooting people or not, do we, Kyle?" his dad asked with a good-natured contrariness. "Maybe she's getting shot."

"She's not shooting anybody or being shot either, as a matter of fact," Kyle informed them, grinning at his father's subversive levity. "She's a *witness*."

Before Van could react to the fact that Kyle did, actually, know rather a lot about the show, his father stepped in. "So that's not so terrible," he observed, decisive. "A witness is an honorable role to play. We are all witnesses to our Lord and his creation. And now Alison is getting paid for it, which is always a good thing for our young people. Let's say grace." He bowed his head, folded his hands, and eased elegantly into the prayer over the meal. "We thank you, Lord, for this beautiful food, prepared with loving hands by Susan and Margaret for our nourishment. Look kindly on us as we gather in your name, and keep an eye on your daughter Alison, who has run off to the big city to follow her dreams. Some of us think that may have been a mistake and that she will need your guidance there, as we need it here. Amen."

There really was not much you could say to that. Dad started cutting his chicken with gusto and told Susan that it all looked terrific. Susan thanked him and said that she had gotten the recipe out of that church cookbook Mom had gotten from St. Bernard's almost ten years ago now. Mom said something about how many good recipes she had found in that old thing, it was maybe the best cookbook in her kitchen. Van took a bite and told Susan it was so good, she'd heard about pecan-crusted chicken but she'd never had it before, she always thought of it as a Southern dish. Bill started to explain how in many ways Cincinnati really was a Southern city, sitting right there across the river from Kentucky, and how it was one of the first stops on the Underground Railroad. They had a lovely dinner, everyone went home early, and nobody watched Alison make her television debut.

five

"I'M SORRY, what was the question?" Alison asked, confused.

"DID SIMON DILLINGHAM INSTRUCT YOU TO LIE TO THE POLICE OFFICERS ABOUT WHAT YOU SAW OUTSIDE THE BODEGA THAT MORNING?" The ADA was really leaning on her. He was incensed.

"No, he didn't," Alison said, defiant. Tears were streaming down her face. "He didn't tell me anything."

"Permission to treat Miss Garrity as a hostile witness, Your Honor," the ADA snapped suddenly.

"*I'm* hostile," Alison snapped back. "You should look in the mirror."

This brought cheers to the small gang of near strangers who were crowded on and around the bed in the corner of Lisa's so-called loft, watching it all on the flat-screen TV screwed into the wall there. "I can't believe you *improvised* that," Lisa announced, with a tone that was not particularly admiring, in spite of the general approbation of the bed full of people.

"It just came out," Alison admitted.

"You could have gotten fired."

"No one was going to fire her over an improvised line," one of the other actresses, Marnie, observed with a careless tone of dismissal. Some people thought Lisa was too bossy. Now that Alison had actually booked a television job and landed herself an agent, Alison was beginning to find Lisa a bit bossy too.

"They stopped the cameras!" Lisa announced, comically outraged.

"Were you there?" Marnie asked.

"I wasn't there, I'm just telling you what she told me. It was not a good thing."

"People laughed," Alison said, trying to defend herself from, what she wasn't entirely sure.

"The *crew* laughed," Lisa reminded her. It *was* sounding as if Lisa had been there, when in fact she had just hung on the phone, disbelieving, while Alison gave her a blow-by-blow of the day, which had gone well—just as the other three days of shooting had gone well.

"I like crews, they're the nicest people on those sets," Marnie observed.

"They're not the ones who are going to be deciding if they should hire you back," Lisa argued.

"Nobody does that anyway; once you've done a guest spot they don't bring you back ever, or if they do it's not for four or five years." Marnie was like a wayward pit bull in this debate. Alison wished they would both shut up, as the scene was rolling by, unwatched now, on the television set. The rest of the gang was getting impatient with the debate as well. Several people started to shush the speakers and then someone called out, "Back it up, I want to see her tell the DA he's hostile again. It's the best moment in the whole show." Alison glanced behind her to find out who it was requesting an encore of her moment of rebellion and saw that it was Seth, the smug writer who had been snotty about her grammar and her undergraduate education in this very loft, not three months ago. He was squeezed into a corner with his back against the headboard and his long legs dangling off the edge, propping himself up at an awkward angle as he slugged back a bottle of beer. He seemed sincerely amused by all of it. "Back it up, back it *up*," he insisted. "Who has the clicker?"

While several people went diving into the pillows and blankets, Seth caught Alison's glance and raised his beer and an eyebrow at her, not smiling, but impressed. Alison turned to get back to the television set and simultaneously grab whatever refill was being offered, which seemed to be a cheapish sort of half-decent pink wine from Argentina. Lisa had informed her not a week ago that she was happy things had never heated up between Alison and Seth because it seemed that this young paragon was now interested in Lisa herself. Lisa and Seth had gone out for drinks after bumping into each other at a screening; one thing led to another, bodily fluids had been exchanged, and Lisa decided that Seth and all his East Coast promise were not meant for Alison after all.

Under which circumstances Alison was not particularly interested in renewing an edgy flirtation with the guy. It was clear that he was now somewhat more impressed with her dubious credentials as an actress and he was still, as she recalled from her first meeting, pretty cute. But the fact that he seemed to have changed his opinion of her because she was on television just annoyed the shit out of Alison. She was beneath his notice three months ago when she was a would-be actress who had gone to Notre Dame, but now he was interested because she had a guest lead on a mediocre cop show? And this was what passed for intelligence and sophistication in the Big Apple?

As soon as the thought flew by—*mediocre cop show*—Alison felt some part of her surge up with pride and defiance. It *wasn't* mediocre, she told herself; it was crime drama, a time-honored form, and all these people who she barely knew had gathered at Lisa's invitation to watch it.

Two years ago, in Seattle, she and her little band of passionate theater friends spent a lot of time making fun of mediocre cop shows, but for an actress in New York, someone who was actually taking a shot at it, someone who was going to try to make it happen, these shows were bread and butter, and besides, some of the best actors in the country were doing them. The actor playing the surly DA was a huge film and theater star, who happened to work regularly in television as well. There was no selling out involved in this experience. This was a major step up the ladder.

And the part, which had been only two lines when she went in to read for it, turned out to be quite a juicy little nugget of a role. The thing just kept growing. Within a day, there were two extra scenes sent to her Gmail, and by the end of the week there were three more. Each came with a brief notification attached, that all scenes were subject to change, and her new agent, Ryan Jones, warned her numerous times that it was great that the part was growing, but it could shrink just as easily. But it didn't shrink. The witness was given her own name—Elizabeth Garrity—and a backstory: She was dating one of the friends of the killer, who had some sort of "he's my buddy" pact with the guy that was more important to him than anything in the world. There was even a great scene added in which she accused her nasty boyfriend, in front of witnesses, of being in love with the killer. Then he tried to slug her and strangle her, and the cops in the room had to jump him and drag him off. That bit necessitated a fight choreographer who for a couple of shots had the other actor throw her across the desk, but the director thought it was too much and declared firmly that he wasn't going to use any of it.

The whole experience was a complete blast, on top of which they actually *paid* her. She had done a couple of scenes in an independent movie while living in Seattle, so she was already a member of SAG, which meant they had to pay her SAG minimums, eight hundred dollars for every day she was required to be on set. Because the new scenes got added so late, they got shoved into the schedule wherever they fit, which meant that Alison was required to be on the set on four separate days. Which broke down to four times seven hundred, twenty-eight hundred dollars for the whole gig, a figure she never would have gotten if they could have scheduled her scenes more tightly. Ryan wanted them to pay her even more—he tried briefly for the top-of-show rate, which was what anyone with a major guest part should have gotten. But everyone knew this was a huge break for Alison already and they weren't going to go the extra mile for an actress who was such a total nobody. Ryan settled for the $2,800.

Besides which, there definitely was some confusion around the way that audition had been booked. As it turned out, Ryan *hadn't* submitted Alison for the two-liner. His *assistant*, somebody named Darren, was the one who put the call in without running it by his boss, which was why the suspicious casting agent had never heard about Alison from Ryan—because Ryan had never heard of Alison either. Alison didn't even know about this angle of the shenanigans until Ryan called her the next day to congratulate her on booking the gig and to ask her who the hell she was. She told him what she knew, as she had been told by Lisa, about the whole hip-pocketing plan, and Ryan informed her that this was all news to him but that he'd love to meet the girl who had managed to convince a writer to build a whole subplot around her in one audition. Once in his reasonably swank offices, Alison had apologized, but she also was shrewd enough to continue to stick to the point, which was that she had actually booked a pretty big job with very little assistance on anyone else's part. The agent, who *was* in truth impressed, was the one who actually explained to her the whole story—how she had wowed the writer so much that he went ahead and reconceived the entire episode, which never happened, and would not have happened if the script hadn't in fact come in eight pages short to begin with. But that specific detail was neither here nor there. Alison had done what everyone told these young actresses they had to do: Grab an opportunity and make it your own. Ryan Jones signed her on the spot.

As Alison found out later, the reason her episode came in eight pages too short to begin with was that in the middle of November the show was hitting a wall; all the scripts were coming in late, and the executive producer, who was an egomaniac and a prick, had spent too much time rethinking every choice anyone made in any of the episodes that had already been shot and so they were days behind schedule and inches away from shutting down production for a week, which would have cost a complete fucking fortune that the network was not willing to spend for a show that was on the bubble. So while the egomaniacal prick of an executive producer was off putting out fires with the network, the episode's writer was left to solve his own problems. When this young actress showed up and actually gave an emotionally charged reading of two fairly mediocre lines of his dialogue, he felt artistically vindicated and knew that this was his chance to spread his wings.

"Everything was for Billy," Alison told the camera bitterly. "It was always, 'he's my buddy'. You mess with that at your own peril."

"This is it, this is the big scene," the real Alison informed the room.

"Did you feel threatened by that?" asked the ADA.

"I felt disgusted by it," Alison told him. "He was always telling me, 'I love this guy.' He said it so many times I thought, why don't you just sleep with him then." Everyone in the room said "Oooooo," like she had really stepped over the line with that one even though no one could give a shit about implications of homosexuality in New York City. On the television set the scene was erupting. The lousy, threatening boyfriend leaped across the room and started strangling Alison. People cheered. And then when he hurled her across the table—someone somewhere apparently did *not* think that was too much, after all, and they used the more exciting shot—everyone cheered again. All in all, the drunken celebration surrounding her television debut was enormously satisfying to Alison's ego, and she didn't pick up her cell when her mother called because she was having too good a time and she wasn't going to let her mom wreck it with some ill-placed remark.

The party lingered on lazily after the episode's conclusion at 11 p.m.; the young would-be actors and intellectuals gathered in Lisa's apartment insisted they wanted to catch up on the news but once the sound was muted during the commercial break no one really turned their eyes to the screen again. For a short while they drank and chattered cheerfully about Alison's debut and how much fun guest leads could be and what upcoming auditions were hanging out there for her now, and then two by two they drifted away to look for cabs. Not quite ready for her moment in the sun to end, Alison hung around, collecting glasses and empty bottles and organizing the detritus of the evening into a slightly more coherent version of itself.

"Leave it!" Lisa commanded. "Benita comes tomorrow, she's got to have something to do."

Alison raised her hands, leaving the glasses in place. "I always forget you have a cleaning lady," she admitted.

"*Cleaning lady*? Oh God, you are so Midwestern," Lisa tossed back at her, pouring the ends of a bottle of red into a water glass. She staggered a bit as she turned toward the kitchen, where Seth was hanging in the doorway, holding a beer and watching the girls with an amused glint in his eye. The whole scene was a little too Tennessee Williams, Alison thought, but she plowed ahead bravely.

"This was so nice of you, letting us come over and watch the episode together. I hate to leave you with such a mess."

"I said leave it," Lisa told her, picking up several bottles herself as if Alison were bound to do it wrong anyway. While she was fairly sure that

Lisa's snarl had a little more behind it than too much alcohol, Alison was in too good a mood to be wounded.

"Okay, well, I'll call you tomorrow then," Alison shrugged, picking up her jacket—a denim relic from high school, so unchic it actually counted as cool—from the chair by the door, where she had dropped it with her purse three hours ago.

"You're uptown, right?" Seth said. "We should split a cab." He downed the end of his beer, leaned back into the kitchen, left it on the counter, and sauntered toward the doorway. He had framed the announcement with the kind of impartiality that made it impossible to tell if there was any hidden meaning in it, but in the lexicon of young New Yorkers, "We should split a cab" could mean "I find you kind of hot and I'm interested in going home with you if it turns out that something develops in the back of that cab." Or it could mean "We should split a cab." Alison had no interest in splitting a cab with Seth for any reason whatsoever, but there was no way Lisa could read Seth's careless announcement that he was leaving with Alison as anything other than a rejection. At the very least, "We should split a cab" meant "I'm not sticking around to have sex with Lisa, in whom I am less interested than she seems to think."

"Oh!" Alison laughed, trying to sound as uninterested in the subtext of all this as she possibly could. "I was going to stop and pick some things up on the way." This didn't come off as smoothly as she wished; it sounded more like she was making a fake excuse to cover the fact that she was walking off with Lisa's boyfriend. Seth raised that eyebrow again and said, "Well, but you'll still need a cab, I'm guessing." With that he opened the door and with a wave of his hand indicated to her *after you*, as if this dual exit were the most natural thing in the world.

Alison hesitated, then smiled back at Lisa and said, "See you! Thanks again!" which also sounded phony. But there was nothing else for it. She preceded Seth out the door and pushed the button to call the elevator. They both waited in silence while the wall hummed and clicked with the sound of the lift approaching. The elevator door slid open, and Alison silently stepped inside the tiny cubicle, which was lined with faux-wood Formica paneling. She concentrated on the line of buttons in front of her, and pushed "Lobby." There was another tense pause until the door finally slid shut. Seth glanced down at her, grabbed her by the waist of her jacket, and pulled her to him.

"Hey," said Alison. "Hey."

The fleeting worry that this would really piss Lisa off was obliterated by the thrill of having a man's torso up against her own and his tongue halfway down her throat. Alison's brain vaguely noted how quickly Seth's right leg shoved itself between hers as he actually lifted her up against the wall, how his hand slid up the back of her shirt, but after that, her brain went on hold, and there it stayed. Her lonely spirit and young body were severely in need by that point, and the brain's concerns seemed less and less relevant with every passing second in that elevator. Seth was momentarily surprised at the visceral power of that first kiss, and so was she, and the heated cab ride home did nothing to diminish their sudden and demanding physical hunger. So when they finally made it into an actual bed the sex was long, complicated, and satisfying.

After they had finished, Seth stretched his arms toward the wall, yawned, and glanced at the cheap LCD alarm clock plugged into the wall at the side of the low futon. "What time is it, three?" he noted. "Shit, I have to go." He stood, naked, and drifted into the bathroom, peeling off the condom he kept so handily in his wallet. He returned moments later and idly picked up a corner of the strewn sheets and blankets, carelessly searching for clothes which had been torn off in an unself-conscious frenzy hours ago. Reason reasserted itself and as he located his boxers and stepped into them, Seth's maneuvering mind moved back into place.

"That was great," he told Alison, as if to reassure her that in fact he hadn't already forgotten how great it was.

"Thanks," she replied.

"I'll give you a call, okay?"

"You have my number?"

"Oh. No, I guess I don't. Hang on. Let me get my pants on . . ." He slipped into his jeans, and found his socks, barely paying attention to her. "You have a pen?" he asked. "Something to write on? You don't have a card, do you?"

"What? We just had sex so you want my *card*?"

Seth sighed; he remembered this about her now—she was difficult. This really was the problem with so many of these women: They wanted a career and a life in the fast lane and love and commitment and a man who would almost fuck you in the backseat of a cab and then pretend that it was love. He had appreciated the fact that Alison was so receptive to his come-on, and that once things were moving in the right direction she didn't seem all that interested in talk. He regretted the fact that she seemed to want to talk now.

"Look, I said it was great, and it *was* great," he reminded her, successfully keeping the impatience out of his tone. "I want your *number*, I think is what I said."

"Well, I'm kind of lying here naked, so I don't actually have a pen, or a card, on me." She didn't mean to sound like she thought he was an idiot, but there was something about this all that bugged her, even in the languid throes of satiation. She wasn't mad at this guy, she really wasn't; she wanted to tell him how much she enjoyed the meaningless sex, the way he was telling her the same thing. There was something vaguely bemusing about this onset of manners.

"I don't need you to say you're going to call me," she said.

"It's not whether you *need* it," Seth told her, zipping up his fly. "I *want* to. I think you're great. Didn't you think that was great?" *Some writer*, she thought, *the only word he can come up with is "great."*

"It was fucking awesome. I have not had sex that amazing in my entire life," she told him. This was, not to put too fine a point on it, the truth. She had had several on-and-off boyfriends in her years in Seattle, in between the torturous months when she was once again trying to work things out with the insistently celibate Kyle. But none of those guys—and there weren't, honestly, all that many of them—were any great shakes in bed. This so-called writer, on the other hand, clearly enjoyed sex, and he was good at it. Sex with tall, arrogant, self-involved Seth *was* fucking awesome. Unfortunately, Alison's cool tone belied her hyperbole, and Seth heard sarcasm instead of truth in her statement.

"Well—you weren't exactly pushing me off."

"No, I was not pushing you off."

"Oh, brother," he muttered. This chick got under his skin in all the wrong ways. And it was too bad, because she really was great looking—those green eyes were killer—and she was a total animal in the sack. But even after sex that good, she was too much work. "What do you want? You want me to say I'm in love with you?"

"No, I'm not interested in 'love.' I think that's pretty obvious."

"Well, then is there a problem here? I really was going to call you. Unless you don't want me to."

"You know, I don't think I do want you to," Alison admitted. Mere moments before Seth's brain had been busily trying to get his body out the door without committing himself to any future contact with this great-looking actress. But now that she told him she didn't want any contact either, he felt wronged.

"Thanks a lot," he said.

"Don't be mad," Alison sighed. *Boys are morons*, she thought. *They act more like girls than girls do.*

"I'm just confused," Seth continued, trying now to sound more like he gave a shit. "Is this about Lisa?"

"Lisa?" Alison asked. Lisa, she knew, would never forgive her this, but Lisa had already not forgiven Alison for actually landing a part from an audition that she helped her get. Lisa hadn't forgiven Alison her uncool mother, whom she had met and deemed "cute." There were a million things Lisa was already finding unforgivable about Alison, and she didn't even know that Alison had utterly betrayed her by falling into bed with the guy she wanted.

"Look, there's nothing going on with me and Lisa," Seth explained, still miles behind Alison in his conception of this situation. "She wanted you and me to get together, she told me to come to that party, whenever that was back in September, just to meet you."

"The demimonde," Alison murmured, watching him wearily through half-closed eyes. She really wanted this conversation to be over. The guy was racing to get out of there minutes ago; why didn't he just leave?

"Yeah, right?" Seth agreed. For a moment he grinned and she felt the stirrings of interest; his amusement at the memory of that moronic argument was the most personality she had ever seen him express, the few times their paths had crossed. The moment was fleeting, though. He went back to his default position of privileged white male egocentrism with alarming speed. "That's my point. Us getting together was Lisa's idea in the first place. She was disappointed when things didn't click the first time."

"She's not going to be disappointed now," Alison informed him with a sardonic edge.

"She doesn't have any claim on me," Seth said, bristling, as if this were really the problem. "Seriously, I've known her a long time and I like her. We went to high school together! And then one night a couple weeks ago things went a little further than usual, that may be what she told you about. But if she told you it's more than that, she's misguided."

"She does think it's more than that," Alison sighed. "So you maybe will want to clear that up with her."

"I will, I totally will," Seth said, not even bothering to pretend that wasn't a lie. He picked up his shirt and studied the front of it, which seemed to irritate him for a moment. "Shit," he observed. "We actually tore a button off." He glanced around the room idly, as if that might yield the missing button, before turning his ADD attention span back to the girl who was lying naked in the bed. "So I can call you?"

Alison felt the sudden urge to start yelling at this guy; his logic was so utterly fucking self-involved. But she was just too tired. "No, you can't call me," she said. "I did think the sex was great. I wasn't kidding when I said that was the best sex of my life. But even though I like having sex with you, I think you're kind of a huge asshole, and I don't want to have to talk to you again. And even though that probably would work for you? That we never speak but we still get together and just fuck every now and then? I'm from the Midwest and we don't do things like that there. So I don't think you should call me." *That should do it*, she thought.

Seth nodded and then gave a little shrug, while he buttoned up his shirt. He even grinned a little, to himself. This chick was a mess. And the sex was great. The combination had its appeal. He dropped onto the bed, coming down to her level. "You're from the Midwest, but you're learning fast," he informed her.

Which, to his delight, made her smile. The smile was crooked, ironic, intelligent. The green eyes, amazing. "True enough," she admitted.

He kissed her. He was fully dressed now but she was naked beneath him, and the one fast kiss was just hot enough to give him the beginnings of yet another boner. He was starting to like this girl enough to pay attention to the signals, though, and decided not to push it.

"I got to get out of here before this goes any further," he informed her.

"Yeah, you do," she agreed.

He stood, and picked up his shoes. "I can't believe you called me an asshole," he told her.

"You *are* an asshole," she said, but with enough good nature, it sounded almost affectionate.

six

AS USUAL, Christmas was shaping up to be an excessive, loud, crowded food orgy at the Moores' house. Years ago, Andrew, the third of the middle brothers, had taken to declaring, "More is Moore, less is Not Moore!" and while it wasn't the wittiest thing anyone had ever heard, the truth of it was undeniable. Growing up, there were eight Moore siblings, plus Mom and Dad, which made the family ten. But as of this particular Christmas, there were now twenty-three—six spouses, seven small offspring—with Megan pregnant with twins and ready to pop any minute and bring on numbers twenty-four *and* twenty-five. She had taken her husband's name, so there would not *literally* be two more Moores, but there definitely would be two more small people, who had been named "Twenty-Four and Twenty-Five" by the exuberant multitudes which regularly gathered at Rose's house. Megan informed them all that she did not want her unborn children to be treated like a football score, but led by the sardonic Andrew, everyone ignored her wishes and chanted "Twenty-four, twenty-five" every time her swelling belly entered the kitchen or the dining room or the family room or any room where two or more of them had gathered.

Alison frankly found all this joviality tedious. Her brothers and sisters were nice enough individually but there was a pack mentality to these gatherings which left her annoyed and alienated. One person wanted ice cream, so eight people would drive to Graeter's. Some niece or nephew needed new shoes, so half a dozen would end up at T.J.Maxx. Every meal was an endless affair which necessitated at least five people running around Rose's kitchen, cooking the multiple gigantic casseroles necessary to feed the hordes. And the lying around in front of the television set! It seemed at times that all twenty-three of those Moores and subsets of Moores took the holidays to mean, somehow, that the television set should stay on *all the time*. People would drift in and out of the family room watching a nonstop stream of football games, cartoons, and Fox News shows until, after days of this, Alison finally asked, "Can we just turn that thing off for a while?" The six or seven television watchers who were in there all the time were so engrossed in what was on—some cartoon about Christmas—they didn't even answer her. She went back into the kitchen and thought about complaining to Rose and Megan and Andrew and his wife, Stella, but they were engrossed in a conversation about the possibility of going to Skyline for chili later that afternoon, so Alison held her tongue. She knew that complaining about that stupid TV would just make her seem a crank and an ungrateful crank at that, because they all had made much of the fact that she had recently *appeared* on television. If she announced that she just wished they would turn the damn thing *off*, she would open herself to days of good-natured derision about being an intellectual snob who couldn't support herself unless she was on television, which she thought she was too good to watch.

Alison's private speculations about the ribbing she would take under the circumstances were not far off. In truth, the general consensus among the Moores was that Alison was bright but misguided, something of a problem child. She was the only one out of the whole brood who had ever expressed any interest in the arts, and it had marked her as odd and pretentious; she wanted to talk about Shakespeare and analyze movies all the time while they just wanted to relax and watch football and have a couple of beers. She had a famously fractious relationship with her father, who was no walk in the park for any of them, but why antagonize him like that? Plus she and Lianne, the oldest of the younger sisters, couldn't stand each other, which constantly created problems at family gatherings. Alison was the source of so much contention that she had no traction in her family. The only siblings who connected with her were Jeff, her smartypants brother, but he wasn't home this year—he was off doing research on APO-E and DNA repair at some Alzheimer's lab in Heidelberg—and Megan, who was deep in the land that pregnant women went to when they were about to give birth. Alison felt more isolated and blue than ever.

In addition, just before coming to Cincinnati for the holidays she had received an email from Ginger which informed her that their third invisible roommate had decided to leave his tour as of the New Year and needed his room back. Ginger herself was doing some out-of-town tryout in San Francisco, so Alison could sleep in the other bedroom for a couple of weeks, but essentially Alison was going to have to go apartment hunting as of January 1. And she was broke again. Ryan needed her to do new fancy head shots, and he had insisted that she get her hair and makeup done for them. He also pushed her to expand her wardrobe into a more sophisticated and upscale style; there was plenty of work for pretty girls out there but you had to look like money. Looking like money, Alison discovered, cost money, and she had been forced to break her own rule about depleting the bank account and running up those credit cards. It was the worst time possible to be told to move out of that lousy sublet; while she might have the wherewithal to come up with a first month's rent on a new place, she didn't have a penny to put down as a security deposit. She was going to have to ask her parents for a loan.

It was a hideous prospect. The night her episode aired, while Alison was off having a one-night stand with a guy she didn't really like all that much, Rose had called and left a tearful message on her cell about how much her father had liked the show and how he "didn't really understand" what Alison was doing but he was "relieved" to see that she really might be able to make a go of this acting thing. Alison knew that her mother had meant it as some kind of apology but in it she heard all the negative assumptions her parents had been trading between themselves for her entire life. Her father had never been terribly subtle about the fact that he didn't think much of her career choice and that he believed she would never be able to support herself; he also had articulated—publicly—more than once that he doubted she would *ever* find someone who would actually want to marry her. She had to put up with this crap on a regular basis, and then everybody got mad at her when she talked back to him! Whatever. After she and Kyle had finally broken up for good, the sniping had just gotten worse. And now this apologetic message, through Mom, that he was "relieved." He might as well just come out and say that he sure didn't want to be on the financial hook for the rest of his life for his least favorite kid with the lousy rotten attitude who nobody would marry, so it was a good thing somebody finally put her on television. And now she had to ask him for money.

On top of all that she was *starving.* This on the unflinching orders of Ryan: She had to lose fifteen pounds, and keep it off. He was very clear when he signed her about the demands of the marketplace. She was by no means fat, he was not saying that *at all*, but it was his job to be straight with her about what people were looking for, and the fact was that the curvaceous nature of her physical package would not be well received. He didn't want her to get all feminist on him and think that because she looked great that would be enough. He wanted her to be a realist: Theater audiences maybe wouldn't care so much if she looked like an actual woman, but all you had to do was watch one night of television to see what the score was there. Inwardly, Alison flinched when she heard the words "actual woman." It was hard not to read that as a euphemism; he may just as well have called her "chunky." An "actual woman"? The directness of his approach did the job. In November and December she had managed to take off nine pounds with relatively little trouble by reducing her lunch and dinner to virtually nothing while adding three extra four-mile runs to her weekly workout schedule. But she was starting to feel hungry all the time now, and the last six pounds seemed to be just stubborn as hell. And now here she was at Christmas in Cincinnati, where every table was loaded down with homemade cookies and chocolates and pies and cakes, and every meal included bread and mashed potatoes and gravy, and anything healthy—like the occasional vegetable—was drowned in cheese sauce and cream of mushroom soup. She was starving amid a sea of fattening plenty, and it was making her cranky.

But even though she was positively light-headed with hunger all the time now, she had to admit it—when you got extra skinny, you did look great. Her cheeks were defined and chiseled, which accentuated her eyes, and it was kind of fun to feel how loose her jeans had become. Her breasts were no longer as luscious as they had been, which gave her a pang of regret, but this was more than offset by the thrill of actually seeing her ribs when she lifted her arms and looked at her slender new self naked in the mirror. The new clothes and the rail-thin new figure which wore them got her a kind of attention she had never had before. When Andrew picked her up at the airport just two days ago, he had noted, "Well, looks like somebody's been living in the big city," but his tone was not as effortlessly dismissive as she had known it to be growing up. There was no mistaking it: He was impressed. Rose was impressed as well. As

Alison shrugged off her winter jacket, her mother actually exclaimed, "Alison! You're beautiful!" Which frankly didn't suck to hear.

"Alison! Hey, Alison, the phone's for you," Andrew called to her. He held out the beige receiver, which was still attached by a curlicue cord to the functionally ugly phone screwed into the wall at the other end of the kitchen. It took Alison a moment to realize that he was speaking to her; the kitchen was hot, everyone was talking at once, as usual, and recently she had noticed that she was so hungry all the time it made her a little slow on the uptake, like her blood sugar levels were really just too low.

"For me?" That seemed unlikely. "Who is it?"

"I think it's Dennis? Dennis, is that you?" He asked the receiver. A moment later he held it out to her. "It's Dennis."

"Dennis?" she asked.

"Ho ho ho," the voice on the phone informed her with a dry, sarcastic edge. "Merry Christmas, Miss Television Star."

"Hey!" she said. "Dennis, hi, Merry Christmas!" No one in New York ever allowed themselves this degree of unabashed enthusiasm and she sounded idiotic to herself, but it had been a long time since she'd heard from any of her old friends, who, since high school, had drifted irrevocably apart. Parents she couldn't talk to, siblings who thought she was weird, old friends who didn't stay in touch, new friends who came and went too quickly: The past few months she had gone on some major crying jags. But here was Dennis, calling her on the phone. It was fantastic.

"I heard you were in town, my brother bumped into your sister at the mall this morning," he informed her. "Gotta love Cincinnati. Two million people, but everybody still bumps into each other at the mall."

"Which sister?" she asked.

"Who can remember; don't you have like thirty?"

"Four girls, four boys, it's very symmetrical."

"Whatever, there are too many of you. I had it all written down on a cheat sheet in high school but I don't know where it is anymore. How long are you here for?"

"You know, a while," she admitted. "Like almost two weeks."

"Jesus, why?"

"Show business," she sighed. She ducked out into the hallway, pulling the phone cord as far as it would go, which was just inside the doorway of the tiny bedroom around the corner from the kitchen. It was exactly the same routine she had perfected in high school, plopping on the floor and trying to get the door to close even though it never would, because of that stupid cord. Why Mom and Dad didn't break down and buy a portable phone was beyond her. "Everything shuts for two whole weeks around Christmas and New Year's. All the people with money and power go to Aspen or Hawaii, so nobody else has anything to do."

"There's nothing to do in New York City over the holidays? I find that hard to believe."

"No, there's things to do, of course, I just wanted to come home. Let my mom feed me for a little while. Free food." She said it lightly, like a joke, which in fact it was because there was free food everywhere here in Cincinnati but she wasn't allowed to eat it. Nevertheless, there was no reason to hang out in New York, which was truly a cold and dreary place if you had no money and no friends and nothing to do. Plus she had to ask her parents for money. That might actually take the whole two weeks to figure out.

"Well, it's good news for me because I'm seriously bored as shit. I'm quitting my job, I don't give a fuck *how* good the health insurance is, I am *not* working for Procter and Gamble for the rest of my life, or even till I'm thirty. Fuck this fucking bullshit. My dad went to Paris with Felicia and I'm house-sitting, so I'm having a party tonight," he informed her, switching subjects on a dime. "I want to see you, you have to come."

"Oh, a party!"

"Yes, everyone you know will be there."

"I don't actually know anybody in Cincinnati anymore, except for my family. That's what it feels like."

"Well, that's fine because I'm not talking about anybody, I'm talking about Kyle." Dennis tossed this off with the devilish bonhomie which was, in truth, his specialty.

"Kyle and I are done done done, as you well know."

"You and Kyle have been done done done so many times, Alison, I've lost track."

"You don't need to keep track. This time he went and got married."

"So you'll come and say hello and get it over with. Seriously, Alison, both of you are being totally fucking ridiculous," Dennis told her, finally plunging into the heart of the matter. "When was the last time you talked to him?"

"Who cares?"

"It was a year ago *August*. You haven't spoken to him in eighteen months! He's married, you've moved on, you're a big fucking TV star, so fuck him."

"I was on *one* television show."

"You were and you looked fantastic and I loved it when the guy threw you across the desk, it was fucking awe-inspiring."

"Is *she* going to be there?"

"Yes, she is, and she is not going to like you one bit and you are going to *hate* her. You still have to come and just get it over with."

"You said she was nice. When I asked you last year, you said she was really nice."

"What was I going to say? She's a cunt?"

"Is she?"

"Is she a cunt? Absolutely."

In high school everybody's parents loved Dennis because he always knew how to charm them, but, honestly, behind their backs he had the filthiest mouth. He also drank way too much every chance he got; plus he was a total hound. But the charm was quite real and not specifically reserved for parents. Calling Kyle's new wife a "cunt" had a very friendly ring to it.

"Come on, you've got nothing else to do, I can hear it in your voice," he informed her. "You're going to be stuck at home with all those millions of brothers and sisters you never liked and what, seven hundred nieces and nephews?"

"I like my brothers and sisters."

"Well, as my memory serves, they only tolerate you. I want to see you! And everyone will make a huge deal about that television show, I swear all of Cincinnati is abuzz. It's the talk of the town. Wear something hot, you'll totally scare the bejesus out of Van, I can't wait to see it."

"Why would I want to scare her, I don't even *know* her," Alison told him, trying to maintain a shred of maturity in the face of this.

"Trust me, you're going to *hate* her. I think he just married her to get back at you, I really do."

"I could give a shit what Kyle does," she lied.

"Then why am I begging you. Just come. I told Kyle you'd be there, and he's fine with it. You just have to get through 'hi,' which is in fact in your skill set. Besides, you love my dad's house."

"All right, all right, all right," Alison caved. "Fine, I'll show."

She returned the old-fashioned phone receiver to its cradle in the kitchen and reported back to the audience that had appeared in the kitchen.

"Dennis is having a party tonight." There were as usual a mob in there—Andrew, Stella, Megan sitting down, Lianne pouring juice for three toddlers, Mom at the stove. Most of them didn't even hear her. It was the way, finally, you dealt with so many people: You just tuned everything out. Except for Rose, who glanced up from the stove, where every burner was covered with some sort of pot.

"Oh, Dennis!" she said, with a fond interest. She was one of his many fans in high school; whenever he came over to hang out, he flirted with her shamefully. "Where is he living now?"

"You know, I'm not sure. He had a place somewhere over in Clifton for a while, I guess he's still there."

"Maybe you should find out where his apartment is before you go to a party there," Lianne advised. *Pure Lianne*, Alison thought. *Can't say anything nice, and in such a stupid way.*

"He's house-sitting for his dad right now," she announced, as if the room in general had inquired as to Dennis's whereabouts. "In that huge place on Grandin Road."

"Well, the kids wanted to go to a movie tonight, so I don't know what the car situation is," Lianne observed, looking at her mother with a worried parental superiority. Alison wanted to smack her but the truth was that every one of her siblings had assumed that tone one by one, as they started having kids. The unspoken addendum to any sentence being *But the kids might need that!* Alison and Jeff and Megan, the last unmarried Moores, had frequently rolled their eyeballs at each other whenever someone started indulging in the whole *you wouldn't understand because you don't have kids* line of logic. But Megan was married and pregnant now and Jeff was off in Germany. Alison just had to weather this one alone.

"Well, we have Andrew's car and Paul's car and your father's car," Rose informed Lianne. "And your car, right?"

"Do we know if Andrew and Paul are doing anything later on? Weren't some people going to Skyline?"

"Oh, they were going to do that around five, I don't think that will interfere with movie plans."

"Well, that's when we would be going, right *around* five. They're little kids, we need to get them home early, Mom. They need to be in the bathtub by seven thirty."

"How many people were thinking of going?"

"To what, Skyline or the movie?"

"Either one."

"Well, that's my point, it sounds to me like *everyone* is going to one or the other."

"I don't think your father is going to want to go to Skyline, or a kids' movie."

"Okay, then everyone *except* Daddy. That's still *everyone*."

"Except for me," Alison inserted.

"But that's the *point*, it's just *you*, taking a whole car, which would leave us sort of stranded."

"Would it?"

"Our car sits eight," Andrew noted.

"Yes, but you're going to Skyline. Which will leave us with just one of the vans, and Dad's car, and Mom's."

"And Paul's car, right?"

"We don't know what Paul's doing."

"If you're going to the movies at five, it shouldn't be a problem," Alison said, trying not to look like her head was about to explode. "I'm sure Dennis is not expecting anyone till at least eight or nine."

"Well, but we might want to go get a bite after the movie."

"I thought the whole point was to get the kids home early." In spite of her best intentions, Alison's tone shifted into something a shred too aggressive and Lianne bristled. She turned back to the sink, started shoving dishes around loudly, and then she sighed, clearly communicating how selfish she thought Alison was being. Everyone in the room exchanged glances with everyone else while simultaneously avoiding eye contact with Alison, who felt herself immediately in the doghouse for having crossed a line with Lianne even though Lianne was acting like a colossal idiot.

"I think it will be all right," Megan said. "Who knows how long the movie will take, but Skyline is so fast! Those guys will be in and out in no time. If Alison doesn't need the car before six thirty, there should be no problem."

"I don't think I'm going to need it until eight," Alison said, trying to sound innocent and reasonable.

"I just think it helps to plan these things out," Lianne commented. "You didn't tell us anything about a party until just this second, it would have helped to have some warning."

"I didn't know about it until this second."

"That's not my fault."

This could have gone on forever, but the transportation problem was in fact sorted out—everyone made it home from both Skyline *and* the movie by seven—so there were cars aplenty. Alison took her mother's, a sky-blue Oldsmobile a shred less massive than all the other vehicles crowding the driveway, and headed across town to the problematic party—problematic in more ways than one—on Grandin Road.

seven

IT WAS HARD to go inside. She stood for a moment, shivering in the December night and wondering what on earth she was going to say to Kyle when she saw him in the middle of a sloppy crowd of drunks, with a total stranger standing next to him as his wife. The last time they had seen each other—almost a year and a half ago now, in Seattle—she had said unforgivable things to him, and then they had made out on her bed with a loveless fury before he abruptly stood and left the room, her apartment, and her life. The morning after this final encounter, as Alison stepped into the shower, she had stopped, in shock, at the sight of her naked body in the bathroom mirror. Her breasts were covered with bruises. He was willing to maul her, but not make love to her, no matter how desperately they both wanted it.

Why did it finally pervert itself into that disaster? So many other times their connection to each other seemed to make one living thing, something with roots and branches. Everything about their relationship had some sexual element to it—arguing about Thomas Merton and Teilhard de Chardin could still turn her on, because she had spent so many hours listening to Kyle trying to explain why their arcane and mystical brilliance might one day transform the earth into something holy. Then he would run his hands up her torso under her sweater while moving her whole body beneath his own, finally getting her just where he wanted her, before leaning in for his first kiss of the night. It would literally make her see stars. He was a truly gifted lover, if you ignored the fact that there was no genital interaction whatsoever other than the most extended and painful dry humping the universe has ever seen. But they were happy—*they were*—when it all wasn't too dangerous to be tolerated. For the whole time they were together, the agonizing simplicity of their physical connection annihilated what otherwise were real obstacles. He was so fucking uptight about the church. She despised lying institutional hierarchies. He wanted to be a Doctor Without Borders. She wanted to be an actress. Why would anyone think this was ever going to work out? The puzzlement was that it just did.

But now, standing out there on the frozen lawn, Alison remembered the night of their final breakup and the morning after as one long moment of heartlessly cold dismissal. It was the poison that she was left with now. "This is stupid," she muttered to herself, gathering her courage as she stalked toward the medieval manor and the warm chaos of the party within. "Fuck Kyle and his fucking Catholicism. It doesn't matter who he married. What's done is done. I can do this." She was grateful the lawn was so expansive. It gave her time to convince herself that this was true.

Whereas parties at the Moores' were known for the mountains of deliciously trashy appetizers, Dennis's were known for their bacchanalian excess. For Dennis, a party was all about the booze, and he always bought way too much of it: case upon case of European and Mexican beers, enormous bottles of bourbon and vodka and gin and scotch with plenty of vermouth and soda and juices and maraschino cherries and olives and anything else anyone might imagine would be a good thing to toss into a cocktail. No soft drinks, and no wine—if you wanted that, you had to bring it yourself. At some point, inevitably, someone got hungry and sent out for pizza, which everyone chipped in for with a good-natured and very drunk esprit de corps. There would also be some drug action—the occasional joint, one or two people doing lines in the bathroom, maybe a few people dropping Ecstasy—but mostly when you went to one of Dennis's parties, you knew ahead of time that people were going to be getting really drunk. That was the given, even in high school, when some kind of parental supervision might have been expected.

Things hadn't changed. Alison cautiously opened the front door—it had been standing half ajar, so there was no reason really to ring—and for a moment watched a bunch of total strangers laugh and shout at one another. She was glad that she had bothered to put on several choice pieces of her new wardrobe; Dennis was hanging out with people who dressed considerably better than she or any of their friends had in high school. These people had jobs and money and they seemed to think that a Christmas party was the perfect opportunity to show all that off. The house was just as she remembered it—exquisite—although the beautiful lines of the mansion's soaring front foyer were obscured by the numbers of partygoers who truly seemed crushed into every odd corner they could find. Even though this was a fancier crowd, the rules of too much alcohol still, apparently, applied. Everyone was smiling and laughing and flirting cheerfully; they had all already had maybe two or three. It was numbers four, five, and six when things got a little wilder.

But as well as she knew this party, she didn't know any of the players, and for a moment she panicked. It was a learned fear, something that she had just picked up in the past few months. In New York, when you walked into a party alone, you really *were* alone, and unless your host had invited you in order to palm you off on someone who was looking to be fixed up, no one was going to even bother saying hello. Up to this moment, she would have said that Cincinnati truly was different when it came to the party scene; when you arrived by yourself, people would welcome you politely, usher you in, and introduce you to their friends, who would ask engaging questions and try to make you feel at home. But now she wasn't sure where she was. This party looked impenetrable and, given her already heightened nerves, downright terrifying. She almost turned and ran.

"Not so fast," laughed a voice at her shoulder. A hand actually reached out and held her in place.

"Dennis! Merry Christmas!" She smiled professionally. Dennis looked exactly the same, his open and sunny Midwestern grin undercut by skittering eyes which were slightly too obvious in their hunger for things which would be bad for him. His dark hair was still thick, thinning only at the temples, which made him look even more sardonic than he was. He gave her the once-over with that hedonist's appreciation she had seen before, but it wasn't a source of real worry; in the past few years, Dennis was consistently too drunk to really try anything more than an inconvenient grope. In high school, he always seemed radical in his decadence, but it was easy to see now what a coward he was. Flushed with drink, hiding in Cincinnati, working at P&G—and she really had no idea what he did there, since he never shared the specifics—hovering constantly around the wealth and privilege accorded to a father he despised, Dennis was now in the full flower of his weakness. *If he'd left Ohio he would have turned into nothing, but it would have made a man of him*, she thought. *He'll turn into nothing here and it will just make him even more bitter than he is already.*

"You look fantastic," she said.

"Well, you look like a scared rabbit," he told her, with a superior glint in his eye. He kissed her on the cheek, lingering just a second too long.

"I don't know what you mean by that."

"What do I mean by 'scared rabbit'? I mean 'delicious,' Alison; you look good enough to eat. The boots are a terrific touch and they make you nice and tall. Well done. Now, let's get this over with." He put his arm around her shoulder and steered her straight into the heart of the crowd.

"Do you think I could take my coat off and get a drink, Dennis?" Alison laughed. Her heart was literally pounding; she could hear the blood in her ears.

"Absolutely, give me that, and what would you like?" He peeled her coat deftly off her shoulders and draped it over his arm. "Van, you have to meet Alison! Alison Moore, this is Van. Evangeline Wallace, she's Kyle's wife, and she took Kyle's name, isn't that right, Van? Sorry, Evangeline." Alison stared. She had had no idea, honestly, that the interloper wife was standing there, right in front of her.

"You can call me Van," Van laughed. She had a perfect laugh, silvery, delightful.

"Yes, but why would you, if the real thing is Evangeline! Isn't it fantastic, Al, someone in Illinois actually named their kid *Evangeline*."

"Well, I wasn't born in Illinois! We're really transplanted Southerners," Evangeline declared cheerfully. "My mother is from Louisiana." She reached out and shook Alison's hand. Alison shook it back, nodded politely, and hoped that her smile was coming off better than it felt like. She couldn't believe it. Evangeline, or Van, or whatever her name was, was no taller than five foot one, and she had a perfect little peach of a figure. Her skin was a creamy kind of pink, and she had startling blue eyes, a blue so dark it looked like a lake in the mountains in the winter. Her mouth was wide and delicate with a crazy fullness in the middle where the upper lip parted from the lower with an unconsciously lovely lift. This chick was a total blonde cupcake. Alison knew that's what men wanted, how could you *not* know, just growing up in America, that every boy out there innately just wanted some sweet little blonde thing to smile up at him, but *Kyle*? That's what *Kyle* wanted, too?

"I've really been looking forward to meeting you," Alison told her, with what she hoped sounded like sincerity. "I'm an old friend of Kyle's."

"Of course I know who you are!" Van smiled. "I've heard all about you!"

"Nothing too bad, I hope!"

"Not at all. Everyone was so excited when you were on that television show. That must have been so exciting for you."

"It was nerve-wracking, but fun."

"Well, everyone in Cincinnati was talking about it, it seemed like. We were so sorry to miss it. We were having dinner with Kyle's parents and his mom was worried it might be too violent. And who can blame her! It's awful, some of the things they put on television, just ridiculous anymore."

Alison blinked. This last zinger was clearly an uncalled-for dig, although who was kidding who? They both were expected to hate each other on sight, and they most certainly did. She was just stunned that a total stranger would feel free to haul out big moralistic guns about what Alison was doing for a living within the first thirty seconds of conversation. Dennis, watching the whole thing, was practically licking his chops.

"Where *is* Kyle?" he asked. "I thought he was here a second ago."

"Oh, he went to get me a club soda," Van explained.

"A club soda? You're not drinking?" Dennis raised that eyebrow again. It was starting to look like he practiced it, in the mirror.

"No, I'm not."

"It's a Christmas party, you don't want even a glass of wine?"

"No thanks." Her tone was deliberately blank, as if she were landing the words without intent.

"Why, Van, you sly puss." Dennis focused his attention on her with a sudden glee.

"What is that supposed to mean, Dennis?" she countered. "You are always acting like you know some big secret."

"Do you have a big secret?"

"If I did, I certainly would not tell you."

"I'll just get it out of Kyle."

"You will not, because maybe Kyle doesn't know."

"Then there *is* a big secret."

"There's always a big secret."

"Not this big."

"Stop it, Dennis. You're terrible. Where *is* Kyle?" Van arched her neck toward the light, as she looked around with eager delight, trying to spot Kyle in the crowd. Alison knew the whole performance was for her benefit, and in a swift moment of clarity she found it terrifically unfair, that they both thought it so clever to torture her this way. She had never done anything to Dennis worse than refuse to hook up with him while she was in love with the boy he proclaimed was his best friend. And this Van, Kyle's new wife? Alison had never done anything to her at all. Yet here they were, performing an excruciating opera—which centered on the pain they must be causing her—solely for their own amusement.

"I'm sorry," she said, suddenly and completely at the end of her emotional rope. "I'm going to go get myself a drink."

"Oh, let me!" Dennis said, smiling his devil's grin.

"I'm not a fucking child, Dennis; I can get my own fucking drink," she told him, pulling out her potent ability with the word "fuck" in an unflinching warning.

"Well, I guess you need one," he informed her, as bitchy as an old theater queen.

"That's right, I do," she shot back, as she turned away from them both. She knew that this would instantly become a part of the lore surrounding her unpromising meeting with Kyle's idiotic blonde wife. *Good*, she thought.

Across the room and behind a pillar Kyle watched Alison turn, her pride and her anger flashing like a sword in battle. Then, there it was:

The color rose to her cheeks and he recognized the quick shame which overcame her every time she let her temper get the better of her. The sight of her—vulnerable, stylish, alone—unmoored his heart beyond reason. She looked taller, somehow, and more slender than he remembered. Her hair was longer, and cut into subtle layers which revealed the occasional auburn highlights buried in the dark, textured browns. He had told himself, in the past, that those hidden streaks of auburn were his alone; as he came to know every inch of her they had revealed themselves readily to his seeking hands while remaining elusive to the unknowing eyes of others. Now that some clever New York hairstylist had uncovered them with a swipe of the scissors, he felt lost and adrift. Those hidden glints of red were no longer his, and neither was she.

But that was on her; it was all on her. She was always the one to end things, usually with no warning; they would be completely drunk on each other in every way possible, and then it was like she would simply turn the spigot off and disappear inside herself. Then the other Alison showed up, the one who was cold and clinical and determined that it was long past time to end this. That Alison wouldn't even discuss things. It was like dealing with someone who had multiple personality disorder, frankly. He remembered all the times he would show up at her house, or her dorm at college, or that exhausted apartment she shared with those hippies in Seattle. Every time she would open the door, his nerves would stand completely on edge, waiting to find out which one of her was in charge. If she smiled and threw her arms around him, they were going to have an amazing night. If she couldn't meet his eyes, not so much.

But the first Alison—the one he was in love with—always returned to him. That was the reason he held on with such determination, even during the months of separation and break-offs. Those times always seemed to be merely necessary, part of the cost of adulthood, and education. They had fallen in love in *high school*, for crying out loud, and even though they started applying to colleges at the same time, there was no discussion, ever, that they might apply to the same school. It wasn't done. They were too young. Too young and too sensible. His parents had sat him down at the well-worn Formica table in the kitchen and told him soberly that they thought it would be a bad idea; they loved Alison and they knew he did too, but college was a time to broaden your world as well as your mind, and going to school with your high school sweetheart would cut you off from all that. He nodded and accepted everything they said, swallowing the panic that threatened to rise up like gorge from his stomach; he was an essentially obedient young man, and the idea of defying his parents on a point so patently established in the local cultural lore was not in his skill set. When he presented this reality to Alison, she thought about it only briefly, then shrugged. Her parents had not given her the same speech—there was too much chaos over at the Moores' for things like parental guidance, honestly—but she had assumed that this would be the lay of the land.

"Well, if they're going to split us up for four years," she said thoughtfully, "we need to get busy." And with that she climbed onto his lap, straddling him with those long legs, reaching under his shirt, and kissing him with a passion that never ceased to thrill him. They were sitting on a floor in the corner of the Moore family room behind the piano; it was one of the few relatively private spaces in that small house full of people but it wasn't like they couldn't be seen, if someone went looking. Alison didn't care; she never did, even after her mother had found them one night so close to having sex they might actually have fallen off that cliff if Rose's spot-on timing—and enraged disgust—hadn't intervened. Kyle remembered every one of those make-out sessions with a vividness which still frightened him; at night, when he would return to these memories obsessively, living in the heat of the past, he wondered if they would ever wear thin. As of this instant, they had not.

It was a spectacularly delusional dance. He truly hated her, and had already laid full responsibility for the creeping mediocrity of his marriage at Alison's feet. But even as he privately nursed this whisper of blame—for a disaster which hadn't even occurred yet—he simultaneously drowned, every chance he got, in the memories of their time together. Outwardly, no one would ever know. He barely knew himself, the cost of holding those two opposing psychological rivers right up next to each other, day in and day out. But he had a powerful mind, and an even more powerful will, put in place by years of Catholic indoctrination. No one would ever have to know.

The question now, of course, was how to get out of there without having to speak to her. He was furious with Dennis, who had told him in no uncertain terms that Alison had *not* been invited, and that there was no chance whatsoever that she would show up. He was furious with Van, who had insisted on coming even though he tried to beg off a half dozen times, on the off chance that in spite of his protestations Dennis actually might try to pull something like this. And he was furious with Alison, who he knew in his heart had come to check out and judge the woman he had married instead of her. *Instead of her.* He hated thinking of the two of them in the same sentence; his past and his future were completely different lives and there was no point in comparing the two women, and even if he did—*even if he did*—Van clearly was the superior choice. She was more beautiful, and there was a supple grace to her blonde loveliness which was, frankly, relaxing. "Relaxing" was the last word you would use in regard to any aspect of Alison. Van was every bit as intelligent as Alison, if not more so; Alison's erratic emotionalism always crippled her in an argument. And Van was loyal. He knew that she would never turn on him, or abandon him, under any circumstance. The same could not be said of Alison.

Who, at that very moment, was pushing through the crowd in the foyer with an unflinching determination, headed right for him. As soon as the thought flickered through his head he had to deny it: She wasn't technically heading for *him*; she was heading for the bar, and the phony Grecian pillar behind which he had hidden himself was positioned just to its left. Two teenage girls in sexy black barkeep garb poured drinks with a slashing efficiency which was called for under the circumstances; Dennis's new friends from Cincinnati's corporate set were predictably alcoholic and swarming, and Alison was temporarily trapped in their midst. She glanced skyward with annoyance and then, as her eyes raked back down in an attempt to gauge her distance from the bartop, her gaze suddenly and unexpectedly landed on him. Their eyes met.

He plastered a smile on as fast as he could, but it wasn't fast enough. She saw, who knows what she saw, but it was seen before he could hide it. Even now! They were stuck in the middle of a crowd of strangers, they had not spoken or laid eyes on each other for almost a year and a half, and yet he could not escape the terrifying probability that she had once again managed to intuit some unknowable aspect of his interior life. This had proven true so many times that she used to tell him he had a glass head. He felt like he had a glass head now.

"Hello!" he said. It sounded like an idiot was speaking.

"Hello, Kyle," said Alison. She had inched incrementally forward in line and he could see that her cheeks were flushed. That could have been the heat. Or the alcohol. Only she had not managed to get herself a drink yet. It was probably the heat.

"Can I get you a drink?"

"Can you what? Sorry. Oh. Sorry, no, I can get myself a drink, thanks." She squeezed past another stranger. "Besides, you look like you have your hands full." Her eyes flickered down to the drinks in his hand. A wilting cup of club soda and a possibly drinkable scotch, served over ice in a plastic tumbler.

"Right! I need to get this back to, my wife." He stumbled over the words at the last minute. Of course he did. He meant to just say her name, *Van*, just toss it out there casually, the name of the woman he was with now, but then it seemed cold, he needed to do better by her, out of loyalty, and also let Alison know that he regretted nothing, he had moved on, he had a *wife* now, that was his reality, a reality that Alison knew nothing of. Sadly there were too many tumbling worries and the words escaped with that slight stutter step which, he knew, made him sound again like an idiot. He felt Alison's eyes looking straight into his glass head. *I didn't ask for this. Fuck Dennis, and fuck her*, he thought.

"Yeah, your wife, I met your wife, we just met," Alison acknowledged. She had finally maneuvered her way through the throng and secured a spot at the front of the line. "White, anything white," she told the sexy young bartender. "Wait. Anything white that's not a Riesling."

"Chardonnay?"

"That would be fantastic." She smiled politely, but the girl was uninterested in the social niceties; she uncorked the necessary bottle and poured. Alison turned back to Kyle with an air of what she hoped would sound like a sardonic hopelessness. "I love Chardonnay. A nice California Chardonnay, I don't know why people make fun of them, I love them."

"Do people make fun of them?"

"In New York everyone's above them. You're embarrassed to order them. Pinot grigio would be acceptable, if it didn't give you a headache. Sadly it does."

"I'm sorry to hear that." God, he sounded like a complete ass. And even worse, he felt the same way he had the first time he laid eyes on her. He had to get away from her. He couldn't move. Alison accepted her tumbler of white wine from the humorless barkeeper girl and then, scooting to get away from the crushing hordes of desperate alcoholics behind her, she slid to her right, holding the drink up high so that it didn't get bumped. She looked backward as she did—either to keep a lookout for who was pushing her, or so that she didn't have to meet his eyes again—but the maneuver sent her unguarded chest within inches of his. He could smell her.

"Sorry," she said with a tight, polite little smile, as she landed herself on the opposite side of him, where the crowd was less crushing. "I can't believe how many people are here. It looks like Dennis invited half of Cincinnati. And I of course know no one!"

"Yeah, I'm surprised to see you here," Kyle said. She looked at him sharply, like that was the wrong thing to say. Was it? His brain was in hyperdrive but it felt like all the gears had locked up and so the whole operation was just spinning uselessly. Every word he uttered sounded thin, small and phony, while as usual Alison just seemed larger than life. Even though she was tossing off social nothings with no content whatsoever, they sounded like so much more. Her glances all *looked* like so much more. They looked like the glances of someone with a soul. He told himself once again that it wasn't that she was a deeper person; it was just that she was an *actress.* A notoriously shallow and unstable breed. Famous throughout the centuries for bringing men to wreck and ruin. That was all she was, and all she had ever been. An actress with green eyes. *She was just an actress with sensational green eyes.*

"You look tired," she informed him.

Those long years of passion and disaster moved through him as if they were happening now. How could he be expected to even say hello to her if just seeing her in the middle of a crowd did this to him?

"The holidays are always a little stressful."

"Oh yes."

"How's your family?"

"Everyone's great. The house is packed. Megan's about to pop, it looks like."

"Yes, I heard she was pregnant. When's she due?"

"Of course you would ask that. And of course I have no idea."

"Oh. I'm sorry. You and she were so close, I just thought . . ."

"No, you're right, you're totally right. I have been shockingly narcissistic with regard to these babies. Maybe I'm jealous of them. Wow, maybe I am." An edge of painful admission had crept into her tone.

"Of *them*, not her?"

"No, of them. They have her now."

"This is her first pregnancy?"

"Yeah. It's two, even. Twins!" It was a little loud by the bar, and Alison was now studying her plastic cup full of white wine with distracted determination. He wished she would look up at him and tell him that he looked tired again, and ask him why, and let the slightest air of her tenderness breathe on him, even though there was no place for it. "She's one of them now, I guess," Alison said, glancing away, suddenly opting for a lighter tone.

"Excuse me?"

"Megan. She's one of the people who have children and, you know. Turn into zombies."

"I hardly think children turn adults into zombies." He meant to adopt a careless tone, like hers, but it came out sounding superior. He sounded like a superior prig.

"No, no, that's not— Well, it is what I said. I didn't mean— I just meant, at least over at our house, it's all kids all the time, and it kind of distorts. You say, I need a car tonight, and it turns into an endless circular discussion about whether or not some child might need ferrying somewhere in the most abstract and bizarre system of logic imaginable, you know, everything is just kind of . . . You would know better. You're a pediatrician, you would know, I wouldn't know," Alison said, breezing right by the edge of his tone with an easy forgiveness. A forgiveness of what? Of everything? If she forgave him everything, he would go home and hang himself. "Wow. It's great to see you, Kyle," she finished, unexpectedly. "I'm going to see if I can find the bathroom." She swiveled and paused, facing the daunting necessity of somehow plunging herself into that teeming hive of alcoholics, and turned sideways. He could see again, now, how thin she was. She downed the rest of her wine, dropped the cup on the bar, and worked her way into the crowd with a determination which did not look back.

She had made her escape just in time. As he watched her go, someone tapped him on the shoulder. "Is that for me?" Van asked, flirtatiously imperious. She poked her head around and reached for the now-exhausted cup of club soda which he held clenched in his fist. "I didn't know where you went!"

"Sorry, it's so crowded," he started. And then, "I bumped into Alison."

"So I saw."

"Yeah, she said that you guys met."

"Dennis introduced us since you wouldn't."

"I didn't even know she was here," Kyle noted. "Dennis told me she wasn't coming."

"And you believed him? I didn't."

"I guess you're smarter than me, then." He finally took a much-needed sip of his now-watery scotch. It tasted dreadful.

"You didn't tell me how tall she was. She's just *huge*," Van observed, searching the crowd for another glimpse of her.

"She's not *huge*," Kyle replied. "If anything, she's thin." *That ought to shut her up*, he thought. Although Alison certainly was taller than he remembered. During their brief conversation he had been so disconcerted by so many things, he had not considered that she was now looking him in the eye, which might have been part of the disorienting effect.

"I didn't mean huge, I meant tall. Which feels huge to me! She's like a tree, she's so tall. And you're right, she is skinny! Well, I guess if you're an actress you have to worry about all that."

Kyle didn't even know how to respond to that one. He took another hit off his scotch and wondered how much time he had to give to this. He knew that they should leave, that even hanging around this dreadful party would be a bad idea, but he also knew that to suggest such a thing within instants of talking to Alison would be incriminating beyond belief. Then there was also the fact that he couldn't bear to leave. The thought that he might actually bump into her again was humming in every cell of his body. And why shouldn't he talk to her? He was married now. All that nonsense with Alison was finally, blessedly over. He could talk to her. He could see her, and talk to her.

"So did she have anything to *say*?" Van asked. He glanced down at her. Her eyes were glittering with an air of exasperation, as if there were simply no reasonable answer to this, but somehow it was his fault that she had been forced to ask.

"She didn't, really."

"What about you, you apparently had a lot to say."

"'Hello' was actually pretty much the extent of it."

"Well, you talked for quite a while, for two people who have nothing to say to each other."

"Were you watching?"

"I was waiting for my club soda, which took you so long to deliver it's *flat*. So yes, I was watching, and you did more than say 'hello' to each other."

Kyle let that one land for a moment before he deigned to respond to it. This harping about Alison was a repeat offense with Van, and sometimes the best way to deal with it was to let her go too far. The silence bloomed, and he took another sip of his watery scotch. He knew how to outwait her. It usually didn't take very long.

"Well, that's great," she said, glancing away with unmasked contempt. "That's just perfect." He considered letting that hang out there as well, but they were in public, and there was an unexpected ferocity behind Van's agitation.

"I don't know what you're mad at me for," he told her. "I didn't even want to come to this party. That was your idea. As I told you, Dennis said she wasn't coming, I didn't fully believe him, just for the record, I'm not an *idiot*, so I said I thought we should stay home. I said it more than once. You were the one who insisted we come."

"You knew she would be here."

"Oh, for crying out loud. That's— I just told you a moment ago that in fact, I *didn't*—"

"You just said—"

"I *said* I knew there was a chance I was being lied to. But generally I try to assume that I'm not."

"Whatever—"

"Not whatever. No. I was told she wasn't going to be here. That is what we both were told."

"I don't—"

"In spite of which, you, apparently, at least so you say, knew she would be here, and you wanted to come! Insisted on it, in fact. Which, if logic serves, would indicate that you were the one who wanted to see her, not me."

"Maybe logic isn't everything."

"Clearly it's failed us tonight. If you don't want to be here now, we can go home."

"Why, because you can't stand to be in the same room with her?"

"Fine, then let's stay, since we're both having so much fun."

"I have no friends here," Van hissed, furious now. "Everyone is your friend, and they haven't been exactly *welcoming*, so if I get invited to *one* Christmas party maybe I might want to go. Even if your ex-girlfriend is going to be there."

"That's ridiculous," he said. "Everybody loves you. My parents adore you. And Dennis thinks you're great." This wasn't strictly accurate. Whenever they met for dinner, or drinks, or a casual movie, the conversation was cool and impersonal unless Dennis decided that Van needed to be flirted up, in which case all burners went on high. In other social situations Van was effortlessly positive and poised, presenting herself confidently as the working wife of a young doctor in Cincinnati. But that's pretty much where things had leveled off. Kyle told himself it was just a matter of time till everyone got to know each other but even his parents seemed to have settled into a kind of withholding formality. Susan was still trying too hard publicly and not giving anything privately. For all her charms, Van had not been let *in*, and he did not know why. The sudden recognition of the pain and loneliness that this exclusion must be causing her softened the irrationality of his mood.

"Look. We should go," he said. "Really. It's not the *only* Christmas party. And if it isn't going to be fun, I don't see any point in staying." He meant it as a kindness, but Van's eyes flickered at this, settling themselves into some sort of sullen, disappointed rage. Why? He was saying, *I can see that this is no fun for you, let's get out of here.* Why would that piss her off?

Whether he knew why or not, it most certainly had. "I wouldn't want to inconvenience you," she replied. "Besides, if we walk out within instants of your little tête-à-tête with your old girlfriend, people will be gossiping for weeks."

"I can't imagine that people find us that fascinating, Van."

"You can count on it, Kyle," she informed him. And with that she plastered on a lovely, bright smile, and waved her hideous glass of dead club soda at Dennis, who was in fact watching them with a shred too much interest from across the room. "Help! Help!" she called with her bubbling laugh. "He's failed me utterly!"

She was so pretty and impermeable. She said things which were clearly meant to express something about her interior life but he simply couldn't understand what she meant, or even what the words meant. It was like talking to a puppet. It was less coherent than talking to a puppet. With a puppet, you could take things at face value, and interpret backward, to what the hidden meaning might be when you worked what you knew about the identity of the puppet master into the equation. But there was no puppet, no puppet master, only words that indicated emotions in a way which revealed nothing, words which simply mystified the workings of the heart even further. If his head was made of glass, then hers was iron, or stone.

"His interview with the great actress was more impressive than mine," Van informed Dennis, who had joined them behind the pillar. "At least it went on long enough for my club soda to lose all its fizz."

"Well, that's a metaphor if I've ever heard one," Dennis noted.

"You told me she wasn't coming, Dennis," Kyle reminded him.

Dennis smirked. "You needed to get that over with," he informed his friend. He took the weakened scotch out of Kyle's hand and leaned through the people cluttering the end of the bartop to return the empty plastic tumblers to the bartender. "Two Macallans, and we would appreciate a heavy pour."

"I'm driving."

"Van's only drinking club soda, she can drive. Besides, you've earned it. That was hard, seeing Alison, and you both got through it. Well done, Kyle. Well done, Van." Van lifted her chin with the slightest edge of appreciation at this and Kyle recognized that once again Dennis had managed to soothe her agitation with a minimum of effort. How did he do it? What did it matter. He took another hit and let his glance float over the crowd. Alison was nowhere to be seen.

eight

ALISON WAS NOWHERE to be seen because she was literally hiding from him. Her immediate impulse—to find a bathroom and hole up in it—had been thwarted by the crowd of well-dressed Cincinnatians who clustered around the doorways to the two half-baths on the ground floor with drunken determination. So she snuck up to the second floor and down the three successive hallways to the enormous marble bath off the master bedroom in the back.

The way was familiar enough; Dennis had given her a tour of the house years ago, when he was babysitting the place the first time his father went wandering the globe with Felicia. *What a ridiculous episode that was,* she remembered. Dennis had eased himself onto the edge of his father's bed and turned on her, with his practiced and wicked glee. "Come on, Alison," he purred. "Let's have sex on Felicia's duvet." A moment before she had been admiring it—it was made of some sort of shimmering material, pewter gray, ˎdged with muted gold braiding and tassels—but immediately it looked tawdry and like the kind of duvet you'd find in a whorehouse. The room was dark and she became aware, in the stillness which followed his proposition, that she was in fact alone in the house with him. She took a moment to consider a saucy retort, something dismissive enough to buck up her nerves and also shut this whole line of logic down forever, but he instantly misconstrued her silence to express some degree of interest on her part. "God, you're gorgeous," he said, moving quickly down the path of his own desires. He grabbed the tail ends of her shirt in his hand, pulling her toward him with a shred too much force. "You have such beautiful breasts."

"Dennis, for crying out loud, Kyle's your best friend." She shoved him away and took a step backward, out of his range.

"He knows I'm not to be trusted. And if he doesn't know that about you yet, he should."

"Who wouldn't leap at that charming offer?"

A swift anger blew through Dennis's expression. "You, I should think. Aren't you getting tired of waiting for it?"

There was a meanness to this that hit her like a physical blow. Had Kyle talked about their sex life with this most disreputable of all his friends? Why did these two even like each other? Alison knew she'd better get out of there, but she couldn't resist a parting shot. "Wow, what romance. 'Come fuck me in my father's bed.' Maybe a therapist could help you out with this, Dennis," she told him. "Your issues are out of my league." Then she had turned and walked out, and he didn't follow her. And nobody ever spoke about *that* again.

Was the surreptitious disaster of this horrible Christmas party just another one of Dennis's fucked-up games? Kyle, she knew, had been blindsided by her appearance; she could see it in his eyes the instant she caught him watching her from behind that ridiculous pillar—Dennis had once again lied to him thoroughly. Alison couldn't help wondering how that worked, how all those Catholic boys made sense of the many ways they betrayed themselves and their girlfriends and each other every minute of every day. Maybe it had something to do with the way all those self-congratulatory priests lied to them about what it meant to be a "man for God" and then turned out themselves to be thieves, drunks, child abusers, and power mongerers. If the priests are all massive liars about everything, why wouldn't their students turn out to be the same? Kyle would never have tolerated *that* discussion; there was something relentlessly rigid about his innocence. Dennis on the other hand would have found it an interesting notion, and then used it to try to coerce her into the sack again. It wasn't worth thinking about. She collapsed on the bed, which luckily had a new bedspread.

"Excuse me."

Alison cracked her eyes open. The girl in the doorway was young, maybe still in high school, even. Her clothes looked expensive but without style; the cream sweater top actually had gold sparkles in it and the wool skirt, cut in straight, unflattering lines, was red. Alison wondered if she had ever dressed like that herself, and concluded that even at the height of her Midwestern ignorance she most definitely had not. She most certainly had never worn her hair in such a deliberately asexual do, tight to the head, with plastered bangs cut way too short for a face that round. Everything about this girl told you she was innately too boring to even look at.

"I'm just looking for the bathroom," the fashionless girl explained. "Is there a bathroom back here?" Her voice was cautious and simple, respectful to a fault. Alison felt a pang of yearning to just be back in New York, where people didn't abase themselves like this just because they were looking for the bathroom.

"It's over there." Alison lifted her arm and pointed to the far wall, but she did not bother getting up. Her eyes, which had only barely opened in the first place, slipped shut again. This girl, who was doubtless a really, really nice person, would come and go more quickly if she wasn't encouraged by a lot of well-mannered drivel about absolutely nothing.

"You're Alison Moore, aren't you? I saw you on television. You were amazing! But I don't want to bother you."

And yet, you kept talking, Alison thought. "No no," she said. "No bother at all." In complete contradiction to her sardonic inner monologue, the words came out of her mouth with an effortless grace. *You can take the girl out of the Midwest but you can't take the Midwest out of the girl.* She didn't want to talk to this person but there was no way to get out of it without being rude, and she just didn't have the energy for that. It was, finally, easier to be super polite.

She should have left. Why run upstairs and hide? Why not just *leave*? Well, where would she go? She couldn't go home and face her interminable family, who would all ask her what she was doing home so early, revisit the mind-numbing wrangling about the car, and then drift into a bunch of boring quips about Dennis and how rich and unethical his father turned out to be. Plus, she wanted to see Kyle again. She didn't want to talk to him; she just wanted to look at him. Her thoughts were ping-ponging now. *His wife is horrible. She's fucking gorgeous. I can't believe he married that person. I can't believe he didn't marry me. I wasn't going to marry him anyway he's too Catholic I hate the Catholic church how could he marry someone else why am I even thinking this shit I should never have come.*

"Can I ask you a question?" Alison found herself hating this girl almost as much as she hated herself right then.

"I guess that depends on what the question is," she said. Considering the fact that she was still lying there with her eyes closed, she sounded ridiculously sunny.

"Well, I just, I love acting. I just love it. Like, I totally think it's what I want to do with my life? And I'm still in high school, so I've only really done a few plays, but I had pretty good parts in both of them, like we did

Charley's Aunt and I played this character who is really Charley's aunt. Like, not the guy in the dress, but the *real* Charley's aunt? And in the other one I played just, like, a servant, who had, like, five or six lines, only, but I had to do an Irish accent, which was really, people said it was really good! And I just wondered if you could give me some advice? About how to pursue it, as a career?"

This was unspeakably dreary.

"People probably ask you that all the time. Because you're so phenomenally successful."

"Oh, boy," Alison sighed. "Successful? I don't—no. I wouldn't say that." She let her eyes drift over the ceiling, the drapes, the black trees and the winter night hovering just outside the window. On the wall across from the bed there was a collection of small but surprisingly well-chosen artworks—one of them, a framed red-and-black cartoon, was an actual Matisse. Felicia's enormous jewelry box sat like a majestic throne just under it, on top of Felicia's enormous dresser. She had a pearl necklace in there, an emerald tennis bracelet, and two pairs of diamond earrings; on that memorable night many moons before, Dennis had told her the prices of everything, mocking his father's lavish spending on his stepmother before inviting Alison to have sex on her duvet. But it was hard to take the trappings of wealth seriously, when you had so little of it yourself. Why would you spend thousands on a tennis bracelet when you didn't have eight hundred dollars to spend on a month's rent?

"But you have an agent."

This kid was incredible. "Yes, I do; I do have an agent."

"Is it hard to get an agent? Like, if I came to New York, and wanted to try to be an actress, would that be something I would have to do? Because I heard that there are lots of auditions you can get, where you don't even really need agents."

Alison decided the kid was just weird enough to tolerate. She liked the way the inane questions kept her from obsessing about Kyle and his gorgeous blonde wife. "Look," she said. "I can tell you all about this? But I need a drink."

"Do you want me to get you one?"

Two hours and four drinks later, the party in the bedroom was in full swing. The kid—her name was Donna—eventually got dragged off by her sister, who needed to meet some people in Mount Adams, but by then Alison had lots of new friends. Every twentysomething who went looking for the upstairs bathroom eventually found a way to the back bedroom. One wily youth snuck down the back stairs into the kitchen, where he snagged a couple of six-packs, several bottles of really good wine—Christmas presents, clearly—and a gourmet gift basket full of cheese, summer sausage, and fancy crackers. Alison observed that this was better fare than Dennis usually served, and everyone agreed so readily that it was established that all present had been guests at his bacchanals more than once.

Cincinnati parties were much better than New York parties, Alison decided. Even the slightly too uptight retro-Catholics in the bunch were major drinkers, and as the evening wore on they grew progressively more jocular. People she had known only vaguely in high school were so impressed by her small shred of New York success that they congratulated her enthusiastically. They asked curious and respectful questions about how television was made, which largely focused on the technical aspects of the process. A few brazenly asked how much money something like that would pay, and she answered with direct specificity, explaining terms like "top of show" and "day player" and how much these definitions might earn you as a neophyte on a SAG contract. Everybody thought that being paid almost three thousand dollars for one week of work—and pretty glamorous work, at that—was impressive. She tried to make the point that she had had to audition for weeks and months on end before she landed that singular job, and all her earnings went into head shots and new clothes for more auditions, but no one found that to be a serious detriment to the whole idea of being an actress. She had done it; she had gotten herself on television; she had arrived. When she tried to make the point that she'd like to continue to do theater as well, no one understood why. None of them had been to a play in years. One girl talked about how she used to go to student matinees in grade school, and how she remembered liking it a lot, but now theater was so expensive and if she had a hundred dollars extra to spend she'd rather go to dinner at a really good restaurant, because that was fun too and the last time she went to see a play it was boring and she felt ripped off. Alison thought about how everyone she knew in New York would make fun of this position, and perhaps even say something unkind about how this girl—who was slightly chubby, truth be told—maybe should take art more seriously than food once in a while. But Alison also thought that the slightly chubby girl was right.

Cincinnati people are nice, Alison thought, and for the first time in a long time, the word "nice" carried no negative connotations. "Nice" didn't mean "stupid." It meant friendly, and easygoing, and easily moved to happiness. It meant relaxing. It meant *sane.*

But the nice hidden party in the bedroom upstairs couldn't be expected to go on forever. The kindly drunken Cincinnati strangers started drifting away, and Alison was searching through the empty bottles for one which might have a few last inches of wine left in the bottom, by the time Kyle came looking for her.

He had in fact been looking for a while, as carelessly as he possibly could. As the evening wore on and he traded light chat with the few people he knew there, he would occasionally let his eyes sweep the crowd swiftly, hoping to search her out without giving any indication to Van that Alison's presence was of the least concern to him. He had followed Alison's coat as well. Dennis had taken it off her, just as she said hello to Van, and then carried it on his arm for several minutes before draping it over the banister of the stairway near the door. At one point it slipped off, or someone knocked it off, and from then on it lay in a heap in a corner by the door, where people kept kicking it aside until someone finally picked it up and folded it nicely before setting it on the steps. It was just a black wool coat, relatively indistinguishable from any number of other coats, but he had been tracking it since the moment he saw it on Dennis's arm, so he knew that it was hers. All night the coat was there but Alison wasn't—this contradiction went on for so long, at one point he wondered if she had left without it.

"It looks like your friend didn't stay very long. I haven't seen her since we got here," Van finally observed.

"No." Van of course would not have been tracking the coat. She would just be aware of Alison's presence, or absence.

"That's too bad. I really wanted to get to know her! We hardly had a chance to say hello." Van issued this announcement with a sweet, good-natured sincerity that was so believable it frightened him. Did she mean this? Just hours ago she was spitting venom because he had spoken to Alison briefly about nothing. Now she wanted to get to know her? Her earnest hope to make friends with Alison struck him as the most dangerous and chilling possibility yet presented.

"I guess she did leave," Kyle said.

"Well, that's a shame. Dennis! We haven't seen Alison for hours! Did she leave?"

Standing as they were near the front doorway, Van could easily intercept him on his endless ramble back to the bar. "*Alison?*" he asked. "No, haven't seen her since she got here." Dennis was steady on his feet, but Kyle had known him long enough to recognize the profound alcoholic glitter in his too-steady gaze. His words were hyperarticulated with a heaviness that indicated the coming blackout was maybe fifteen minutes away. "Fled, apparently. You scared her off, Van."

"I didn't!"

"You're for*mid*able. And gorgeous. Kyle always gets the best girls."

"You're terrible."

"I could be much worse, Van; keep an open mind."

"That's enough of that." Kyle draped his arm around Van's shoulder and pulled her back to him. "She's mine." This made Dennis raise his eyebrows and Van blush with pleasure. She loved flirting with Dennis and seemed to have no idea that he was not fully kidding. Or did she? Maybe she was hoping to stir some sort of mysterious plot between the two of them. He didn't know and less did he care, for he knew from years of experience that as soon as Dennis passed out, the party would dissipate quickly. If he was going to get a chance to speak to Alison alone for even one minute, he had to go looking for her now. "I'm *starving*," Kyle suddenly announced. "Is there *anything* to eat around here? Ever?"

"Food is overrated," Dennis informed him with a laconic grace.

"Funny, they didn't teach us much about that in med school. I wonder why. I'm going to go find some crackers. Behave yourself," he warned Van. She laughed and glowed at him with the charming radiance of a high school girl whose crush had just smiled at her on the way to class. Is that really all it took? Did she want so little, was that the secret? Most of the time it felt like she wanted far, far too much.

He knew the layout of the house well, as he had been there often. Down a short hallway, past a leathery den in which several people were playing a computer game on an enormous flat-screen television. Just past the den the hallway turned into the kitchen, a butcher block, stainless steel cavern which always looked like it should be crawling with minions and never was. One of those chilly bartender girls was at the sink, rinsing glassware; it was later in the evening than he thought. Up the back stairs, into a deserted passage which led to the bedrooms before curving around toward another, much larger space which Felicia had dubbed the "screening room." If Alison was hiding out on the second floor, that was doubtless where he would find her. The floor was coated with a plush white wall-to-wall substance which he knew must be wool, but always seemed like snow to him. It silenced all footsteps.

Which was how, after thinking about her all night, he almost missed her. His approach was silent, and she was not where he expected. In fact he had passed the door to the master bedroom without even glancing in. It wasn't till he was three steps farther on that he heard the clink of a glass and the whisper of clothing, someone moving on the bed in the room behind him. He turned simply out of instinct.

They stared at each other through the open doorway. Alison was on her stomach, on the bed, her head lifted in surprise, a half-empty bottle of wine in her hand. She had clearly just retrieved it from the floor, where a half dozen other bottles lay scattered on the snowy carpet; there, a long dark line of red wine drops wound away from her like an accusation. "Oh, God," she said, looking up at him helplessly. "I didn't do it! It was some guy who snuck down into the kitchen and brought the red up. Which I told him not to; he clearly just went into the secret stash of Christmas presents, this stuff was probably worth a fortune."

He took two steps toward the door, toward her. Suddenly appalled at herself, she couldn't bear to look at him.

"Shit, look at this, it's a disaster," she said, biting her lip. This was a disaster, indeed. She looked adorable.

"I'm sure they can have it cleaned."

"Right, I know, that's right. Red wine on white wool, I'm sure that will be the easiest thing to just, make go away."

"It looks like you had quite a party in here." He hated the sound of his own voice around her; it sounded unfeeling and distant, and angry. She caught it too, with a quick glance that let him know she heard the wounded possessiveness behind the words. Well, what *was* she doing up here, hiding in the master bedroom with a bunch of guys? Is that in fact what she had been doing?

"It was pretty claustrophobic downstairs and I didn't know anybody. I was just getting some air, and then, you know, people kept coming."

"I thought you might have left. Not just me," he added immediately. "Van, actually, and Dennis, were wondering. They hadn't seen you. So they thought you left." It came out sounding like the opposite of what he meant to imply, which was that it wasn't a big deal whether she left or not. Obviously it was a big deal or he wouldn't be making such a big deal of it. Glass head.

"I didn't leave, no," she admitted, before glancing up at him under those long bangs. "I thought about it. You know, Kyle, honestly, I am sorry about— Dennis told me that you knew I was coming and that you agreed it was time to just say hello and get it over with. And then when I showed up, it was so clear you *didn*'t know I would be here. But that wasn't, I didn't, I wouldn't have come—"

"It's fine."

"Obviously it's not fine. Honestly I would like to *kill* Dennis. He's such a *liar* and a pig. I'm amazed you'd leave him downstairs alone with your wife. She's so pretty he's surely started putting the moves on her by now. It's not safe, you know it's not."

"He was on the brink of passing out. I'm sure he has by now."

"Well, that's good news. Honestly he's such an alco*hol*ic," she said, standing in front of her ex-boyfriend surrounded by dozens of empty wine bottles." She laughed at her own joke, and made a little wave of her hand over the bottles before her, as if she were blessing them.

"I was going to mention it but I thought it would be rude." This sounded more real, to his relief, friendly even. She started to pick up the bottles, with the apparent conviction that straightening the room would keep things light.

"Anyway, I am glad we have a minute. I mean, I know it's just a minute."

"Yes."

"I wish it was more than that. Because because because what happened, in Seattle—"

"You don't have to—"

"I do, Kyle. I'm so ashamed of myself, the things I said to you."

"It was a long time ago." At some point he had stopped counting the days; it was when Van had appeared in his life and provided such a blessed distraction. Then later, when the memory of Alison began creeping back into the corners of his brain, he would rouse the specter of time as a weapon—*can't even remember how long it's been, more than a year, almost thirteen months since you've even seen her, she's been out there throwing her life away for fifteen months already.* But that line of logic finally turned on him: *It's been eighteen months since you've seen her, and the rest of your life is going to feel like this.*

"Anyway, it's great to see you," he announced. "Really great. Do you like living in New York?" The only way to keep this going, he knew, was to be as much like a normal person as possible. She smiled at the question—*thank God*—and set the bottles down on the bookshelf behind her.

"It's okay. It's kind of lonely. You know they say that about big cities, they're the loneliest places? That turns out to be true."

"I couldn't live there."

"No, I *know* that," she said. "I'm not likely to forget it." There had been a few dreadful conversations about his moving to New York, which went nowhere. It would have been impossible for him to live in a city as large and dirty and impersonal as New York, it was too far from his parents, and it just wasn't an environment that interested him in the least. "You thought my fascination with it was, what did you call it? De*lu*sional?"

"Was I wrong?"

"I don't know, Kyle, there's nothing I can do about it. It's where you have to be if you want to be an actor. That or Los Angeles. Which didn't interest you either." Her ironic tone was starting to drift into bitterness, which she pulled back on immediately. "But there's no point, honestly, is there? We don't have to go back to that stuff anymore. The answer just turned out to be so obvious! Stop torturing each other and you can both live where you want. Ta-da! Not so hard after all."

"No." The cold admission of this startled him back into the present—the *real* present, the one in which she didn't in fact exist. This was not reality. In reality, she was about to evaporate.

"You look thin," he said.

"Anorexia one oh one, the required class for all would-be actresses," Alison nodded, recovering with what sounded like a practiced, tossed-off laugh. "And I'm supposed to lose another six pounds! I don't know how, or where it's supposed to come from."

"Someone's telling you to lose weight?"

"My agent," she said, shrugging as if agents were something everybody had, although it was an entirely new entity in her life, as far as he knew. "It's not his fault, honestly. He's just telling me what people are looking for. Casting people want actresses to be thin, so, if you want to work, you have to starve yourself. It's business."

"Not art?"

"I don't know about art right now. I'm just trying to survive."

"You always made fun of that."

"Did I?"

"Didn't you? Everyone who straight out of college took a money job, you were mad at all of them."

"God, I was insufferable about it."

"It just wasn't what you wanted."

"No, I had big unrealistic and delusional dreams. Shakespeare and Chekhov."

"I should never have said that."

"I said worse things, Kyle. About you and *God*, your boyfriend *God*. How are things with God?"

"He's fine."

"Tell him I need a job. Or if he could just send cash, that would do." This admission seemed to cost her. She dipped her head, continuing her search for stray bottles behind the bed.

"I'll do that."

"Your wife seems nice," she said, abrupt.

He felt an interior panic rise up and threaten to annihilate him. She was right to mention Van. But it left him adrift, two selves. He turned and looked at the door, knowing he should go now, before he broke down in front of her, or before he evaporated entirely. Those were the choices, as far as he understood them. He needed to leave.

For once Alison misunderstood; she seemed to feel that she had crossed a line and needed to make amends. She put her hand up, palm forward, which she meant as an apology, or a request, but which momentarily seemed to imbue her with a mythic grace.

"No, come on, Kyle, don't go away," she said. "I just meant . . . well, you love her, right?"

"Of course I love her."

"That's great, then."

"Yes, it is."

She cringed. That judgmental harshness had reappeared in his tone.

But there was no way to apologize for it without taking back the certainty of his declaration of love for Van. "She's great. She's incredible. She has a terrific job at a firm downtown. What she really wants to do is public advocacy, but she needs litigation experience first."

"So she's a lawyer?"

"A litigator. That is, yes, she's a junior associate." God, had he just repeated himself? This whole situation was intolerable. Why had he come up here?

"You're still going to Ecuador, though? Or Honduras? I can't remember. Someplace where you could get away with pidgin Spanish. That's what you said, after you had to give up on the Navajo Nation because the language was so hard. Remember? All we could ever figure out how to say was 'I love you.'" She had meant that one to come out lightly. When it didn't, she flailed. "Anyway . . ."

A bolt of rage sliced through him. Whatever he was doing, or not doing, with his life was none of her business anymore; she was in no position to question his choices, or speak to him about his dreams. She rejected those dreams long ago by insisting that her own dreams would be paramount for her. Acting! The most self-indulgent, narcissistic choice imaginable for someone with her strength of mind and will. She was built for a life of service. But she wanted to be an *actor*, as if that would be God's choice for anyone. *Acting.* On *television.*

"Kyle? Are you okay?"

"I'm fine."

"You just kind of went away there."

"No. I'm here." And now he was ashamed of himself, still judging her choices like this. He had no right. But it was impossible to apologize for something he hadn't even said. Their lives were so divided, there wasn't even air between them. She was watching him, her eyes alert, curious. She nodded with that new sadness.

"Well. I hope you do go to South America. Or the Navajo Nation. Wherever. I thought that was a great idea."

Alison pushed the empty wine bottles onto the top of a bookshelf under the back window. It was only five or six feet away, but it struck him like a blow. This short interview was ending.

"Alison."

She was crying, and trying not to; she had turned away from him specifically so that he couldn't see it. But she caught herself with a stern little shake and cut him off. "Anyway, I'm glad that I got to see you, because I do want to say that I'm really happy for you," she announced. "That it's all working out for you." She stopped talking and didn't try again. The silence which rose between them and filled this foreign bedroom could not have been more complete.

Kyle glanced over at the open doorway. With one fluid gesture he pivoted on his right foot, reached for the door, closed it, and locked it.

Alison lifted her head, startled by the swish of the closing door, or perhaps the tiny ping of the lock falling into place. Kyle looked at her. Her mouth parted open, then closed. She looked down, and ran her right hand along the edge of the bookshelf, a delicate move, no move at all really, except in its direction, which was toward him. He waited. He knew her, still; he knew that she was not going to be able to stand this as long as he could. It had been their pattern for six years.

She took a step, following her hand. "Oh, fuck it," she said.

It was impossible for Kyle or Alison, in that moment, to understand how kissing each other in this locked bedroom, unseen and unknown to everyone in their world, might be considered a betrayal. The obstacles to their feelings for each other had been so numerous and complex over time that they had come to identify themselves as the victims of a vast conspiracy which involved America, God, culture, gender, capitalism, Catholicism, parental obligation, personal responsibility, youth, age, reality, dreams, and sex. Sex being the worst betrayal of all, because they were, frankly, the two of them, so good at it. When Alison came to him, it was not with a clumsy rush of despair, but rather with deliberate certainty. Her life wasn't making a ton of sense. Engaging in physical contact with Kyle, the most irrationally destructive thing she could possibly do, made more.

After yearning after him for nearly two years, having Kyle's tongue down her throat sent Alison's consciousness reeling. His hand went immediately up her back, under her sweater, where it had always belonged. Her hands peeled at his shirt with desperation; she could not tolerate any inch of him remaining untouched. He pushed her backward onto the bed and she fell willingly, letting him burrow into her neck while his hands dug underneath her bra, insisting on finding her breasts with an unflinching determination. She knew they would be bruised again, and was glad of it. His erection, pressed up against her, was welcome and familiar. She was only wearing a pair of sheer leggings, which meant that once again he was all but inside her. She gripped his back and gasped, silent, for the shred of a moment left to her before he lifted his head and found her mouth again.

And why not? They both had been so unhappy for so long; they both had fought through months of regret that things had ended so poorly between them, regretting even more the choices they had each made which sent their lives spinning farther and farther away from each other. There was no question in either of their minds that it had never been their destiny to go through life without each other; in spite of the repeated finality of their many betrayals, it was not their intent that things should have ended between them ever. This secret tête-à-tête, hidden from everyone who knew them and had ever known them, felt not like a misstep or a temporary slip into madness. For Kyle, it felt as if he had reentered the world. But that was not what was happening.

Kyle's fierce determination to finally claim Alison irrefutably led him to do what he had stopped himself from doing far too many times. Holding her entire body under his, he reached down with his right hand, grabbed at his belt buckle, and started to unfasten it. His new willingness to just *do it*, finally, was met with no resistance from Alison, whose hands reached up and onto his hips, desperate to just get him out of those pants, and into her. But even as he yanked his belt open and leaned back, momentarily, to tear his trousers off, she pulled away. *She* pulled away. It was so unexpected, to both of them, that it could not be mistaken for an insignificant pause, but Kyle was frankly in no condition to be sensitive to whatever qualms of conscience might be rising out of her primordial cortex. He kissed her again with such total determination she almost succumbed. *Why not why not why not*, she allowed herself to think for one last moment, although too much of her already had remembered what it was she knew.

"We have to stop. Kyle, Kyle, stop. You have to stop," she gasped, pushing his chest away from her own. "You have to stop."

"No." It was all he could say. He did not have any other words left in him.

"Seriously, Kyle, stop."

He paused.

"We can't do this."

Kyle could not comprehend what was happening. Alison had never had any respect at all for the rules which required them to stop at this moment; she had relentlessly begged him to continue in the face of commandments from too many sources that insisted, irrefutably, that they stop. In his determined innocence, all those years, he had protected them both. Now that he knew—as she had told him so many times—that the laws of God were a lie, the idea of *stopping*, now, at this *moment*, seemed so perverse that he had the urge to strike her.

Instead, he stopped. He looked away. Then he looked down at his belt, and once again did as he was told.

"I'm sorry, Kyle. I shouldn't have done that. This. I shouldn't have done this." *As if it were your idea*, he thought, *I came looking for you, and for this, it wasn't you who did it. You were too much of a coward to do it. You ran away, and you hid. I was the one who came looking. I was the one who was willing to sacrifice everything for you. You who sacrificed nothing for me.*

"You need to talk to your wife," Alison said. "She has something she has to tell you."

You know nothing about anything, he thought. But he would not speak even to curse her. He opened the door, stepped through it, and closed it decisively behind him, without looking back.

Alison lay back on the bed, her heart pounding. How could she be the one to tell him? He clearly did not know. He was willing to throw everything away, but to throw away this would have been beyond thinking. It would have poisoned everything even more than it already was.

You could have done it just once, her animal brain informed her, pissed. *Nobody even knows you're here. You could have done it and walked away and at least you would have done it.* The part of her which understood Kyle better than he understood himself dismissed this. *He wouldn't have been able to live with himself*, it said. *Wanna bet?* said the animal. Alison barely tracked the back-and-forth, as she listened for the sound of a car door, in the distance, slamming shut, the turn of the motor, the gentle crunch of the gravel under the wheels as it moved off. *That wife better be driving*, she thought. *Kyle is drunk. But she's not. She's not drinking, because she has a secret to tell him.* She listened to the end of the night for what seemed a lifetime. Finally, the sounds came: The car door slammed. The gravel crunched. The car drove off.

Alison remained on the bed, staring at the ceiling, the walls, the Matisse, the jewelry box, the wine bottles, the dark air beyond the windows. She heard the rest of the party drain off. Dennis was doubtless passed out on some couch in some room somewhere.

Alison's reptilian brain, thwarted in its main purpose for coming—a purpose so nearly achieved—was clever and determined, and no longer willing to take no for an answer. There was no reason to stay in Cincinnati; the entire city and her history there was a trap and a disease and a punishment. She had to get out, and get out for good.

She waited another ten minutes. Then she got off the bed, went to the dresser, and opened the jewelry box, emptying its contents first onto Felicia's duvet, and then into one of the many handbags Felicia had so helpfully left on a shelf of her walk-in closet. Alison then crept down the back stairs and peered into the kitchen, which was deserted. The house was empty. Alison made her way back to the main hallway, where her coat waited for her in a tidy little heap right by the front stairs. She picked it up, put it on, and left, and the following day she informed her parents that she needed to return to New York immediately. Over their heedless protests, Megan drove her to the airport, where she took the first standby seat available.

By the time Dennis's father and his wife returned to Cincinnati three weeks later, the trail was cold. No one could say when or how, even, the robbery took place. Two months later, Alison put down a security deposit on a tidy little studio apartment just six blocks from the Atlantic/Pacific Street subway station in Brooklyn. Three months later, she booked a pilot.

part two

nine

THE SCENE WAS A MESS. A good mess, but wow was it taking forfuckingever to figure out how to get the thing to click. It wasn't like there were a ton of extras to wrangle, and God knows there wasn't any fancy camera work going on, but there were about eight entrances and exits and meaningful shreds of conversation that were interrupted by plot elements from six other story lines and then yet more buildup to the climactic fight between Tara and Rob that was supposed to get to some place of white-hot rage in a back room of this location, and then end with them having sex on a pool table.

So there were plenty of unhelpful twists and turns but there was fantastic stuff too. Alison flipped through the pages quickly, reviewing, then let the script drop onto the polished plywood bartop and stood, rolling onto the tips of her feet, stretching out the backs of her calves. Her arms floated up over her head and her fingers met, unbidden, in a reflexive yoga stretch which calmed her nerves and made the black cashmere sweater she was wearing creep up to her midriff, making her look for a moment like a world-class belly dancer. The costume designer,

Alec, really knew his shit. That sweater fit like a glove but it would come off as soon as Bradley touched it.

She looked around, trying to spot Bradley, but he wasn't on set yet. It was one of his behavioral trademarks, to make the set wait; he was the show's acknowledged antihero and he had absorbed his character's easy contempt for reality and rules. There were better-looking actors on the show, but Bradley's bad boy with a heart of gold owned the Internet. The websites oozed with estrogen gone haywire; the guy was a certifiable rock star, as far as the lonely ladies of America were concerned. He continued to drift down to the set on his own schedule, no matter how much the crew griped about it. But there was no question that today he deliberately was working her nerves. He had been abrupt in the makeup room, commenting on the way she was "letting them" ruin her hair, and announcing to Donny the hair guy that he didn't want to have to deal with some insane twist on the back of her neck while also figuring out how to actually have sex on a pool table. When Donny earnestly tried to explain that the director had already approved the look, Bradley snapped.

"I have not had sex with her for a *year*," he told Donny. "I'm not taking the time to do anything but grab her, get her on the pool table, and fuck her." Before anyone could think of anything to say to *that*, he turned on her. "It's your hair. Can you take care of this, please?"

She wanted to snap back at him, but she knew to save it up. "Sure," she said.

"Thank you," he replied, with an impatient edge that was much more pointed than the words. As she watched him go, she could see Irene from makeup make a small face while concentrating on the difficulties of cleaning a clotted eyebrow wand. Donny tried to recover some of his pride. "Queen Bradley is on the loose," he observed. "It's going to be a long day."

"Yeah," Alison sighed, trying to sound like she was dreading all this. "Let's just take the pins out."

"I love your hair up like this. You can see your face!"

"He's right, it's not very sexy, Donny."

"You don't get to the sex until the end of the scene, you're sitting at the bar for three whole pages. And it will be so pretty, when your hair comes down, it's classic, all he has to do is take a few pins out. Neil already approved the look."

"Don't throw Neil at me," she sighed. Neil was one of the too-many executive producers who did nothing but swan around and collect a paycheck for having mediocre opinions about television shows. Honestly he was nice enough but he was sixty-seven years old and gay gay gay; what he knew about hetero sex was absolutely nothing. She was not surprised to hear that this dumb idea about taking pins out of her hair had come from him.

"I don't want to be the one who tells one of the executive pro*du*cers that the *actors* don't like his taste in hair and makeup," Donny announced. He was gay gay gay as well. It was ridiculous how they all stuck together. Alison wanted to scream but she knew that if she did they'd all be ready to take her head off as soon as she exited the trailer, and that it would get back to somebody somewhere that she was getting *difficult*.

"Donny, this one's not worth fighting," she informed him. He turned away and unplugged his heating iron with a swing of the shoulders which informed her that in spite of the fact that she was really being pretty nice, he was going to report that she was difficult anyway. Behind him, Irene caught her eye. She was in for it too; when Donny got mad at someone, it was everyone who paid. "I'll take them out myself," Alison sighed, and to make her point she did it right there, pulling the pins out and tossing her hair about with as much sexual verve as she could cook up at a makeup station. "Okay, that was fun but we can do better than a couple of fucking *hairpins*." As long as she was pissing him off anyway, give him something to report.

But of course everyone wanted a piece of the show today; Tara and Rob getting back together counted as a Big Event. Marketing was putting together a whole promo campaign that had already started even though the episode wouldn't air for six weeks. They had pulled a lot of shots from last season, singles of her and Bradley turning toward the camera with smoldering determination. She felt like Scarlett O'Hara, about to be ravished by Rhett Butler; their reunion had legendary status, and they hadn't even shot it yet.

Everybody knew it was going to be a blistering scene. During their initial stint as network television's hottest couple, she had loved having fake sex with Bradley, who was great looking and funny and unabashedly turned on by her. The first time they made out for the camera—almost two years ago now—he whispered jokes in her ear and made her laugh, then stuck his hand up her shirt and his tongue down her throat. It was a definite shock, but good Catholic girl that she was, she just went along with it, until take three, when she decided to enjoy it. On take four she even reached for Bradley's belt buckle, which all the cameramen loved. When she went back to her trailer to change into her street clothes, the PA who served as her bodyguard made a quick dry comment about Alison's "chemistry." Alison didn't see the footage until it was all cut together on the air six weeks later, and she was shocked at how raw the sexuality seemed. They were only kissing, for crying out loud! But the high-def camera caught an astonishing level of detail, physical and otherwise. Even though the kiss was shot in close-up, the moment she reached for Bradley's belt was caught in the specific shift of her shoulder, which left no room for doubt about what else was going on here. Bradley's answering shift—it was more like a grind—left even less doubt about what he was doing and where that would go, if he had any say about it. On top of which, by cutting the first and last takes together, the editors created a mysterious moment in which the defiant intelligence of Alison's gaze seemed to simply evaporate as she fell into the kiss. After the show aired Rose called immediately, asking point-blank if Alison was going to be involved in "all that sex" they put on "shows like that."

Alison felt like hanging up on her. But she didn't. *Don't be ugly*, she thought, it was becoming increasingly clear that her mother had always been right about that one. *Be nice. Be pretty.*

"There is going to be some sex involved, yes, Mom," she said.

"I just don't know why you have to do all that." Rose was, apparently, just revving herself up. This could go on quite a while.

"Hey, there's someone on the other line," Alison replied, trying to be nice and pretty. "I'm so sorry, Mom. If you don't want to see me doing that stuff, then just shut your eyes at those parts. Because I'm pretty sure that I'm going to be doing all that stuff."

She was right. The fans loved all that stuff, and Rob and Tara's explosive first kiss made Alison a bona fide television star. The blogs which obsessively shredded every moment of nighttime television were entranced and turned on. "Tara and Rob tsunami report," one anonymous blogger announced. From then on, every scene they had together came out under the hashtag #TsunamiReport. "I wanted to fuck them both," one viewer noted in some comment stream. That got retweeted, too.

Which is why, of course, the writers had to break them up. After almost a year of scorching up the airwaves, Rob discovered that Tara had had a one-night stand with Marcos, and that was the end of everything. It seemed, to say the least, a tad forced—Rob had betrayed Tara about sixteen times, by the time she slipped up—but when she had tried to point all this out to Neil and Craig and Vernon and one or two of the other endless executive producers, she was met with a hostile civility which chilled her to the bone. Bradley actually backed her; he liked playing Rob's asshole side, but when it got too irrational it became truly hard for him to make the scenes work. Screaming at her incessantly about what a lying, deceiving traitor she was for doing this one teeny thing while he had done so many that were patently worse was honestly too crazy for him to act. He also thought, quite rightly, that it made his character unsympathetic. So both of them stood their ground, together: They understood the need to break up Tara and Rob so that you could spend some time getting them back together, but you didn't have to make them morons to do it. All the interchangeable executive producers got more and more heated because there was no way they were going to admit that they were wrong and they certainly weren't going to go back to the even more useless idiots at the network and tell them that Alison didn't want to play what was written. People got on the phone to her agent and she was told to do what she was told, and if she didn't like the writing they could arrange for her to be released from her contract.

That was a year ago. This was today. Alison felt a tingling along her jawline; she was nervous. Because of the bitter estrangement that had been tricked up between Tara and Rob, the writers had condemned them to long months of soul-searching looks, near kisses, and contemptuous verbal takedowns. But now Tara was going to tear down the barriers between them, force Rob to admit that he had never stopped loving her, and fuck him on that pool table in the back room. The crew, to give them credit, behaved beautifully on days like this. Whenever someone said, "This scene is sensitive" to a bunch of union guys, they understood that meant more than *no drooling.* The less-classy writers would gather at the monitors and watch every take like spectators at a porno film, but the muscular, tattooed guys who were out there on the set with the actors, pushing the cameras in and out while they faux fornicated, behaved like utter gentlemen.

The lighting was complicated. The cameras had to do a bit of fancy footwork, which amounted to not much more than scooting forward and back and then zooming in, but it took time to sync it up with the lights.

Alison was seated at the corner of the bar for all of this, and finally, Bradley was there too, ignoring her with a maddening deliberation. Some actors, she had heard, were tender and careful with their scene partners when a big sex scene was on deck. Bradley took the opposite approach. He floated from table to table, refusing to acknowledge her presence even as he got closer and closer to where she was, as if being pulled to her by the inevitable tidal forces of his desire. That's what the stupid director had explained at the read-through—"He's pulled to you by the tidal forces of his desire." *Honestly*, Alison thought, while listening politely. *These jobs pay so much money, why do mostly stupid people get them?*

This guy was an A-one example of the breed. Before he had even finished blocking the whole scene he had decided he was worried because Tara was sitting there by herself for so long and she was such a *presence* in the scene, and such an important *character* to the show, that she wasn't active enough. So, what she would be doing, he felt, was *flirting* with the bartender.

"You want me to flirt with the bartender?" Alison tried to ask the question respectfully. "Oh. I'm—but—is that in the script?"

"Not like, *heavy* flirting," the director said, also respectfully. "Just smile, check him out. He's cute. Like that."

"But I'm, aren't I sort of obsessed with Rob right now? By the end of the scene I'm going to, you know, do him on the pool table."

"You're not thinking about that right now. Of course that's not what's on your mind."

"Actually it hasn't been much *off* my mind for the last three months, I'm constantly whining about how much I miss him to anybody who will listen." "Whine" wasn't a good word. She was already miked, so if any of the writers had their ears on, they would hear it and get mad. "Not whining, I don't mean whining, but seriously, I've been talking about it a lot," she amended.

"Right, but he doesn't need to know that. You don't want him to know that. You want him to be jealous."

"But he's not paying attention to me."

"He's drifting toward you relentlessly."

"No, I know, I just meant that he's at least *pretending* to not pay attention. He's seriously talking to everyone else in the room, and he's not looking at me, so . . ."

"That's why you have to grab his attention."

"By flirting with a bartender?"

"Right."

"Okay. I get it. I'm just a little, because the bartender doesn't have any lines, does he? And I'm pretty sure my only line to him is 'I'll have another,' which, I'm not, it's kind of hard to flirt on that. Unless you really want me to lean into it, like, 'I'll have a*no*ther,' which it's hard to do without looking really slutty. But if that's what you want . . ."

She hated talking like this. But it was somehow the rule of television, you had to discuss even the most inane questions as if they were utterly serious.

"I'm not asking for much. Just a little flirt." An edge of real annoyance had entered the director's tone. Another fight not worth having; she would need to have this guy on her side when they got around to rewriting dialogue and having sex on the pool table. Time to cede ground.

"Okay. Sure. I see." She smiled at him with what she hoped looked like a sweet impulse to cooperate. "I think I know exactly what you mean, Jace."

"Really?"

"I . . . will have another," she informed him, with a saucy tip of the head. She let her fingers drift up his arm playfully, and grinned at him, flirting. He blinked with surprise at the sudden shift. "Let me play with it." She turned to head back to the bar, a good little girl ready to flirt with whoever she was told to.

"Didn't we decide to put your hair up, in some kind of knot?"

Alison froze. The director was staring at her hair with a rapt certitude which made her want to hit him.

At which point an arm crept around her waist, and someone buried his head in her neck. "God you smell good," Bradley whispered. She felt her knees buckle, but his grip was firm. "Her hair looks amazing," he informed the director. "I'd do her right now, in front of everybody, if I wouldn't get arrested for it."

"Save it up, Bradley," she said, pretending to take a professional tone. "It's going to be a long day."

"This is a nice sweater," he responded. "I can't wait to ruin it." He actually wagged his tongue at her in the sudden brutal gesture of a truck driver in heat.

"Oh, gross, get away from me," she said, shoving him.

The director got down to business. "So Tara's already here, at the bar, when you enter," he explained, flicking his hand toward the proposed action as if it had already played itself out. "And you spot her, across the room, flirting with the bartender."

"Well, that'll piss me off."

"That's the idea," the director agreed, pleased that Bradley intuited the brilliance of this. Bradley followed him across the floor, gliding like a cat, nodding intently, and just as intently now ignoring her. Annoying the shit out of her, flirting with her, having hot sex, then ignoring her again—it was just like being in a relationship, only you didn't have to wake up with the guy or share a bathroom with him. You did everything *but* go all the way, because they were paying you to do it, on film. And then you broke up. And then you got back together and did it all again.

The similarities to her on-again, off-again relationship with Kyle were not lost on Alison. She had boldly made the associations herself, publicly, laughing at her entire past as if it were a joke, many times. The first time they had fake sex on camera—some eighteen months ago, just six episodes into season one—Bradley had brought a bottle of champagne to her dressing room, and they drank it and gossiped with Alec from wardrobe and a couple of day players. After one glass she was giddy and she spilled the whole story to half a dozen people she barely knew.

"That was my relationship with my boyfriend for six years," she laughed. "I went out with him for *six years* in high school and college and we would do absolutely everything ex*cept*. Aside from the fact that there were no cameras? It was exactly the same."

"You would do everything except *what*?" Bradley asked, with a gleeful leer. "You're so Midwest. Except what, except anal sex?"

"God, no! We couldn't even say the words 'anal sex,' we're too Catholic."

"Trust me, your priests know about anal sex," Alec observed with a wry grimace.

"Well, obviously, but they're still teaching the rest of us that it's a mortal sin."

"Anal sex is a mortal sin, they teach that?"

"All sex is a mortal sin. Anal sex might be okay. I think the position is, all sex with *women* is a mortal sin. I think actually that's true; I think that's how all those priests justified it."

"I don't want to talk about the priests, I want to talk about Alison and the boyfriend she wouldn't fuck for six years," Bradley interrupted. He was drinking out of the bottle now.

"No no no. I did, I wanted to fuck him," Alison clarified. "He wouldn't fuck me."

"That's amazing," Bradley informed her, serious. "Because honestly—seriously, Alison, you're pretty hot."

"Thank you, Bradley."

"Very hot," agreed one of the day players.

Bradley smacked the kid on the shoulder. "Down, boy, you're just a day player," he warned him.

"So?"

But Bradley was intent on keeping the story on track. "So you didn't have sex with this guy—excuse me, he didn't have sex with *you*—because it was a mortal sin?"

"You could have sex, but it was like television sex," she explained, draining her cup of champagne. "You could strip down and make out for hours, fingers, everything—"

"Blow jobs?"

"Yes, blow jobs."

"You can't do that on television."

"We didn't do it either, I just knew that theoretically, it was possible. We were more into the whole torture each other for hours—"

"Torture? Like whips and chains?"

"No, more like I love you but I won't fuck you."

"How literary," Bradley observed. He smiled at her with an intimacy that surprised her, while pouring more champagne into her plastic cup.

"It was extremely literary and extremely hot," Alison admitted. "If it hadn't made us both completely insane I probably would have married him."

"You were going to marry this guy who wouldn't have sex with you? That *is* insane."

"Right?" The champagne was going to her head, she couldn't stop laughing now. The whole thing seemed absurd, childish, stupid. She knew telling the story this way was a complete betrayal, but it was what she wanted. She wanted the betrayal, even though no one but herself would ever know it had happened. She wanted revenge on Kyle and her family and her own soul; she wanted her past to be something you could grind into nothing and dismiss. "I finally got sick of it and told him off," she giggled. "I mean, we were breaking up and getting back together like *forever*—"

"And you never cheated on him? You were—be still my heart—you were still a virgin?" Bradley asked. He was enjoying this as much as she was.

"Don't get a hard-on," she warned him.

"Too late for that, I've had a hard-on all day!"

"Okay, I did cheat on him."

"Thank goodness."

"Well, yeah, I was like twenty-three years old and my boyfriend wouldn't have sex with me. What was I supposed to do? Besides, he was in med school in Ohio and I was in Se*at*tle, so I just, I just—had an affair with this musician."

"Oh, 'musician.' You mean 'loser'?"

"I needed to have sex; I didn't care who I was having it with by that point!"

"You were twenty-*three*?" asked one of the day players, a pretty blonde who looked like she weighed about eight pounds.

"Don't distract her; I sense that we're getting to the good part," Bradley advised. "So you slept with this loser—"

"I slept with this incredible mu*si*cian who was also Irish"—this brought cheers—"who had a fantastic cute accent and he was great in bed. And he was also sleeping with about eight other people, which was a bit of a shock—"

"You were using protection, right?" asked the teeny blonde.

"Yes, of course, he was a mu*si*cian, so I knew he wasn't some great innocent—"

"Like your boyfriend."

"Yes, exactly, but nevertheless I did think in the moment he was not sleeping around—"

"Did he tell you he loved you?"

"Yes, he did—"

"In an Irish accent?"

"Oh yes."

"What was his name?"

"Brendan."

"Oh, God, *Brendan.*"

"Yes, Brendan the cheater. So he was out there cheating away—"

"While you were cheating on your boyfriend—"

"Because he wouldn't sleep with me, yes, and I found out about the cheating, of Brendan the cheater, in a kind of horrible way, a mutual friend, someone I barely knew came over the house and said you know I have to tell you this thing I bumped into Brendan at a bar last night and he was with this other girl, and they were making out and then he went home with her."

"Who is this person, the one who was ratting out Brendan?" Bradley asked.

"His name was George."

"Did he want to sleep with you?"

"As it turns out, yes, he did."

"Of course he did."

"But I didn't find out that until later. Because when I went to talk to Brendan about this story he went on and on about how much he cared for me."

"In an Irish accent."

"Yes. So we ended up back in bed, and I decided he had just slipped up, until a couple weeks later when I was over at his apartment, and I went to the kitchen to get a glass of water and one of his roommates called me Kathleen. So then Brendan and I got into a screaming fight and I went home and Kyle was there."

"Who's Kyle?"

"Oh, sorry, he's my boyfriend, the one who wouldn't sleep with me."

"He was at your apartment? While you were out cheating on him? I thought he was in med school."

"He came to surprise me, it was a surprise visit."

"He came and surprised you while you were out cheating on him."

Alison was starting to feel tainted by it all. She hadn't meant for it to go this far, certainly, when she started to tell the story. She just wanted to be cool and hip and *urban*, a New Yorker, a New York actress, someone who ran through lovers willy-nilly and didn't think twice about it. But these people were strangers, and they were laughing.

"How could she be cheating on him if he wasn't sleeping with her?" This from that skinny blonde, a girl whose name she didn't even know.

"Oh, come on, there was no question she was cheating." That from another one of those day players, a boy with black hair and black eyes, a dead ringer for Brendan himself, truth be told. Someone else she had never really known, not really.

"I was cheating; I was," she admitted.

"You're too hard on yourself." This from Bradley, in the corner, who was watching her so diligently she knew he was still thinking about having sex with her.

"But I was! I was cheating, and Kyle—Kyle caught me! And then I was so angry, that Brendan had been cheating on me—"

"Even though you were doing the same thing to Kyle—"

"*Yes*, even though *I* was doing the *same thing* I was angry at Brendan and Kyle too because honestly I thought I'm sick of dealing with this whole no sex thing, that was just *crazy*, and so I told him I had been having sex with a lot of people."

"*What?*" Bradley sat up, alert and gleeful even, at this turn of events.

"Yes, I told him I was doing all sorts of— Well, I told him I was—" She stopped, suddenly and completely ashamed of herself, for having cheated, for having lied to Kyle, and now, more than anything, for telling the story to a bunch of nobodies. These people were nobody to her. Nobody.

"You can't stop now!" Bradley shouted, happy.

"I don't think I'm drunk enough for this part."

"Someone give her more champagne!"

"There isn't any more," said Alec, pensively turning the bottle over and looking for stray droplets.

"Does anyone have any, in their trailer or anything?" asked the skinny blonde, drunk herself but ever hopeful.

"No no no, she has to tell the rest right now, right now. Get it off your chest," Bradley insisted.

"I have to save up some secrets," Alison informed him.

"Not from me," Bradley grinned. There was no question why he was a TV star. He had thick dirty blonde hair and crazy brown eyes, actual gold flecks in them, a crooked smile. The smallest of scars ran along the right side of his jaw, the souvenir of a bike accident when he was seven. "I'm your destiny, baby," he said. Rob had already dropped that destiny line on Tara about twenty times. Alison thought it sounded idiotic but the writers seemed to love it. Destiny. Tara and Rob were each other's destiny.

Whatever that meant, Bradley did stick around after everyone split that night, and he and Alison of course ended up having sex in her trailer. They were quiet, more or less, but it was a tiny three-banger which rocked mightily, so there was no question that the security guards and the teamsters and the craft service people all knew what was going on in there. Certainly the next day there were enough crew members who were being overtly discreet, in the way that people who know secrets are. And then somebody phoned in a tip to Page Six about the two of them, which ran next to a picture of them innocently talking on a street corner. Alison felt completely shamed, just as she had when she came home from her ill-fated tryst with that feckless Irish shithead only to find Kyle waiting for her on her doorstep.

Well, that was then. Her showmance with Bradley fizzled as soon as it started—it was actually more of a one-night stand than a showmance, the rumor mill notwithstanding. And without any further ado Alison fell into the spectacular life that luck had handed her. Being a pretty girl on network television was more work than she had imagined, but it was more fun too. She was invited to gallery openings and screenings and parties at private clubs, where her picture was snapped relentlessly. She was interviewed by morning talk hosts and late-night comedians. She was given free clothes and jewelry from designers who wanted their wares seen draping her body. She was pursued by total strangers, both men and women.

The anonymity of it all was startling. She was constantly surrounded by people, but none of them seemed to want to talk about anything other than parties and dresses and sex. For a while she wondered if these people had forgotten that there was a real life, aside from what was printed in the cheap glossy magazines which more or less passed as female pornography these days. Certainly when Alison tried to make fun of those things, no one reacted very well, and when she heard one of the writers murmuring behind a door that Alison was "really smart," she understood that brains were not necessarily a good thing around here. Not that you weren't allowed to be smart—there were plenty of people, especially the crew guys, who were shrewd enough, God knows. But more and more she realized that people judged her as they saw her—a pretty girl, who looked good in clothes, who photographed well, and who knew how to lift her leg for men and sparkle with a saucy wit for the women who wanted those men put in their place. What was that word? *Manqué.* She was a phony person, a *manqué.* Lying on her bed, alone in her apartment, the word popped into her head and made her laugh, and she thought briefly about that idiot reporter who thought she didn't understand the word "demimonde."

The lights shifted; the scene was about to start. Alison took a breath. Bradley was suddenly at her side, leaning over her, intent.

"Are you following me, Tara?"

"I was here first, Rob, which kind of suggests that *you're* following *me*."

"This was supposed to be a private party. It's Sheila's birthday. And you weren't invited."

"I didn't have to be invited because this is a public place, you moron." A flash of humor passed through Bradley's eyes. That "moron" was not in the script.

"What happened to Paris?"

"It's still there, last I checked. Hasn't gone anywhere."

"You were supposed to be on that plane."

"I postponed."

"Why?"

"You know what, Rob? You don't get to ask. You're here with Sheila on her *birthday* and you and I are *done*. And we've been done for long enough that I don't have to tell you *anything* about *anything* ever again." This was another new line; she was supposed to say something inane about questions and the past, which honestly made no sense at all. His cue was completely screwed up, but he loved it when she messed with the words; Bradley actually was so bored with acting that he loved being thrown off balance. She decided not to wait to see what he improvised in response and just started moving. As she took a step away from him he grabbed her wrist and yanked her back. She staggered with a sudden impetuous anger, tried to pull away. The physical contact was intoxicating.

"Get your hands off me," she warned him.

He didn't comply. "This *isn't* done," he informed her, simply and inexorably going back to the script.

"It is," she said. But her resolve was weakening as quickly as it had built. Still gripping her arm, Bradley took a step inward, which surprised her and threatened to push her off balance, but she held her ground and they ended up in an intimate close-up instead. At moments like this her height was a real advantage; no other leading lady could go toe to toe with Bradley, who hovered, in stocking feet, above six foot two. But her five foot ten plus heels made a shaky clinch the easiest thing in the world to shoot. She wobbled but Bradley's left arm caught and held her around the waist. The Steadicam operator crept in, danced around them, capturing the moment of indecision.

They were so close to kissing, and they had been waiting for that kiss for too much time, and so had the fans. Alison felt herself fading into an ancient longing to be held and valued and even worshiped. Bradley held her, uncertain—the scene was meant to go much longer, and the fight was meant to be more fierce, and the collision of lovers was meant to be more violent, more filled with disappointment and pain and a rash hunger for sexual connection. But in that stumbling half step, where her body instinctively refused to back away and her scene partner felt no more urge to push her, the two actors knew they were meant to represent the union of man and woman, and that further rage and conflict was not necessary. Bradley leaned in and kissed her for both of them, and their sojourn in the wilderness, and also for the fans of the tsunami, who wanted not so much a ruthless and relentless fuck on a pool table in some tawdry back room, but an answer to their yearning for relief from the exhaustion of what it meant to be human.

"Cut cut cut! Okay, that was great, guys, but we left a lot of the script on the floor," the director moaned at them from the darkness behind the cameras, but they could not let go of each other. *Fiction, this is all fiction*, Alison reminded herself, *the whole of my life is fiction.* Bradley's hands were inside that perfect sweater. Some of this take might be usable. In spite of the fact that they had gone completely off script.

Rage and wrangling ensued. They shot the scene the way it was written. Alison went home to her empty apartment, and Bradley went home to his wife.

ten

THE OLD PRIEST made a terrible patient. Slumped forward on the edge of the examining table, his eyes gazed up at Kyle with watery disinterest.

"How is your digestion? Is there any reflux? Up in your throat, do you feel a burning sensation?"

More staring.

"Bowel movements regular?"

Kyle felt a vague tension creeping along his jawline. He knew that the monks took a vow of silence, but he had been told that it wasn't anything they adhered to rigorously. How was he going to diagnose this old man's digestive malfunction, whatever it was, if he wouldn't even answer a simple question?

"I realize that you have taken a vow of silence but you will have to communicate with me, Father. If I ask you a question, can you write down the answer? That's all right, isn't it?" The priest continued to simply stare, but there was a whisper of movement behind him, and a hand was laid upon the doctor's shoulder with such tender grace that for a moment Kyle thought that in fact he was the patient, not the old man.

"He has dementia. Some days are better than others." The second monk, bespectacled, was nearly bald, but rigorous, clear, and sensible, decades younger. He took the old priest's hand as he spoke. Lifted so lightly upon the younger man's open palm, Kyle now could see the palsy there. "Father Timothy, this is the new doctor, he's going to be with us for a whole week, while Dr. Murrough has his operation in Louisville. This is Dr. Wallace. He needs to ask you some questions about why you've not been eating. Can you answer his questions today?" Father Timothy stared at the young monk with the same indifference he had directed at Kyle mere moments before.

"I'm sorry. I wasn't aware," Kyle began.

"I apologize for that, someone should have mentioned it. On his good days he's fine. People want to believe that means he's on the mend. He's very beloved." The younger monk continued to hold the old priest's hand with such simple affection that Kyle felt his throat tighten with emotion. The unself-conscious use of the word "beloved" caught him by surprise. Father McManahan, the friendly parish administrator who had informed Kyle that the Abbey of Gesthemani monastery needed a doctor to oversee their infirmary for a week, had filled him in on barely anything and Kyle had arrived carrying the slenderest set of facts: The regular physician, one Dr. Murrough, was scheduled for hernia surgery. The doctor meant to replace him had come down with a bronchial infection. They needed someone right away. The monastery was a good two-hour drive from Cincinnati, so it would be best for him to be in residence there, where they could put him up in the retreat hall. They realized it was a lot to ask, but it would be only a week. Kyle's internal monologue had a quick enough answer to all of it: *Only a week? My daily life is a Gethsemani. This one might be an actual break.*

Which of course was completely unfair, absurd even, or at least it would have seemed that way to anyone who knew him. The past three years had slipped by with an idyllic ease. He was successful and well liked at Pediatrics West and had even been encouraged to take on some of the practice's shifts at the local hospital. He and Van lucked into a charming prewar house in an exclusive section of Hyde Park, which they would never have been able to afford under normal circumstances, but the market was wobbly and the sellers were desperate. He hadn't wanted to take on the debt, but Van's parents stepped up and released the money they had been holding in trust for her from her grandparents. It was her money and she was his wife; there was no way to refuse, and why would he? The property was beautiful, with old-growth trees and dazzling azalea bushes, and the kitchen had just been redone with a Sub-Zero freezer and a chef's stovetop. The wood detailing was stunning, the neighborhood impeccable. Van was in love with the location and the eccentric charm of the architecture. And there was money left over to pay off almost half of his med school loans! He was in his late twenties, and already he had money, health, looks, a great job, a gorgeous house, and his wife was beautiful, sociable, and educated. No one would have called his life a Gethsemani.

Still. When he mentioned to Van that he had been asked to take on this one week of service for the monks at the monastery, she had feigned enthusiasm for the idea with the clear implication that she would be enthusiastic about anything that would get him out of her hair. At two and a half, Maggie was the charming center of Van's attention; they lived in a world of gold ringlets and stuffed animals and sticker books and fairy princesses. Oh, and new babies. In her seventh month Van was blooming, as they say, with expectant hopes that her second child would be a little brother for her spectacularly adorable first. The three of them—the second child already had such a vivid reality it was hard to think of it as a fetus—traveled in a kind of bubble apart from him. People stopped them on the street to coo about how lovely Van looked, and how cute Maggie was, and how the second pregnancy was going. And could these total strangers put their hands on her belly to see if the baby within would obligingly twitch on their behalf? At times Kyle wanted to partake in all this delightful nonsense, but it was a world that held him at bay with an insistent feminine disdain. He had heard that some little girls preferred their fathers, and he had even seen it, at the pediatrics practice, girls clinging to men who haplessly admitted that it created real problems at home when she wouldn't go to bed for her mother. This would never be Kyle's fate, at least not with his first child, who was so patently averse to him no matter what he did that he was convinced that behind his back Van had been poisoning her mind with tales of Kyle's dark and loveless heart.

Was his heart dark and loveless? It certainly never felt that way, although it would have been difficult for him to use the word "beloved" for the women in his life with the ease of this young monk, whose gaze upon the ancient priest spoke eloquently of that blessing. Now that Kyle had been forced to slow himself down and quiet his nerves, he could see that the old man—what had the younger monk called him? Father Timothy?—must be in his eighties. He glanced at the chart before him. Father Timothy was ninety-four.

Kyle felt a stirring of panic in the pit of his stomach. He shouldn't have missed that. But the drive from Cincinnati had been stressful. There was more traffic than he expected and the directions he had pulled off the internet were just a shred too convoluted to figure out while simultaneously operating a car. Having crawled through the city traffic, he found himself wandering down circuitous country lanes which carried him past luscious horse farms before going nowhere, so he'd had to pull into gas stations twice to make sure he was on the right road. When he finally arrived he was already tired, even though it was only ten in the morning. The monk at the front desk of the retreat house had kindly suggested he say hello over at the infirmary before he took his things to his room, but when he got there the receptionist assumed he was already settled in, and she handed him a chart as soon as he walked through the door. Now here he was, in the middle of an examination before he had even landed. No wonder he'd missed a few clues.

"Ninety-four," he commented. "That's impressive."

"Our community is aging," the young monk explained. "Father Timothy is one of the oldest, but over half are in their seventies and eighties." His statements were so simple. They bespoke a world of trouble, but there was no trouble in him. His calm goodwill toward both Kyle and the old priest was preternatural.

"I'm sorry, what is your name?"

"I am Brother Peter."

"Ah." Kyle had the urge to shake Brother Peter's hand, but it wasn't extended. A patient silence bloomed around them as the two men sat before Kyle and waited for him to explain what he knew, which wasn't much.

"Do you see Father Timothy often enough to give me a sense of his symptoms?" Kyle glanced down at the useless chart and presented his inquiry with a confidence he didn't feel. He should have asked a few questions before he took this on. But when McManahan had told him of the monastery's predicament, all his Catholic boyhood training kicked in and flattered some deep sense of wounded pride. He had taken on the study of medicine because he wanted to work with the poor, to heal the sick, and it was humiliating, every day, to find himself once again trapped in that hyperprivileged country club version of a medical practice called Pediatrics West. Although he was popular with the nurses and most of the other doctors there, he had never felt comfortable with the suburban parents and their round pink children who wore him out with their blatant lack of need. This opportunity to come work with the monks, even for only a week, entered his private conundrum and moved through his spirit like a balm. It had never occurred to him that maybe he wouldn't be qualified.

"We all eat, pray, and live together, and many of us work together too, although Father Timothy has become too frail of late for the real hard labor," Brother Peter said with a smile at the old man. It was meant to be a light attempt at teasing, but Father Timothy was completely out of it. Kyle had a hard time believing that "some days were better than others"; from what he could now see, the dementia was advanced. "This past week several of us noticed that he really hasn't been eating anything at all. Obviously it is a concern to everyone."

"Are there any other symptoms of distress? Does he suffer from incontinence or diarrhea?"

"No, he is as you see. No distress."

"Do people try to feed him?"

"Yes, of course, we try to get him to eat something at every meal."

"And he doesn't take anything? No liquids, nothing?"

"He takes soup, yes. And occasionally he will eat a bit of ice cream. Other than that, nothing."

"How are his teeth?"

"His teeth are fine. He just doesn't eat. We are very concerned, as you can imagine."

Kyle let out a small breath. They didn't need a pediatrician here; they needed a gerontologist. "You have to eat, Father," he informed the old priest, as if the poor man could understand a word anyone was saying. "You need to stay strong, to pray for all of us. We need your prayers." The old priest trembled, but that was the palsy. As far as Kyle could see, there was nothing in there; he was gone already, and his body was trying to follow. He turned his attention to Brother Peter and summoned up the nerve to just tell him the truth. "I am not an expert on the maladies of the elderly, far from it," he admitted. "I suspect the dementia is advanced and is an associated cause of the lack of appetite, but I cannot say anything for certain. I do have several colleagues whom I can consult about this. Unfortunately, I just got here fifteen minutes ago, and I haven't even had time to put my things in my room, and I need to do that, and catch my breath, and then make a few phone calls. Would it be possible for me to see him again, later in the day or even first thing tomorrow? I apologize, I really do feel like I've been caught flat-footed and I don't want to make a quick diagnosis under the circumstances."

"No apology is necessary. On the contrary, I should apologize to you. Of course you need a moment to orient yourself. We should have been more considerate."

"You should have, perhaps, found yourself a different doctor. I'm not at all sure I'm the right man for this."

"That is for God to say," Brother Peter observed. He smiled at Kyle with a quiet confidence which suggested that they both understood that this was, and would always be, the real truth of the situation. Then he placed his left hand under Father Timothy's trembling arm and helped guide him off the gurney and out of the room. The old man could barely shuffle to the door. *He doesn't need a gerontologist*, thought Kyle, *he needs an undertaker.*

That's for God to say, his brain reminded him. Kyle felt his internal thoughts splinter and come together with a sardonic edge. If only God really had an opinion about things, about anything. He remembered how easily his mother used to toss that phrase around—*That's for God to say, Kyle, honey; finish your cereal*—but for years it had been buried underneath all the other inanities he was taught as a child. *Learn to share. Clean your plate. All you have to do is work hard and do your best.* That one was really a joke. Working hard and doing your best *wasn't* all you had to do; not by a long shot. If it were, what was he doing here, surrounded by all these failing monks? He sat on the edge of the examining table, wondering how he was going to pull this off. The sheer challenge of the medicine would have been enough; on top of it, the nearness of so much apparently authentic spirituality was unnerving. This wasn't just the easy pieties he and his neighbors recited every Sunday at Mass. The muscle in his head which reduced his patients—necessarily reduced them, otherwise how else was he supposed to do this terrifying job—to blood and bones and muscles and bacteria felt frozen, bewildered. He thought about just walking back out into the parking lot, getting in the Volvo, and jumping ship.

Instead, he just sat there. Moments later he found himself in the capable hands of Brother Luke, who informed Kyle that he had been asked to show the young doctor to his room in the dormitory of the retreat house. As he followed the brother at a respectful distance—it seemed to be expected somehow—he took more careful note of those ubiquitous brown and white robes. The simple design of the hooded brown shift tied at the waist over a long white robe looked both practical and holy, a light and comfortable cotton linen which was machine washable while simultaneously whispering of the eternal nature of God's grace.

His cell—there was no other word for it—was predictably Spartan. White walls, a window, a dresser, a bedside table with a lamp, and a single twin bed with a simple orange coverlet. There wasn't even a chair, which he found weird until he thought about whether or not he would need one. *Do you really sit in a chair, when you're in a bedroom? No, you sit on the bed. Then you don't actually need a chair, do you?* The voice in his head was more and more bemused; its judgmental edge seemed to be tempering those swift and nasty observations Kyle had come to accept as second nature. That plain room was inexplicably comforting.

"Cell phones do work here, but we try to observe silence in the retreat areas and the dormitories. There is an area out by the parking lot which people use to make their calls. We hope that won't be an imposition."

"Not at all." The idea that he would have a room all to himself, where no one could speak to him, even on a cell phone, felt like a miracle.

"Would you like a few minutes to unpack? Or would you prefer to see the rest of the complex? It isn't large."

The possibility that the rest of this place might reveal itself to be as mutely appealing had in fact already occurred to him. "I'd love to get the full tour, if you have time," he admitted.

"Of course." The brother nodded, content, even pleased in a gentle monk-like way. As Kyle set his single bag beside the single bed, Brother Luke drifted out into the narrow white hallway. Kyle followed.

The monastery grounds were apparently large, as it had previously functioned as a working farm. Black-and-white photographs of monks in those timeless robes riding tractors and holding up garden hoes lined the walls of the small hallway adjacent to the cafeteria. The carpeting was industrial gray, and the few chairs stacked in the corner were monotonous, standard-issue office furniture, the kind anybody could pick up in the back of an OfficeMax or Staples. Institutional Catholicism always looked the same, he thought. Bad furniture, fluorescent lighting, industrial carpet, men in dresses.

"This is Brother Albert, you'll see him often as he is usually here at the front desk," Brother Luke told Kyle. "This is Doctor Wallace, he is going to take over the infirmary this week, while Dr. Murrough has his operation."

"That's very kind of you," Brother Albert nodded, as he offered his hand.

"It's an honor to be asked," Kyle replied, and he meant it. He felt like his best self, the self he always hoped he would someday be, was somehow waking up and taking charge of the show all of a sudden. Without even doing anything these monks were improving his manners.

"I hope we don't give you too much trouble."

"I'm sure you won't."

"I'm sure we will," Brother Albert replied. His tone carried an acerbic edge.

"Brother Albert is one of the oldest members of our community," Brother Luke observed, as if that were a real distinction here.

"Oh my yes, I'm certifiably ancient."

"If you have any question about the history of the monastery, he's your man. Or if you're a Merton fan—"

"Which I am *not*," Brother Albert interrupted.

"He was his secretary, for a number of years."

"You *knew* him?" Kyle asked.

"He was a good writer, but a bad monk," Brother Albert informed Kyle, as if he had asked his opinion of the great man. "He was a child. He was allowed to be a child. He was just terribly neurotic. Oh, don't get me started. The things I know. I opened the man's mail!" He beamed at them with a schoolboy's wicked glee.

What was the story? Merton was a womanizer of some sort, but the specifics eluded him. Not a womanizer, per se—that was Augustine. Augustine, that terrible prude; once he'd sown his wild oats, he turned on sexuality, it was the road to hell, and women were culprits who would lure you there. *That's right, you could talk to women but only if you were guaranteed not to have any sort of sexual relation to them. A meeting of the minds alone.* The guy had a blissfully fulfilling relationship with his mother, whom the church had obligingly canonized after her death. Still, Augustine was better than Aquinas; that guy had announced that women were nothing better than deformed male fetuses. Kyle remembered the sniggering delight with which he and his friends had received this information from the Jesuits who taught them religion in high school. The memories were so close to the surface here. Lousy cafeterias. The terrifying and fascinating otherness of women. Alison.

She had never had much use for the Catholicism which completely drenched every aspect of their lives. That was apparent from the first time he laid eyes on her, at a Friday night football game, of all things. Saint X versus Moeller High. A crisp October night, white lights pouring over that mythic and insane ritual which taught boys to leap and attack one another for the sake of catching a ball. Desperate to make any kind of connection with the guys he knew from school, he agreed to go to these things even though he didn't like them. He barely understood the rules. And then there she was, straggling behind a gaggle of Catholic school girls. Hanging out in the parking lot, clearly hoping to meet boys.

Dennis, of course, knew one of the girls in her cluster and when he sauntered over his group followed. This was the real ritual of Friday nights in Cincinnati, high school boys prowling, girls gathering to be prowled.

Those eyes of hers really were something. A green so startling, the edge of the iris melted into a darker rim, utterly unique, that you felt like you were looking into the eyes of a wood goddess, or maybe just a trickster. Because she grinned at him, as soon as she saw him, as if they had known each other for years. He was young, and pathologically lonely, even then. How did this girl with the astonishing eyes know him, already?

At sixteen he had no defenses. He had no game either. Some utterly forgettable and forgotten girl said, "This is somebody, and this is some other girl, and this is Alison." The whole evening was a blur from then on. She was funny and shrewd and sure of herself, and he followed her around like a dork, barely coming to life when she agreed she hated football.

"Oh, God, it's awful," Kyle admitted. "I don't know why the church condones it."

"Oh, the Catholic church, they condone pedophilia, what do you expect?"

"Well, it's a little more complicated than that."

"Is it?" Alison turned to give him a full blast of those eyes. He knew he'd never recover. By the end of the evening they were making out under a corner of the bleachers, the crowd roaring around and above them. Apparently it was a pretty good game.

"I'm going to show him the chapel, and then the rest of the grounds," Brother Luke told Brother Albert.

"Thank God I don't have to go to choir anymore," Brother Albert replied. "When I turned eighty-four, they decided to let me off the hook."

The tour concluded with a visit to the bookstore, which looked like an unexceptional gift shop, crowded with books and fudge and prefabricated figurines of Mary and Joseph and the baby Jesus. But the ladies behind the counter, the first women he had seen all morning, were straightforward and friendly, and they welcomed him with a cheerful Kentucky twang.

"You're not going to want to leave, that is what I predict," declared the older of the two, a large woman with bright blonde pigtails affixed to both sides of a round face. "People come down for the retreats thinking just to stay for maybe two days, but some of them come back and back and back, they find it so restful."

"Oh yes, it's just wonderful here, we love it here," agreed the other, a luscious young thing in tight jeans and a pale blue tank top. "I heard you saw Father Timothy this morning; we've been real worried about him, he looks like he's just wasting away and no one can get him to eat a thing! He's real confused, too."

"He's very frail," Kyle said, trying to acknowledge her concern without assuaging it. "I'm going to see him again tomorrow." It was a trick he had worked on for years: Don't sound like anything is too dire, but don't offer hopeful assurances either, even tonally. In a pediatrician's office these guarded pronouncements rarely extended to concerns past the effects of a flu shot. It had been a long time since he had had to withhold so much professional judgment around questions of life and death.

"Well, God willing, you'll be able to help him, 'cause he is real special to me and Leeanne," asserted the round-faced woman. "Here, let me ring that up for you." She reached over and took the two books he held out of his hands. "*The Seven Storey Mountain* and *The Sign of Jonas*, anything else I can get for you? You didn't want any fudge or cheese?"

"No, thank you."

"That'll be thirty-two fifty-three."

Kyle paid and then headed to the infirmary, where he spent the rest of the day acquainting himself with its limited resources and doing internet research about dementia in the elderly and its associative symptoms. He downloaded several articles about Alzheimer's disease and nutrition. He studied Father Timothy's files and put a call in to Dr. Murrough, who returned it immediately—that hernia surgery wasn't scheduled till the next day—and got him to fill in the blanks on Father Timothy's medical history. Then he waited and read, uninterrupted; there were no further patients that afternoon. At 5:30 Kyle called it a day and went back to his monk's cell to unpack his few things before dinner.

The room was spare and silent. He sat on the bed and considered taking his phone out to the designated area underneath the trees next to the parking lot, so that he might call Van and tell her about this place. The image he carried in his head, of her and Maggie going about their daily routines in the kitchen and the backyard and the park, seemed distant and irrelevant. Or maybe it was he who was irrelevant. A sudden panic jolted through him. This affectless cell was substantial in a way that he was not. Why had he come here? What was he looking for? Time and space opened around him like an empty balloon. The thought that God might make an appearance and explain a few things to him shot through his mind as a complete, terrifying absurdity. What was the use of faith itself, when it went hand in hand with the knowledge that God wasn't going to show up? The longer he stared at the phone, the less he felt like making any move to communicate to anyone at all, much less his wife. And now, ever, and again, there was Alison crawling around the corner of his brain. Making out underneath the bleachers. Cool night air. The memory of joy, of first young love.

He looked at his watch. It read 5:52. Dinner was at 6. He had eight minutes to kill. His mind was restless, refusing to look at itself, but also refusing to be silenced. His roving attention landed on the paper bag on the bed and was caught with the quick efficiency of a hook landing firmly in the mouth of a trout. He picked up the small package and tilted it forward, allowing the two books inside to slip into his hands. *The Seven Story Mountain* and *The Sign of Jonas.* He had bought them both almost out of a sense of duty, wanting to let all these nice people know that like everybody else who made a pilgrimage to this monastery he was mightily impressed with the famous monk. He glanced at *Seven Story Mountain* and rejected it because that was the one everyone read. The cover of *The Sign of Jonas* presented a photograph of a monk in those robes—which had come to impress him more and more with their straightforward beauty—striding across a lonely landscape. He opened the book and started to read.

Five minutes later, he set the book down, his eyes smarting. The voice of the writer, landing with astonishing clarity across the years, smote him. "I have a peculiar horror of one sin," the monk wrote. "The exaggeration of our trials and of our crosses."

Kyle stared at his hands. He felt his heart move.

eleven

Alison Moore hits the big time. It wasn't that long ago that she was a total nobody he felt perfectly justified in snubbing at a nothing cocktail party. Now look at her. A gorgeous brunette with a crazy sexy haircut. Shocking green eyes. Great smile. A standard PR shot from some after-party during the Tribeca Film Festival. *Didn't see that coming.*

Seth clicked the server off and turned his attention to the fucking pile of press invites which had been dumped on his fucking desk in his fucking cubbyhole. There must have been fifty of them, and he was expected to cover them all, in twenty-two days.

The sheer physical impossibility of needing to be two or three places at one time was not actually the problem; the real problem was how utterly fucking boring it all was. He had been on the culture beat at the *Times* for only four months but it was seriously ruining his life. His job was, literally, going to parties and then writing about them, and then fielding phone calls from hysterical press representatives who didn't like the way he covered the parties. *BAM 50th Anniversary Gala! Tribeca Film Festival Opening Night! 1,000 Stars Fashion Benefit for Breast Cancer!*

Come Celebrate the New Wing at MoMA! Come Celebrate the Award Honoring Somebody Ridiculously Famous Who Really Doesn't Need Awards! The exclamation points were plentiful, the graphics gorgeous, the paper stock superb.

Everybody who knew anything knew this was a total shit gig. *Hi, Jessica! You look fantastic! Can I grab you for a few minutes to talk about your know-nothing role as a gun-toting whore in* Evil Dead 12? *Matthew, hey, how are the kids! Fantastic! How do you feel about being overlooked by the Tonys this year? Nicky, hi, can I grab you for a minute? Just heard about the deal you signed with Warners, congratulations!* You stood in a line and got two minutes of their time as they paraded off the red carpet, on their way to the cocktail event. And then you went to the next one of these things, asked the same questions, and then you went back to the office to type this shit up, and then you went home and thought about murder.

But of course he was surrounded by idiots who thought this whole song and dance was so *exciting.* The would-be models and actresses he met at bars and clubs and parties all over the city couldn't get enough of it. He had never really had any trouble getting laid, New York was a wonderland of party babes, truth be told, and half the guys in town were gay. A relatively decent-looking, moderately successful writer who had gone to Harvard was never going to have a problem here. But this beat had taken his sex life to a whole new level. The girls who fluttered around these A-list events were international beauties—Brazilian, French, Italian, Swedish—who floated back and forth between Los Angeles, Buenos Aires, Cannes, Lake Como—on the arms of some of the ugliest men Seth had ever laid eyes on. They were never terribly interested in talking to him at the different events, where the photographers got much more of their attention, but they were happy to say hello at the private clubs and downtown hipster bars to which he had been suddenly granted insider status. The guy from the *Times* who covered "culture"—God, he couldn't even *think* of the word now without putting it in quotes—was someone everyone wanted to know.

Arwen the office intern once again had clipped the collated schedule of events to the back of the packet of invites. It made him irrationally angry; he had *told* her repeatedly that he preferred the schedule clipped to the *top* of the pile, where he could glance over it without going to all the trouble of unclipping the entire packet, which made a mess. The fact that she had also left him a red velvet cupcake with a little note pissed him off even more. *Dial it down*, his brain warned him. *She wants you to like her she wants to be a writer you are her hero she doesn't even get paid don't hurt her feelings.* He slumped back in his Aero chair and sighed. A cupcake, a fucking cupcake. They were omnipresent these days. You came by them so easily, they had ceased to be special.

He opened the note. HAPPY BIRTHDAY!!!! the note announced, in capital letters: HAVE A GOOD ONE!!! For a moment his impatience with this overexcited piece of punctuation almost clouded the information that had been presented to him so unexpectedly. But there it was. HAPPY BIRTHDAY!!!!

It's my birthday? He thought about it for a moment. *Is it really?*

He clocked the date on his computer screen. September 9, that was it all right. How Arwen had found it out was more of a mystery than the fact that everyone else had forgotten it. Birthdays were passé, and generally the source of slightly too-aggressive ribbing in his so-called band of brothers. *How old are you? Thirty-three? Where's the Pulitzer?* The names of those who had won Pulitzers in their twenties were not something you wanted to think about on your thirty-third birthday, when you were on your way to the red carpet at Fashion Week, so you could write a snappy three-paragraph column for the internet edition of the fucking *New York Times*. Birthdays were a pain in the ass. *Red velvet. What the hell is that, anyway?* There was some news item floating around about how they were using ground-up insects as red food coloring because the other stuff had chemicals in it. Ground-up bugs equals *organic* food coloring. Another Pulitzer-worthy bit of information. He picked up the cupcake and tossed it in the garbage can at the side of this desk.

The tents in Bryant Park looked like they had floated down from some other universe. The air was fresh and cool, as an early autumn breeze had swept through Manhattan and contributed to the festive spirit. Elegant men in black suits opened limo doors and held their hands out to the mysterious figures in the backseat, in a gesture of benign invitation. *Come out come out.* Before barreling across the street to plunge himself into this mess, Seth stopped, suddenly taken by the timelessness of the city's rituals, on a night that was touched with stardust. He would not have been surprised to see twelve dancing princesses hurry by him at the streetlight, eagerly throwing themselves into the celebration.

No such luck. The red carpet tent was packed and while the evening was cool, there was a sheen of humidity which had gathered, a literal wet blanket, right on top of the crowd of photographers and reporters. Someone should have turned on the air conditioning—he felt sure somehow they knew how to air-condition those fucking tents—but apparently the freshness of the late summer night had fooled the event organizer and her three assistants, who were walking around smiling serenely even though tiny beads of perspiration were popping up all over their faces. As usual, there was a problem, squishing that many bodies into a space that had no circulation. And for all the humid claustrophobia, this didn't look like much after all. The pretty girls in the photo line were obvious nobodies, certainly nobodies that he was not going to be able to write about for the *Times*. Not even for the online edition.

"Hey, Fraden." A voice called to him from the crowd of reporters, a hand with a Bic pen lifted itself above their heads.

Most of his fellow culture beat scribes were serious-minded girl reporters with digital recorders, who asked the same questions over and over and nodded professionally as they did so. Lou Schaeffer, on the other hand, was two hundred and forty pounds of sweating romance. Schaeffer thumbed his glasses back up his nose and squinted past Seth, as if something, anything worth writing about, might be hovering. The guy always looked completely out of place at these things. A beached whale with stringy hair, Schaeffer always had three or four pens clipped to the pocket of his bargain-basement cotton shirts; he would have fit in better at a sci-fi convention. But his prose was impeccable. If they actually did give out Pulitzers to losers who wrote about culture on the internet, Schaeffer would have six or seven.

"Who are these chicks?" Seth muttered, squeezing past the tiny girls to take his place next to the beached whale. "Is this the B-list? Are there two press tents?"

"You missed Clooney and the wife, Aniston, SJP, Damon was here, Susan Sarandon, David Geffen showed up—"

"Come on."

"You're asleep at the wheel, my little friend. We started an hour ago."

Was that possible? Seth checked his watch and ran the times through his head. *Seven p.m., the invite said seven and the screening over at the Ziegfield starts at eight. Is tonight the Ziegfield or is it the fund-raiser for PEN?* He felt a pebble of sweat creeping down the side of his face. *You missed Clooney.* That was a mistake, someone over at the *Times* was going to make note of it. Clooney always stopped to chat with the clowns in the press line, everybody in town would have a decent quote. Except for him.

"Hey, Marissa! How you doing, you look incredible." Schaeffer waved at a pretty teenager in a peach mini dress. Brown hair curled down her back and a wide belt with the biggest silver buckle he'd ever seen cinched the dress at the waist. Her eyes were bright but honestly, the kid looked like an anorexic ten-year-old. "She's only got a few minutes, guys," her publicist announced. He hovered sternly, to make sure they didn't take advantage.

"What are you working on, Marissa?" Schaeffer was on it. Seth just listened and scribbled down the answers.

"Well, I just did four days on the new Noko Matsui film, that was a total blast."

"Oh yeah? You like working with Noko?"

"Oh my God, he's a genius, he's such a genius."

"What's your favorite movie that he's made?"

"Is that a trick question?"

"Not unless you don't know the answer."

"You're awful," she grinned.

"I'll pick one for you. You get to do any action sequences?"

"No, I just got shot."

"You get to fall off a roof or anything?"

"I did! How did you know?"

How did *he know?* Seth was convinced that Schaeffer just sat around his apartment all day, surfing the internet and storing every meaningless fact he could find in that fucking big brain of his. One time over drinks Schaeffer admitted he had a photographic memory, which may have been a lie, except for the fact that Schaeffer wasn't exactly proud of it. He was drunk and morose, and confessing that he had gotten kicked out of MIT for some ridiculous cheating scandal, hacking computers or selling prewritten papers to terrified freshmen, something totally needless and stupid. And now here he was, chatting up starlets and writing dazzling paragraphs about who these pretty girls were dating, or what talk show they were going to be seen on next. Seth didn't get it. But he liked the guy. Compared to all the vapid know-nothings who regularly showed up on this beat, fat Schaeffer had the air of a tragic desperado about him.

In fact, at that very moment Schaeffer was waving wildly at the next starlet down the line. He was flushed with delight, or that might actually just have been the heat. The whole thing was dreary as hell. Seth started digging through his shoulder bag, looking for the ultra-handy celeb cheat sheet that Arwen always stuffed in there, to let him know who and what to expect at these things. He couldn't find it. "Shit. I'm taking off," he said. "Did I really miss everybody? 'Cause if it's just B-list from here on in, I got two other parties I have to cover before midnight."

"You telling me you wouldn't want to tap that?" Schaeffer muttered, by way of reply. Seth glanced up, finally, so that he might make an informed answer to the everlasting male question. The answer leaped rather quickly to mind.

I already did.

Alison Moore, in a skintight lavender mini dress, clocked his presence. Then she leaned over and kissed Schaeffer on the cheek.

"Hey, Schaeffer, you look awesome. Hi, Seth. I heard you were covering these things for the *Times*, but I've never seen you at any of them."

"He's always late and often lazy," Schaeffer informed her. "You look fabulous."

She did look fabulous. Her figure was flawless in that dress, and the color was so fragile and pale it took you a moment to register that it was there at all. Cascading seed pearl earrings were her only accessories; she didn't carry a clutch. Those great long bangs were still there, the long legs too. Her eyes were even greener in person, but maybe that was the dress. She looked free, spare, and fearless, like someone who might split and duck into your Chevy, take a road trip to Montauk, and make out in the backseat all night.

"What are you up to, Alison?" Schaeffer asked her.

"Show's on hiatus, so I'm out and about," she shrugged.

"You think you'll get an Emmy nod this year?"

"Absolutely. Best sex on camera, they're giving me a special award." Schaeffer was a puddle of adoration.

"What show is this?" Seth asked.

She shot him a glance which scorched his eyeballs. "No, seriously, I'm not trying to be an asshole," he protested. "I just don't watch much television. I'm out most nights."

"Yes, I see that, you clearly have much more serious things to do with your time." That got tossed off with a throaty laugh. She had gotten somewhat better at hiding it—the laugh was fantastic—but she was still trigger happy. He remembered that temper, how easy it was to wound her. He also remembered how great she was in the sack.

"It's the best show on television," Schaeffer gushed.

"Thanks, Schaeffer."

"I was so relieved when you got your pickup for next season."

"Yeah, we were on the bubble a little bit this spring."

"Until you and Rob got back together. You are holding that whole show together."

"Don't tell anyone," she warned him.

"All the chat rooms are saying the same thing, that you absolutely saved the show," Schaeffer continued, with an OCD insistence. "I know you don't read what they're writing about you, but you really should check it out, the past few months you have been on fire. Seriously, this is a total breakout year for you."

Schaeffer was notoriously unabashed in his star worship, but this was whole new territory for him. The poor guy's fat cheeks were positive pink with excitement. It *wasn't* just the heat. "Why don't you get a selfie and make it your background photo, fan boy," he observeed, only half to himself. Schaeffer turned, surprised for a moment that Seth had intruded—it was an unspoken rule that you didn't interrupt; everybody got their thirty seconds to ask a question, no matter how inane. The idea that you would make fun of a fellow reporter? Schaeffer's bewilderment was innocent, then confused, and then the pure understanding of Seth's careless dig landed. A lumbering embarrassment rose to his face. He turned back to Alison, sheepishly. "Sorry," he said, trying to laugh. "I just like your work."

"You don't have to apologize to me," Alison told him, firm. "Your friend's a know-nothing asshole."

"Hey," Seth started, but she was taking no prisoners.

"Excuse me, prick. Know-nothing *prick*." The PR reps were starting to turn their way. And why not; Alison was speaking loudly enough for everyone within a square block to hear.

"Come on, Alison." Seth glanced around, aiming for the merest shred of discretion. But Schaeffer was already starting to put two and two together. Like everyone else.

"Lou Schaeffer is a fantastic journalist," Alison continued, certifiably pissed. "And if he is kind enough to say a few words of support for my work, then who the fuck are you to tell him to shut up?" This was getting the attention of every reporter in shooting distance.

"Whoa, wait a minute." The eyes and ears of the blogosphere were turning their way. But Alison was just getting tuned up.

"You didn't even show up for the fucking press line. Which gives you, I would say, no rights at all in this situation. You arrogant fuck." Someone actually clapped at that. It was because he worked for the *Times*. They were all jealous. And now those press reps were all pouncing, handling her ruffled feathers with crispy finesse.

A short skinny guy in a nice suit descended, apparently her personal PR handler. "That's it, guys. Thanks. Alison, this way." Alison swiveled and stalked off. For a second, she wobbled. Was she drunk? *No. She's just not so good at walking on those fucking heels*. Beside him, Schaeffer exhaled softly. "Va-voom," he whispered.

And not two hours later, thanks to the magic of the Twittersphere, their idiotic exchange had made it into every major New York gossip blog. "The press line at Bryant Park provided its own drama Tuesday night, when *New York Times* reporter Seth Fraden traded words with television actress Alison Moore. Fraden, who apparently was annoyed that he had missed the chance to interview some of the night's biggest celebs, was on a rampage about the 'B-list' stars, such as Moore. Moore didn't seem to care, calling the reporter several choice and unprintable names." *When did the coverage become more real than the thing being covered?* His cell phone was blinking and buzzing furiously, as everyone in the known universe texted him about his moment in the sun. It was a disaster. And over what? How had it exploded so fast? The sullen realization that the whole needless mess was his own fault did not make the situation any easier. Sitting alone in the back of a shitty bar in the Garment District, downing Jameson on the rocks, didn't make the situation easier either. The clipped text from his editor—*call pls*—also didn't help.

"It's a complete misunderstanding," he said, as soon as Eric picked up.

"Okay, just tell me one thing: Did you sleep with her?"

This caught him so unawares he felt his brain do a half step. "Whoa, what?" he said.

"Oh, God."

"Hey, Eric, no, I didn't," he lied.

"Tell me again that you didn't."

"I didn't!"

"You know there's a lot of talk about you. You're partying with these girls, you're using your position to get laid."

"Okay, that is—"

"Spare me."

"Look, if I'm being accused of something—"

"You ever hear of sexual harassment, Seth?"

"Okay, that's crazy. That is—"

"Using your power and influence to coerce sexual favors. This is no joke. You understand me?"

"I know it's no joke. I'm saying it's completely no joke, and no, I didn't do it."

"I don't care if you did it or not. Did you leave us open to a lawsuit? That is what I want to know."

Of course that was all they cared about. *Fucking politically correct bullshit. Those girls throw themselves at you and if you take them up on it you're the one with the problem. Since when did it become illegal to fuck a woman?* His thoughts were racing now, or trying to race. He regretted having had that third drink, which he had downed unthinkingly on this, his most pathetic of all birthdays. Sexual harassment. If they fired him over the merest suspicion of something like that, his career was toast. *What career?* For a brief moment he had nothing but contempt for all the choices he had made since swanning into New York on the wings of that overhyped Harvard BA. Everyone wanted to take a meeting with the culture editor of the *Crimson*, but what had come of it over time amounted to less and less and less, clouds floating in a queer blue sky. He had spent eleven years writing nothing about people who were doing nothing.

In the rising of his self-doubt, he unwisely let the silence go on too long. "Answer the question," Eric snapped. He should have taken more care with Eric. There were plenty of writers out there who wanted his idiotic column—there were plenty of writers, in fact, who would happily shoot him in the head if they thought they could crawl over his body and grab that stack of party invites.

"No. No. No lawsuit," he promised. "Just give me a minute, would you? Alison and I are old friends, and we were, honestly, Eric, we were horsing around."

"You're 'friends'?"

"Swear to God. We've known each other for *years*. She was like, best friends with one of my old girlfriends, and I hadn't seen her for a while, so we were just, you know—"

"I don't know, Seth, which is why I'm asking. 'Cause the shit I've been hearing about you, it is not good."

"Eric, I don't know what you've been hearing, but I know you wouldn't just go flying off the handle because of some whispering campaign. Everybody talks shit on each other in this business, but that's all it is. As I think you well know."

This time, Eric paused. It was a fairly played hit; Eric had been famous for his cocksmanship in the day. He was tired, he was pissed, the job wasn't any fun anymore, all that was a given.

"You want Alison to make a statement that this is all a big misunderstanding, I can call her and ask her to do that," Seth offered. "But I think it's making too much of it."

"There are plenty of people who have already made too much of it."

"That's my point."

"No, that's *my* point." An edge of exhaustion had drifted into Eric's side of the conversation. "Just take care of it," he sighed. "Get her to call somebody over at Page Six and set it straight."

"Page Six isn't going to do us any favors."

"Then get somebody *else* to do us a favor! Get her to tweet about it! I don't care where it shows up, but someone has to print a story that exculpates you on this, or so help me God you'll be writing obituaries for the next six months."

Seth raised his finger toward the bartender; this warranted another Jameson. Thirty-three years old, a degree from Harvard, a byline at the *Times*, features in every major magazine that still existed, and now he was going to have to get on his knees and beg some actress to publicly vindicate him for telling the truth for once.

"Today's my birthday," he told Eric.

"Yeah, happy fucking birthday," Eric said.

Seth hung up the phone and stared at it. Who would have Alison's cell number? Didn't he get it from her—when was that even—three years ago?

He sighed. The only person who might know how to get in touch with her was Lisa, to whom he hadn't spoken since the night he stepped out on her—which had been, in fact, three years ago. This was going to be an endless saga of sucking up.

twelve

ALISON STARED as the tribe of waiters marched into their private dining room, *twelve* of them—all in black tuxes, even the women—carrying course number eight, pork belly with wilted chard. She had been warned ahead of time that this was going to happen; this restaurant was duly famous for serving ten-course dinners and a flight of wine with each. But it was one thing to hear about it and another thing to experience it.

"They're small courses, but it's definitely a long-distance event. You have to pace yourself," Ryan informed her. They had gone out for cocktails to discuss how things were going with the oh-so-shiny movie director who had a lot of projects she "might be right for." An invitation to a private dinner party with his closest friends and their wives and girlfriends indicated that things were progressing nicely. But as usual Ryan had a lot of advice. "Wear something tight. It'll show off your figure, and keep your appetite in line. One bite of each course. That's it."

"You said they serve the most beautiful food in New York."

"Beautiful food is for you to look at, and other people to eat," he warned her.

"Can I at least get a doggy bag?"

"No, you cannot, and don't say the words 'doggy bag' within three blocks of me ever again."

"I miss food." She was actually eating the olives from her martini with a little too much gusto, she realized; a tiny pile of pits had piled up on the bartop in front of her. Ryan eyeballed them, and her, a dangerous warning in the tilt of his head.

"Trust me, the food you will be served tomorrow night will be exquisite."

"But I'm still only allowed to look at it."

"You're allowed to *taste* it; I never said you couldn't taste it. But there are ten courses! Some of them very rich. The coddled egg is legendary."

The coddled egg was legendary for good reason. Course number two, it was so delicious and she was so hungry, she absolutely gobbled it down, breaking every promise she had made to Ryan. Every other dish—oysters, goat cheese and frog legs, diver scallops drizzled with a basil reduction, lamb medallions, lobster tail, even the foie gras, which came nestled in a bed of fresh creamed corn—she took one bite and then set her fork woefully to one side, while she wallowed in the explosion of flavors for as long as she could make that one bite last. But the dress presumably was worth it. A rich green satin, skintight, narrow skirt, boldly strapless, it was so cinched at the waist that her figure looked like Ava Gardner's in *The Barefoot Contessa*. The thing was so tight it even made her boobs look big, the way they used to, when there was more of them.

But there was a problem with the plan: course number three, the wildly delectable foie gras. When Alison took her one bite and dutifully set her fork aside, the gorgeous chicklet sitting on her left took note. "That's all you're going to eat?" she asked.

"I'm just not very hungry," Alison lied.

"You came to Per Se for a ten-course meal and you're not *hungry*?"

the girl asked, loud enough for the whole table to hear, and gleefully hostile enough to make Alison blush. Immediately, of course, the entire table was watching her turn beet red. Her accuser saw her moment and held on to it. "How much does a dinner like this cost? Don't tell me. If you have to ask, I know. But that's got to be fifty bucks' worth of foie gras!" This hideous slut's name was Suzy something; she had been in a studio feature last year, eight lines, she was brash and nasty, apparently that was her whole skill set. She made a little stabbing gesture, like she was going to nab the food off Alison's plate. No one laughed, which made her even more aggressive. "And what about the poor goose who was force-fed for our delight?" Fearing that Suzy might actually start acting this process out, Alison took charge.

"This dress is not going to be very forgiving," she said, feigning a graceful humility. "If I eat too much I'm going to pop out of it."

"Keep feeding her," advised some guy in a suit two people to her right. The casual leer made the men chuckle and the women smile politely.

"It is a beautiful dress, and she is beautiful in it," Lars informed the room. He actually raised his glass to her. "I would hate to see it come to harm."

This brought another polite chuckle and a couple of "here heres" from the men. Lars turned to the gentleman to his left, to make some private observation about something, signaling that the possibility of a ritual hazing had been put to rest. Instinctively Alison remained ramrod straight, until Lars glanced back and caught her eye. He gave her a slight smile. She offered him a breath of a smile in return.

Lars Guttfriend. Lanky blond hair, and a preternatural tan which seemed to be somehow genetic. You'd think he was an Icelandic prince, but in fact, he was from Philadelphia. He claimed to be the son of wealthy socialites, and that "Lars" was a family name, but there was something a little too Gatsby-esque about all that; Alison didn't buy it. With or without a tan, all these East Coasters started to look and sound the same to her after a while—the edge too consistently inauthentic, the social manners too practiced. Everybody had so many agendas running you couldn't make heads or tails out of what was going on in anybody's brain unless you put it all down to just constant power plays, which she found too wearying to even contemplate. In any event, Lars kept looking at her like she was some sort of strange yet wonderful art object. It seemed a little practiced, like the sort of thing a movie director was supposed to be doing, constantly eyeballing pretty actresses and wondering what their best angle was.

But he could stare all he wanted. Alison's attention turned to the next temptation, course number seven, halibut in sea butter foam. She decided that since it was fish she was going to just go ahead and eat the whole thing and then shamelessly lick the plate. She knew that Ryan didn't actually give a shit if she put on a few pounds. The not-eating rule had more to do with some total fantasy he was having that Lars would invite her back to his fabulous penthouse suite at the Soho Grand and ravage her, which would not be quite as sexy on a full stomach. Ryan's cooing obsession with Lars was a little extreme frankly; he seemed to have some sort of major crush on the guy. *He'd probably have a better shot than I do*, her brain observed idly, and as soon as the thought skittered through her she stopped to look at it. Three weeks ago, she was dreading the possibility that she might have to sleep with this movie director just because. *Because that's what starlets do.* So this idea was maybe good; maybe Lars was gay, and she was going to be his beard for a little while, and maybe she'd get a few auditions out of it, and she'd meet some important people, and that would be that. The question of whoring herself out could be put on a shelf for another couple of months.

"The halibut *is* delicious," noted the woman to her right. *What is her name? Is she married to one of these men in suits?* There was no boy-girl-boy-girl nonsense going on at this table; Lars had directed everyone to their seats, but the plan seemed to be to put the girls on one side of the table so the boys could do business on the other.

"You know what, Kate"—*what a save*—"the halibut is so awesome I'm throwing caution to the wind," Alison told her.

"You've been very good all night." Kate actually reached for a roll and buttered it. The butter, they had been told by their master waiter, was artisanal. It came from cows who only fed on the first clover of spring, or sage leaves and pea sprouts, something like that.

"I'm a little mad at myself," Alison admitted. "This food is amazing and I should not have worn this stupid dress, I should have worn a big baggy sweater."

"You actresses have to be so careful," Kate noted. "I couldn't do it." The woman was lovely, silver haired, probably over sixty, but the fact was she was definitely on the larger side. Her boxy jacket did nothing for her figure either. Alison realized with a pang of regret that she had assumed that the woman was not so important, because she didn't carry herself with the same smug arrogance all the skinny people had. And of course half the men, across the table over there, were sizable to hefty. The other half were as wraith-like as medieval monks.

"How do you know Lars?" Alison asked.

"Oh, I gave him his first job, whenever that was, fifteen years ago?"

"You gave him his first directing job?"

"His first 'job' job. He was a PA. I was the line producer."

"What are you now?"

"I'm myself now. I'm too old for your game."

"Surely not," Alison said politely.

"It's not an easy business. It wears some of us out," Kate informed her dryly. She reached for her wineglass with the definite air of someone who had finished the conversation.

Alison found herself strangely jolted at that. With that momentary inanity—*surely not!*—she seemed to have lost some unexpected chance, even if it was just a chance to tell a secret to a total stranger. The older woman was already looking to her right, as if considering the possibility that the brainless actress on that side of her would have something more interesting to say.

"I don't like show business either," Alison admitted, under her breath. It wasn't the most brilliant of observations, but it snagged the other woman's attention, momentarily, anyway.

"You seem to be doing fairly well for someone who doesn't like it," she said.

"It's wearing me out. Sort of like this dress," Alison said. "You can't have a decent conversation with anyone. I don't know how to talk anymore. And I'm so hungry all the time I can't think. I'm ready to stab you in the heart over that roll with the butter on it. That's all I'm thinking about half the time. And I'm so lonely."

The older woman considered this, and set her wineglass down. "You're very pretty," she finally concluded. "It distracts people."

"Oh." Alison's disappointment at the banality of that couldn't be disguised. But Kate Whatever Her Name Was was waxing philosophic now.

"People don't know how to talk to pretty girls. Especially when they're wearing dresses like that. People generally don't want to talk to dresses. They want to do other things to dresses, and with dresses, but conversation is not high on the agenda."

"They still seem relatively important," Alison pointed out.

"Oh yes. One would have to say that history has been kind to pretty dresses. Less kind to the women who wear them, overall, but kind enough to the dresses themselves. Anne Boleyn. Mata Hari. Jackie Kennedy." This Kate woman smiled at that, as if she had just said something wise.

And then she reached for her wineglass, punctuating the finality of this observation.

"You're not suggesting that I stop wearing them."

"Not at all, they will serve you well, until they don't." A cryptic smile. Alison wanted to hit her.

"What are you two conspiring about?" Lars asked. The question floated across the table with a faux playfulness. The other guests rustled and turned.

"Your young actress is regretting her choice of attire for this truly exquisite evening, Lars," Kate told him.

"I don't," he replied.

This again made the men chuckle. The weirdness of this whole dinner party never quite congealed into something she could explain. A cozy private dinner that Lars was throwing for twelve of his closest friends? There wasn't anything cozy about the way the men leered anytime they got a chance, and the chick to her left, the one who had been so aggressive five minutes ago, was back in the action.

"You know you guys are animals," she told them. "I'm offended on behalf of this darling girl in her teeny tiny dress—what's your name again?"

"Alison." Alison smiled, keeping the demure crust of good humor firmly in place.

"I'm offended on Alison's behalf. You're all looking at her like she's part of the dinner! Okay, not the dinner. The dessert. Or the after-dinner drink. Or the after-dinner snack." And now Miss Aggressive was putting her *arm* around Alison's shoulder and leaning in, performing the role of the offended feminist friend. "What's that fairy tale where they eat all the women? Red Riding Hood! The big bad wolf eats Red Riding Hood *and* her grandmother, which is really perverse if you think about it." She started to make animal sounds, growling and miming that she was going to take a bite out of Alison's bare shoulder. "Arroooooo," she howled. She actually howled.

"Jesus Christ, Suzy." One of the suited men, across the table, was smiling with an air of cheerful chagrin. "How much wine have you had?"

"Don't change the subject. I saw you looking at this nubile young thing's cleavage. I'm going to tweet about this. 'Leering lemur eyes babe's boobs, hashtag Per Say What?'"

"Where's the ladies' room?" Alison asked, trying for graciousness now and landing somewhere closer to embarrassment.

"Oh no no," the bombing comedienne countered. "These guys are not getting treated to a sweet view of your tush running off in shame to the 'ladies' room.' We're going to have this out. They're ogling you like you're hot lunch."

"Now we've moved on to lunch?" Lars asked, cool and perplexed.

"She's your date, Lars, so presumably the dress is for you. Lunch and munch." She grinned and leaned over the back of her chair, as if to physically stop Alison from escaping. "Presumably that's the plan."

"Knock it off, Suzy," someone murmured. Both outraged and excited to have another target for her meager satire, Alison's tormenter turned to see who had spoken. Alison took the opportunity to squeeze by her and stagger on those painful heels into the main dining room.

The place was calm, gorgeous, serene. A cool blue glow suffused the room; dusk was settling onto the city beyond the wall of windows, and the other diners—*civilized, they look so civilized*—were deep in quiet conversation. As she neared the waiters' station, the master waiter looked up and immediately assumed a helpful air of propriety.

"Are you looking for the ladies' room?" he asked.

"No," she replied. "The elevators."

He nodded without comment and gestured simply for her to follow him. Nothing made sense; she just wanted to get out of there. Which now seemed much easier than it had any reason to be. She had had the foresight to pick up her utterly useless clutch, a teeny handbag so small it could barely hold a credit card and fifty bucks.

"Do you need anything?" the master waiter asked. There was no judgment, no cunning, no desire. Just the question.

"No," she said. "Thank you."

She stepped into the elevator. And after all that—after all *that*—it wasn't until fifteen minutes later that anyone wondered where she had gone.

thirteen

TO BE A PEDIATRICIAN who doesn't like babies was to know oneself to be absurd. Kyle watched his new daughter yawn and stretch and mewl in her mother's arms and wondered if this is what sociopaths felt like. Dissociated, repulsed, a bit annoyed with the expectations from others as well as himself that he should have warm feelings for something so patently distasteful.

Van of course was oblivious. She sat in the corner of their beautifully decorated Victorian living room and cooed at the blob in her arms with a picturesque maternal splendor. It would have been an even prettier picture if their first daughter, the photogenic Maggie, had been sitting at her feet playing with her dollies. But Maggie had somewhat predictably hated the baby on sight. When she wasn't screaming for her mother's attention she was hiding under a bed somewhere, sulking. Kyle occasionally went looking for her, hoping that she might sense his own appalling aversion to the new baby, and that this might actually turn into some sort of unspoken bond between them. But Maggie was strong-willed, and Kyle was not the parent she wanted. His few attempts to lure the child over to his side were met with such screaming resistance that Van was forced to intervene, pointing out with acidic grace that she "had enough on her hands" without Kyle making things worse.

According to Maggie's infantile logic, she hated the baby because it was a girl. In spite of all Van's convictions to the contrary, it wasn't a boy that she had been carrying after all, it was another girl, and while everyone knows that girls are just as good as boys, occasionally they're really not. Through his years of daily servitude at Pediatrics West, Kyle had come to understand the unspoken pattern of gender preference in the subtle behavioral lexicon of new families. A firstborn who is a girl is good! Not quite as thrilling as a firstborn who is a boy, but not so far off. If the firstborn is a boy, that's fantastic, and then a second boy? Unbelievable good fortune. A firstborn girl with a second-born boy is also unbelievable good fortune. A second-born girl is good, if the firstborn is a boy. Two girls? A subtle breath of disappointment enters the discussion. Are you going to have a third, and try for that boy? The fact is your odds don't go up, the more girls you have. The highest chance you will ever have of having a boy is 50 percent. If you've popped out two girls already, then the chances are actually better that you'll pop a third. Statistics are just statistics, but they're statistics for a reason.

Kyle knew that Van had wanted a boy, and why not? Little boys really did love their mothers with an unadulterated wonder. He had seen it often enough in the examining rooms at PW; the way the young mothers and their little boys looked at each other was truly enough to break your heart. The opposite scenario was also assumed to hold true. Two girls and a gorgeous wife should have meant nothing but uninterrupted adoration for Kyle Wallace. It didn't quite work out that way. When faced with the complete catastrophe of living with three females who really had nothing at all to say to him, he folded his own truths into whatever corner of his brain might hold them. It is possible that they festered there.

For today, the issue was the grocery store. The glorious health which Van always enjoyed had taken a hit during her second delivery; her placenta tore and there was a bloody trauma which would have been the death of her in the nineteenth century but was handled with a quick shot of oxytocin in the twenty-first. Still, she had lost a lot of blood; she was consequently anemic and her milk didn't come in properly, and no matter how much she pumped and breastfed night and day, the baby remained unsatisfied and colicky, struggling wanly to stay on that prescribed growth curve. Kyle hated growth curves—*what about the children in Ecuador, anybody worried about their growth curves?*—but you couldn't get around the fact that his infant daughter was hungry and there wasn't enough milk. Sadly some useless neighbor who had read too much La Leche literature had drilled into Van's head the dangers of nipple confusion and whatever else an occasional bottle of baby formula held in store for their daughter, and Van was in anguish. But the baby was unhappy and hungry and she wasn't growing. Finally, in a burst of exhausted tears, Van told Kyle to "just go and get it then!" as if it were his fault.

So there he was, standing in front of a veritable wall of infant formula. Everything in yellow and white—*no pink or blue, hypothetical babies are gender neutral*—powder and liquid, now there were pouches too, something you could just screw a sterilized nipple onto and stick right into the wee thing's mouth without worrying about mixing or boiling or dishwasher safe! Those pouches were even vacuum sealed, so presumably there were no bubbles, which might mean no need even to burp the kid. There was literature on all this stuff down at the office that he had never, truthfully, looked at. But the baby needed to eat, and he had to come home with something, and Van was going to have a lot of questions about what he picked. Nothing he chose would be accepted on face value as the right choice; he was going to have to defend himself. Surely half of them had objectionable chemicals. Or cow's milk. What was infant formula made of, anyway, and why didn't he even know?

"Kyle?"

The voice was so familiar, it was like the voice inside his head. Or not the voice inside his head. It was the voice that the voice inside his head was always talking to.

He turned around.

She looked incredible, even in oversized sweats. Incredible, but too thin. There were circles under her eyes, and her hair was strangely straggled around her face, like a waif's; it needed washing. And the color of her skin was off, slightly gray, or maybe just paler than normal. Whatever normal was; the only time he had seen her in the last three years was on television, where she had so much makeup on that she looked like she belonged to an entirely different race of beings. And here she was, wearing oversized sweats, no makeup, it even looked like a couple of pimples were showing up on her left jawline. A worried crease had appeared between her eyes, apparently having settled there with common usage. Still. The color rushed to his face. It couldn't have been less appropriate, to stand there stuttering like a schoolboy while he was buying formula for his starving infant daughter.

"Alison! Hi. Wow. Hi! I didn't, I wasn't, did uh, are you in town?" And now he was laughing, like a lovesick idiot. Some part of him was trying to get control of this but it was taking much too long.

"Yeah, I just kind of dropped everything and came home to see my folks. Wow, I didn't expect to see anybody I knew at the *grocery* store." Her hand flicked to her hair, unconsciously self-conscious, like she knew she looked terrible. "So, like, do you live out here now? I thought you lived in Walnut Hills or something."

"I, oh, no, Hyde Park, I have a house in Hyde Park. We have a house in Hyde Park." Horrible, having to admit that *we*. Even worse to stutter over it. "But my practice is out here and I needed to pick up some things, on my way home."

"Baby formula?"

"Yes. Oh yeah, we—"

"You had another baby?"

Could this get worse? "Yeah, we did. We did."

"Congratulations! Two kids, that is crazy."

"A little bit, yeah."

"What kind? So, like, what kind?" Her hand creeping to her hair again, pushing it back off her face.

"A girl, we had another girl."

"That's fantastic, Kyle. I mean, congratulations. Two girls, that is so, so great."

"Thank you." He hated how he sounded. It was a sound he heard constantly in the world he lived in, upper-middle-class suburbanites multiplying and buying homes and congratulating themselves on the wealth and security they accepted as a birthright and then bragged about as an accomplishment. Everyone he had known in high school, yearning for a life of the mind or the heart, half his friends wanted to be musicians or writers or actors or activists and they had all settled so quickly into careers as lawyers and bankers and doctors and now they all had adorable babies and nice big houses in Clifton and Hyde Park and Indian Hills. And there was Alison, too skinny, too restless, unmoored, but at least she was out there still throwing her dreams at the idea of being an actress. "And you! Wow! Things seem to be going so great for you! I mean, you've been busy I guess. Becoming a big television star."

"Oh, I don't know about that," Alison tried to laugh, self-deprecating. "Have you seen that show?"

"We don't have a television set."

"You don't have a television set?"

"Van—my wife—thinks TV is bad for the kids."

"Oh, that's right, she said that, whenever that was."

Kyle blushed. That night, at Dennis's party. He saw Alison remember what had happened, that night, and shrug it off, like she couldn't afford the memory. Neither of them could, really. The wary grief that sped across her face, through her eyes, the breath of her disappointment, anointed him.

"It's just while they're little," he reassured her. "She worries about all the colors, and the light patterns, there are so many studies about what they do to kids' brains."

"No studies about what that bullshit does to adult brains?" Alison asked. She was looking off now. "Well, it's great to see you, you look really good, Kyle," she said. The polite whisper hovered behind the goodbye; what was the point of even talking? Life quite frankly had forbidden them to speak. Another step past and she would be gone.

"How long are you in town for?" he blurted. She hovered for a moment, dragged backward by the hook of the question.

"I'm not sure," she acknowledged. There was something there, some kind of exhaustion, wariness, something she couldn't say. Of course he had no right to ask her anything.

"Well, if you're here for a while, you should come over," he informed her.

"Come *over*?"

"Why not?"

"Why *not*?"

He laughed, finally, at that. "Are you just going to repeat everything I say?" he asked.

"Am I going to repeat everything you say? I don't know, maybe I will," she shrugged.

"I have a pretty full plate at the office this week, but I'm usually out of there by seven. You could come over for dinner some night."

"*Dinner?*" She actually grinned at that one, awakened by the absurdity of all this into the moment, and he finally could see her again, wry, complicated, quick to amuse. *She's in there*, he thought. "I don't know, Kyle, your wife just had a baby," she reminded him. "It's probably not the best time to just have people over for dinner."

"She'll love it," he assured her. "She's stuck in that house with two babies all day and the only chance she has to talk to anybody at all is when they show up on our doorstep." His invitation was sure-footed, buoyant with the ring of a truth he was inventing on the spot.

"Maybe you should ask her," Alison suggested, with enough of a raised eyebrow to acknowledge that there was a reality between them more authentic than this polite conversation might suggest.

"She'll be thrilled." *Is he insane?* Alison thought, but Kyle kept pushing through. "She's always wanted to get to know you. God knows she's heard enough about you."

I bet. "I'm sure you have better things to talk about than me."

"You're a big television star! We don't watch it, but everyone else does. My father is addicted."

"Your *father?*" Kyle had tossed that one off casually but Alison inwardly cringed. Mr. Wallace had always had a soft spot for her, and she remembered fondly his steadiness of character and his concern about whether or not you were making the kind of decisions you can live with. She really didn't want to hear that he had been watching her fall in and out of bed with the losers who were constantly traipsing through the universe on nighttime television. "Seriously, don't tell me that your father is watching that junk, the very thought makes me want to crawl under a rock."

"He watches it religiously. My mother hates it but he seems to love it."

"Terrific."

"Right?" There was something different here, a lightness which she hadn't felt with him for years. Well, she'd barely *seen* him for years, only that once, but before that too everything had been so brokenhearted and operatic. This seemed almost normal. He was actually *laughing* at her discomfort, not in a mean way, more like an old friend who is just happy to tease you. It was distinctly weird.

"I'm so glad that you think it's amusing, Kyle, but it makes me kind of uncomfortable to think of your dad watching me on television."

"After what I've watched you do on television, I don't believe anything makes you uncomfortable."

"I thought you didn't have a television!"

"We don't! But sometimes I just—see ads for it." That was clearly a lie, but why? Did he secretly sneak off and watch nighttime soaps with his father? The new male bonding. That seemed unlikely.

"You watch it online," she guessed. "In between patients, you dial it up on Hulu."

"As if there was a minute to do anything between patients. Other than argue with insurance carriers. No no no, I've just seen ads." No question, he was lying. But then he grinned at her. What did it matter, they were finally talking to each other like actual human beings. Hanging out with Kyle hadn't gone this well for—well, *ever*, maybe. There was no worry that this might all suddenly erupt into a huge awful fight which would end up with them *almost* having sex.

"Really, how long are you in town for?"

"I'm not sure."

"But you're at your mom's?"

"Yeah, I'm at my mom's."

"I'll give you a call there."

"Okay, sure."

And so he finally walked away from her, approaching the line of cash registers at the front of the store with his baby formula under his arm, the rules of suburban America respected and complete. It was just what it was, two people parting with the past left like a bland linoleum floor between them. The absurd clarity of the fluorescent lights left no shadows around him to haunt her imagination.

fourteen

HER MOTHER WAS less convinced that Alison's chance meeting with Kyle was as insignificant as all that. "Oh, Alison," she murmured, her hand to her breast in simple and yet utterly melodramatic acknowledgment of the heartbreak Alison must be feeling.

"Mom, it was really no big deal," Alison informed her.

"I would love for that to be true, I really would," Rose replied. "But might I remind you, the last time you saw him, what was it, more than three years ago? You flew out of Cincinnati like a bat out of hell."

"I needed to get back to New York."

"And we haven't seen you since!"

"And I've been really busy."

"That's what you said," Rose sighed.

"Mom—seriously. I have not been *avoiding* the entire city of Cincinnati just because one of my ex-boyfriends happens to live here. That would be ridiculous." Her nerves were too frayed for her to tread into these waters. But the frayed nerves might have had more to do with the eight phone calls she had not returned to her alarmist agent who wanted to know where the hell she was.

"How did he look?"

"Who?"

"Kyle!"

"Oh. He looks good. Tired, but you know, he has two little babies and a full-time job, so of course he's tired."

"She doesn't work, I heard."

"She just had two babies!"

"A lot of women work these days. You made it very clear, you were not going to give up your career to have a family."

"Only an idiot would ask me to give up my career to have a family."

"Well, that was apparently important to him."

"Mom, maybe she quit her job because she wanted to quit her job. Some women want to quit their jobs."

"That's what I'm saying. He wanted to marry you."

"Mom—he didn't marry me, and he never asked, by the way."

"He would have."

"*Didn't* beats *would have*."

"You know very well—"

"Mom, we're not talking about whether or not I should have married Kyle! That's a nonstarter, it's a different life, come on."

"You said he looked tired," Rose noted, suddenly concerned about Kyle's health.

"As I believe I just mentioned, he has two little babies and a full-time job."

"But the wife stays at home."

"Her name is Van."

Rose ignored this. "Has he put on weight at all?"

"What is *that* supposed to mean?"

"Why are you jumping all over me?"

"I'm not jumping all over you, I'm just asking why you would ask that. That is such a terrible thing to ask, like it would be so awful to put on a few pounds." Alison sounded defensive for a reason; she had put on six pounds since arriving in Cincinnati just four days ago. How, you had to ask yourself, was it possible to put on weight that fast when it took so damn long to shed it?

"The last time I saw him I thought he looked a little heavy, that's all."

This was news. "When did you see him?"

"I don't know when that was, a couple months ago. Your father and I bumped into him at a baseball game."

"You didn't tell me."

"Alison, it is impossible to get you on the phone. And you have made it crystal clear, might I add, that you are not at all interested in hearing about Kyle Wallace. You have made that crystal clear."

Rose had taken to repeating herself these days, whenever she landed on a phrase that seemed to do the job. If it sounded good once, it would sound even better a second time. And in this case, she also had a point. After fleeing Cincinnati those years ago, Alison had given herself permission to indulge in an unforgivably hostile surliness whenever Kyle's name came up. Any reminder of her near miss with him was terrifying to her, in no small part because it led so swiftly and immediately to an act which, if ever discovered, would lead to legal and personal consequences too dire to contemplate. She had only ever heard vague reports from her mother that "someone" had "taken some things" from the house during Dennis's party, some of them quite valuable, and that the police were called in. All of it repeated by her mother as suburban gossip, the underlying tone carrying a whisper of Catholic righteousness, *that wouldn't have happened if Ronnie Fitzpatrick hadn't broken up the family and gotten above himself and married that woman who spent all his money on fancy jewelry.* Alison couldn't remember if she had actually heard her mother say those words, or if she had just heard her think them. In any case it was true that anytime that accursed Christmas party made its appearance in a chatty phone call, Alison rather immediately needed to go. Rose had put two and two together and come up with Alison's crashing regret to have lost so definitively the love of her life.

And who's to say she was wrong? God knows it was actually easier to bury the memory of the larceny. There was something so frightening about what she had done she couldn't afford to look at it, and not looking at it meant for the first time since she had met him that she didn't have to look at Kyle or the memory of Kyle or the hope of Kyle. Her ability to cling to some idiotic dream of Kyle was the collateral damage of that night.

Only there he was, big as life, traipsing around Cincinnati, Ohio, buying baby formula.

"So how does he look?"

"He's still great looking. Those gray eyes. Good God."

"What a mistake that was."

"Mom, stop it," Alison ordered. "He's married, he has two kids, I think we can safely say we've both moved on."

"I'm not saying you haven't! I'm not saying anything! I'm not saying anything." She went back to the pot of mashed potatoes on the stove, and Alison caught, in the light over the stovetop, how gray her hair had gotten. She looked old. She was wearing a thin beige cardigan with little embroidered flowers at the collar. It had at one time been a simple pattern, etched in white and brown silks, little daisies and leaves with off-white faux pearls floating among the threads, but most of the pearls had been lost over the years, the threads torn. The pattern was more memory than anything at this point.

"You used to wear that sweater when I was in high school," Alison remarked. Rose looked down at it, surprised.

"Did I? It was my mother's." Alison remembered that too, suddenly, how Rose had gone through Grandma's things when she died and saved whatever clothes she felt that she could wear. But that was years ago, at least ten years, and here she was still wearing her dead mother's clothing. Was she trying to keep the memory close, or was it just another expression of a nature that was pathologically thrifty? Eight kids, of course she had to make do with anything there ever was to make do with. But surely there was more money now, and God knows there was stuff out there to be had. Malls, department stores, one-click shopping, all those television commercials you had to wade through to get to three minutes of storytelling, the whole universe just seemed to be about *stuff* now. She remembered her own childhood differently. The specificity of items. Childish treasures carefully accumulated and arranged on a tiny pressed wood desk—a single line of Pokemon creatures, a Lego starship she had inherited from Jeff when he decided Legos were lame. A colored pen collection. And all her clothes for so many years, nothing but hand-me-downs. Boy, that was a drag, but there was no convincing Mom to buy her something new when there were clothes around that still had some wear in them. As Megan used to say, *Mom could make a nickel bleed.* It seemed another era, simple and humble by comparison to the thoughtless excesses of the present. Or was that yet another one of those strange dichotomies between the Midwest and the East Coast which seemed to multiply every time she turned around? Yet another way Cincinnati was different from New York: They didn't have as much stuff here, and the stuff that was here just wasn't as good. *They don't have as much dough.* Not to put too fine a point on it.

Or maybe she had missed something. Maybe the fact was that her parents were poor. Maybe she'd grown up *poor* and somehow never put two and two together. That was actually possible and would explain the astonishment she had felt when she landed in New York and found herself crippled by her own financial pragmatism. In Cincinnati, if you didn't have money, you figured out how to make that nickel bleed. In New York, you just pretended you had it, because if you didn't have it, you didn't count. That had never even occurred to her before, but now that she had fallen into the deep end of the pool in show business everything looked different. People looked different. Money looked different. The past looked different, and honestly it wasn't that long ago; it was just days ago, it seemed, that she and Kyle were wrapped so entirely in each other that neither one of them could see straight. They were all getting too old too fast. Alison wished that someone had warned her about this while she was in high school. *People get old really fast. Take it easy and learn to forgive.* She wondered if she would have known what that meant in high school.

"Anyway, I think it's a good thing that I saw him," Alison announced, and she was careful to make sure it sounded like a good thing. For extra measure, she went over to Rose and hugged her, reassuring. It was easy enough to do, hug your mom, why don't you do it all the time? Rose certainly responded, smiling up at her with such instantaneous gratitude that Alison felt her heart clutch. Why all the sniping at your mom? What was the point? "You don't have to worry so much, Mom," she said. "I didn't lose the love of my life! He's just a high school boyfriend."

There was a finality to this that felt fine. Years of idiotic behavior were put in a box and labeled, stuck in a corner of the basement along with old art projects and worn-out Halloween costumes. "At some point, seriously, what's past is past and you're an idiot for hanging out in a place that doesn't even exist anymore," she declared, definitive. "That thing with Kyle is just done done done. We have to figure out something else to talk about." The floating awareness that this was merely true breathed through her with something resembling hope. "You know what?" she said. "I have to go wash my hair." And then that was what she did.

THE "SURPRISE VISIT" she had decided to make was welcome and easily explained, especially since she hadn't yet met Megan's twins, who were already toddlers. Rose was happy to see Alison and so even was her father, whose skepticism about his wayward daughter had eased considerably since she had started making money. He was still never around, always off golfing or at the gym, but when she did catch a glimpse of him he was nice enough. In his distant dad way, he was proud of her for being on television and didn't care that the show was crap. Megan, meanwhile, was pregnant again and desperate for help and companionship, so Alison's glamorous irony was entertaining when she drove over to Walnut Hills and tried haplessly to lend a hand with those twin toddlers. There was a kind of joyful and unthinking chaos that carried everyone through Alison's sudden arrival, but after a few days she knew that they were whispering behind her back. What, after all, was she doing there? And how long was she going to stay?

She herself could not have told them, although she was not as ignorant of her heart's maneuverings as she pretended to be. She knew the nature of the storm that was gathering on her horizon and she also knew that there was no way to run from it. Not that she precisely *wanted* to run from it. The universe had come calling, and she felt the reckless joy of having summoned it. She also wanted to kick it in the face. So many girls in her position turned into utter nightmares at this juncture, making surly and constant hysterical demands, exacting a cost for being given everything everyone told you to want. But any hunger for self-indulgent rage around Alison's personal choices had never been acknowledged. She was from Ohio. People didn't act like that here.

In fact, they didn't act like this anywhere else. Disappearing into the Midwest was not generally considered even a possibility in the Hollywood playbook; consequently, it was a tactic with a short shelf life. The very day after Alison's chance meeting with Kyle, her mother's phone rang, and Rose answered it.

"Why, yes, she is," she informed the caller. "Just a minute." She held the receiver out to Alison, who was sitting at the kitchen table, eating a bowl of Cheerios. "It's for you."

Alison glanced up, surprised, and took the phone. "Hello?"

"You don't answer your cell anymore?"

"Ryan?" She had a moment of thinking, *How on earth did you find me*, but then that would imply that she didn't want to be found. When in fact things weren't at all that clear.

"I've left messages everywhere, are you avoiding me?"

"Why would I avoid you?" Her mother behind her, eyes going wide, looked worried suddenly. Alison waved her off. "It's my agent, Mom." This announcement seemed to worry Rose even further. People didn't have agents in Ohio, and she clearly thought Alison should treat this important person with more respect. Alison dragged the receiver back to her bedroom and slammed the door on the chord.

"I just needed to go home and see my family."

"For a whole week?"

"I needed to see my sister, she's got these twins now, they grow up so fast. My mom's been bugging me. How did you find me?"

"You have a lot of loyal fans. Your Wikipedia page is very informative."

"You got my parents' phone number off my *Wikipedia* page?"

"Listen, I was getting desperate. I was about to start tweeting all your stalkers, to find out what they knew."

"That joke is in poor taste."

"So is bolting New York when the hottest director around has taken a very special interest in you."

"I'm sick of interest," she muttered.

"Not this kind you're not. Louise Nagler just called, to check on your avail, for the spring."

"Meaning?"

"She's casting *Last Stop*."

Last Stop was Lars's movie. An eighty-million-dollar epic about a bunch of heroic American black ops who go rogue and take down an evil drug cartel in Mexico. The twist? The secret leader of this merry band of reprobates was a woman. Lars had talked about this project incessantly with the lunatics he did business with, at the dinners he had been dragging her to. She had heard him describe it repeatedly as his dream project, although that seemed to be a term that all these people used a bit casually. Other terms being used were "tentpole" and "international blockbuster" and "mega hit." The names that were being tossed about for the female lead included all the hottest stars in features. There was never even a whisper that Lars or his cohorts would even consider the possibility of casting an unknown. The idea seemed too ludicrous to even entertain. "Oh, for crying out loud, Ryan," she said. "She's being polite."

"No one inquires about avails to be polite."

"How do you know?"

"I think I know a little bit more about show business than you do. They're concerned about your series, whether or not your dates would conflict."

"They are not."

"How do you know, Miss Thing? Who's the agent, me or you?"

"Don't do that."

"Who's the agent?"

"Ryan—it's ridiculous to even talk about something that far-fetched anyway. Besides, I have a seven-year contract on a terrible television series and they aren't going to let me out."

"Let's just take it one step at a time, doll," he replied. "When are you seeing Lars next?"

"I'm in Cincinnati, Ryan," she started.

"Yes, but—"

"I'll check with my mom," she said. "I think she wanted me to be here for some brunch thing she's doing this weekend."

"It would be great if he could see you before then," Ryan informed her. "I'll let you work it out." The fact that there was no wheedling in his tone made it eminently clear how serious this might be.

But how serious could it be? Show business was all talk and money and kind of nothing else. She could fly herself out to Los Angeles and sit in any number of indistinguishable offices and talk to faceless men in suits for months on end, and it would amount to nothing. Or it would amount to something, for reasons which no one could begin to comprehend. Alison knew that she was going to end up sitting in those tragic offices eventually, was there really any reason to rush into it?

It was all so hard to explain. Megan stopped by with the twins to pick up a peach pie Rose had made for her and Phil, and Rose immediately launched into her version of events, reinterpreting the thumbnail sketch Alison had just finished narrating.

"Alison's agent called, she's being offered a big part in a big movie," Rose began excitedly. She was in pre-dinner mode, which entailed a lot of straightening of the kitchen, so that when Dad arrived back from his day of adventures as a retired businessman the house was tidy. Her actions were both conscious and unconscious, the patterns of a lifetime. Megan barely noticed the fact that her mother barely noticed her as she steered those twins out of the kitchen and into the family room, which was still, after thirty years of offspring, littered with toys. Alison did her best to keep up with the swooping women, as well as the fierce and unremitting confidence of their dialogue.

"Oh my God! That's amazing!" Megan started.

"I haven't actually been offered it," Alison cautioned.

"But they want her for it."

"They didn't actually—"

"He called here, to tell you that you had to go to Los Angeles—"

"They just want to talk to me."

"Well, they want her," Rose repeated. She was so determined that this was true, and so honestly excited that Alison didn't have the heart to contradict her again. "The director asked for her himself, which has to mean something, doesn't it?"

"Who is he, is he a big deal?" Megan's question was cheerful, innocent, full of her own delight at all this. She had subscriptions to *People* magazine as well as *Entertainment Weekly*. Showbiz gossip was like a bag of M&M's to her.

"He's not a big deal. He's kind of a big deal," Alison admitted. Only a total art snob would pretend that Lars Guttfriend was not a big deal. "He directs action movies. You know." Her head drew an utter blank trying to remember the action movies Lars had directed. They all sort of blurred together after a while, you had to admit that, even if you weren't an art snob. "I don't know him that well. We went out a couple times."

"You're *dating* a movie director? Oh my God, I have to tell Suzanne, she will just flip *out*." She pulled out her cell and started to text feverishly.

Suzanne was Megan's best friend, they seemed to be joined at the hip by their iPhones.

"We're not dating. It was just a couple of dinners!" The absurdity of all this was starting to amuse Alison, as well as panic her. She couldn't remember the last time anyone in her family had thought anything she did was cool.

"Do you tweet about it?"

"No, oh God, no—I haven't figured tweeting out yet."

"You're dating a movie director, and he wants you in his movie, you need to tweet about it." Megan was hardly paying attention, the toddlers had stumbled back into the kitchen and they were everywhere now. She kept scooping them up and feeding them Cheetos out of a small Tupperware container. They gobbled the Cheetos with such single-minded pleasure that Alison could not stop herself from reaching over and helping herself although she knew that if she was flying to the West Coast on Friday she had better start the starvation diet again, pronto.

"How come you know so much about tweeting?" Alison asked. "You're a young mother with twin toddlers, everybody expects you to be brain-dead for another six years at least."

"The only thing I have time to read is tweets, they're nice and short, and they're funny."

"I don't even know what a tweets is," Rose announced.

"It's stupid, Mom," Alison reassured her. "It's a lot of people with nothing better to do throwing their brains away."

"Oh my God, you are such a snob!" Megan protested. "Mom, you know about tweeting, I showed it to you. People talk to each other on the internet. A lot of people all over the world are tweeting now and it's a big tool for social justice." Rose had, in recent years, become interested in the plight of the poor. She was apparently hanging out with a bunch of nuns who got together and prayed for the suffering of people all over the planet. It seemed harmless enough but it did call to mind stories her mother had told them, in childhood, about how she used to collect money for pagan babies. Another activity instigated by a bunch of nuns, just one that wafted even further into the past, ever further into her mother's unwavering innocent heart.

"It's not for helping the poor, Mom," Alison contradicted. "Tweeting is just a lot of people saying absolutely inane things because they want to be famous."

"That's why you have to do it! You're famous now," Megan insisted.

"I'm a television actress, that doesn't make you famous."

Megan was having none of it. "Everyone in Cincinnati tweets about your TV episodes as soon as they come on," she informed her. "My friend Suzanne tweets about you constantly. When she hears you are going to be in this movie, honestly she is going to flip."

"Why does your friend Suzanne care about what I do?"

"It's just fun, it's a fun thing," Megan said. "It's something cool that we can talk about." One of the twins was getting to the tail end of her Cheetos, and her orange face was starting to register exhausted bewilderment. Alison didn't know much about kids in general, but she knew enough to recognize Megan's precious seconds of adult conversation were coming to an end.

"Well, I haven't been offered any movie, and you cannot tell your friend that I'm dating this movie director because it's just not true," she warned her sister. "I mean it, don't go telling people that. I could get into a lot of trouble if something like that showed up on some dingdong's Twitter feed." Because she was afraid, this pronouncement came out more forcefully than she had intended. Megan picked up her orange-faced baby and tried not to look hurt, and Alison wilted inwardly. *That's not what I meant*, she wanted to blurt, but too many years of being the black sheep kept her mouth shut and Megan turned away from her, fussing with the children, closing herself off from what had mere moments before seemed like pleasant, nonsensical banter.

Honestly, everyone in her world treated her like a complete idiot. Her agent, her publicist, every director she ever met, bloggers—with the exception of Schaeffer, that nutty guy who seemed to think she hung the moon. Now here she was in Cincinnati, and they all thought she was an idiot too. Only in a more Midwestern, *you're so ungrateful* kind of way. And it wasn't what she meant! She loved that Megan was tweeting with her friends about Alison and her slightly silly television show. She liked her fans, they were pretty nice people, when she bumped up against them. They were all so happy to have their pictures taken with her, and gossip about what was happening on the show.

"Here, come help Grandma with the soup." Rose lifted one of the twins into the air and handed the kid a piece of chopped carrot. "You just put it in there. Perfect!" For indeed, the tiny fist had immediately hurled the bit of vegetable into the giant pot of water on the stovetop. With an unconscious ease, Rose handed the second twin her own bit of carrot, so that both children would have a turn. The simplicity of the moment was weird and graceful, plugged innately into a kind of knowledge Alison couldn't penetrate. How did these women know so instinctively what those kids wanted? Even chopping vegetables was a mysterious enterprise these days. It was a given that you would just buy them already chopped, at Dean & Deluca.

The phone rang. Everyone's focus had so completely moved on to the task at hand—dropping vegetable bits into that giant pot of water—Alison was the only one available to pick the thing up. "Hello," she announced.

"Alison, hi." Time flipped. The past and the present kept smashing into each other in completely untenable ways. How did people do this? Why was she so bad at it?

She called upon the actress. Chipper, bold, secure. "Hey, Kyle, hi!" Megan glanced up, but somehow managed not to raise an eyebrow. They were all moving on.

fifteen

KYLE'S WIFE SEEMED to float. She was gliding around the glorious open kitchen, a kid on one hip, pushing a perfect wisp of a blonde curl off her forehead, turning with a faint look of confusion and then smiling, welcoming, couldn't be happier to see Kyle's ex in her fantastic home. *Wow,* Alison thought. *She's like a painting.*

She *was* like a painting, a painting of a wife inside a painting of a house. As she hurried across the room to greet Alison, the illusion of perfection gave way to a kind of harried happiness, which seemed even more perfect. She was so pretty it was like a state of being; she clearly had carried it with her from childhood. Alison knew these girls. There was something about being told you were pretty from the second you were born; it did something to your brain.

"Alison! I am so glad you could come."

"Thanks! Thank you, Van." Alison was abashed in the face of the other women's lovely enthusiasm. Van seemed like such a *nice person*; of course Kyle would marry a nice person. "Here, I brought you this." The standard offering, a generic Malbec, the guy in the store had promised it was good. Van laughed at it, finally a slight note of brittleness.

"Oh, I wish I could! I'm breastfeeding, I can't have a drop of anything. And my milk is so erratic. I know you saw Kyle buying formula, which I *so* didn't want to do, but my placenta tore, there was blood everywhere and I was a*ne*mic for three days, the milk just didn't come and didn't come and you'd think being married to a pediatrician they'd warn you what that might mean—"

"I did warn you," Kyle noted, reentering the room with another guest. Thank God, this was an actual party, there were going to be strangers to meet who would keep the whole thing complicated and social. "Alison, this is Martin Emory. Martin is a friend of ours from St. Luke's. Martin, this is Alison Moore, she's visiting from New York."

"Of course I know who you are," Martin assured her. He was plain-spoken, with an open face, good looking perhaps if he would compose his features into some kind of expression, but that hadn't occurred to him, or maybe he didn't actually know how to do it. His absolutely ordinary face seemed to simply want to be pleasant. These people really didn't exist in New York; they just didn't.

"Nice to meet you, Martin," Alison responded.

"When Kyle said you were in town, I thought, terrific! I really want to meet her," Martin explained.

"Oh, thank you," said Alison. This was different from her fans, who gushed a little more effusively and always took a selfie. Martin was considering her now with a quiet and expectant enthusiasm. He seemed to want her to say something more, but what? Or maybe this fuzzy silence was enough for him. He smiled and nodded, and for a moment Alison thought that he might start bleating, like a sheep.

"So you're from Cincinnati!"

"I, yes," Alison agreed.

"But you live in New York now?"

"Yes."

"I thought all you actresses lived in Los Angeles."

"Oh—well, a lot do," Alison acknowledged. What was with this guy? He didn't come at her with the alpha male energy of a New Yorker, but there was an undertone that implied that he knew absolutely everything, even though he was from Ohio. On her way over Alison had told herself that a party at an old boyfriend's house in Cincinnati would be a cakewalk compared to the shark-infested dinners and screenings and openings and club nights that were her usual fare. But she was already feeling the troubling misconnects of people who lived and believed different things. What had Kyle just said, he knew this guy from *church*? In New York no one admitted that they *went* to church, unless they went to temple.

Martin was still smiling, but there was that edge of something else underneath that fuzzy Midwestern bonhomie. Superiority? "I was in Los Angeles once, the weather's nice but the traffic was so horrible. I don't know how anyone lives there."

"I can't stand LA," she agreed, although the few times she had gone on press junkets out there, they had put her up in posh hotels and treated her like a movie star. It didn't precisely suck.

"New York is worse," Martin continued. "All those homeless people? Who wants to see that?"

Kyle swooped in with a glass of wine for them both. "When was the last time you were in New York, Martin?" he asked, as if this were a serious conversation.

"I've never been," Martin announced, again with such an air of authority that Alison started. She had been immersed in the innate New York dismissal of the Midwest for so long she had forgotten, frankly, how thoroughly Midwesterners returned the favor. This clown had never been to New York, but he still thought he knew enough to dismiss it? Dismiss *New York*? The whole thing?

"You must come!" she said, smiling winsomely, completely pretending that he hadn't insulted her life choices six times in two minutes. "It's actually such a crazy interesting and dynamic place. It truly is a melting pot, it's so amazing to live with so many people from so many different cultures. I love it."

"I'll take your word for it," Martin informed her.

"How long have you been there now?" Kyle asked.

"Wow, I guess it's been—four years? Five years?" She wasn't feigning; at some point time did blur and that point had been passed long ago. Which was why, presumably, she could stand in the kitchen of Kyle's glorious home and chat with total strangers about nothing. In the distance a doorbell rang. Kyle's pretty wife floated by, greeting people, making sure their coats were put in the proper bedroom. A gorgeous little girl ran after her, golden curls flying. Kyle was apparently living a Victorian fantasy now.

"How do you and Kyle know each other?" Martin asked.

"We dated in high school," Kyle said.

"Oh." Martin made a face, putatively impressed. "Kyle! You have an eye for the ladies."

"Well." Kyle smiled and offered up a self-conscious little shrug, *what can I say*? There were more people now, drifting into the kitchen, cooing hellos. He turned to greet them and to collect drink orders.

"You and Kyle dated?" This Martin person apparently had concluded that Kyle's offhand mention of it made their personal history fair game.

"We did, yes."

"So how'd you let him go?"

"Excuse me?"

"Good-looking doctor, isn't that what you girls all want?" *Leering*?

Was he actually leering? "You're an actress, you're going to need someone to take care of you. Unless you were looking to trade up."

"Oh, look who's here!" *What a fucking creep.* "Excuse me, I really do need to say hello."

Tragically there was really no one she knew there, but she headed across the room with a purposeful determination. The guests who were slowly filling the house were a different sort from what she was used to. The women were dressed up; Ann Taylor or something like, tasteful fitted dresses off the rack, a lot of beige brushed wool, a flash of houndstooth, low heels. Their husbands in dress slacks and sports coats, ties, Alison honestly didn't know any people like this anymore, and there were so many of them here, standing around holding wineglasses and chatting. They were all clearly educated and well-off, young adults who seemed like old adults. She felt like a slightly dysfunctional teenager next to them; her black jeans and loose violet-striped top seemed boho and unsophisticated and rebellious, when in fact she had hoped that something so simple and chic might help her fit in. *You look hotter than anyone else in the room*, her brain reminded her. *Stop worrying.*

This particular bit of internal advice bucked her up, made her feel strong, independent, more like a television star and less like a loser actress. She gave herself permission to temporarily ignore the little pods of people who were ignoring her, and drifted over to the wall of bookshelves to read the spines of the books and find out what Kyle and Van were reading or pretending to read. She and Kyle had both been book junkies back in high school but she always went for a good novel while Kyle was constantly struggling with the serious thinkers who were utterly over her head. He had been so sure she could join him in his fascination for theological and philosophical ephemera, but while she had loved listening to him read to her, she actually never understood a word. Although she did develop a true fondness for Teilhard de Chardin, that old brainiac priest who had fallen in love with a woman he couldn't have sex with.

And there he was, the intellectually impenetrable and physically chaste Jesuit, represented by at least six or seven volumes, next to Henri Nouwen, another high school favorite, and there at the end of the shelf four volumes of Thomas Merton. Another one of those priests who couldn't consummate their lust for the women they loved, because of the church. They were their own Boy Scout troop, those guys. The Merton books were newer, while the other books sported the battered covers of those read years ago. Probably the same ones he'd read to her in high school before she would finally get sick of it and climb all over him. She thought about reaching up and taking a peek, hoping to find one of the passages he had read to her back then, but decided against it. *No more of that*, she reminded herself, as she let her attention drift to the other shelves—volume after volume of medical textbooks and then shelf after shelf filled with books about childbearing and child-rearing—*What to Expect When You're Expecting, Wise Woman Herbal for the Childbearing Years, Bearing His Fruit: Stories About Godliness for Children.* Were Kyle and Van some sort of Jesus freaks now? Some of these books looked more like mindless Christian middle-stream tripe.

"You checking up on my reading?" Kyle asked, stepping up beside her.

"Absolutely," she admitted, and she gave herself permission to grin at him. "You still reading this stuff?"

"Mostly Merton now. I went down to his monastery in Kentucky, it was really beautiful."

"You went to a monastery? What, do they give tours?"

"Not a tour," Kyle explained, smiling a little at her cheeky ignorance. "More like a retreat. Their doctor needed some time off, so I went down for a week and took care of them, and prayed with them." He bumped a little on the word "pray." Kyle knew her attitude toward that sort of thing, or at least he knew that her attitude toward that sort of thing had probably not changed over the past years. She had never been openly disrespectful about the seriousness with which he regarded his Catholicism, but it was impossible not to notice that her views were a shred hostile. One time she had actually posited that she might not believe in God; that was another big hurdle.

"So you're a bigger Catholic than ever, I guess," she observed.

"I guess I don't have to ask where you stand," Kyle replied.

"That whole horrible religion sucks," she informed him. "Although I do still have a soft spot for Caravaggio."

"The murderer."

"He was a genius who broke some rules. Like your favorite Jesuit."

"Chardin *didn't* break rules, that's the point."

"He so did too, Kyle, that much I remember. The church told him to shut up, which he didn't—"

"He did."

"No, he didn't, he kept writing."

"But he didn't publish until after he died."

"They were creeps, they should have let him do what he was doing, discovering Piltdown Man."

"Peking Man."

"Whatever. They sent him to China, right—"

"Yes, that's—"

"As a way to shut him up and stop him writing about evolution, even though he knew that God wanted him to be doing that."

"That's not exactly—"

"You told me the story enough times, and then when they banished him to China, what do you know, the biggest find of the century, Peking Man, is right there. So that's either irony or God. You can take your pick."

A charming laugh flashed out of nowhere and skittered between them like a butterfly. "What are you two arguing about?" And there was Van, smiling, rosy, the blonde child propped on her waist. "Reminiscing about your great romance?"

The shock of Van's direct allusion to their "great romance" clipped Alison right across the back of her neck. She turned, polite, racking her brain for a sufficiently lighthearted comeback, but Kyle was ahead of her. "Hardly," he said. His indifference to the accusation put him effortlessly on firm ground. "We were arguing theology."

"Hardly that either," Alison echoed. "I never understood a word of it."

"Not so. You're very good," he informed her. "More wine?"

He turned and reached over to a side table, where several opened bottles waited for a host's attention. Van's smile floated over them, and back to her guests with an adorable, bemused exasperation.

"She was the love of his life, you can't blame a wife for suspecting the worst," she announced cheerfully.

Alison remembered how at Dennis's Christmas party Van had proved herself so adept at the art of inflicting wounds in public.

"Well, I want to hear about the theology," Martin announced. "An actress, arguing theology! You don't see that every day."

"She's quite intelligent," Kyle stated. He wasn't looking at her.

"I'm sure." A cute chuckle from that fucker Martin, what an asshole.

"The best actors are brilliant, they have to be, to understand Chekhov, Shakespeare, Molière," Kyle informed him. "You can't approach the world classics without some spark of genius." That was her argument, made years ago how many times in the face of his insistence that she'd be throwing her life away. "What would the world be without our great artists? Or our great actors?"

"You're on television, aren't you?" This from the cheerful woman in the houndstooth, Alison hadn't even met her yet.

"I don't know if I'd call that brilliant," said Martin.

"I wouldn't either," Alison agreed. "It's a good job, though. I get health insurance." This was meant to be a joke, but Kyle did not look up from the glass of wine he was refilling with such concentration and diligence. His face was set, severe. Was he angry?

"You're being much too modest," Van insisted, kissing that blonde child on the head.

"I'm an actor, we're not a particularly modest tribe."

"Do you see that as being your goal, then?" Kyle finally lifted those pure gray eyes of his. She'd seen that look before. He *was* angry, but not at the creeps who kept pawing at them. *He's mad at me*, she realized.

"I—it's more of a job, I don't know about *goals,*" she stuttered.

"Meaning?"

"Well, television shows don't last forever."

"But you'll stay in television."

"Why wouldn't she?" Somebody lobbed that one in from the back of the crowd. "They pay like, crazy money, don't they?"

"Who are you people?" Alison laughed lightly, to let them know she was kidding, or maybe the laugh was just to take the sting out of the fact that she *wasn't* kidding. "Do you really hang out in Ohio and speculate on what television actresses make?"

"What *do* you make?" This from one of the men. They had all gathered around her, like she was a science exhibit.

"What do *you* make?" she tossed back.

"I'll tell you if you tell me."

"What are those things you aren't supposed to talk about, at dinner?" Van asked.

"Politics and religion," Martin answered.

"And *money*," Van finished. Underneath that angel in the house, there was something implacable and she was not happy. Having started it all, this whole scene wasn't going the way she wanted.

"They already broke the rule about religion!" Martin protested. "All bets are off." The assorted party guests chuckled at this shrewd point.

"We weren't talking about religion at all," Kyle said. "We were talking about art."

"I don't know if I'd call what I do *art*," Alison countered.

"You used to."

"You gotta eat." Now that idiot Martin was stepping into this on *her* side? How could this keep getting worse? All the other guests were nodding; this was a version of the world they understood. Being an actor was a ludicrous idea *unless* you were on television making a lot of dough.

"I still want to do Chekhov, is that what you're asking?"

"You *still* want to do Chekhov?" Kyle was implacable, and unamused.

"Doing television is hardly selling out. If I get big enough, they'll pretty much let me do—all the things—I want to do." This was such crap she couldn't believe she had actually said it. But it was what they all said; every actress she knew who was stuck on a shitty television show at one point or another ended up explaining to anyone who would listen that she had bigger dreams than sitting in a trailer all day for the chance to wear pretty dresses and spout bad dialogue. Besides, putting her in a position where she had to defend her choices to a bunch of strangers was really the limit. They didn't even know each other anymore! "And television isn't exactly a wasteland," she added. "The best storytelling in America is happening on television."

"I just thought you had bigger dreams," Kyle said. The thread of bitterness lying under all of it revealed itself, pricked her.

"I thought you did too," Alison countered. "I thought you were going to South America to set up health clinics." Kyle's jaw stiffened, another one of his tells. But who was he, after all, to judge her?

"Oh, sure," said Martin, that charmer. "South America!" He laughed, as if he even knew what any of this meant.

"It's true, it's the whole reason he wanted to be a doctor, it was all tied up in this idea of service to the poor," she announced. "God's calling. He wanted to take care of the masses."

"Well, there are certainly masses of people down at Pediatrics West," Houndstooth Woman observed. "Everybody's still out there having babies."

"That they are," Kyle interjected, with a finality meant to settle this line of argument. Alison was moving ahead, though, pushing straight toward the coming train wreck. It was her worst failing, and her greatest virtue, this recklessness. Kyle had loved and hated her for it, back in the day.

"It's just not what you said you wanted to do."

"What did he say he wanted to do?" Van was looking at her now like she was insane.

"He wanted to go to Ecuador to set up health clinics. Didn't have to be Ecuador." She waved her wineglass in the general direction of somewhere else, both insisting on her point and dismissing Kyle's past with an insouciant social flare. "Could have been anywhere that they needed him. He was studying Navajo at one point so he could go work at the Navajo Nation."

"Navajo?" Van was beyond astonished at that one.

"You know how they say 'I love you' in Navajo?" Alison asked. "They don't have a word for it, really. Because they don't believe in possession. You can't possess another person. You can't possess anything. So they say 'I'm glad about you.' That's how you say 'I love you.' I'm glad about you." She looked over at Kyle, who was seriously about to kill her. She didn't care. "Look, he still has the book," she noted. And there it was, on the shelf, *Navajo Made Easier*, in with all the other books they had wrangled over. Learning Navajo, another complete delusion, long since tossed aside.

"How charming."

"It's not anything, Van."

"The dream of your youth? That's not anything?"

"It wasn't a dream. It was nothing." *Did he actually say that?* The hours Alison had spent listening to him describe the need for doctors in developing countries, the call to social justice, the hope to work for WHO. The whole problem between them, his missionary's heart and her selfish vision of being an actress. They had never even talked about getting married and it wasn't the Catholic church that was the problem. What was a Doctor Without Borders going to do with an actress wife?

But what was he doing with this one? What was he doing with a nice house in the suburbs and a pretty wife and a charming toddler and a baby upstairs? What was the name of the place he worked? *Pediatrics West*? That's what he gave it all up for? This wife and this house and Pediatrics West?

He knew what she was thinking; of course he did. At least that was clear, they still tracked each other's inner lives with alarming specificity. It wasn't Alison's careless reference to their long-buried romance. He was embarrassed before her, the accusation that she had abandoned her dreams had doubled back on him with devastating accuracy.

Why had they given up everything for so little? And if they were going to give up their dreams anyway, why not give them up for each other?

Questions that didn't have to be answered. Blessedly the door opened behind them; another guest arrived, and another. The blanket of civility descended. It was a dinner party! No one had to account for their souls.

sixteen

"I'M HAVING DINNER with Dennis tonight," Kyle informed Van with casual indifference. He was still at the office, in front of his computer, his eyes bleary from the hours of emailing his practice now required. It was so much cheaper to consult with patients online, there was no way the insurance company would allow him to require office visits when a few keystrokes would do. It didn't mean less work of course—it meant more patients, given less care. His rage at the failures of the medical system got filed into another corner of his brain while he waited for Van to respond to his announcement.

"You're having dinner with Dennis? When did this happen?"

"He called this afternoon."

"And you didn't think to ask me?"

"I'm asking you now."

"You're not asking me, you're telling me."

"I'm asking you, that's why I called, because I'm asking you." A peeved silence bloomed on the other end of the line. This had been the norm for weeks now, ever since he had, according to Van, "humiliated her" at the dinner party he had insisted on throwing for "his old girlfriend." The endlessly circular arguments went nowhere, no matter how many times he reminded her that the idea of the dinner party had been *hers*, *she* was the one who thought it would be fun, she wanted her friends to meet the baby and she was bored, that was really how the whole thing had come to pass—no part or whole of any discussion or argument mattered.

And he could not, finally, dismiss the spirit if not the letter of her indictment. It wasn't the fact that he had gotten into an argument with his old girlfriend. It was what they had argued about. The swift if fleet eruption of accusation between himself and Alison had carried too much information, finally. Van could forgive the social faux pas—they had in fact gotten so heated that they were all but yelling at each other—but what Van couldn't forgive was the fact that Kyle had never told her, even once, of the missionary dreams of his youth. That he had once wanted to go to Ecuador, or Nicaragua, the mountains of Peru, to work in a health clinic. That Alison knew an essential truth about Kyle's soul that he had never even mentioned to Van. That she had blurted it in front of their peers. These facts informed every corner of their lives now.

They ticked away, unspoken, in the silence of the phone. He managed to keep his voice impersonal and cheerful. "Is it a problem?"

"Would it matter to you if it was?" He could hear the baby gurgling in her arms, and behind, Maggie chattering away with the cooler tones of Van's mother, who was in town. The happy contentedness of the life he was providing for all of them breathed through the airwaves. If he had come home for dinner, everyone would tense up and hide and burst into tears over nothing, and she was complaining because he figured out how to give them all a night off?

"Of course it matters, Van, come on," he said, allowing his voice to sound suitably conciliatory. "I just thought you'd like to have the time with your mom."

"So what's the plan, Dennis is going to *cook* for you?"

"No, we're going to meet downtown, maybe at La Cucina or something."

"Maybe? You don't know?"

"Yes, we're meeting at La Cucina, he was going to call ahead and get us a reservation." This of course now sounded like a lie, because that's what it was. He opted for more conciliation, rather than ratcheting things up. "I can come home," he said. "You sound upset. Did something happen?"

"It's fine. It's fine," Van announced, clipped.

The gurgling happiness of background noises had been silenced by all this. "I'll come home if you want me to," he said. "I didn't mean to upset you."

"No. You should go out. One of us at least should have a life."

"Well," he said. "I won't be late." She hung up without saying good-bye.

How had it come to this? He no longer even tried to sort it out and simply pulled up his calendar to get a sense of his late-afternoon workload. You couldn't cure everything online; the insurance company still allowed Pediatrics West to offer evening hours twice a week. Sometimes kids get sick at night, and a number of parents were juggling two careers and daytime appointments were impossible to schedule when Mommy's real estate practice was taking off while Daddy had to go to a conference in Dubai. He glanced at his appointment sheet; ten patients back to back, no breaks. Some of them you'd be able to get in and out in less than a minute, but no parent was going to stand for that after sitting out there in that waiting room for more than an hour.

The kids, honestly, were great. Sniffling, feverish, lethargic at one end of the spectrum and bursting with life at the other, they all seemed preternaturally present, their innocence and energy presenting its own kind of wisdom. You wouldn't suspect that these adorable creatures were going to evolve into the greedy and largely dim-witted race which had spawned them, although there was a creeping arrogance which showed itself when they got a little older.

His next appointment, luckily, was a four-year-old, Caleb. Wide brown eyes and a yogi-like slouch. Red curls. He looked up at Kyle with mournful expectation.

"Am I going to have to have a shot?" he whispered.

"I don't know, what's wrong with you?" Kyle asked him, matter-of-fact. He touched the kid's forehead lightly. Definitely hot.

"We think it's the chicken pox," the mother announced. A slender woman in a skirted suit, she pocketed her iPhone quickly and gave Kyle her full attention. This one wouldn't be snarling about a short appointment, she clearly wanted in and out. "Or at least that's the hope." *Oh, boy*, he thought.

"Then can I assume Caleb has not had his immunizations?"

"Okay, I know some of you don't approve, but this is an ethical issue for my husband and I," the mother announced. "We don't want that stuff in him."

Kids dying all over the world, and she thought vaccinations were unethical. Caleb looked up at him with those eyes. "I don't want a shot," he informed Kyle. His little cheeks were flushed, and now that he had gotten a second look, Kyle could see that the poor kid's collapsed posture was probably due to muscle pain. Kyle had to resist the urge to pick him up and cradle him. The little boys, especially, seemed so vulnerable.

"No shots," he said, trying to sound neutral, although he really hated the careless way these people endangered their children, and everyone else's too. How not to judge that. Yet another mystery. "Let's see if we can just make you feel better."

After two hours more of this, he finished, poured himself into his car, and drove over to the back streets of Clinton, the site of Dennis's elegantly crumbling apartment building. There were plenty of high school cronies who had settled, over time, in Cincinnati, but none of them somehow had the staying power of his pal, who had self-destructed in such a spectacularly public way. Dennis's excessive drinking had cost him his job at Procter & Gamble, and to "teach him a lesson," his father had told him in no uncertain terms that he was "on his own." That meant that the monthly allowance Dennis got was really not anywhere near as large as it could have been. It was also not small enough to force him to get another job. Instead, he invented his own peculiar brand of thrift. His Victorian apartment was small—eight hundred square feet—and because it was in the back of the building, inexpensive. The place was crumbling, but it was not a dump; instead, he had managed to choose a few pieces wisely, culling them from attics of relatives and family friends. A gorgeous bedspread, an antique lamp, leftover pieces of Limoges china, the detritus of weddings long gone by. He lived in two rooms which were, truth be told, elegant and fluid with the touches of decadence. The only thing he had paid for in the whole place? A sixty-two-inch TV.

This spectacular appliance was one of the lures which drew Kyle repeatedly back into Dennis's sphere. There was little or no television watching in the Wallace household, as Van had never moved off her determination that it was bad for the children. No *Teletubbies*, no *SpongeBob*, not even any *Sesame Street*; there was something in the pixels and the light which apparently seared their little brains and gave them autism. The fact that Kyle was even vaguely resistant to this notion undermined him even further in her eyes. He begged her to show him the studies around children and television watching so that he could perhaps provide a calming perspective on the whole thing. Also, he was hoping she might let him watch the news once in a while if he could prove that there wasn't in fact radioactivity blasting at them and infecting the whole house, even when the kids weren't in the living room. No go.

Of course, the underlying suspicion breathed through the house: The real reason Kyle wanted to watch television "occasionally" was that he wanted to see the completely trashy show his ex-girlfriend was on. And in point of fact, Kyle *had* once or twice watched Alison's show over at Dennis's apartment, although he would never admit as much to Van. The thing was stupid, but given the larger questions of his own life—a wife who disliked him, daughters who were afraid of him, a medical practice that was drowning him in paperwork, a God who appeared and disappeared at will—he found its inanities cheerfully soothing. Particularly since Alison has shown up, out of the blue, and reminded him that she still lived on the planet.

"You missed a good one last week," Dennis informed Kyle, upon his arrival. "Alison making out with a naked police officer. In a swimming pool. It was riveting."

"I thought she was back together with what's his name."

"Rob. They are back together, yes. Last week was a repeat. Well worth repeating, too, I must say." He handed Kyle a whopping glass of scotch and refreshed his own. Dennis still went to AA, but mostly for the amusement factor; he took perverse pleasure in getting those chips while drinking on the side. Kyle had registered his protest—really, as a doctor, he couldn't be expected to think it was a good idea for Dennis to destroy his liver—and Dennis had shrugged him off. Alcoholism was in the eye of the beholder, he supposed. And in fact Dennis had a point: Why didn't those people at AA even suspect? Or did they? If they did, why did they keep giving him those chips?

But Dennis was too valuable to him, finally, to press the point. Van had banned him from their house, probably because he had made a pass at her at one time or another. Kyle wasn't sure, but nothing would surprise him; Dennis had twice made passes at Alison, that he knew of.

While Kyle was dating her. It had pissed him off of course at the time but what were you going to do with someone like Dennis, he was just an asshole. Anyway, that was all in the past. Dennis's devilish approach to living was now a balm. And the scotch, and the television set.

"I got Chinese. Dumplings, moo shu pork, kung pao chicken."

"Sounds great."

Dennis unloaded white cartons from a brown paper bag while Kyle dropped onto the couch and reached for the remote. The set flickered to life, and he checked the listings of saved shows in the DVR. He knew that what he was about to indulge in over scotch and Chinese food was the worst sort of psychological scab-picking. But the option was going home to Van and her mother and those two bewildering little girls. There was no question: It had been a mistake to invite Alison to that misbegotten dinner party. But there was nothing to do about it now. Van had not forgiven him, and his brain hadn't either.

Alison's face loomed on the screen, emerging like a mermaid out of the blue water of a pool in the night. She looked straight into the camera, those unforgettable green eyes flickering with confusion and desire.

"I can't believe you had a dinner party and you invited Alison and you didn't invite me," Dennis rebuked him. He dumped the white cartons of food on the coffee table in front of them. Chopsticks, paper napkins, plastic forks. There was no standing on ceremony with Dennis.

"It wasn't me, it was Van. She thinks you're a bad influence on the girls."

"Not yet, but someday, definitely."

Was that even funny? It wasn't worth remarking that it might not be. Dennis was already watching the television set. "She looks hot," he announced, as if this were news.

"She's too skinny."

"She was that thin two years ago, at Christmas."

"It wasn't two years ago. It was three years ago," Kyle replied. Alison was arguing with someone now, it was hard to tell who. The sound was off.

"What was three years ago?"

"Your Christmas party."

"The *Christmas* party." Dennis nodded, digging into the kung pao chicken, wielding his chopsticks with an elegance that was somewhat surprising in a perpetual drunk. "Oh yes, that wonderful Christmas party. Remember those boots she was wearing? Thigh-high gray suede—"

"Yes, I remember the boots."

"Is that bitter?"

"Why would I be bitter?"

"I don't know. I know nothing, Kyle, you are ridiculously discreet, it's one of your worst habits. You invited her to your house for dinner with your wife—"

"And ten other people."

"Yes, and ten other people but not me. So I know nothing about your current standing with Alison. For all I know, you've been carrying on a torrid affair with each other via the internet this whole time. For all I know, she flies in twice a month and meets you in a hotel in Covington."

"If I were fucking Alison, do you think I'd need to watch her do it on television?"

There was a shocked pause at this, and then Dennis laughed with glee. "Well well well, well well—" he started. Kyle stood. If he could have punched himself in the face, he would have.

"This is stupid," Kyle said. He looked around for the clicker, but it was buried, somewhere, under those cartons. The silent movie of Alison, her green eyes, her body rising out of the water, was interminable. "Where's the fucking clicker, I'm not watching this junk."

"Dude, far be it from me but if we were in an AA meeting, there would be about sixty people telling you that you need to talk about it," Dennis informed him.

"I don't need to talk about it."

"No, you just need to drink about it." Kyle glanced at the tumbler in his hand. It was true; he had already powered through the sizable bolt of scotch, in a matter of minutes. "Where's the clicker," he asked.

"You can turn it off if you want, I don't care," Dennis shrugged. "I just thought we were going to watch it. And I didn't get to see her when she was here, so I was kind of looking forward to it. But I can watch it later if you can't handle it."

"I can handle it, Jesus, that's not what—fine." The silent television continued to flicker before them, but Kyle deliberately ignored it, concentrating on his own set of cheap wooden chopsticks, splitting them down the middle without yielding splinters. It calmed him.

"So you and Alison got into it."

"We didn't get into anything."

"Liar."

"Dennis—"

"What? I want to know what happened, of course I want to know. She was at your house and now you're watching her on television and talking about how you wish you were fucking her."

"That's not what I—"

"And you're drinking rather heavily, which may be normal for me but is not for you. So maybe you need to talk about that."

"I don't actually need to talk about why I'm drinking. I know why I'm drinking. What I don't know is why you're so interested in my sex life."

Dennis started, then laughed, enjoying the nasty turn. "Ooo la la, latent homophobia," he grinned. "Goodness gracious, there's always all that Catholicism, right there when you need it."

"Screw it." Kyle was sick of this. He finally found the fucking clicker and pointed it at the television, which for a second refused to go off.

"You're holding it backward," Dennis informed him. Kyle stared at the device in his hand, turned it around, and pointed it at the television. It still didn't work. Alison was silently laughing at some young Adonis now. She had a towel wrapped around her and her hair was wet. The towel slipped suddenly, revealing a black bikini underneath for a moment before she glanced down, picked up its edge, and pulled it close again.

"I should have just slept with her," he said.

The sentence fell between them, clear, final. He looked around for that scotch bottle. Dennis picked it up from the floor beside him and passed it over.

"You really never did?" Dennis asked. "You always told me you never did, but seriously. You never did?"

"That night at your party," Kyle admitted. Repeated pressing got the remote to work and blessedly, the television set went blank.

"Wait a minute. You fucked her, at my Christmas party?"

"I didn't."

"You just said—"

"We almost did." He couldn't believe he was admitting this, but he was tired, and drunk, and it felt good to tell it, finally, even to Dennis. "We were up in your dad's bedroom, and we were drunk, and—you know—"

"No, I don't know," Dennis said. He was laughing, delighted. "You did it in my father's *bedroom*? How did I miss this?"

"We didn't do it," he clarified, for the second time. "It was late, I was leaving. Who knows where you were. You were passed out somewhere. And she was up there, hanging out, and—" He paused, feeling the buzz from the alcohol, and tried to tell the story without getting the sequence wrong, or confusing the words. Dennis was just watching, finally, and finally serious. "Van and I were in a bad place. It just felt like we had, like the whole thing was a mistake, and I was trying to keep everything steady but then Alison showed up, and I wasn't—and then it was, honestly we didn't even have a chance to even talk to each other. And it was terrible, we hadn't seen each other since we broke up, in Seattle, I, you know, we *couldn't*, I know that's why she, and I was so fucked up but I didn't blame her." He was frustrated that he was rambling, and not making his points. If he had been locked in a confessional and blathering on to some somnolent priest, it would never have passed muster. But Dennis, for all his drunken narcissism, Dennis might actually understand what it was he was trying to admit to, if he could simply find the words and admit to it.

"I was in some crazy space back then, I know it was ridiculous, I wouldn't have sex with her. And I knew, Christ, it's not like I didn't, man, all those years. To want something that entirely and not be able to, but all the shit they shoved into our heads? And that's no excuse. Seriously, I'm not making excuses. She wanted to. And I was the one. I was a fucking moron." He reached for the scotch bottle. What did it matter how drunk he was, now? "It was a power play. I was just, I wanted to win. I knew it was driving her crazy. And I'm not, listen—I don't think it was a game for her. I don't think that. I think she was just, we were, when we were together in it? Nothing else, you know. I'm such an asshole." It felt great to admit it. Every shred of his stupidity laid open to the air. "I was a fucking child. And then she was gone. And it was like I woke up, one day, and I had a wife who really didn't like me, and there was Alison, at your house, at a really stupid Christmas party. Wearing those boots. And then we didn't have a half second to even talk, because Van was so paranoid. Which, why wouldn't she be? But there was so much that Alison and I, we hadn't finished, we weren't anywhere near finished with anything, between us, and then she disappeared, it was like she vanished. I thought she had gone home. It was the end of the night, everyone else was either passed out or had taken off, and I was just, I thought maybe—her coat was still there, on the steps, so I thought she might still be there." Having relived the memory so many times in the past three years, this part of the mystery was exquisitely present. "And then there she was, in your father's bedroom. And we, honestly I can't remember what we said. It didn't matter. Maybe it's just that we were tired of punishing each other. That's what I thought. I was just done with all the shit in my head. She was there and I didn't care about anything else. And then she, you know, I don't know, she . . ." As much of a relief as it was, he couldn't, finally, describe the moment. Dennis was hanging on his every word, and Kyle couldn't tell it. "Anyway," he shrugged. "We almost did it." He took a breath.

Dennis waited for a moment, then another. Then another. "Wait. *Wait*," he erupted. "You *almost* did it? That's all I get? You *almost did it*?" He looked completely outraged. Kyle would have felt sorry, but he had in fact noticed that Dennis had a growing boner, strategically disguised behind the mustard-colored throw pillow he held oh so casually against his thigh.

"Yeah, we almost did it," Kyle admitted, abrupt. "And then she stopped it, and I went home, and worked things out with Van."

"You 'worked things out,'" Dennis sneered. Kyle, wavering on his feet, didn't understand how this confession had gone so far awry. It didn't matter. The spell cast by his own words had splintered. He felt the shame of all of it, doubly, yet again. Why had he said so much, so unwisely, after holding it so close for so long? The television was a blank. He was drunk. A fractured family of unhappy women waited for him to return, and create, for them, a misery.

That's ridiculous, they love you, he told himself, as he had told himself so many times before. *You are being ridiculous. Alison is a fantasy. She's not a real person anymore. Van and the babies are real. They are waiting for you. They are love.*

He had no way to determine, anymore, if what his brain told him was true.

seventeen

BY THE TIME Lars finally allowed himself to undress Alison, he was so obsessed with her body he had a vague urge to hurt it. The unfolding of her white back as he lifted the straps off her shoulders was exquisite. The dress, a simple black silk slip, dropped to the floor with an erotic grace as he turned her toward him. She wasn't wearing underclothes.

He always made them wait. Actresses were as a breed too volatile; you couldn't let them get the upper hand too early, as that would be the end of everything. But this one had not accepted his feigned indifference to her body with anything remotely resembling insecurity. She accepted his invitations to dinners and screenings with professional ease, and performed her duties as arm candy with the practiced charm of born royalty. She never intruded on his privacy. And then she disappeared. She literally just bolted—from Per Se, at a dinner which had cost him a thousand dollars a head—and then was utterly unreachable for two full weeks. He thought for a while that she was just fucking with him, and his interest cooled. He didn't have the time or the energy for a difficult actress. But then she returned, just as quickly and inexplicably. She called and apologized for leaving so abruptly. She had had a family emergency in, of all places, Cincinnati. She was sweet and funny. She wanted to take him out, to make up for it. He had his assistant Josh arrange a date for the following week; she would join him at a business dinner. When she showed up at the restaurant, she was wearing the thinnest of thin dresses. Another check in the plus column.

They sat next to each other on the banquette, facing a couple of the countless suits he had to deal with from one studio or another. He was glad that she looked so hot, as that was what those clowns expected. As usual she ate next to nothing, again something those shitheads approved of; the guys from headquarters were always suspicious when they saw a woman eat. She was winning and witty, laughing at their slightly too-sexual jokes, but never losing her poise. You could see the hint of her nipples underneath that black silk. He wanted to fuck her right there.

He waited through the drive back to his apartment and invited her up. While he turned her body toward him, she reached for his shirt. Conveniently, there was a condom in his back pocket, so they made love, for the first time, up against the door.

"Just like in *The Godfather*," she whispered, laughing, as he entered her.

The following morning, when Lars woke to find her in his bed, he studied her naked body with the eye of a connoisseur. Was she a notable beauty? It wasn't clear. She had certainly participated in behaviors which would increase that perception in the general public. Her hair had moved through a series of colors and cuts and extensions and curls, and had settled into a breathtakingly tousled brunette mop. Having gone back to starving herself since her return from Cincinnati, she was once again thin as a teenage tomboy with a glorious curve to her hips. As she turned and stretched, the hint of those green eyes lifted to him under the black smudge of mascara and eyeliner still more or less in place in spite of the vigorous night before.

Which of her predecessors did she call to mind? Elizabeth Taylor, another raven-haired beauty with extraordinary eyes? Ava Gardner? That was perhaps more like it. The ruthless duality which had made Ava a star had begun to assert itself in Alison's being. The eyes were too vivid. The soul was too big. She was both body and self. As he reached for the condoms in his bedside table, Lars let the thought skitter across his brain: Men would want that. It was marketable.

Lars had been intuitively aware of this possibility from the first moment he saw Alison Moore on a television trailer which had been forwarded to his email account from his otherwise generally useless agent. He was constantly being told to "take a look" at these girls and in fact it was a part of the detritus of his job that he enjoyed. Girls were always being offered up to him; he was expected to taste and determine which ones might develop into more than a taste. His agent had told him that Alison was "something special," but they said that about all of them, and most of them were anything but. Even in their early twenties, they had been sculpted and painted into an abstraction of beauty that was cheap and pornographic: the silicone breasts, the tiny nose, the strangely voluptuous lips, enormous eyes, tight, perfect skin. These were the girls who came to Los Angeles with a fierce and unexamined ambition to be a star, and each and every one of them proved willing to subsume any shred of individuality in the quest for that prize. Lars had railed about the contradictions mercilessly during drunken arguments with producers: None of these girls *were* anyone! Why do you need to turn them all into Kewpie dolls? Where is the next Monroe supposed to come from? You would have dismissed her for being fat. Streep? Funny chin. Bette Davis, Joan Crawford, God forgive us, those two horsefaces wouldn't have made it out of the starting gate. They all laughed at him, and had another martini. The next day he would get another ten emails, with footage on ten more identical starlets. When Alison's demo showed up in his inbox he didn't dismiss her immediately simply because she was a brunette. Perhaps if he had been less bored by all the Botoxed blondes, he wouldn't have given it any attention at all. But he *was* bored, and Alison was having sex with some good-looking hunk. The chemistry with her costar was impressive, and so were the green eyes. Having now tasted the wares, he could congratulate himself on the unerring accuracy of his instincts.

Alison stretched. As she drifted back into consciousness of what she had been up to the night before, she had to admit that making Lars wait had not been such a bad idea after all. Having finally landed herself in a movie director's bed, she also had to admit it was not a bad place to be. Lars was handsome, rich, and emotionally unavailable. After their second round in the sack they took a shower together, lounged around the apartment until noon, and then had sex again on the blond wood floor of his pristine dining room. The next day a pair of stunning silver earrings arrived at her apartment two hours before he did, carrying two bottles of Veuve Clicquot and one of the very finest olive oil. The olive oil was not for cooking.

"Well, you must have had quite a weekend." Ryan was positively cooing over the phone lines. It was only Monday afternoon.

"What are you talking about?" Alison felt a quick panic. She already knew that Lars had an absurd, even paranoid obsession with privacy. If he thought that she was out there bragging about their sexual escapades, the whole thing would immediately fall apart. "Tell me what you heard and who you heard it from." It crossed her mind that Lars might have had security cameras taping their activities in his apartment. She prayed there were no crazy photographs or sex tapes on the internet.

"I didn't hear anything! But you have been getting some very interesting attention from some very interesting people."

"Stop being coy or you're fired," she announced.

"That's my little spitfire! Louise Nagler just called. Lars has talked to the studio. They're moving ahead with an offer for you on *Last Stop*."

Her heart stopped. Would he do that? Would he cast her because she had fucked him? The idea seemed too ludicrous to even entertain. "Oh, for crying out loud, Ryan," she said. "That's—impossible."

"Oh, no it's not, my dear." His tone was brisk, excited, confident. "You don't need to think about this side of it. Let me do my job. You just keep doing yours."

The words went through her like a knife. "I didn't sleep with him to get a job offer," she protested.

"No no no, of course you didn't. That is not what I meant. I meant acting. You are a brilliant actress. Stay focused on that. That is why they want you."

It hit her sideways. Kyle's accusation, that she was "brilliant." This was all moving too fast.

"Ryan, it's not *Sophie's Choice*. It's an action flick in the middle of the jungle."

"Okay, fine," he replied. "You don't have to do it, if you don't want."

"Of course I want to do it, I just—you know, I'm surprised. I didn't see this coming, I really didn't."

"Alison. Get excited. This is tremendous! Just give yourself a minute to be happy, okay? I'm going to get you everything you deserve. And then some. Now, go kiss your boyfriend, he's going to make you a movie star."

Boyfriend? She had spent the weekend having sex with the guy, and now he was her *boyfriend*? The radical disconnect between Lars and Kyle—with whom she had spent so many years, *not* having sex—was not lost on her. After that ridiculous dinner party where she and Kyle had accused each other yet again of so many mysterious failures, Alison had just decided to get back on the track of her own life. Calling Lars up and apologizing to him was simple good manners. Wearing a black slip dress with no underwear to a dinner date was something else entirely, but Lars was sexy, she was lonely, and she was mad at herself for even talking to Kyle in the grocery store, much less going to a stupid dinner party at his house. Having a hot date with a movie director seemed like a reasonable idea, in the wake of that nonsense.

This new development—he wanted to offer her a part in his movie?—was the last thing she had looked for. She had spent half the day wallowing in a walk-of-shame insecurity; having wild sex with a big Hollywood director for two solid days had truly made her feel like a slut, the fact that she had enjoyed every second of it notwithstanding. There was no question of love involved; obviously they did not love each other. *What is this then, a business arrangement?* Her brain was having its way with her; she wanted to tell it to shut up. In any event, when Lars's assistant called at six to find out if she could meet him for a late dinner at ten, she agreed immediately. She didn't hesitate when he let her know that Lars would love it if she could meet him at his apartment.

She also didn't think twice about wearing the maroon silk Prada mini dress which showed up at her door minutes later. Lars's eye was, not surprisingly, impeccable; the dress fit beautifully and the color was both slutty and glorious in its classic grace. Alison looked like a whore and a goddess. It was the first breath of an inkling as to what Lars was going to try to do.

eighteen

AGAINST ALL ODDS, the script was good. Having expected it to be total junk, Alison was caught off guard. The dialogue was sharp; the jokes were funny. The hero was world weary but determined—because of his tragic past he had lost all hope, but a shred of the hope for hope remained. The action sequences were terrific and on the whole the script was surprisingly careful not to kill extra people. Those who lost their lives in the black-op showdown with the local drug dealers were mourned. There was no meaningless carnage.

And her character—well, it wasn't her character *yet*, but the one they were considering her for—was fantastic. Laila was a hippie waitress who had split the States three years ago, following a boyfriend to the middle of Mexico. He subsequently disappeared, carelessly informing her he was going to Belize for a weekend from which he would never return. The girl stayed on and became a local legend. She ran the only decent restaurant within a sixty-mile radius of Salusito, the mountain village in which she found herself. Her cook, Diego, was fiercely loyal and protective of her. She fronted for some of the local kids when they tried to play rock and roll in her cantina on Friday nights. The whole town adored her. *What a part*, Alison knew. Her Midwestern practicality informed her quite firmly that the chances of her actually getting it were slim to none.

And of course the offer didn't come, did it? After being told that it was on its way, both by Ryan and by Lars, it simply didn't show up.

"How many times do I have to tell you, these things are complicated," Ryan reassured her on one of their daily phone calls.

"Oh, Ryan, please stop. You know I love you. I think you're a great agent, this isn't about you."

"I *know* it's not about *me*, who said it was about *me*?"

On days like this she really wished she wasn't dealing with such an *agent*. The layers of show business bullshit were like some sort of very strange, sticky cocoon. "I'm just saying it's been a long time since you told me this offer was coming through, and it was a long shot to begin with. I'm not *stupid*." She suddenly felt overwhelmed that she even had to mention that. No matter how cataclysmically she had been misunderstood by every single member of her giant family, no one had ever underestimated her intelligence. And now here she was, being conned by idiots who expected her to care about a shell game. *Where is it where is it? Where's the ball?* A reasonably smart canine would have picked up on this useless bullshit years ago and refused to play.

"It's okay," she said, suddenly humiliated by her own stupidity. "If I'm not getting an offer, it was a long shot."

"I thought things were going well for you and Lars."

"Lars and I are fine, that's not—look. You know that's not why he offered it to me. He's not offering me the part just because he's screwing me. Oh, God. I can't believe I just said that. Particularly because as far as I can tell he's not offering me the part at all."

"What does Lars say?"

"Lars—Lars says they're offering me the part."

"Well?"

"WELL, IF THEY'RE OFFERING IT WHY IS IT TAKING SO LONG?"

"Back down, tiger. We've been through this. They are offering you the part, they just have an internal situation they need to work out."

"What does that even mean?"

"Alison. Alison. Do you trust me? Do you trust me?" For a moment Alison remembered that snake, from *The Jungle Book*, who sang a sweet little song to Mowgli to get him to go to sleep, so that he could eat him.

"Sure, Ryan," she said. "I trust you."

"How *are* things going for you and Lars?"

She took a breath. "Lars and I are fine. We're great."

"That's all you need to think about. The rest is my job. Let me do my job."

Things *were* good with Lars. "Good" was as usual a relative word, but she would have a hard time describing her relationship with the Icelandic Prince in more unsavory terms. Lars was gorgeous. He was sexy. He was romantic. He was remote, but in a way that you would expect out of a global film director. It was true that sex with Lars, while exciting, was a little unnerving. He would do things like suddenly grab her by the hair, pull her toward him, and kiss her with complete, unself-conscious abandon. She could be sitting on the couch eating popcorn and the next thing she knew he was on top of her, with his fingers shoved up her vagina, her back arched over the armrest, moaning with pleasure. She felt like a total slut at times like that; she had never known that sex could be this overwhelming, and there were moments when she wanted him inside her so much that she wondered if maybe she shouldn't go see some therapist about sex addiction. It was like a fever dream, half the time, and she would have been embarrassed by her own behavior if he were not even more creatively hedonistic in this arena. If one of them was a sex addict, it was Lars, but she was pretty sure that wasn't it. This was the thing she couldn't possibly tell Ryan: Lars was obsessed with her.

He sent dresses to her apartment and then came over at all hours to watch her model them, before undressing her in creative ways so he could fuck her. He brought her exotic Moroccan oils and showed her even more exotic ways to use them. And then one day he brought actors with him.

No big deal, he explained; he just wanted to have the guys read a few scenes from the movie with her. Her apartment was so small, and so marked as Lars's sexual territory by then, the addition of the two strange boys was unnerving, bumpy. On the other hand, the idea that Lars wanted to work on the film seemed promising. She had practically memorized the script by then, and the chance to actually say the words and show what she could do with the character jazzed her. There was no way to say no. Why would you?

And of course it was fun, at first. Snappy little scenes where she flirted with the boys, bossed them around, acted all cool and witty while nursing a secret crush on the too-tough leader of the crew. It was lively and they were enjoying themselves. And then they got to the sex scene.

The living room, with so many men in it, had gotten a bit too warm and one of them—Carl, the one playing her love interest—had conveniently stripped down to his T-shirt.

"Let's try this on the couch," Lars told them.

It wasn't a difficult scene. In fact, there was nothing to it. Laila was sitting on the edge of her bed, and the guy came in, kissed her, and then they had sex.

"You want us to do this scene?"

"Is that a problem?" Lars didn't even look up from his script.

"There's not much to it."

"Let's just take a shot at it."

"You want me to sit here and make out with Carl."

"I want you to act the scene."

She actually started to do it. She sat on the couch, brooding—that was the direction in the text, *Laila, brooding, sits on the edge of the bed. Her shirt, loosely unbuttoned, has slipped off her shoulder, revealing the nipple of her perfectly formed right breast.* Carl sat down on the couch. He shifted, took a moment to settle, then leaned gently toward her.

And then it didn't feel like so much fun anymore. "Hang on, cowboy," she said. She turned to Lars, who was considering her with a slightly too-deliberate curiosity. "You want me to open my shirt and reveal the nipple of my perfectly formed right breast?" she asked.

"That would be fine," Lars informed her. She didn't know if he was kidding. It seriously wasn't clear.

"You want me to make out with him? Right now? Like, right here on the couch?"

"We're doing a scene, Alison," Lars reminded her, with a condescending Icelandic superiority.

"Sure we are, Lars."

She sat in silence for a moment. Carl looked back and forth between them, then stretched his hand down his back, like he was warming up for a wrestling match. "So do you want me to . . ."

"I need you to take off, Carl," she said. "All of you, take off."

"Oh," said Carl, surprised, and clearly disappointed.

"There are still several scenes I'd like to look at," Lars told her.

"Well, I don't feel great, I really don't feel up to this right now and I'd love it if everyone left."

The two actors turned and looked at Lars for direction. It was enough to make your head explode. "Hey, numbnuts," Alison snapped. "This is *my* apartment. I get to say who stays and who goes, not him. This is my home. I want you out of it."

"Oh, sure, I just wasn't sure what—" the poor dope started.

"IT DOESN'T MATTER WHAT HE WANTS TO DO. I'M CALLING THE POLICE IF YOU GUYS DON'T GET OUT OF HERE RIGHT NOW."

That did the trick. The two guys picked up their backpacks, their eyes averted, mumbled their apologies and good-byes to Lars, and then shuffled to the door and split.

It was so sheepish and guilty, Alison knew immediately that they were all in on it. "You told them they were coming over here to fuck me," she said. "You told them that I would do it. In my apartment. You told—two total strangers—"

"They're not strangers, I've worked with them on several projects."

"Did you honestly think I'd do it? You fucking ASSHOLE." She did like Lars, and she was afraid of him too, but it felt good calling him an asshole.

"I just wanted to see when those Midwestern values would finally assert themselves," he said, observing her coolly. The whole situation was appalling. How had she gotten here? *One step at a time.*

"You need to get out of here now."

"Do you really think I'd want to stand here and watch someone else make love to you? That would be torture!"

"Then why did you do it?" Alison could not stop her eyes from filling with tears. Her voice was cracking.

Lars looked at her intently, those blue eyes alight with cool imperial wisdom. "I wanted to see the saint in you again," he said. "I know the whore now. I wanted to see Joan of Arc."

"Lars, please. You have to go. I mean it. Don't make me yell anymore."

"I like it when you yell."

"Well, I'm tired, I'm really just so so so—tired." There was a moment of silence as they considered each other. *God*, Alison thought, suddenly praying, *please make him understand that I'm not kidding. Please, God.*

Lars went to pick up his glorious shoulder bag, where he had dropped it near the door. *Thank you, God*, Alison thought. Then Lars moved back into the room, reaching for her. *Fuck you, God*, Alison thought, *what new hell is this?*

Then he kissed her on the forehead and finally, blessedly, left.

So when Alison insisted to Ryan that things between her and Lars were "fine," she was not strictly telling the truth. This whole fiasco had just been three days ago, and she hadn't seen Lars since. He had sent flowers twice, and this morning another dress had come, a vibrant, frankly disturbing pink. *I've seen the saint, now I want to see the whore again*, was her guess what he would say.

But when she finally tried to tell her stupid agent about all this, he would have none of it. "Lars is notorious for knowing what he wants," Ryan told her. "That's what makes him a great director. And the fact that he is so committed to casting you is a total game changer."

"In spite of the fact that there's no offer."

"You cannot get hung up on that! People know you're being considered and that's enough!" On some sick level Ryan was telling the truth. Ever since the word went out that Lars Guttfriend was going to cast Alison Moore as the female lead in *Last Stop*, the scripts had been rolling in. Managers were calling for interviews. Publicists were begging to take her on. This was her moment. *Careful what you wish for.* This is what she wanted, wasn't it? Who would decide to be an actress, then try to back out of the whole thing when someone said, *Okay and now we're going to make you a star*? None of her friends, what passed for them in the acting community, had any sympathy—they were all too jealous. She had gone out for drinks with Lisa and her trust-fund pals and they all got so brittle when she mentioned it, she had to make it seem it was a near impossibility she would actually even *get* the part, and quickly changed the subject. Her friends from the show, no better. She hadn't even tried to tell her mother what all this involved because she had been so thrilled when that first call came in. How could she explain these hypersexual machinations to her *mother*? Her father would see dollar signs. Her brothers and sisters would think she was making it all up.

The door buzzed. Lying prone on her unmade bed, where she had spent much of the past three days, Alison had a hard time deciding whether or not she should answer it. She had no doubt that Lars was finally making his appearance, to find out if he was forgiven, to see her in the pink dress. The buzzer sounded a second time and she sat up.

Mom is right about this, she thought. *Even the Catholic church is right—this loveless sexual power game is a sin. In some stupid primal universe this is the shit that gets you sent to hell.* She had to cut Lars off. It's not like she didn't know how to do it; she had broken up with Kyle something like thirty times, and she *loved* him. Lars, she didn't know what that was, but it was nothing remotely resembling love. *They weren't ever going to offer it to me anyway*, she knew. *This is all nothing, it's nothing at all.* She opened the door.

nineteen

THE HAIR WAS pulled back in a ratty knot at the back of her neck, and she wore a pair of naughty-librarian eyeglasses. In the past three years, Alison had somehow become the kind of beauty who could look stunning in sweatpants and a T-shirt, which was what she was wearing.

"Dennis," she said. "*Dennis!* I—have never been so glad to see anyone in my *life*." She threw her arms around him and dragged him through the door.

It wasn't what he had expected, but it would certainly do.

"Alison, you look sensational."

"Don't tell me I look pretty, I'm sick of it. What are you doing here?" The buzz of familiarity, the relief of it, had been replaced by a terrifying jolt of guilt. What *was* he doing here? "Do you want a—seltzer, or a juice with some soda or something?" She strode briskly back to her kitchen, gathering her wits. And acting. *Just keep acting.*

"Actually, my flight was ridiculous, you don't have any vodka, do you?"

Alison turned and looked at him with stern, good-natured disapproval. Dennis grinned. "Don't you laugh at me, I'm serious, Dennis, I heard you stopped."

"Oh, yeah, who'd you hear that from?" he asked. He smiled at her, knowing.

Something in her chest tightened. "All of Cincinnati was talking about it," she informed him. "Don't change the subject. Did you fall off the wagon?"

"Darling, I fell so very far off the wagon so very long ago you can't even *see* the wagon from the pit of iniquity into which I have so recklessly tossed myself."

"Oh, Dennis."

"Oh, Alison—really it's not as bad as all that. I'm not the desperate character I used to be. I have learned how to drink responsibly."

"Sure you have."

"No, I have, I really have." His insistence was so underwhelming that he actually rolled his eyes at himself. It was fine; it made her laugh. Really she was always such a forgiving girl. "You never knew me, in my sober days, anyway," he reminded her, leaning against the clean blond woodwork of her very chic little kitchen. "You haven't been back to good old Cin City for so long, you completely missed my resurrection and subsequent decline. It was quite the nonevent. Where is my vodka?"

Alison handed him a glass with ice over a bare inch. "I don't care if you're drinking again, but if you say you're in control of it, I want to see it," she warned him.

"Puritan."

"Oh, God, have you been watching my television show? I'm hardly a Puritan. They've got me fucking anything that moves." Dennis laughed with delight. She looked so pretty in her sweats, and if anything she was saltier than ever. There was some disturbance running through her that added a warmth to her cynicism. No, that wasn't new; that had always been there. All that intelligence and heart. A disappointed innocence. *And morality.* That was why she and Kyle had been so right for each other. They both believed that the universe had rules. They just never agreed on what the rules were.

"How's Kyle?" she asked.

As tactics went it wasn't a bad one. At least it got them onto familiar turf.

"I did not travel a thousand miles to merely talk about Kyle, forget it," he warned her. "I will tell you this, his marriage is a disaster and he deeply regrets that you two never consummated your lust. But other than that I'm telling you *nothing*."

"That is so not fair."

"*Not fair* is you taking off and completely cutting yourself off from me for three years. I'm really angry with you. And you were in town *and* you went to a dinner party at Kyle's—"

"Don't remind me, it was horrible—"

"I don't care, I'm really hurt no one invited me," he said. "There is no food in this refrigerator."

"There's food," she started, but he held open the refrigerator door and waved at it, a careless magician. The thing was an empty cave.

"Celery, nobody eats that. Yogurt, the Greek kind with no sweetener. A bag of carrots. A teeny tiny container of hummus that looks like maybe a rabbit has been nibbling at the edges of. Six cans of diet root beer. Is that your secret vice? You don't even have a frozen pizza around here?"

"I'm an actress, they don't let us eat."

"Yes, I've heard about that." He swung the door shut and turned to her. "Okay, so what are we going to do for food? Where are the takeout menus? I want Indian."

"Okay, but no bread."

"I traveled a thousand miles just to see you, of course I'm allowed to have bread."

"I'm not kidding, you can't do it to me. If I eat one piece of bread I'll blow up as big as a house. And I can't have it here or I'll eat it. Order lentils, or rice." *Why was he here?* All of this too-friendly banter was starting to wear on her nerves. The cheerful indifference to facts. A plummeting guilt racked her for a moment but she ignored it. What's done was done and for three years it had never come up. But then why was he here?

"I want bread," he announced.

"Dennis, what did you come here for, to make me fat?" She made it sound light. This bit you had to keep light.

What did he come here for? Dennis had spent very little time considering that. But he was moving forward now, it was a good mode for him, people generally did whatever he wanted them to when he just pushed a little. His whole life, it had been that way. A little flattery, a little fun, a little alcohol. *Voilà.*

"Yes, hi, I want to place an order for delivery," he informed the Indian voice on the telephone. "We're going to want lots of bread, what's that kind of bread that you deep-fry, it poofs up?"

"If you order bread, I'm telling you, I'm going to make you go out into the hall to eat it."

So she wasn't going to eat any bread. But otherwise you'd have to say things were going well enough. She had lost interest in the question of how much he was drinking virtually as soon as she raised it. That was the lovely thing about alcohol; everyone really did want to drink it. *The man takes the drink, the drink takes the drink, then the drink takes the man.* That was the mantra of some old lush he'd met at a meeting and he knew every syllable was true, and not just for raging alcoholics. Even so-called social drinkers got taken in the end. The whole human race was nothing but a bunch of drunks. And the ones who didn't drink were nothing but dry drunks.

"Nice place," he informed her.

"Oh, it's awful. It's not awful. It's just a bit plain. I haven't even painted. And there's not enough stuff on the walls. It's just, I never have people over and honestly I'm never *here.* I can't believe you just showed up like this. The odds of me being home on any given night are not good, in general." She swept through the small living room, clearing magazines off the coffee table.

"What are you reading?" She was so clearly embarrassed by the fact that there were so many celebrity rags lying around that he simply couldn't let her off the hook without catching her on it, just a little.

"It's just stuff my publicist sends over. You have to look at it and make sure they're at least pretending to be accurate, otherwise the whole thing gets too weird too fast. You end up with three-headed babies, shit like that."

"You're *in* these? You have to let me see."

"No. No—Dennis, come on! You'll just make fun of me, stop!"

"I won't make fun, it's so impressive, you're in trashy magazines, Alison, well done, you've made the big time." And of course she had let him wrest at least a few off the top of the pile. He plopped onto the Naugahyde couch and started leafing through page after page of gorgeous girls in couture gowns, standing on a faux red carpet and smiling inanely at some photographer. "Oh, yes, very nice. Ooo, look at her."

"I told you it was stupid, you're the one who insisted on looking at it."

"I'm looking for you!"

"So, seriously, Dennis. What are you here for?" Dennis glanced up at the sudden shift, but her smile was simple. Which was interesting, considering what a simple girl she wasn't.

"Kyle asked me to come find you and bring you back to him."

"Ho ho ho," she said. "I saw him, and I met his family. He seemed really happy."

"There you are! That's a pretty dress." He waved an open magazine at her; he had in fact found a photo of her on some receiving line. She was wearing a daring black gown with a plunging neckline and a gold cinched waist. "I can't believe they let you out in public in this thing. You could start a riot."

"That is generally the idea," Alison admitted. She took the magazine out of his hands, grabbed the rest of the pile, and carried them all into the teeny bedroom just behind him.

"Aw, come on. I want to see the pictures. I think you look pretty!" Alison reentered and dropped into her chair. He grinned at her. "You know, Alison, I have to say, you really have turned into a looker."

"Oh yippee."

"I also have to say, you know very well that Kyle is not happy."

"He has a gorgeous wife and a gorgeous house and two gorgeous kids and he's a rich doctor, and my impression, from that dinner party, is that he is *happy*." This was a colossal lie but so what, human beings lied all the time. "And I have a very hot movie director boyfriend, and I'm happy too," she lied.

"Tell me about your big-shot boyfriend."

"Well, he's really talented. And handsome."

"Do you love him?"

Alison momentarily regretted having dumped the subject of Kyle, thus opening the door to this line of inquiry. "Okay, you don't love him," Dennis said. "Moving on. What do you like about him?"

Alison paused, trying to make it look like she was being careful about choosing her words, instead of just making shit up. "He's interesting. He's smart. He knows so much about how this world works, and it's reassuring, in a way, to have someone like that in your corner." Dennis wondered for a moment why Alison was such a good actress and such a bad liar. There was probably a reason those two things went together, but he wasn't curious enough about the intricacies of psychology to run down that train of thought. He just made his face as sympathetic as possible, and let her hang herself. "He's crazy attractive, he's like—trust me." She blushed; that meant the guy was good in the sack. "He's got a lot going on, so I don't see him for a while, then it's like twenty-four seven. And he knows, just everybody. It's a bit more glamorous than I'm used to. I've been to these amazing dinner parties in the Hamptons, they fly you out in helicopters. I know that sounds a little—excessive."

"Alison, remember who you're talking to. I did not inherit any Midwestern snobbery about wealth. Far from it."

"No, I know. It's just weird for me a little bit." The blush was back again. He let the silence hang. "Anyway. He's also famous, you know, he directed these big movies. "

"You mentioned."

"He's completely attentive. I get flowers and gifts all the time. Jewelry and dresses."

"Dresses! You let a powerful man—a movie director—buy you clothing? And then does he dress you up?"

Alison bristled, and Dennis felt the hairs on the back of his neck rise, just a little.

"Don't get mad," he cautioned.

"I'm not mad."

"You are definitely mad, and I didn't mean—"

"You did too, Dennis, of course you did."

"Okay. You're 'dating' a powerful guy—"

"Don't put it in quotes."

"Okay. You're fucking a powerful guy—"

"That's not what it is."

"You're not fucking him?"

She took the hit. Let it land. The girl had such integrity, in her own fucked-up way. "Yes. I am fucking him," she said.

"And he sends you things. So that's cool! He's rich, he should send you things."

"I don't want to talk about Lars," she said.

"Oh no. Don't run away from this. Alison—"

"What are you doing here?"

"I'm just visiting! I had a weekend off of work and I thought I'd come to New York."

"It's Wednesday."

"I took a few days off." He reached for the vodka bottle. His hand was still steady. "Come on. You were so glad to see me just fifteen minutes ago. I think it's great this guy is buying you dresses. He *should* be buying you dresses and having great sex with you. This is the way things are meant to be, Alison. The way they were with you and Kyle—that did not work out for a reason. And the reason is, Kyle is no fun."

"He's fine."

"I love him. But he's a mess. I want to see you in one of these dresses."

"Oh no no."

"Oh yes! Come on. Please? Do you know how long it's been since I've seen a pretty woman in a really pretty dress?"

"I don't know who you're dating, these days."

"I'm dating nice Cincinnati chicks who think 'couture' is spelled with three O's."

"I'm a nice Cincinnati chick."

"Alison, you never were before and you most certainly are not now."

"Whether or not I am, there are plenty of beautiful young women in Cincinnati who know how to wear a pretty dress."

"There are, but my dad cut me off and I'm living in a shitty little apartment in Clifton, where everyone dresses like starving hippies."

The tossed-off admission—*my dad cut me off*—did its work. Her heart constricted. Dennis kept smiling at her. "Come on. This director sends you dresses. I want to see one. Come on."

"Oh, for crying out loud," she sighed. "There's a new pink one."

"Well, put it on!" He smiled.

She hadn't even tried it on yet, but there was no worry that it would fit; Lars knew her body better than she knew it herself by this point. The slightly crazy fuchsia was truly electric, and the fit made it more so. She had to hold in her breath and try the zipper four times before she managed to get it up. In her childhood, that would have meant that the dress was just too small. In show business, it was never possible that the dress was too small. The neckline was gorgeous, a subtle heart-shaped curve, and the skirt was slit with the same subtle touch—three inches, no more. As she looked at herself in the mirror, she knew that Lars was making a point. *Not a saint, not a whore, but definitely a bit of both*, she thought. If this was what she owed to Dennis Fitzpatrick for sins of the past, so be it.

When she swung the bedroom door open, stepping out into the living room, Dennis did not immediately respond. The look in his eye was unnerving.

"Well?"

"Sorry. Oh, sorry. That looks—amazing," he told her, with a deliberate coolness.

"It's a bit tight," she said, making a face and pulling at the side like a ten-year-old. It was a self-conscious attempt to lighten the mood, which had shifted into something decidedly more treacherous. She should have paid more attention before, when they stopped bantering. Humoring him about that dress was maybe not the best idea she had ever had. She didn't want to think about why, but she knew she had better get out of it.

"Ugh, I'm taking this off," she told him.

"Oh, come on, you just put it on!" Dennis protested. "You have to at least let me see it with shoes."

"Dennis—"

"It doesn't look right! It needs high strappy heels, like they wear on television."

"I'm not putting on heels for you."

"Why not?" There was no question anymore. There was a meanness, a demand in his tone. She swallowed.

"I'm just not," she said.

"Come on, Alison. You just told me, not ten minutes ago, you'll do pretty much anything you have to."

"I didn't say that."

"You've been saying it nonstop since I got here. You hate being in trashy magazines but you have to do it because that's what they expect you to do. You don't really like this Lars character but it's nice to have a big director in your corner, so you fuck him and take clothes from him."

"I like Lars a lot."

"Just put some shoes on! What is the big deal?" He was sitting on the couch, his arms and his legs spread wide, like a drunken despot. Alison let her gaze drop momentarily to his glass, and the vodka bottle. She hadn't paid enough attention.

"Okay. Okay!" She smiled, her most dazzling smile. "As you may well suspect, I do have a pair of strappy sandals, very high heels, which will look sensational with this dress. I will go get them."

He stood. Even though he was clearly drunk now, he was steady enough. Which made it worse somehow. The apartment was so small, it only took him two steps to position himself between her and the door to the bedroom. His left hand lifted, letting a pair of black slingbacks dangle from them with an elegant confidence. "How about these?" he asked. "I found them under the coffee table."

"Oh, God, I'm such a slob," Alison laughed. She hated this feeling, the knowing that things were getting bad and the only way through it was to keep it light. "Let me put them away and find those sandals."

He handed her the shoes, that part was easy enough, but then there was no way past him. He considered that pink dress with something resembling hunger, or hostility. This was bad.

"Come on, Dennis," she said, quiet, placating. "Let me go get the right shoes."

"You're just going to go in there and take it off, because you don't like the way I'm looking at you," he said. He reached out and touched the fitted waist. She wanted to back up, but she didn't want to raise the stakes any further, or any faster. Instead, she placed a hand on his chest and feigned the affection she had felt for him years ago.

"Dennis, knock it off," she said. "You're drunk."

"I am drunk," he admitted. "And you're beautiful."

"And we're going to have Indian food, remember? That'll sober you up. I should never have let you drink that much on an empty stomach."

"How much I drink is not up to you, or to anyone, Alison," he informed her, and there was enough disappointment in his tone to suggest momentarily that perhaps she had mistaken his intent.

"Come on, you got to sit down. Seriously, you need to sit down and tell me what is going on with you. Why you're here." His other hand had crept onto her waist as well now, but he was falling into some sort of morose stupor. He actually laid his head on her shoulder.

"You're a goddess and I'm a mess," he muttered. And for that moment, it was true, and it was all that it was.

"You're all right. You're all right," Alison promised him. She patted his back, reassuring, and gently began to unwind their tattered embrace. "Sit down, I'll get you a glass of water." He didn't move other than to sway, momentarily unsteady on his feet. She waited and instead of pushing harder, patted him again on the back. "Dennis?"

"What is this material?" he asked, closing his hands around her back. "It's so nothing, it's nothing is here." His hands were slipping down, now, pulling the skirt up.

"Dennis, stop it," she said. No more back patting. "I mean it, let go."

"You're so soft," he told her.

"Stop it." Even drunk, he was so fucking strong. She heard and felt the fabric shred as he pulled the skirt up, sudden. "Dennis, stop, *STOP IT!*"

For a moment he didn't, and then he did. It was like a breath of reason, moving through a tomb. He just let her go. She pushed him away and he let her. And then he sauntered back to the coffee table, picked up his glass, and poured more vodka into it. As if nothing had happened. No one said anything for a moment, which made him feel great. She was scared; he had succeeded in that at least. It wasn't nothing.

"I know what you did," he finally said. "Kyle told me. That you guys were up there, in my dad's bedroom." Alison was as still as she could be. "And then he left. He left you up there. And then things went missing. Didn't they. Alison."

She didn't answer.

"And the cops never thought of talking to you, you were long gone, everybody thought it was somebody on the catering staff. Or me! That was what my father thought. Felicia certainly thought so. But no. It was my dear friend Alison Moore. *Stole* jewelry worth, do you know what that stuff was worth?"

She still couldn't speak, or look at him. Her brain was frozen with the truth of all of it.

"When Kyle told me you were up there, not having sex yet again, I thought, oh what the fuck, *you* know what I thought. And did you ever stop to think what happened, what happened *to me*? My father was furious. Whatever happened, there was no question it was *my* fault." The fullness of his betrayal came back again. "I lost *everything*. So under the circumstances, a little friendliness on your part might not have been amiss."

His anger frightened her into the barest attempt at an argument. "Dennis. You need to stop drinking and and and—"

"Don't tell me what I need to do," he warned her. The alcohol had leant a righteousness to his disgust. Laying his hands on her seemed like nothing compared to what she'd perpetrated. "I'll tell you what you need to do, is you need to write me a check. Five thousand—who am I kidding—ten, ten thousand dollars. You have it, you can't tell me you don't have it." She didn't answer. "I'm fucking broke. But we'll just, ten thousand and we'll call it even."

When he turned his gaze back to Alison, she seemed like a strange, poisonous flower. Her back against the wall, wearing that ridiculous pink gown. She was scared as shit. That wasn't nothing.

"You don't have a checkbook?"

"It's in the desk." She tipped her head. He glanced around the apartment, which was spare to the point of absurdity, truth be told. But yes, there in the corner, a tiny Ikea desk, something you might find in a dorm room.

"Go get it," he told her.

"You step aside," she answered.

"Oh, relax. I'm not going to *rape* you, Alison, although some people surely would think you deserve it." He downed the last of the vodka, barely tasting it now. The drive toward oblivion was familiar, his old friend. But he did as he was told, and took a step back toward the couch.

After a moment she eased herself out of the corner and walked across the room with as much dignity as she could muster in that pink dress.

"You make yourself look like that, and then you're surprised that men want to fuck you?" he asked.

That one she had no answer for.

part three

twenty

THEY ENDED UP going darker with the hair and everyone had to admit that Lars's preoccupation with the exact color was pure genius, because Alison looked devastating. Face framed by feathers of raven curls, her complexion drifted into a pure, vulnerable alabaster. Those green eyes were even more startling in their intelligence and cunning, but now there was the whisper of hurt there too, a panic which occasionally flickered to the surface before it was willed away. It wasn't precisely Ava, or Liz either; for both of them, the black hair had a Samson-like power: Those girls knew how to snarl. Alison had something more wounded-bird going on, and the whole effect was startling. It was, in fact, that rarest of commodities, for Hollywood: It was not merely familiar; it was also new.

Unfortunately, getting the hair to that exact color wasn't easy. Alison's natural brunette was so dark the stylist, a fierce and competent young woman who was covered in slightly scary tattoos, explained that they would actually need to strip Alison's natural brunette and lay in the raven, which had less red and more black in it, on top of the stripped hair. So then they needed a high-volume peroxide in order to activate the bleach and remove the color, and then they had to shampoo, remove the bleach, and do the whole thing again. The bleach had a high lift, which removed the color well enough, but a pale orange cast in the stripped hair was tenacious. After two days of this, the intimidating hairstylist—her name was Rocky, of course it was—pointed out that all this manipulation could permanently damage Alison's follicles as well as the hair itself. In other words, if they kept this shit up, it could ruin Alison's hair *for life.* Determined that when he got her to Los Angeles to meet the studio royalty she would be as close to perfection as he could make her, Lars fired Rocky and hired a second, and then a third stylist, flying them both in from London. They made all sorts of wild promises and in fact delivered one hell of a cut and color, but just when Lars finally approved a stunningly accurate deep brown-black, Alison's own roots, with those hints of auburn, were starting to show. The second as well as the third stylist confirmed what Rocky had been fired for saying: Much more of this, and her hair would be wrecked for good. Ryan got involved, and in the end they compromised: You can touch up the roots for the screen test. After that, you're going to have to wig her.

In the moment, the compromise was acceptable. Alison's meeting with Gordon and Norbert and Barry and David and Ron and half a dozen other white men was set, and it proved to be a superb exercise in feminine charm. She wore a skintight pearl-colored georgette slip dress that left little of her figure to the imagination. The dress was so low-cut she was convinced that her nipples might slip out at any moment and ruin everything, but Lars had insisted it would keep the room on edge (it did), and more important, it was the kind of thing that a screen goddess would do. She'd sit there in a dress like that, acting like a perfect lady, and letting them all fantasize about fucking her on the floor.

"Yeah, but most of them are gay," Alison pointed out to him, afterward. "They don't want to fuck me at all. They want to fuck you."

"They want to *be* you," Lars informed her. "That's better."

"I don't know, Lars," she sighed. It seemed weird, frankly, the way these guys obsessed on her every detail, like she was their own favorite Barbie doll. Lars seemed to care more about the shade of her lipstick than what kind of car he drove. And the hair thing was totally bizarre. He wanted her to look exotic, confident, Audrey Hepburn–like in the knowledge that no matter how boyish the cut, she still knew she was a ravishing beauty. The flip side danger of a cut that short was that she would look like a lesbian. He went back and forth relentlessly about it, as apparently there was nothing in the universe less sexy to all men, gay or straight, than lesbians. But she had made it through that essential meeting with flying colors, and finally he could relax, and express approval. "You look amazing," he told her, studying her from behind. His hands were creeping around her waist, slowly pulling up the georgette. She wondered how much of this crap Ava or Liz had to put up with and immediately regretted even asking herself the question. Her brain whispered back to her, *A lot. They had to put up with this a lot.*

There were plenty of stories out there about how continuously Ava was preyed upon. Maybe not Liz, who looked like she could defend herself, but Natalie Wood, yes, Marilyn Monroe, certainly. There were a billion stories about old Marilyn getting raped at parties by the biggest guys in Hollywood. It wasn't a surprise, if you thought about it. *Dennis was right.* Turning yourself into a person who men wanted to fuck all the time, what else was going to happen? The memory of what had almost happened shot a bolt of panic through her. It wasn't anything she hadn't learned to handle, but she wasn't going to let Lars just have his way with her either, especially from behind. She let him paw her breasts for a moment, press that perpetual erection up against her, and then she shrugged, deliberate, a gesture that was unmistakable: *Not now.*

Lars was never one to misunderstand body language. His power, her power, her lack of power, her appreciation for his power—it was an ongoing board game of unspoken one-upmanship. He wanted to have sex, she didn't; he wouldn't push now, because that would be begging, which he didn't do, he was indifferent to sex, except that he thought about it all the time, and he was furious now that by shrugging her shoulders she had acted on her own power which was a threat to his power which meant he was going to have to make her pay for it later without making it look like that's what he was doing. Alison was well aware of the nuances of this dance, and she rarely bothered to push her luck. Lars was no better than any of these guys, but he was in her corner. If letting him dress her up like Ava Gardner and have sex with her constantly was the price, so be it. But once in a blue moon a shred of defiance was not only inevitable, it was necessary.

The memory of the way she used to yearn for sex rose from the back of her mind. The way she and Kyle used to torture each other with their hunger? Those were the days, when you were just a kid whose mom was always yelling at you for making out with your boyfriend on the family room floor. The distance from there to here seemed impossible; everyone agreed on that much. But everyone else seemed to think that the impossibility of that journey was something astonishing, brilliant, celebratory. *Careful what you wish for.* But had she even wished for this? She didn't actually think she had. And now here she was, trapped not by her own dreams, but by the dreams of something else, something weird and inhuman but generally accepted as truth.

She would never have been able to explain this to anyone, but there was no question that she understood it. She understood power and she understood that she didn't have any. Sitting around and letting men fantasize about fucking you, seriously? That was not all it was cracked up to be. *That is the thing everyone figures out too late*, she thought, as she swung open the minibar and grabbed a couple of airplane-size vodka bottles.

"We're having dinner with Norbert and Gordon," Lars reminded her. "It's only the most important dinner of your life, so I'd suggest you show up sober."

"It's for you," she explained, with a well-performed air of apologetic surprise. "I thought you'd want to celebrate! It went well, you know it did." She cracked open the absurdly small bottle and dumped the contents into the rocks glass which had been so usefully situated for them right there on a scalloped paper doily. She floated by him, and delivered her little offering to the gods with a cocky smile. Checking his emails on his cell, he barely glanced up. Sex or the cell phone, either would do for Lars.

"What are you going to wear?" he said. Sex or the cell or her clothing, that was actually door number three.

"I don't know, what do you think?" At this point, it would be madness to answer any other way. The idea that she might know anything at all about what looked good on her had been dismissed months before, along with the insane idea that something loose and comfortable might occasionally be fun.

"Something with color. I would say pink if that weren't too much to ask."

It was a reckless, careless dig. Pink was off limits, and he knew it. But he wouldn't fucking let it go.

She had never told him what happened to the pink dress. How could she? Would he have wrapped her in his arms and comforted her? Would he have hunted Dennis down and beaten him to a pulp? Would he have done anything that any number of characters in one of his stupid movies would do? Not likely. She had taken the torn dress and thrown it in the garbage.

And then she refused to talk about it. There was nothing to say, any lie that she might have told—*I spilled coffee on it, I returned it, I didn't look good in it, I loaned it to a friend and she ripped it*—would have been shredded. So she said nothing.

Which, perversely, worked. The day after it arrived, Lars called and left a message on her machine. "I hope you like the dress," he said. "I can't wait to see you in it. Give me a call." She didn't. The next day she got another call, this time from his assistant, the interminable Josh. "Lars asked me to call and make sure that you got the package he sent on Tuesday," Josh told her machine. "Could you touch base with the office and let us know that you got it?" She didn't call him back either. So then Ryan called. "Alison, it's me. Give me a call." She didn't. He emailed her. And then he called again. "Alison, where did you go? Did you run away to Cincinnati again? I'm going to be really mad if you did. Call me back. It's serious." *Fuck you*, she thought. But after three days of locking herself in her own apartment and taking long showers, she got ahold of herself and called Josh back.

He was so relieved to hear from her, he practically jumped through the phone and hugged her.

"Alison, hi, *hi!*" he gushed. "Wow, it is so great to hear from you, we were getting worried!"

"Were we?"

"Yes, Lars has been really concerned."

"I went out of town," she lied.

"We tried your cell," he informed her.

"Oh, it's out of juice."

"Okay, well—uh, Lars was wondering if you got the package he sent you? It should have arrived on Tuesday."

"That's what Lars wants to know?"

"Well—I'm sure he'll want to talk to you about a lot of things. "

"Great, why don't you tell him to give me a call."

"Should he use your home or your cell phone?"

"Either works." She didn't care how inane this all sounded. She really didn't.

"Okay, well, I'll have him call you," Josh said.

"You do that, Josh," she told him, and then hung up the phone. She didn't want to be mean; she knew that Lars had probably been taking the poor guy's head off for the entire three days. But what the fuck, why was Lars having his fucking assistant call his *girlfriend* anyway? Not that that's what she was. Who knows what she was.

Lars was waiting for her at the table when she arrived in the restaurant, which was good. Disappearing for three days had clearly been effective. For one unguarded moment, there was a flash of something that skittered across Lars's face—*was that relief?*—before he stood and kissed her elegantly on the cheek.

"You've been elusive," he observed.

"Not really," she countered. "I needed a little breathing room."

"The last work session was intense," he admitted. *Oh yeah, you mean when you wanted to watch me pretend to have sex with two actors I'd never met, while you watched?*

"A little intense, yes," she said. She really didn't give a shit. The whole fiasco of that so-called work session had been annihilated by subsequent events. Still, he wanted to see her in the dress. In the middle of all these nonapologies, the pink dress was the real apology, and he wanted to see her in it.

"Did you like the dress?" he asked.

"The dress is gorgeous," she informed him.

"I was hoping you'd wear it."

"This is what I wore."

"A black sheath."

"Yes, a black sheath, makes me look like I'm going to a funeral, I picked it out just for you."

"That's a bit edgy."

"It's Audrey Hepburn."

"Audrey Hepburn would never have worn a sweater with it."

"I was chilly."

"You can take it off inside."

"I'm still chilly." She didn't want him to see her arms, which Dennis had in fact bruised rather noticeably.

"It's just a very sober look."

"I'm feeling sober."

"I see that." His jaw was getting tense now. All this backtalk clearly wasn't fun for long.

"It's just a sweater, Lars," she told him. She put her hand on his. "I really have been fighting a cold, and I'm honestly not feeling quite myself. But I wanted to come have dinner with you. I wanted to see you. Can't we just enjoy ourselves?"

It did the trick, but not for good. Over time, the dress question appeared and reappeared as a running battle of wills.

"I still haven't seen you in that dress."

"No, you haven't."

"Didn't you like it?"

"I didn't say that."

"I'd love to see you in it."

"Why are you so obsessed with that dress?"

"I just think it's a beautiful dress."

"There are lots of beautiful dresses out there."

"Did you not like it?"

"I didn't say that."

"Then why won't you wear it?"

"Why do you want me to wear it?"

This could go on for hours, as far as she was concerned. It was like being in an Ionesco play. She had done a scene from *The Bald Soprano* in an acting class in college. It was easy, light. Mean.

"I just don't understand why I can't see it on you."

"Then you do need to talk about the dress." And then, finally, she couldn't help herself. "Because I would prefer not to."

That "I would prefer not to" line was a stunner. Lars was so surprised by it he actually twitched. He stared at her. She could positively hear him thinking: *Is she fucking with me?*

Is she indeed, thought Alison. She smiled at him, dazzling, and the questions about the dress went on and on and on. Eventually the subject mutated into a discussion about the color pink, is it *pink* that you object to or that specific pink (*who said I objected to anything?*), what color pink would you agree to wear if you were theoretically going to agree to wear pink? The rage behind the triviality of the discussion revealed itself in the sheer insulting relentlessness of it all. But Alison never faltered. How could she? The dress no longer existed. And there was simply no way on earth to explain to him why.

twenty-one

VAN WAS FINALLY HAPPY. Since Georgia's birth, she had taken to wearing flowing white frocks, which made her look like a pre-Raphaelite goddess—a startling distance from when they first met, when contemporary fitted sweaters and narrow skirts showed off her figure. But the loose new look suited her. She was now letting her hair air-dry, so that it fell in untamed locks to her shoulders. The whole picture was stunning, frankly. And it was definitely easier to live with. The hardened determination which had ruled their lives for years seemed finally to have run its course. She was wistful and dear with the girls, kissing them and making much of Maggie's small accomplishments, but not demanding her undivided attention with anywhere near the same ruthlessness as she had commanded in the past. She gave the baby up to Kyle regularly, with a surprising ease. For all his hours with the many patients who came through his office, he remained surprisingly awkward with his own children, but Van made no more cutting remarks about it. Rather, she would smile encouragement to him, touch him lightly on the shoulder, and move on.

It was a magnificent autumn day. They had gone to his parents' for an early supper, and his father was taking advantage of the weather to grill hamburgers and hot dogs outside one last time before the winter frost set in. Van had brought special veggie burgers for Maggie, who was hopping up and down with delight while her grandpa fussed slowly around his rusted old Weber grill. Over the ironwork patio table, Kyle's mom was carefully laying a tablecloth with a homey red-and-white check, which Kyle could swear he remembered from his boyhood. He suddenly felt strange and old. But when his mom turned to him, her face blossomed with delight.

"Give me that baby," she laughed. "Oh, she's so big! Goodness, you're such a big girl." She held the baby's glorious little body up to her face. He thought his mother had never looked so lovely.

"Almost a year," he agreed.

"Yes, she is a *big* girl, a whole year old! What will we do for your birthday? Maybe we can go to the zoo and see all the baby animals, the baby *bun*nies and the baby *cows* . . ." Maggie turned at this, jealous and interested.

"I want to go to the zoo and see the baby bunnies," she informed them.

"Of course you'll come, what fun would it be if you didn't?" Grandma asked. "It would be no fun at all."

Reassured, the child turned her attention back to her mother, who had stretched out in a lounge chair to enjoy the afternoon sun. Maggie had a spectacular red oak leaf in her hand, which she was presenting to Van as the treasure it was. "Look, Mommy," she said.

"Oh, goodness, that is *gorgeous*. And so big!" Big was a big thing that day. Van took the leaf into her hands and showed Maggie how it was almost as big as her face. Maggie squealed with delight.

"We can't wait to hear your news," his mother told him. He looked at her, surprised, and found her positively bursting with smug, unspoken joy. She leaned in and kissed him on the cheek. "I am so glad that you and Van have worked things out," she whispered. And with that, she cradled Georgia on her hip and sauntered over to the grill, to watch silly old Grandpa cook.

Kyle turned his gaze to Van and Maggie. Looking for more leaves, Maggie had skipped back to the one large tree that graced the suburban yard. Van followed her with her eyes, her left hand shielding her face from the afternoon sun. The white dress had settled; for once it wasn't billowing around her like the sail of a boat. Lying there in the flickering afternoon light, she looked content, regal, a princess in repose. A thoroughly pregnant princess in repose. The flimsy dress, when it wasn't billowing around, was revealing as hell.

He had known it intuitively for weeks. Her pale skin ripening like a rare peach, her energy shifting not away from the girls, but toward something more internal, something that demanded her secret attention. There were none of the usual telltale signs; if she was throwing up or eating weird things, she had managed to hide that business from him. But the dress asserted quite clearly that things were progressing on this front. She was a tiny person, and so she would show early, she was maybe three months along. But she was definitely pregnant.

He didn't wonder for one moment why she hadn't told him. She hadn't let him touch her since the baby was born; they hadn't had sex in over a year. Unless the good Lord really did occasionally descend from on high in order to impregnate pretty women, Van was having an affair. Which might explain how happy she was.

She was having an affair, and she was having someone else's baby. She was sitting on his parents' back patio watching his folks make dinner for their two daughters, and she was pregnant with someone else's child. She was lounging in the sun, contented, filled to the brim with her joy, drinking iced tea, smiling at his father, while her body grew a baby for someone else's lovely family. The level of the betrayal was so vast, and came upon him so quickly in the late afternoon air, that he felt light-headed, dizzy even. *But you knew,* his brain reminded him. *You've known for weeks.*

Yes, he replied to himself. *But now I have to talk about it.*

It was the rising of the truth to the surface of the world which finally and utterly filled him with rage. So much of his life had become his own secret. His wife didn't love him, so be it. His children were afraid of him, so be it. His wife had gone into the bed of another man, *so be it.* He had what he valued more than all of that—he had silence. He also had bitterness, grief, fleeting joy, struggles with the devil, conversations with God; he had within himself a universe of hope and disappointment and that was fine, it was what he had learned to make do with and even love. But *no one else was allowed to see it.*

It was the strength of that conviction which enabled him to make it through the rest of the afternoon, until the blessed exhaustion of both baby and toddler claimed the day. In fact, his ability to perform his life while living it somewhere else inside his head was so refined by this time that his mother would say, as she kissed him good-bye, "This is the nicest day I think we've ever had, Kyle. You have the nicest family I could wish for."

"Thanks, Mom," he said. She smiled at him with all the benign glory of her aging motherhood. *What a fucking idiot,* the bad side of his brain sneered, gleeful. Kyle was shocked at the malevolence of the thought, but what did it matter? She would never know. Thoughts like that came and went with lightning speed, and no one ever knew.

Both girls were asleep by the time they pulled into the driveway, which Van had predicted, so they were both already in their jammies. She carried the baby into the lovely house as Kyle lifted Maggie out of her car seat.

"Mommy do it," the sleepy child muttered, still and always her mother's girl.

"Tell her I'll be in to sing her a song," Van called back to them. "I'll be right there, honey."

Folding the sleeping children into their adorable bedrooms took seconds. But Van had all the time in the world. She sang a lullaby while tucking the baby into her crib. She made sure the bars were settled properly and the bumper wasn't all bunched up. She went up to Maggie's room to make sure she was really asleep, and not faking, and if she was in fact awake (she wasn't) to see if she needed a cup of water or a story. She went back to the baby's room again, to do who knows what. Exiled as always from this relentless ritual, Kyle sat alone on the edge of their bed, in their bedroom, and waited for her.

He had taken the precaution of turning the light off. For the past months Van had developed a very active schedule in her evenings. The dinner dishes took longer and longer to rinse and put into the dishwasher. On the nights when the girls went down easily, she had developed a fondness for late-night reading. Kyle didn't mind the threadbare flimsiness of these tactics; he knew that she was avoiding their bedroom until she thought he was asleep. He sat silently in the dark and waited for her to grow weary of whatever the phony diversion was this time, and come to bed.

The whisper of that white dress. She appeared in the dark, floating through the room like a ghost.

Kyle turned on the light.

"Oh, for crying out loud." Van put one hand on her stomach and the other on the edge of the bed. His bad brain allowed itself a shiver of delight, that he had frightened her. The other half of his brain managed to maintain a clinical distance while Van collected herself. She turned her back on him and headed for the closet. "I thought you had gone to bed."

"I was waiting for you."

"In the *dark?*" she asked, exasperated at the idea of this insanity.

"Yes, in the dark," he replied.

"Well, that doesn't make any sense."

"I don't need it to make sense."

"Honestly, Kyle, is there a point to this? Because I am really tired."

"Why?"

"What do you mean, why?" The breath of a defensive uncertainty was taking hold under her impatience. It had been so long, years even, since he had called her out on any of her bullshit, and she was smart enough to recognize that something different was coming her way now. "Because I was out*side* all day, taking care of two children, in case you hadn't noticed. As usual." This last bit was muttered under her breath, a hostile last-minute tag.

But these games were done now. The whole thing was done. "That's why you're tired? Are you sure? Are you sure it's not because you're *pregnant?*"

It was spoken with too much anger. The bad part of his brain was winning. A look of panic flew across her face, but so quickly. She smiled at him, just as quickly defiant.

"Keep your voice down," she commanded him. "I won't have you waking the girls."

"You won't have me *what?*" he asked. "You have betrayed our entire family, and you are telling me, what are you telling me, not to *yell?*"

"Betrayed, that's a joke."

"No, it is NOT." He managed to land this without breaching the walls of the bedroom, but she was having none of it.

"I'm not talking about this here. I mean it. We should go downstairs, to the kitchen, where—"

"I am not going *downstairs* and neither are you." He shut the door and positioned himself in front of it to make this point. "You are not ordering me around like a child, and you are not making me the problem here."

"Lower your voice."

"Whose *baby* are you having, Van? Because we both know it's not mine."

"I don't have to answer that." She tipped her chin at him defiantly and "drew herself up," that's what they used to call it, this phony moment when the person who is the most in the wrong pretends to be taller than she actually is. He watched her mind settle into some far-off place where its righteousness was unassailable. It was astonishing.

"You don't have to answer that? You don't answer, to your husband—"

"You were *never* my husband."

He had expected some narcissistic retelling of their history, *you haven't been a husband to me since the baby was born*, something that completely erased the fact that she was the one who had kicked him out of the marriage bed. But "never"?

"I have no idea what that is supposed to mean," he informed her. "That is just fucking crackers."

"Please refrain from the use of obscenity, it's highly offensive." *Here we go*, he thought, *here we go.*

"Okay, Van. Great. I won't say anything. You go right ahead. Explain this situation to me. You are pregnant, yes? You're showing, so I would like to warn you, as a physician, that a denial at this point won't do you any good. Because eventually a baby is going to show up. And that's going to be a challenging thing to explain, if you're not even pregnant."

"Babies are not things."

"No, they're not; they most certainly are not," he admitted. "So may we expect a new human *being* to show up around here, in the next six or seven months? And if that human being does show up, do you want to care to hazard a guess as to why that might happen?"

"You're ridiculous."

"'Cuckold' is actually the word, but yes, it is widely understood that it makes a man ridiculous, when he is *cuckolded.*" God he sounded like an ass. How was he losing this argument? He had all the facts on his side, and all that was right and good, and the girls too, *his* girls, all on *his* side, he had everything on his side, but she had folded her arms now and was looking at him like he was nothing more than a cheap bully. She was a skilled and devious opponent in an argument; over the years she had taught him the bitter rules of engagement with a will that refused to lose anything at any cost. *Okay then.* He leaned against the closed door and folded his arms. *If you want to do this all night, we will,* he thought. He couldn't tell anymore who was in charge inside his head: bad brain, indifferent brain, victim brain. Was there a good brain anywhere? *No. There isn't.*

"I am pregnant. Yes," Van said, defiant. *Why was she defiant?* thought one part of his brain. *Because she's a fucking idiot*, another answered. "It is not your child." *No shit.* "I think it's clear that we haven't been getting along for a long time." *Again, no shit.* "I met someone. You don't need to know who, it doesn't matter. But he and I, we fell in love, and I'm sorry if this news hurts you, but honestly, it's been so obvious for so long that our marriage was simply a huge mistake from the start. And I want you to always have a good relationship with your daughters, that is important to me. Maybe more important to me than it is to you, frankly, you don't seem all that interested in them, most of the time. But that is an unkind thing to say and I really, I never meant to be unkind or unfair in any way. So."

A pause.

"*So?*" In spite of the fact that most of his brain was feeling colossally aggrieved, the last shred of his logical mind couldn't help but want her to finish her fucking sentence. So *what*? The lack of apology was maddening. Not the lack of apology, but the crazy conviction that this complete disaster was somehow his fault. And his failure to fall to his knees and beg *her* for forgiveness was even more reason for her to heap blame on his unworthy head. His many years feeding at the malign teat of gender sensitivity rose in his chest like bile. Those everlasting feminists needed to take a lesson from Van. All that moaning about injustice and patriarchy and victimhood? She could teach them a thing or two about how to avoid *that* bullshit.

"*So* I don't see the need to belabor this," Van sighed, full of disappointed regret. "I would not have broken up our family in this way," she informed him. It was a phenomenal performance. "I didn't choose this."

"Well, *I* certainly didn't choose it!"

"That's my point, Kyle, neither one of us chose this."

"And yet only one of us *cheated*."

"Is that right?"

"Yes, Van. I am not the one who went out and decided to have a *child* with another person."

"You would if you could."

"What? What, what on earth—"

"Don't act all, don't—"

"What are you accusing me of?"

"You *know* what I'm accusing you of, and I don't think, frankly, I *don't* think you should make me say it."

"Make you say what?"

"You know." The accusation was profound.

This was all going so wrong. *Well, because she's insane. Is this a surprise, that she's insane? She's not insane. Then what is insanity/ what is it/ she's right you've been unfaithful/ never/ she knows/ I should go to bed have to get up at four Lord Jesus Christ.*

"Dennis told me."

The strangeness of this was perhaps the only thing that reached him. The room was so dark, so still. The one light on the bedside table beside him, beside the closed door, really made no impression at all, on the darkness. If she hadn't been wearing that absurd white dress, she would have been invisible, a black hole, nothing.

"Dennis told you, told you what?"

"Now who's lying?"

"I don't know, Van. I guess you think I'm lying but the fact is I don't know what you're talking about, what did *Dennis* tell you?"

"You are still in love with her! When you married me, you were still in love with her, and that wasn't fair, Kyle. Not to me, not to the girls, to bring them into a loveless home was not fair to any of us." She was so aggrieved he thought his head would explode. The only thing to do, the only thing he could even think of doing, was to stick so excruciatingly to the facts that the hope of reality might hover around this nightmare of a confrontation.

"I assume you are referring to Alison Moore."

"Yes, you *assume* correctly." The sarcasm was dripping with timeless indignation.

"I have not seen or spoken to Alison in a year. It's more than that now, I haven't seen or spoken to her since that stupid dinner party, so I don't know what Dennis told you—"

"He told me the truth. That you had sex with her, up in his father's *bedroom*, you had sex with her while I was pregnant—"

"What—"

"That you are still obsessed with her, that you go over to his place, you lie to me and go over to his *apartment* and watch her, you make him tape the shows and then you watch her having sex—"

"That is completely ridiculous. It's beyond ridiculous. I have been completely faithful to you, *I am not the one who cheated.*" That shut her up. He decided to stick with a winning strategy and just repeat it. "I am not the one who cheated, Van. I never cheated on you. You are carrying someone else's baby. You cannot make this my fault."

"You never loved me. Our marriage was never a real marriage."

"Well, that's interesting, because it certainly feels like a real marriage." There was another silence at this. He didn't know if that meant he was winning or losing. He didn't know which would be better. "So Dennis told you all this shit—"

"The truth, you mean?"

"Whatever. Why were you off gossiping about me with Dennis?"

"It wasn't gossiping—"

"Is he the one, he's the one you slept with?"

"Oh, please. That's disgusting."

"*That's* disgusting? None of the rest of this—"

"You are so distorting this situation."

"How would that be possible, Van, seriously, I don't see how I could possibly distort this any further."

"I did not sleep with Dennis. He's your friend. I would never do that."

"But you would have another man's baby."

"I knew you would say that."

"Say *what?*"

"All your Catholic righteousness, it flies right out the window when it's convenient. Well, let me tell you something. I am not getting an abortion. I would never do that. I would never, *never* do that."

"Did I ask you to?"

"Didn't you? What is my choice? If you don't want me to have another man's baby, what does that mean? That I should kill it? Isn't that what you're saying?"

"I'm not, I'm just—trying to get to the bottom of this!"

"That's not what you're trying to do."

"What am I trying to do then?"

"If you had come to our marriage with a pure heart, none of this would have happened. If you had tried to love me. But you never did, it is so apparent to everyone, and our marriage never even *existed* and I want a divorce *and* an annulment."

"An *annulment?*"

"It's the *truth*, it's the truth of our marriage. You never loved me, you always loved that other *person* and it was never a true marriage."

The pins were starting to drop. He never actually knew what that old phrase meant before this moment, *what the fuck are dropping pins*, but he saw them now, in his head, metal rods in a clock-like contraption, pieces fitting together so that the mechanism is complete.

"He's Catholic," Kyle told her. "You met him at church." He took a couple of steps closer to her, so that he could see her better in the gloom. He felt like Sherlock Holmes. But how had he missed it? Holmes would never have missed the clues of what was happening right under his nose. "Who is it?"

"It doesn't matter."

"It matters to me."

"You don't know him, Kyle, so it does not matter."

"Is he married?"

"I'm not talking about him. He is none of your business."

"It's none of my business. You're cheating on me, you're pregnant, you're talking about destroying our marriage—"

"It was never—"

"I've heard, Van; I know the arguments, okay? I know the whole stupid annulment argument, I know the whole crazy Catholic set of rules, *I WAS RAISED CATHOLIC*, and I understand the logic of the technicality, if some consortium of elders in the Catholic church proclaims that the marriage never existed, then you're free to marry again within the church. Which means that somehow you have managed not once but twice to fall in love with a practicing Catholic. Which is impressive; honestly there aren't that many of us out there anymore." His anger was spent. Somehow explaining Catholic dogma to this devious, pretty lunatic had brought him back to himself.

Van watched him, uncertain. "So are we finished, then? Because I really am very tired."

"I—guess—we are finished."

She reached for a pillow. "I'll go sleep in the baby's room. It's a miracle you didn't wake her, but she'll be up soon enough."

"It's okay, Van. I'll go somewhere else."

"I don't want Maggie to find you sleeping on the couch. Until we get this settled about how we're going to proceed, I don't want her to have to worry about, you know. Why is Daddy not sleeping with Mommy? She needs to be protected."

"Maybe you should have thought of that before."

"I did *nothing* but think of that before," Van flared. "Do you think this has been easy? It has been hideous. Every thought I had was for those girls. You feel nothing for them, that is so clear to everyone. So don't, just don't you *dare* throw that at me. I am a fantastic mother. You don't have any right to accuse me, on that level."

Would this never end? "I will not sleep on the couch."

"Where will you sleep?"

"I will sleep somewhere else."

"Please don't go to your parents'. We really do have to talk to lawyers first."

"I will not go to my parents'."

"Where will you go?"

"I . . . will go to Dennis's."

"Of course." She smiled at this, triumphant, her point made.

Really, would this never end?

Dennis, drunk and sympathetic, was also completely unrepentant about whatever part he had played in this increasingly sordid drama. Kyle threw back a huge glass of Dennis's best scotch—*how can he afford this stuff he never has a job*—while Dennis explained how Van had played him like a violin, had poured her heart out about her insecurities, had demanded the truth about Kyle and Alison, had been assuming something so much worse.

"Seriously, Kyle, she was way out on a limb. She had a whole thing going on, you were flying to New York behind her back and having sex with Alison, it was crazy, she had dates and times all worked out. It was completely insane. And that's what I told her."

"And then you told her—"

"I told her that the only thing I knew was that one night, at the Christmas party."

"You mean the night I *didn't* have sex with Alison? You mean that night?"

Dennis shrugged. "You were up in that bedroom alone and it didn't sound entirely innocent, my friend. I put the best spin on it but what can I say, it wasn't exactly innocent." Dennis's tone moved off of reassurance and on to something darker but it bounced quickly. "What she did with it, I have no idea. She's an interesting woman, your Van. How you two ever got together is a mystery to me. She's a killer."

"She wants an *annulment.*" Blearily, he reached for the scotch bottle. "This is going to kill my parents."

"Come on, parents are generally sturdier than we think."

"Mine aren't." He was drinking much too fast, he knew it, but if ever a person had earned the right to pour booze down his throat, it was him, and the moment was now. "They're like children, both of them. My mother, *Jesus*, this afternoon she was *congratulating* me on my happiness with Van, how we both finally seemed so *happy* and seeing me so *happy* made her happy and it was the best day of her whole *life*. This was, oh, four hours ago."

Dennis simply shrugged at this news. "If you don't tell them anything about what's actually going on, how are they supposed to know any better?" He swung himself out of his one good chair and headed back to the kitchen. It wasn't actually a kitchen; it was a kind of old-fashioned kitchenette space that boasted a tiny refrigerator and the smallest four-burner stove imaginable. Dennis's little apartment was both sparse and suffocating. Next to the charms of the sprawling Victorian mansion Kyle shared with Van and the girls, it looked pathetic.

But Dennis considered his singular ice cube tray with the focused confidence of an aristocrat. "Well, I'm sorry if my little foray into the truth got you in the shithouse with Van. But for fuck's sake, Kyle, the woman is a nightmare. I would say if she wants a divorce you should be *celebrating.* Do not pass go, just get out of jail free."

"It's hardly that simple."

"Stop being such a pussy. You've been miserable for years. You never had the balls to just take what you want. Catholicism is *stupid.* Everybody else knows this; why don't you? You're supposed to be so smart, the *doctor*, start acting like it!" This last bit was delivered with a flash of mean pleasure. It moved quickly, but it was startling in its sneering superiority. Something in Dennis had begun to edge into bitterness; he was turning into the definition of a nasty drunk. The clinician in Kyle recognized the signs and behaviors of the toxicity, how thoroughly the alcohol was taking hold of the organism. Dennis needed months in rehab. He needed his family to step in, not that they would. His father had washed his hands of him years ago. *Can you do that? Can you wash away your children?* The sacrament of baptism, the washing away of sins. *Can you wash away your life?*

I need to get out of here. Kyle stood, swayed briefly as the oxygen hit his brain. He needed to find an all-night diner, and get four or five cups of bad coffee into him.

"Where are you going?" Dennis asked. "Kyle! Where are you going?" *What's he so pissed about?* Kyle's bad brain seemed to finally have gone to sleep. Why, he couldn't say. Maybe it was the sight of Dennis, drunk, proud, withered, old. "Are you going to New York, to finally *do it* with your long-lost love? Let me tell you. You haven't missed that much. Seriously! She's still not giving out. Not to the likes of us, anyway."

What was he saying? Kyle knew he was trying to get a rise out of him. He knew, also, that Dennis was a liar, that he *had* told Van whatever he could, that he had thrown bombs into his marriage, that Dennis was every bit the man he claimed to be—charming, dangerous, completely and utterly destructive in every way. He reached for the doorknob behind him.

"Yeah, you heard me!" Dennis jeered. He sounded like a kid in a schoolyard, daring Kyle to punch him. "I went to New York, I saw her!" Kyle turned back and looked at him. "She's totally sold out. She's fucking some director, she's fucking anyone. Anyone except you and me! She is what she always was, Kyle. She's nothing but a *whore*."

"Stop." Kyle was exhausted by the breakage. The breakage of everything. Dennis wove in and out of focus. He was wearing a dirty plaid robe—*what an affectation*—over a T-shirt and sweats. His face was full-on purple, the color of someone about to have a heart attack. How had this happened?

"Did you even hear what I said?"

"You should go back to AA, Dennis," Kyle told him. "You're not well."

"That's hilarious, coming from you."

Kyle turned the doorknob, swung the door open.

Can you wash away your life?

twenty-two

MOVIES WERE FUN. The makeup trailer was boring, and it was a drag to have to get out of bed at four in morning all the time, and everybody obsessing about your hair was boring, and having your picture taken and talking to reporters all the time was also dead boring. But the rest was a blast.

A movie set is a like an aircraft carrier. One of the grips had told her this. A big guy with a plain blue tattoo on the back of his left hand, Stu had been in the navy for sixteen years before they sent him to the Gulf, where he saw some honest-to-God action. According to Stu, who was also a huge flirt, everything in the navy was built toward that aircraft carrier. It was the *tip of the spear.* The fighter pilots were the tip of the tip. They were the movie stars. He would grin at her, point. She was the tip of the tip here.

Not that Alison *was* a movie star. Not yet. But the dailies were phenomenal. She had been warned not to watch them, and in fact she wasn't *allowed* to watch them, but the buzz on the set was "phenomenal." It was a peculiar word, when you heard people say it over and over; it sounded insecure and phony, so she didn't believe it when it first started floating around the bubble of their own little biosphere. Of course people in show business were always pumping themselves up and no one ever wanted to be caught up saying anything negative, that was the sort of shit that could get you fired. But at some point a different sound entered all the narcissistic chatter. There was, apparently, *buzz.* The suits started to show up on the set. Everyone started to take credit.

Everyone especially started taking credit for *her.* "I was thrilled when Lars brought up her name, the first time," Norbert told *Us Weekly.* "Gordon said from the start, we need to make a star with this one and I took one look at Alison and said, she's the one."

"She's been on everybody's radar for a while," Colin told *People.* "It was just a matter of time until she made the leap into features. I had seen tape on her a couple years ago, people were talking about her then. I said to Gordon, you have to see this girl. And Gordon totally agreed."

This account was politely contradicted by Gordon. "She was my idea, from the word go," he told *Entertainment Tonight.* "I told all of them, you guys need to look at this tape on this girl before you do anything else. It was Lars who needed a little convincing."

"So what's the story? *Gordon* fixed me up on a *date* with *Lars*?" Alison was endlessly on the phone with Ryan now; it was like he didn't have a single other client. Day or night, she had the hot line.

"You are not to worry about the *story,*" he informed her.

"People ask, Ryan! People read that stuff and they believe it and then they ask me, did Gordon really fix you up with Lars? What am I supposed to say? You and I both know he fought tooth and nail to keep me out of this."

"Darling, if Gordon didn't want you in this movie, you would not *be* in this movie," Ryan reminded her.

"That's not true, Ryan! You told me yourself—"

"I *told* you there were reservations at the studio level—"

"Oh, bullshit, you told me that Gordon wanted a big star—"

"Alison. Alison. Alison." She hated it when he did this, it sounded like he thought she was eight years old. She was already struggling with the fact that everyone treated her like a complete child. Whenever she was in hair and makeup, they actually sent a production assistant over to walk her to the set. Usually a total nitwit, someone fresh out of college who had a dad who pulled connections and got little Heather or Connor or Jamie a job on a movie set, where their responsibilities included fetching cappuccinos from the coffee truck and making sure the star didn't get lost. Not that she was a star. Yet. There was always that caution. She wasn't a star *yet.* She had a long way to go, and to get there, she would have to play nice.

What that meant, though, was anyone's guess. Who was she supposed to play nice with? Lars? She had, and she did, and that situation only got more complicated. Impossibly, he was even more obsessed with every detail of her; every vowel she uttered came under excruciating and never-ending scrutiny. If the line was as simple as, "What do you want, Ben?" there were still thousands of ways to modulate it. He would put her through take after take focusing on a lift of an eyebrow. And then there were the ever-increasing demands on her time off the set. Lars wanted to have sex all the time and it was exhausting, frankly, especially on nights when she had a 4 a.m. call. Also, especially, since his potency waned even as his demands increased.

It was too much. He was tired, and she was tired, and she had to get up at least two hours before he did, to sit in a makeup trailer while they made her glorious twenty-eight-year-old face even more photogenic. What was he trying to prove? He wasn't enjoying the sex anymore; that was perfectly clear. *She* certainly wasn't enjoying it, although that didn't seem to matter to Lars one little bit. The vigor and ingenuity of their previous lovemaking laughed at them from the corners of hotel rooms, a mocking and prurient ghost. *It was never anything at all*, she thought, while Lars pumped away at her. Most of the time, he had his eyes closed. Why couldn't he even look at her? She was the living visitation of movie magic, a sex goddess in the flesh, made incarnate by his own hand. It didn't matter. His eyes remained shut, his face slack, while he concentrated on whatever it was inside him that might entice him to come. Most nights she truly wanted to shove him off her. But the pressure was on, and she had to play nice.

The movie itself was good. An action movie, with eight hot-blooded American boys on a mission in the jungle, with a swell girl who might have been a lesbian but also looked like Ava Gardner? The peculiarity of if it crossed over into something original, weird, even magical. Alison had never actually understood what Lars was doing with his pathological control of her look, but once they were shooting, the fierce intelligence behind the peculiar filmic elements began to reveal itself. It was *Day of the Locust* meets *The Misfits*, with a few grenades tossed in. A couple of times, Alison actually was the one who got to toss the grenades. David, the DP who had worked on three other films with Lars, knew instinctively that Alison's more classical features required a shift in the way the film itself was shot, and so he hypersaturated the colors. While the gun battles were shot like hallucinations, the love scenes drifted into haunting movie moments redolent of the heyday of the film greats. Alison actually did know how to tip her head back and look at her hero with tragic yearning.

"The young Bergman," the second camera op muttered. Stu the grip nodded, equally impressed. They were a gang of seasoned pros who had worked with pretty much every star and starlet under the sun, and many of these young stars treated the crew like servants. But Alison's good Midwestern manners never failed her, and the grips, the PAs, the wardrobe assistants, and the lady who helped her with her coffee at the craft service table were all treated with good-natured respect and gratitude. The crew loved her.

And as days rolled into weeks the camera recorded the possibility that Alison was in fact The Real Deal. Pretty soon, they all said, she was going to be able to do whatever she wanted. She didn't know what that meant, but so many people said it to her so many times, it was hard to pretend that it might not actually be true. Even strangers, especially strangers, gushed and warned her gleefully of the coming tsunami of global attention. Reporters who showed up on the set hovered, watched, flirted with her. Men in suits whose names she could never remember came and watched with a reptilian bonhomie. The sequence of writers who showed up on the set invariably ended up writing extra scenes for her.

Gordon, the head of the studio, meanwhile, joined in the obsession with every detail of Alison's hair, her makeup, her dialogue, and her close-ups. Her clothes especially were cause for brutal interference. The day Lars decided that Alison should be wearing a narrow pink silk sheath—all the better to seduce a drug lord at his birthday party—Gordon weighed in passionately. He liked the color, she could wear the pink, it was a terrific color and it looked good on her. But shouldn't the dress be more "special"? This was often the language of their parlance: Gordon was "underwhelmed" by the dress. It needed to be "more special." When you pressed him as to what he might mean by "more special" it turned out that what he usually meant was "sequins."

This news was delivered to all of them during a costume fitting in the wardrobe trailer. Alison thought Lars's head was going to explode.

"*Sequins*? Is he fucking insane? Where the fuck did they find *sequins* in the middle of the fucking *jungle*?"

"Well, for that matter, where did they find a pink silk sheath?" observed Molly, the imperturbable costume designer.

"She *had* it. She brought it with her from the States, it's been in her backpack for six years."

"Oh."

"Don't say *oh* like that's impossible, it's not *likely*, but it's *possible* that she would squirrel away a piece of her previous life as a *debutante* but it is *not* possible that she would carry around a pink *sequin dress* for six years, that's in*sane*."

Alison kept her mouth shut and sat there. They were surrounded by hundreds of dresses and scarves and steam irons. Lars preferred issuing orders and having them intuitively understood by someone who had decent and reliable taste, like Molly, who had worked on three films with him; this being summoned to the wardrobe trailer did not suit him.

"I can email them a rendering in half an hour," Molly explained, the soul of patient cooperation.

"He doesn't really want to see a rendering, he wants to see her in the dress." This from weirdo Norbert, the producer-slash-factotum who always insisted they implement any demand the studio put forward, bar none.

"But we don't have a dress, we will have to build the dress, and this is supposed to shoot tomorrow," Molly explained. "If he really wants her in a sequined dress—"

"He definitely wants the sequins, it's really important to him. The dress really needs to be more special."

"Well, we can do that but—"

"We are not *PUTTING her* in a *sequined dress*!" It was the first time Alison had ever seen Lars's cool Icelandic prince act start to crack. What was the big deal? The whole idea that she had any dress at all stuffed into a backpack for six years was preposterous. The whole sequence in fact was ridiculous, and had actually just been added to the script last week, apparently as a total excuse to put the hot young female lead into a slinky dress and watch her play Mata Hari for a couple of minutes while the boys ran around and placed detonators on the periphery of the drug lord's compound.

Lars finally threw in the towel. The compromise—if you could call it that—was *gold* sequins. But it came at a cost. Lars never threatened to walk off the picture, as that was not his style. But, Ryan told her in a whispered phone call, the entire *town* was talking about the degree of interference that the studio was inflicting on him. It was un*heard* of.

Rumors of studio intervention were flourishing everywhere. The band of brats (so titled with a saucy sisterly flair by Alison) tossed the unverifiable information about carelessly as they sat to the side and waited for the DP to finish lighting.

"I heard they're going to reshoot all the bar sequences," Evan observed.

"I heard we were going to reshoot all the action sequences," Robbie countered.

"Gordon hates all the sets, he says it looks cheap."

"He wants to rebuild all the sets?"

"He wants to send us to *Mexico*," Robbie insisted. "That's what my agent says."

"Cut it *out*." Lars had fought valiantly for a location in Mexico, but the studio bean counters had put their collective foot down. There was a drug war going on in Mexico—not a pretend one, a *real* one, where *real* drug cartels were shooting *real* bullets at each other and anyone else who happened to be in the vicinity. Under these circumstances, the insurance company had decisively declined to offer any kind of coverage to this particular production. So Mexico was out, and Colombia too, and the farther south they went in their search for an authentic Latino jungle the more the complications flowered and decayed. Finally, the only answer was building a Mexican rain forest in the desert hills just outside downtown Los Angeles. Which cost a small fortune. Now Gordon didn't like the sets and he was going to send them into the middle of the Mexican jungle and put all their lives at risk after all? Well, anything was possible. Alison was learning: Any amount of insanity, not to mention dough, was tossed about these movies like confetti.

Although Lars never blew his cool (other than during the War of the Sequins) the disagreements with the studio became increasingly intense, making their presence felt on the set with a weary regularity. The editor had put together some rough cuts of scenes which Gordon asked to see well before the DGA rules allowed him to get a look at it. Rightly, Lars refused to let him look at the footage. But some exec managed to sneak a flash drive out of the editing bay and he took it straight to Gordon's office, so Gordon did in fact see footage he had no right to see, and he wasn't happy. In spite of everyone's delight at the dailies, he expressed his unhappiness with the direction of the scenes, the look of the sets—that rumor turned out to be true as well—and demanded substantial reshoots. After hours of wrangling with executives, Lars refused to reshoot a single frame, at which point Gordon threatened to pull him off the movie. Phone calls were made to and from the DGA, and agents and execs screamed at each other regularly, and one day the lunch break extended into two hours while it was determined whether or not Lars would return to the set, which if he didn't would put the entire movie in jeopardy as well as cost the studio millions. Then, suddenly, it all got settled somehow and everyone went back to work.

Several weeks later they did spend half a day reshooting scenes that really were fine, and then a week after that there were more reshoots. Lars had won the battle and lost the war.

It was the third time Lars reshot one of Alison's scenes that her nerves began to fray. Protected by the early buzz, she had managed to stay out of all the wrangling by simply being agreeable, doing a good job, and never showing up late for anything. Actresses who showed up late were regularly dismissed as the lowest form of life by everyone on the set. But when Lars came to the set one day and explained that they were going to have to reshoot for a third time the scene where she was talking to her mother on the telephone, and looking at herself in the mirror, she made a mistake. She asked him why.

"We just need some more colors," Lars told her, abrupt.

"What kind of 'colors'?"

"It would be great if you could be putting lipstick on. Looking at yourself and putting lipstick on."

"While I'm talking on the telephone?"

"Yeah, while you're talking on the telephone."

"Do you still want me to start in the kitchen, and then walk over to the mirror?"

"Yes."

"Yeah, but this isn't—"

"Isn't what?" Lars was testy. Which was entirely unfair; the boys talked back to him all the time, and he never got testy with them. She should be allowed to ask a *question.*

She had the phone in her hand. She held it up for him. "You can't actually—okay. Look." She marched over to the kitchenette part of the ratty apartment set and held the phone to her ear. "Okay, I'm on the phone," she announced. "I'm talking talking talking to my mother in the States. I walk over to the mirror to look at myself, I'm not sure why, but I do it, and now I reach for a lipstick which you need two hands to open, so in spite of the fact that I'm on the phone I reach for the lipstick and do what, hold it on my shoulder, while I open the lipstick? It's a *cell* phone. You can't hold a cell phone with your shoulder, to your ear."

"Set the phone on the dresser."

"Like, while she's talking?"

"I would really like you to put lipstick on."

"But—"

"*Just do it, Alison.*"

"This is the third time we've shot this stupid phone call," she said, and there was no question, she was tired and edgy. "What is the fucking deal?"

Lars turned and stormed off the set.

The fucking deal, as it turned out, was that Gordon had decided that he wanted to see Alison putting on lipstick while she chatted on the phone. The first time this request had come down the chain of command to Lars, all the intermediaries had interpreted Gordon's request with too much complexity: He wanted to see a more sexualized version of the character. Alison was playing her too soft. She should be more cunning. These instructions had been delivered with so much determination that Lars had shrugged and agreed finally to the first request for a reshoot. But the first reshoot was unsatisfactory. She was playing it more cunning, yes, but where was the lipstick? Why wasn't she putting on lipstick? When this question made its way down the chain of command to Lars, it was a bad day. He couldn't believe that the head of a studio would be thinking about an actress putting on lipstick. He also was in no mood to cooperate. Gordon had recently fired the fifth writer the studio had hired to do petty rewrites and they were now scrambling for some other WGA hack who would cost an arm and a leg while delivering nothing but shit dialogue. And then the bean counters would call and scream at him about going over budget. The studio was out of control; his producer Norbert was a useless, incompetent toady; and the budget was soaring, not because he couldn't control it but rather because Norbert couldn't control Gordon and Gordon couldn't control himself, and kept insisting on more of everything: more costumes, more extras, more writers, more sets. Doing a second reshoot of Alison in front of a mirror was insane. He would do it, but it was insane. He put a different costume on her, hoping that Norbert and Gordon would feel like the studio had been placated, and left it at that. When Gordon came back a third time with the demand that he see her putting on the lipstick, Lars hit the roof. But, as one underling pointed out, that was *always* what Gordon had been asking for. Gordon had a right to be angry. It was the simplest of requests, to see Alison putting on lipstick while she talked on the phone! He was the head of the studio. What was the big deal?

Alison, of course, had no way of knowing that this shit was the backdrop to her reasonable but impertinent questions about why they might be reshooting such an idiotic little scene for the third time.

So when Lars stormed off the set, she was left exhausted and appalled. Of course everyone knew that they were sleeping together, so there was no way to interpret Lars's explosive reaction as anything other than a fed-up lover whose fuse had finally been lit. And while everyone liked Alison, Lars was the *director.* She was doing a great job but everyone also knew that she wouldn't even have this part if Lars hadn't handed it to her. Within seconds the delicate balance of collegial affection which had kept the set afloat evaporated. Ronnie, the first AD, called out, efficiently, "Everyone take five!" and scurried after Lars. The sound guy scurried forward, to carefully disconnect her mic and her wire. Everyone else scurried away.

The whole thing was so stupid, but there was something truly frightening about how quickly everyone had evaporated, as if cued by some offstage god in a paranoid nightmare. Bewildered, Alison stood alone on the set for just long enough to realize they weren't kidding, and then she went back to her chair, guessing without guidance that maybe she should stick close to the set while Ronnie and Norbert and Lars worked out what to do next, in consultation, of course, with the studio. But the small island of slingback chairs which had been placed near the set for the actors to lounge in was also deserted. None of the few crew members who lingered nearby would meet her glance. She considered taking her chair and waiting, like a good girl, for everyone to return, but her heart choked her. She stood up, confused and impatient. *When they wanted her back on the set, they could just come and ask.*

The closest path back to her two-banger was through the soundstage. The set of the mocked-up apartment where she was supposed to be putting on lipstick was tucked back in the far corner; she cut through it, and through the Mexican bar where she waited tables and where the black ops regularly got drunk, before turning to the loading dock, which opened out onto a hard, featureless concrete pathway. For once there was no twenty-two-year-old production assistant walking ahead of her while reporting her location to someone else on a walkie-talkie. She turned a corner and found herself face-to-face with a small army of union carpenters who were hauling a magnificent Mayan temple out to another loading dock, where it would be picked up and shipped out to the nearby desert hills which were being transformed into yet another jungle set. Seeing the deconstructed pieces of the set being placed so neatly on the silent concrete gave Alison a sudden rush of panic. *I like this job*, she thought. *I really like this job.*

She walked around another corner, wishing desperately that there was someone whom she could call. Her mother was no good; she never lost her tone of mild judgment whenever Alison even inched toward telling her what her life looked like. Megan was lost in her children, and Jeff—the one brother who had, long ago, in their youth, almost understood her—she hadn't talked to for almost a year because he was off on another grant somewhere, maybe in Hong Kong. She was tired of talking to Ryan, who would just tell her to go suck it all up, that she was going to be a star but she wasn't yet and she owed everyone an apology. She wondered what the guys would say if she showed up at whatever trailer they were hanging out in. At least *they* liked her. They seemed to like her. They enjoyed working together. Alison took a few steps toward the line of closed trailers and remembered that none of them were called to the set today; when they rescheduled this third reshoot they gave everyone else the afternoon off. The alleyway with its line of trailers was empty, still and ruthless in the afternoon sun.

She knew that something dreadful had just happened to her, but she honestly couldn't tell what. Having been skeptical for so long about the different steps she was required to take up the path to where everyone wanted her to go, she finally had allowed herself to relax into the delights of all the delightful things which were being showered upon her. Pretty clothes, flirty boys, nice hotel rooms, terrific sushi—seriously, the sushi in Los Angeles was so good it temporarily made up for the sunlight and the loneliness. But the whisper of fear was back upon her; she remembered in the moment poor Pinocchio, hanging out with the wrong crowd, allowing them to drag him to that terrifying amusement park where they all turned into donkeys. She wondered briefly if she might be sprouting a tail.

The problem with all this light and heat, she thought, *is there's no place to hide.* Maybe that was why people just flattened out, finally, it was less risky to just let go of whoever it was inside you that made you a person. There was no time for that stuff out here anyway. You had to go to the gym, to sit in the sun, to make an appearance at restaurants where people went to see and be seen. She hadn't started hanging out in clubs yet but she knew that was next on the agenda; Ryan told her definitively that she was going to have to "come out" from Lars's "shadow" and claim a place in a hipper, more current crowd. After practically throwing her into Lars's bed himself, Ryan was ready to move on; Lars Guttfriend, one of the biggest action directors in the business, was yesterday's news. People weren't people out here, they were moves on a chessboard in a town where no one knew how to play chess.

What her next move was, she had no idea. She turned a corner, lost, and looked around.

She looked pretty. Ridiculous, but pretty. They had her all dolled up as a sort of femme fatale, but with a modern twist, low-slung khaki trousers, one of those tacky wife-beater undershirts, a little bit of belly button showing, just in case the boys weren't being driven crazy enough by the rest of it. She looked mad, fed up, almost like she was about to start crying. There was a charming dissonance to it all.

"Hey, movie star," he called.

Alison raised her hand to shade her eyes in that endless sun. He wondered for a moment why she wasn't wearing sunglasses, when she smiled.

"Man, they'll let anyone on these lots," she observed. "What the fuck are you doing here?"

It was more auspicious than their last meeting, at least you could say that. "I'm stringing for *Entertainment Weekly*," Seth informed her.

"Meaning?"

"You're in *Entertainment Weekly* often enough, you don't know what that means?"

"I don't know what 'stringing' means, it sounds like a complicated Ivy League insider code word."

"It means sucking up."

"Just Hollywood then."

"I have a friend in the PR department here, I'm trying to get them to throw me a bone," he admitted.

"What happened to the *Times*?"

"Newspapers are a dying breed."

"You got fired," she guessed.

"I didn't want to work there anyway." This got him the flash of a grin, not a full laugh. He couldn't quite tell if she was upset or her makeup was askew. Or maybe it was the hair. It made her seem frail. The few times they had met, he had found her to be many things, but "frail" was never one of them.

"What are you doing, wandering the lot alone, I've never heard of such a thing," he noted, glancing about. "Where are your minders? Where's the entourage?"

"I escaped while they weren't looking."

"Escaped what?"

"Oh, do you think I'm going to answer that? You're a *reporter*."

"That is using the term very loosely." Okay, *that* made her laugh. For a moment, her whole being came into focus and then evaporated. She shot a look over her shoulder, the swift paranoid glance of someone under siege.

"What's with your hair?"

"Don't you like it?"

"I just like your normal color."

He hadn't meant it to wound her; he had hoped that it would make her laugh again. But she reacted strangely. She turned and looked behind her, making sure that nobody had heard that—at least, that's what he thought she was doing—until a mere moment later, when she reached up and yanked at the black mop on her head, and revealed that underneath there was another head of hair.

"It's a wig," she announced. "They wigged me."

He didn't know what to say. She didn't either, for a moment. Then, in a simple unself-conscious moment of exhaustion, her hand fell to her side, her fingers loosened, and the wig dropped.

"Can we get out of here?" she asked. "I mean, do you have a car, or anything?"

"Of course I have a car, it's LA," he told her. "Do you need a ride?"

"A ride would be great."

The wig lay forgotten at her feet.

She never specified where she wanted a ride to, but they ended up at Venice Beach, where they sat on a bench and watched the crazies and the Rollerbladers. Alison took off her shoes and ran to wade in the surf, which was a worry, as the East Coaster in him was certain the water was full of pesticides and jellyfish. But she was having so much fun he couldn't bring himself to mention either pesticides or jellyfish, although he didn't go in himself. He just watched. She was gorgeous.

Seth knew he was being stupid. She wasn't a person anymore; she was a story, and a big one. He could sell this as *Roman Holiday* for starlets, complete with surreptitious candids taken with his iPhone, but it would create real problems for her if he did. Would it be worth it? He watched her, alert, as she rolled up her khakis and splashed around with the unthinking abandon of someone who had grown up without an ocean nearby. *That's a costume*, he remembered. *She's still wearing her costume.*

Alison was drenched by the time he insisted she get out of that filthy water, so he bought her a Venice Beach sweatshirt, and a pair of sweatpants too. As she ripped off her wet clothes and changed in the backseat of his rental car, he willed himself not to watch in the rearview mirror. That made her laugh too. "It's not like you haven't seen me naked," she reminded him. But to him it felt as if while they had been moving forward in time, he had somehow slipped backward into a more innocent past. Maybe it was her; she was in all seriousness kind of acting like a twelve-year-old. She climbed over the seat in her ridiculous sweats and dropped into the seat beside him, looking around with an unguarded curiosity. "There presumably is someplace to get a drink around here," she announced.

There were many places to get drinks three blocks from Venice Beach, but she rejected them all ("sleazy," "gay," "yuppie bullshit") and in the end they bought a bottle of vodka and parked in a turnaround up on Mulholland, where they could look at the lights in the valley and get drunk without anyone bothering them.

"So is *that* the demimonde?" she asked, tipping the half-empty bottle toward the city flung beneath them. The night sky was clear, and the sun having just set, the mountains hovered in a silent, crisp blue shadow. The lines of light spilling toward them across the miles of uninterrupted plain were eerie and beautiful.

"That's the valley," he answered. "I would have to say, definitively, that the valley is *not* the demimonde."

"Why not?"

"Too many poor people."

"There are plenty of losers with no cash in the demimonde."

"Not in my demimonde."

"*Your* demimonde?"

"Are you kidding? I'm an *entertainment* reporter. The demimonde is my turf," he informed her.

"The demimonde is *my* turf," she reminded him.

"Well, then you know I'm right. The valley is not the turf for the demimonde. The demimonde is up here in the hills, in the hidden homes of movie stars such as yourself."

"You know, it's so weird. I would have thought that you had to *want* to be a movie star, to be a movie star. All those people out there trying desperately to be movie stars. Like, working at it. And with me I'm just hanging around one day and someone says, 'Here, put on this wig.'"

"I have a feeling it was a little more complicated than that."

"Not all that much."

She took another hit off the vodka bottle with just enough exhaustion to lead him to suspect she was lying. "The wig isn't what's made you a movie star."

"I'm not so sure it *isn't* the wig," she said. "Or the wig and the dresses. Honestly, the acting isn't anywhere near as difficult. You spend hours in hair and makeup, and wardrobe, you spend *years* in wardrobe, and then like sixty people change their mind about your costume and your hair, even the head of the fucking *studio* is obsessing on what I wear, it just takes forever. And then I get to the set, and the scenes are really not all that—you know, half the time, I'm just running from one set of rocks to another, yelling, 'Come on!' Occasionally I get to throw a grenade. I was doing more acting on that terrible television show."

"You have good scenes in this." She looked at him, surprised. "I have a friend in the Xerox department. She slipped me the script."

"A friend in the Xerox department. That's a euphemism if I've ever heard one."

"It's not a euphemism; they have Xerox departments, and I have friends there. And none of them are in the demimonde, let me reassure you. There are no Xerox departments in the demimonde."

"There are no actresses there either, let me assure you."

"No, the actresses are all in the theater, starving." He knew plenty of them, and they were no fun. OCD losers who lived in a constant state of rage because they couldn't get cast in anything, and when they did get cast the plays were so bad no one came to see them. Plus they got paid next to nothing. Then they proceeded to lord their Commitment to Art over any actor out there who did manage to land a money gig. Like Alison. He was sure they all hated her. Certainly her old friend Lisa had nothing good to say about her.

"You ever hear from Lisa?" Alison asked, as if she were reading his mind.

"Now and then."

"She won't talk to me. She's convinced I stole you from her."

"That's not what she thinks."

"Oh ho." Alison glanced over at him. "What does she think?"

"She thinks that the demimonde would be a fun place to live, and she's jealous that you get to live there, and she doesn't."

"So how'd *you* end up here?" she asked. He'd asked himself that question, on plenty of drunken nights. How was it that no amount of money, looks, talent, pedigree, education could extricate him from this petty, demeaning, and meaningless livelihood; why couldn't he shake himself out of it, write that novel, run off to Africa to report about child soldiers, research a book on China's stunning takeover of global capitalism? Why couldn't he do that? He himself had taken every step down the path to the nihilistic cultural abyss which was entertainment reporting—there was no choice that he hadn't made with full knowledge of where it was leading. But there had been some whispered promise along the way, *this is how you get to where you're going, this isn't the destination, this is power, you need to build up your power, make a name for yourself, get to know people, this is how writers rise.*

"We're not talking about me. We're talking about you," he reminded her.

"Is this an interview?"

"You're lucky it's not. You could get in big trouble for saying shit like this to a reporter. You know not to do that, right?"

"Lancelot, where have you been all my life?"

"Hey, listen, I'm serious." She arched her eyebrow in surprise. For all her flirty irony, she really was, somehow, a total innocent. "You need to call somebody, tell them where you are."

"Why?"

"Because you're a commodity, you're like a valuable thing to them. You can't just run off, it freaks them out."

"They should be freaked out. They treat me pretty shitty, if you want to know the truth."

"They treat everybody shitty. You have to take it until you have enough power to treat them shitty."

"Why can't they just treat me well, and then when I have power, I won't want to treat them shitty?"

"Because that's not the way it works. And besides which, they don't think they're treating you shitty. They put you in a movie and they're making you a big star, they think that's pretty nice of them."

"But they don't talk to me like I'm a human being!"

"You're not a human being."

"I am too."

"Well, you have to try and forget that for now."

"That's right, you had to *apologize* to me because you were so mean to me on the red carpet."

"I was not mean to you. But I did have to apologize *and* get it out into the Twittersphere that I wasn't sexually harassing you. Because if I didn't it would have wrecked my career."

"Such as it is."

"Well, precisely. I know what I'm talking about. You need to call somebody right now and tell them where you are and that you weren't feeling well and you're so sorry you had to go home and get some rest. Have your agent do it."

"I don't have my cell phone, I left it in my trailer."

"You can use mine." He reached into his pocket.

"Do I have to do it right now?"

"Yes, you have to do it right now."

"Once I do it, this will all be over," she warned him. "Like, we escaped, we really did, for six hours. And once I call in, we won't have escaped anymore."

You really need to kiss her right now, his brain informed him. But the cell phone was already in his hand, an anchor holding him in place. Its cold weight tugged him back into the reptilian subcortex which innately understood the narrower rules by which the demimonde operated. Something she had said earlier had been lurking there.

"Gordon is personally approving your costumes?"

"Yes, it's a complete pain in the ass. They have to send him *swatches*."

"What do you mean, swatches?"

"For all the dresses. They have to make them, because he was like, he didn't like anything that they shopped, so they're building all these dresses for me and he's more or less hyperobsessed and you know. He wants to see fabric swatches."

"The head of the studio. Is looking at fabric swatches. For your costumes."

"Stupid, right? Plus he can't make up his mind, so they have to build like two or three versions of every dress. It costs a lot of money, everybody's all worried about the budget but he keeps going, 'That dress sucks,' and he keeps reshooting things."

"He's ordering a lot of reshoots? For what?"

"No one knows. Or at least they're not telling me. No, wait, the one we were supposed to do today? They reshot it three times, and now it turns out he wants me to be putting lipstick on. While I'm talking on the *phone.* Which you know is harder to do than you'd think, and besides which, nobody does it. If you're going to put lipstick on, you set your stupid cell phone *down.* Which is, that's all I was saying and then everybody stormed off the set."

He had heard a lot of crazy things as an entertainment reporter, but this creeped him out. And it was bad, that she had dropped the wig. You just innately knew that people were not going to have a sense of humor about that. "You have to call in, Alison," he said. He held out the cell phone. "You have to do it right now."

She grimaced and for a moment it seemed like she was simply going to refuse. A fierce argument hovered, just behind her lips. It reminded him of the moment they had met, when she was so quickly irked by his pretentious babble. He wished that he had just taken her home that night, and fallen in love, and married her. *Maybe you should just do it now.* But she had taken the phone, and she was dialing dutifully. She smiled at him with a rueful obedience.

"Ryan, hey, it's me, Alison," she announced. "No no, I'm fine, I'm fine. There was just a kind of misunderstanding at the set and I didn't know what was going on, it sounded like we were finished for the day, so I took off and— Uh-huh. Uh-huh. Ohhhh. Wow. No no, I am *so sorry.*" She actually was a good little actress. At least the phone call was a masterpiece. "Oh, God, no! I was ready to do the shot, and I was asking a few questions and then everything seemed to erupt, so—of *course* I'll call Lars. I lost my cell phone, I didn't—oh, it's in my trailer! Of course it is. Well, I'll call him right now. You call him too. It's a total misunderstanding. Thanks, Ryan. Thanks."

She clicked the phone off. "This whole movie business is retarded," she announced. "It's a fucking police state. No kidding, they went into my *trailer* and found my *cell phone.* I have to call Lars *immediately* and apologize. When *he* was the one being mean to *me.*" She sighed and started to dial again. "I warned you, once I made a phone call, all the fun would be over."

Yes, she had warned him, and she had been right.

twenty-three

MARRIAGE COUNSELING was hideous. Van was eight months pregnant, and uncomfortable. And she didn't want to be there. She had to be told point-blank that if she didn't go to counseling with Kyle, he would refuse to even consider an annulment. The whole argument was circular and coercive: Unless you try to talk things through and save our marriage, I won't admit that the marriage never in truth existed.

Poor Van. She had more or less entered this miserable marriage because Kyle felt duty bound, as a Catholic, to wed the woman he had deflowered. Not, actually, that he had deflowered her. But he had deflowered himself. Which at the time had somehow seemed to be the same thing. And now she wanted to escape. But apparently she had fallen in love with a man who was every bit as Catholic as Kyle. He wanted that annulment, and he was not going to marry her without it. She was stuck.

Kyle didn't want to be there either. But the kindness of the monks to whom he'd fled for wisdom could not absolve him of the worldly responsibilities he had taken on with this marriage. No one ever said as much;

in fact, those quiet, decent men said pretty much nothing at all. They accepted his sudden arrival as if it were the most natural thing in the world. They took him in; they gave him a bed; they let him sleep. For two days, no one asked him anything at all. They were simply content that they had something to offer him. They accepted that he understood the value of peace, and time, and prayer.

And pray is what he did. He got up at four in the morning and sat in the plain wood loft, listening to the brothers chant below him. He went back to his room and slept, then got up at seven and went back to the chapel for more of the same. Then he wandered the grounds until he could go back to the chapel and listen to them chant some more.

He phoned the office—*emergency family leave*—and then he texted Van to tell her where he was. Not that she cared, but he wasn't going to give her any excuse to sue him for abandonment or in any way damn him further. The spectacular permutations of her logic in laying the blame for this at his feet overwhelmed him daily; a terrible rage would unleash itself like some sort of mindless undersea creature determined to strangle the life out of him. Her declaration that *he* was to blame for her infidelity, that he was *responsible* for her utter betrayal, after everything he had suffered, lost, mourned, on her behalf. His dreams of accomplishment and joy, gone. His children, taught to see him as an enemy. His parents, yearning for grandchildren she willfully held away from them. The woman was a fucking holy terror.

He did not know how long this bitterness might consume him, nor did he know how long the good brothers would allow him to live among them without finally asking a question or two about his plans. By the end of his second week in retirement from the world, the steady hum of prayer and spiritual good will actually began to do its work, and he could go for longer stretches between seizures. He texted Susan, asked her to let his parents know he was on retreat at Gethsemani. He knew that simple detail would ease their anxiety, and in this moment of bewildered compassion—*they must be worried sick*—he began to find his way back.

Brother Peter joined him in the cafeteria for a 5:30 breakfast one morning, and after they had prayed over their eggs and toast, he asked a gentle question.

"Have you found comfort, in your time here with us?"

"I have, yes," Kyle responded, a little too quickly. It made him sound glib, which was the last thing he wanted. The few words you might use in a place like this should all matter.

"How long are you able to be here with us?"

"I would like to stay forever," Kyle confessed.

The brother nodded. So much silence. It was different from his own silence, which too often placed a wall between himself and Van, or the girls, or the nurses. He remembered that Alison once accused him of using silence as a weapon.

"My wife," Kyle began. He faltered. What was there to say about Van? Was she really his wife? She said she wasn't, but if not, then what was it that they were to each other? "She wants to end our marriage."

"That must be painful."

Was it painful? Certainly the rages which overwhelmed him when he considered her vast betrayals were painful. Less so the distance, the time, the fact that he didn't have to face her determined disappointment every single day. "The situation is painful, but I find my time here to be wonderful," he said. "I don't want to go back."

Peter nodded at this and even smiled, rueful. "Everybody's trying to escape," he admitted. "Most days, I'd give anything to escape from here."

"What do you mean?"

"You don't find it a little prison-like? Those tiny rooms? The marching to chapel every three hours to pray for half an hour? The work details? The monotony?"

"I think it's great."

"Try it for ten years." It sounded like blasphemy but Peter was completely content to admit it, and seemed to have no fear of being overheard. "But life isn't something we're meant to escape. Or rather, we are meant to escape it, profoundly, in death. While we are here, we are meant to live it."

"Then you don't see the monastery as an escape."

"For me it was a choice. Were I to abandon it, I would be abandoning myself. Which would be the same as abandoning God. So I wish to escape, but I choose to live through that wish, to discover what wisdom God might choose to bestow."

"Might?"

"Yes, that's the problem, isn't it? He might just decide to bore me to death. But I suspect he has better plans, for both of us."

This ruthlessness of choice was completely belied, of course, by the life of their saint Mr. Merton. Kyle was finally permitted to accompany one of the older monks to the site of Merton's hermitage, down a simple path through a few charming thickets to a clearing where a humble cinder-block structure stood. He had long known the story of the famous writer, who actually couldn't decide between a life of prayerful seclusion or a life in the world. But those fates were afforded to great men. The longer Kyle stayed and pondered God's will, the more he felt the constrictions of his psychological trap. These good monks would not send him back to his life, but neither would they make him one of their number. Unlike Merton, who found a way to straddle two identities, Kyle would be left floating between them. And so he got in his car and drove back to Cincinnati.

Which frankly threw Van into a rage. When Kyle reappeared on the threshold of his own home, she practically spit in his face, and not over the fact that he had left in the first place. It had actually suited her just fine to have him disappear for a whole month; she was free, in that time, to do as she pleased. She and the girls had fallen into a routine that fit them, and her besotted suitor had even taken the opportunity to begin insinuating himself into the role of husband and father. Not that Van admitted as much; Kyle had put that one together when he found a half-eaten grilled rib-eye in the refrigerator and she had fumbled her explanation of what it was doing there. The whole thing was appalling, but he wasn't going to get into some circular argument about it. His new goal was simply to make his choices functional. He called the parish office and asked for a recommendation for a couple's counselor.

Van had no intention of making this marriage work, but once he registered the problem with parish leadership, she had nowhere to run. Refusing to enter counseling would have made it impossible to get that annulment. And once they were stuck in that room with Roger, their kindly, white-haired Teutonic mediator, no amount of determined and circular logic passed muster. Old Roger had a truly excruciating idea of communication: He insisted on slowing everything down to a snail's pace, and then once you were down there with the snails, you had to explain every thought three times before you were allowed to inch forward to another one.

"So what you're saying, Kyle, is that you were upset when Van admitted to you that she had been unfaithful to your marriage."

"Yes."

"Could you tell that to Van?"

"Van, I was upset and hurt, actually, when you admitted you were unfaithful."

"He wasn't hurt, he was enraged. He was furious! And terribly threatening."

"Okay, we'll get to that in a minute, Van. What I'm hearing is that you felt frightened."

"Of course I felt frightened, he frightened me."

"But I really need you to take this one step at a time. When feelings run away with us, it's hard to understand what is at the core of the misunderstanding."

"It's not a misunderstanding. He never loved me. He was in love with another woman when he married me and he never pretended otherwise."

"I was not in love with Alison."

"LIAR."

"I hadn't seen her in YEARS."

"Whoa whoa whoa. You see how quickly this can run away from us! We're going to slow this ship down. Slooooow dowwwwwn. Just repeat back to Kyle what he said to you."

"What he said was a lie."

"That's a judgment, Van. We're not going there, remember? What I heard, from Kyle, is that he was upset and hurt that you had been unfaithful to your marriage."

"So?"

"Is that what you heard?"

"Yes, I heard him say that."

"Could you tell Kyle that that is what you heard? And that's all we need you to say." He started to coach her. "'Kyle'—"

"Kyle," she snapped. "I heard you say that you were upset and hurt that I was unfaithful to our marriage." Admitting that Kyle had in fact strung those dozen words together clearly felt like an outrageous loss of the moral high ground she had staked out with such unflinching determination.

"Good. Good! Marriage is about communication. We're just here learning to communicate. Now that you have told Kyle what you heard him say, let him know how that made you feel."

"I already told you; it makes me feel like he's an insane liar."

"That's a judgment, remember? We're going to try and stay away from those. Let's just stick with feelings for now." Kyle wanted to strangle old Roger, but he couldn't help enjoying how panicked it made Van to have every single word put under the microscope like this.

"I feel—frustrated," she finally said.

"That's good, you feel frustrated."

"How is that good?" she asked, with bitter common sense.

"It's good because now Kyle knows what you felt, when you heard him say that he was hurt and upset when you—"

"I did not 'betray' our marriage. How can you betray a marriage that never existed?"

Roger nodded at this, endlessly patient. "We'll get there, Van. We will get there. One step at a time. Kyle, what did you hear Van say?"

"She said a lot of things," Kyle pointed out.

"Let's just stick with the one statement. How she felt when she heard you say that you were hurt and upset—"

"How come we have to hear that again?" Van asked. "How many times does he get to repeat that—that—"

"Van," Kyle interrupted. "I heard you say that you feel frustrated."

"Good!" Roger was ridiculously pleased that Kyle was cooperating. "And how do you feel when you hear that she is frustrated?"

"I feel sorry about that, actually. I wish she wasn't frustrated."

But Kyle's trivial success in maneuvering the rules of this absurd exercise only annoyed Van further. When they got home, she informed him in no uncertain terms that she thought that the counselor had already taken his side against her, and that she found the whole process unfair in the extreme. Kyle thought momentarily about pointing out how unfair it was of her to blame him because she had cheated on him and was having another man's child. Instead, he thought for a moment, and said, "What I hear you saying, Van, is that you find this whole process unfair. Is that what you said?" Van just stared at him. "So that makes me frustrated." At this, Van stalked past him, into the kitchen. He heard Maggie coo, "Mommy, Mommy!" and then the sound of the back door slamming, as Van blew by her daughter so she could go outside and call her lover on the phone.

Kyle was well aware that she spoke to the guy six or seven or eight times daily. She was careful not to use their landline but he dug through her purse one night at three in the morning; the cell phone was chock-full of calls placed to and received from "RT." He then went to the parish phone book and paged through all the R's and T's; none of the names popped out at him as a likely suspect. Which led him to understand that even the initials were a code, a secret language, between this utter stranger and his wife. Before he could go any further—*just hit send, call him, insult him*—his better brain stepped in and reminded him, with mournful dignity, that this unhappy situation called for more wisdom, not less. While Van clearly felt that taking the girls away from him and putting a new household in place around this other father was what needed to happen, Kyle had to consider the endless years of shuttling children back and forth between double homes and double parents, not to mention ever-multiplying sets of grandparents. The scenario filled him with unspeakable dread.

The whole situation was already a mess. The girls knew that Mommy was no longer theirs; she drifted by them with the kind of self-contained indifference she previously had reserved only for Kyle. She still tended to their snacks and crayons and diapers and dresses, but a weary impatience had set in. Neither one of them was Mommy's beloved anymore. That was reserved for the baby in her belly, and the man who had put it there. Increasingly, Kyle found himself trapped in an unrelenting worry for these small strangers. He started sneaking little treats into the house for them—Waffle Crisp cereal, apple juice, those long squishy Go-Gurt things. Maggie somberly tried to tell him that she wasn't allowed to eat Go-Gurt, and then she burst into tears. He held her on his lap and the two of them, together, figured out how to open the plastic tube and squeeze out the sugar-hyped goo. Van was out somewhere; who knew where. It was easy these days to sneak such nutritional outrages into the home. Her attention was not there.

"I feel worried about the girls," Kyle asserted clearly at their next session.

"Van, how do you respond to that?" queried their guide to marital communication.

"That's hilarious, is how I respond to that."

"What I'd really like you to do, Van, is repeat what you hear Kyle say—"

"I am aware. Kyle, what I hear you saying is that you are worried about the girls."

"Is that what you said, Kyle?"

"Yes, that is what I said."

"And Van—"

"Yes, I know what comes next," she informed him, suddenly deciding to behave. "This is how I feel about what you have said, Kyle. I feel frustrated that it has taken you so long to express any interest whatsoever in the well-being of your children."

"Kyle—"

"Thanks, I think I have this, Roger. Van, I hear you say that you are frustrated because you feel that it has taken me a long time to express interest in the well-being of our girls. Is that what you said?"

"Yes, that's what I said." No matter how much you distilled this stuff down, there was still so much attitude attached that there was no way not to know that she held him in the highest contempt for his neglect of the children.

"I feel frustrated that you feel that way. I feel that you have deliberately, over the years, held them away from me. I feel—"

"Kyle—"

"Why don't you just let me finish the thought here, Roger; I promise you this really is only one thought. I feel that there were many times, Van, when you wouldn't let me love them. And that made me sad."

"That's ridiculous."

"Van—"

"*Okay*." She was pissed now, but like a trapped bird she was learning to acclimate to the rules of the cage. "I hear, Kyle, that you are frustrated with my frustration. I hear that you wanted to be a good father and somehow I stopped that from happening."

A disappointed silence drifted over all of them. For a moment Kyle thought that Roger had fallen asleep; his eyes were shut and he was utterly still. The silence continued. Kyle decided to close his eyes as well. And for a moment, for the first time in months, the unbearable tension of utter disappointment lifted just the tiniest bit.

God is in the silence, Merton informed him. But Merton had told him a lot of things. He had read and reread those journals and books, hoping against hope that at some point the great, confused monk's wisdom would kick-start something in his own soul. Why did it never happen? The hours and days he spent wandering around that monastery, wondering how so many men could find so much peace and he could find none at all. Praying and suffering and begging God not to let his meager little life drift away, yearning for a renewal of passion and connection but unable to even remember what those feelings might attach themselves to. And now here he was, fighting to the death for a marriage nobody ever believed in. Except, maybe, his parents, his forlorn, hopeful parents, who had been treated so badly by Van, year after year, cut out from the lives of their grandchildren and estranged from their only son by his own willful determination that they would never know the depth of his psychic exhaustion. He was so desperate to appear happy he held them at bay and told them nothing.

His body started shaking, and he realized that he was sobbing; his body was sobbing. He could not bring himself to open his eyes, wet with tears; he didn't want to see Van's horror-stricken and pitiless dismissal of his broken heart. He wanted to simply feel what he was feeling, until he was through feeling it. Which wasn't easy. The sobs moved through him violently, but he could barely understand why. Only briefly was there a moment when his grief passed through some barrier in his throat and into his brain. There was a sudden rush of sparks behind his eyelids, and he heard himself gasp, and then a deep silence which was held in some sort of darker wound. There was something there with him, in the sadness. His mind stopped wandering and waited. It was very quiet.

"Kyle, do you want to tell Van what you're feeling?" Roger's voice was soothing but a little too hopeful. Kyle wanted to hold up his hand, to try to keep him from saying anything else—he wanted to wait in the quiet just a moment more. But the world was rushing in.

"I think it's my turn to say what *I'm* feeling." Van's voice was completely exasperated. Kyle could not yet bring himself to open his eyes.

"It's not a matter of taking turns, Van," Roger informed her with his professional kindness. "We're really trying to get to some basic communication skills. That's all we're trying to do." Kyle continued to breathe. The wounded calm was easing, but more slowly than he had feared it would. He realized that he might be able to open his eyes without entirely losing whatever it was that was standing there with him.

"I'm feeling sad," Kyle said. "I feel very sad."

He opened his eyes. Roger's tiny office seemed to be glowing. He realized that this was just a trick of the light: The walls were paneled in a lovely blond wood; it was 5:30; the sun was going down, and light was flowing through the venetian blinds on one side of the room and bouncing off a large, simple mirror on the other. The dust motes hovered, reverential. Van, in her ever-white dress, was caught in a halo of light. The news that Kyle was sad seemed to have completely unmoored her. The silence extended between them in the golden room.

"I hear that you are sad, Kyle," she admitted, finally. Her own disappointment entered the room and sat down with them. "I am sad too."

"I hear that you're sad, Van," Kyle told her. "And I feel sorry that I have made you sad."

She nodded. Roger for once kept his mouth shut. The light floated over them like a blessing. Then she sighed.

"Okay, so we're both *sad*," Van announced, with a sudden impatience. "So what? I mean, isn't that the *point*, that we're both *sad* and why should we stay married if we're both so fucking *sad*?"

Roger thought about this, and answered for both of them. "One step at a time, Van," he said. "One step at a time."

twenty-four

Last Stop came and then it went. All the wrangling with the studio had taken its toll; the air of trouble had settled on the movie itself, and the critics generally categorized the whole enterprise as an entertaining mess which didn't live up to the fun of its premise. Lars was lightly rebuked for making yet another cynical action movie. On its opening weekend the movie cleared forty-two million domestically and a hundred and twelve worldwide, which was considered a disappointment for the studio and an embarrassment for Gordon.

And then an article appeared on an entertainment website, a scandalous exposé of the real reason that the promise of *Last Stop* had floundered and then fallen into chaos. The fault, apparently, lay with Alison Moore.

It was a good old-fashioned character assassination. According to the blogger—who Alison had never heard of—the reviews missed the truth of the matter, which was that Alison's lack of talent and experience was actually what sank the film. Alison was an arrogant, narcissistic flirt who thought that everyone was in love with her. After failing publicly to seduce the movie's star, Colin Cudahy—pictured with his wife and their newborn baby—she tried to seduce every one of the young bucks playing the black-op sidekicks. One of those young bucks was anonymously quoted as saying, "It was embarrassing! She was in a relationship with Lars—who got her the job—and then she was all over the rest of us. We didn't know *what* she thought she was doing." Someone in hair and makeup reported that Alison was completely unprofessional, always showing up late and eating up hours in the makeup trailer, and that it was impossible to please her with regard to her costumes. "She totally thought the movie was about her," this person whispered. "We were all like—sorry, isn't this your first film?" Of course the wig incident was recounted, and new, more damning stories were told. One nameless source described how Alison endlessly tried to suck up attention from the press. "Anytime there were reporters around, you could lay money that she would be falling all over them," this person claimed. "Colin was really nice about it. This was a big picture for him, he's a producer on it! And actually they did not want to hire her but he said no, she's the one. But I don't think he'll ever work with her again." An unnamed studio executive delivered the coup de grace. "Her performance was just bad. Why do you think they did so many recuts? The whole editing process turned into a hash."

And so a sloppy piece of so-called journalism sprinkled with the unholy perfume of insider gossip was blasted onto the internet, where it was picked up and re-reported and retweeted tens and hundreds and thousands of times.

Alison first heard about the story from Ryan. "We need to talk about a publicity thing that's come up," he said.

"What kind of publicity thing?" Alison asked. She assumed it was some red carpet event, a gala or a screening, some party that they wanted to sprinkle with young celebs.

"It's actually this thing that's just come up on the internet. Nothing serious, but I don't want you hearing about it the wrong way."

"A thing?"

"A story. It's just a lot of very negative stuff about *Last Stop.* You need to be prepared, there's going to be some noise coming at you."

"The movie's been out for three weeks, isn't that ancient history?"

"Absolutely, that is the position to take. The whole thing is stupid, and no one's even heard of the reporter, who is clearly some sort of complete hack. And it's on a website no one's ever heard of. It will come and go, you really have to just ignore it."

"Why, does it say mean things about me?" Alison managed to make this sound like a joke even though she already knew this was not going to be funny. Ryan continued to speak in a voice that was ever more soothing.

"It's just not anything you need to worry about. And I seriously don't want you reading it. You have nothing to gain from even giving it that much of your attention, Alison. Anyone who calls you about it, you direct them to me, or the studio's publicity people. You should not even be answering your phone for the next week. Let it go to voice mail, and then send anything that needs attention to me."

"What did they say?"

"It doesn't matter."

"Who said it?"

"No one would talk on the record."

"So they printed a bunch of shit about me and didn't talk to me, and I don't even get to know who is saying what?"

"Alison, it is going to disappear by the end of the week. Just turn off your cell phone and let us handle it."

Alison felt sick. The lead-up to the release of the film had been grueling enough, and now this? So many days and nights and months going to screening after screening, giving hundreds of interviews to reporters who all asked the same questions, being handed off from one underling to another, makeup artists constantly in your face, stylists flinging you in and out of dresses, before-parties, after-parties, everyone drinking too much champagne, waking up with a headache every morning, half crippled from those fucking shoes they always insisted that you wear, Lars no longer speaking to her, *he never even bothered to break up*, even the fun of the gang from the set evaporated because all the guys were already moving on to other jobs—*plenty of parts out there for boys*, she was told, *it's different what you're trying to do, you're a leading lady, that's a much bigger deal, they're going to wait to see how the movie does, then the parts for you will start rolling in.* That promise was still out there, *you'll be able to do whatever you want*, but every time she made it through one obstacle course another magically appeared. *Wait until the movie comes out, and we'll see how you do.* Well, she did just fine, the movie tanked but that wasn't her fault. And movie offers did come in but the payoff was so much smaller than she had been promised. A couple of indie films that were all right but little more, and none of them had their financing. When she pointed this out to Ryan, he laughed. Nothing, apparently, had its financing anymore. The movie industry was in the toilet! Nothing decent is getting made! *So why would I want to be a movie star?* she wondered. She knew better than to ask.

And now this. There was nothing else for it; she turned on her computer and read the story trashing her and her talent and her work ethic and everything about her—everything Alison Moore was or ever hoped to be.

Seth knew about the piece a full twenty minutes before Alison did. Fat Schaeffer had texted him, in a rage.

some bitch on line is trying to take down our alison, Schaeffer wrote. He was a terrific writer, but Schaeffer was one of those dudes who had forgotten how to punctuate. Seth had thought it an annoying affectation until he started doing it himself and realized how much faster you could write if you didn't worry your little head about capitalization or commas.

???? Seth responded.

Schaeffer sent him the link.

The thing was a hatchet job. It was so poorly written and so generally mean-spirited it was surprising that even a third-rate website would print crap like that. The piece itself was sandwiched between some pretty marginal stuff—funny photos of pets, nonsensical lists about *The Ten Ugliest Celebrities! Who Wore It Worst?* Talk about the detritus of culture. And there was Alison, right in the middle, taking it on the chin. *Where does shit like this come from?* he wondered. Once asked, it wasn't actually all that difficult to muddle through that one; all you had to do was run down the list of who benefited. Not Colin, not Lars; they had seen worse flops and publicity disasters in their day; *Last Stop* to them was a blip on the radar. One of the producers? Gordon? Unlikely that he would dirty his hands with something like this but it wasn't out of the question. It reeked of vindictive cunning, someone who knew how to needlessly put attack dogs in motion. And this writer, whoever she was, had smelled her chance. What the fuck. Shit like this happens.

His iPhone blipped. Schaeffer again.

did you read it?

it's bullshit, Seth typed.

i fucking want to kill that bitch who the fuck is she anyway

never heard of her

i wiki'd her, she's got like two bylines what a bitch who would talk to this person?

it's fucked up for sure but stay out of it schaeffer it will go away. This should have been unnecessary advice, but Schaeffer was an animal when he got worked up.

how is alison she must feel like shit, Schaeffer wrote.

haven't seen her since la when they were shooting that piece of shit, she's in the demimonde, Seth replied. He didn't hit send. That wasn't what Schaeffer was asking; he wasn't *asking* for gossip, a tricked-up bit of information about an actress in a muddle. Alison liked Schaeffer for a reason. He was all heart, that guy. Peculiar, for a gossip columnist on the internet. Unheard of, even. Seth deleted his response and wrote another.

i'll get back to you after i call her, he typed. *i'll let her know you were worried and that you think this reporter is a douchebag piece of shit.*

douchebag piece of shit is too nice, Schaeffer wrote.

If she had any sense at all, she wouldn't be answering her cell phone, and emails would be off limits too. He tried both anyway, as well as texting. *Schaeffer says douchebag piece of shit is too nice*, he wrote.

He heard back within ten minutes: emoticon heart, emoticon tear.

where r u, he wrote.

She texted him her address and an hour later he was at her door. "You brought food, thank God. Not that I can eat it. Eating? Food? What a stupid idea, EATING." She was rattled, rattling; he wanted to reach out and hug her, but she seemingly could not stop moving. "You know what happens to you if you eat like, one bite of carbs? You look like a whale, seriously. That happens! Get that away from me. They'll say I'm fat. In addition to everything else I'll be fat after starving myself for five years. This person who is writing complete shit about me online will say I have no talent and I'm fat."

"You shouldn't have read it."

"Somebody is writing complete shit about me online and I'm not allowed to read it? Someone who I never met *I never met this person* and she's writing terrible things, LIES about me and *publishing* them, but it's my fault if I read it?"

"Hey hey—"

"Don't tell me, hey hey. I didn't do anything except wake up this morning, and now I find out that my career is *over*—"

"Your career isn't over."

"What do you know. You're one of them—"

"HEY!"

"You are, you make excuses for all this bullshit."

"I'm not making excuses! Would you relax?"

"I don't *want* to relax. They're all LIES and they're printed out there, and who would do that? Who would say those things? Did she make them up?"

"It's doubtful she made them up."

"I never—did—any of that—"

"You threw the wig."

"What is the big deal about the stupid wig? God, the shit they did to me every day, the shit I've been putting up with for years, how come nobody reports about the bullshit *they* do? What kind of reporting is this?"

"It's not reporting," he sighed. He hated having to explain the world to this actress who, God help her, seemed to still have something of an innocent heart.

"Can I sue? I want to sue."

"It's not worth suing."

"People say that because they're scared to fight for themselves—"

"People say that because these people who write this shit are the lowest form of life and they can claim that they were just reporting what someone told them and it's not slander if they're just reporting what someone said."

"Well, can I sue the person who said it?"

"It's doubtful she'll give up her source."

"Well, isn't that FUCKING CONVENIENT." She grabbed her

drink, which seemed to be some huge shot of vodka over ice. God knows he'd been there often enough; the morning after he almost got fired for sexually harassing this very actress, he went to the office, apologized mightily, pointed to the Twitter feed and the two blog posts exonerating him, then went to the bathroom and puked for five minutes.

"I'd be careful with the vodka," he suggested.

"It's water," she retorted. "I don't drink anymore. I got scared of drinking. All those people drinking all the time. Me too. I was drinking all the time. But I *could* use a drink. Did you bring any vodka?"

"We're going to stick with water," he said. He opened one of the cartons of takeout, mu shu something.

"I don't want any food, I'm serious!" she told him again.

"It's for me, I'm hungry," he informed her. She was on the move again, ignoring him. He rooted through her mostly empty kitchen drawers until he located a lone fork, and then followed her into the tiniest of living rooms. She really didn't have any money. All the dresses and shoes would have been provided, the jewelry too, those girls looked like a million bucks but how much were they really worth? Agents, publicists, stylists, business managers, everyone got a piece, and what were her credits after all? Two seasons on a trashy TV show, and one movie that bombed. Because she was a neophyte film actress they would have paid her pennies. That's why they hired those girls: because they were all interchangeable anyway, and the new ones were so fucking cheap. They didn't hire her because she was a star; they didn't see women as stars. They saw them as fodder, and then they used them up. What had this one done to piss them off so badly that they would send attack dogs after her?

"Who do I talk to?" she asked. "You're a reporter."

"Alison, you don't want to draw any more attention to this. Seriously. It's just junk on the airwaves."

"If they're allowed to put junk on the airwaves why can't *I* put junk on the airwaves?"

"You can, but it will make it worse. You have to let other people take care of this, Alison. I mean it."

"I'm not even allowed to say this is bullshit?"

"That makes you sound defensive."

"Defending myself makes me sound defensive? That's terrific, Seth, I never thought of it that way! Let's NOT defend ourselves then. Wouldn't want anyone thinking that DEFENDING YOURSELF WHEN YOU'RE ATTACKED IS A GOOD IDEA." He had never seen her like this. The size of her anger was impressive as hell: She was a titan. The idea of wrapping all that up and putting a little bow on it suddenly struck him as the height of absurdity. *They don't know what she is*, he realized. *They never did.*

"You have to let someone else do it," he started.

"I ASKED you to do it, and you said no," she retorted. "I think that was like a minute ago, I ASKED you to do it—"

"I can't do it, because I almost got fired for sexually harassing you, remember?"

"That's why you should do it!"

"Schaeffer will do it. You don't even have to ask him. He's probably already done it." She was about to spit something back at him, but her complete faith in Schaeffer silenced her. It was weird, and touching. The mere mention of Schaeffer seemed to spark a fragile hope somewhere in her that everything would be all right. *Schaeffer to the rescue*, he thought. And why not? "He was the one who planted all those pieces that saved my job," Seth reminded her. "After you almost got me *fired* for sexually harassing you, which need I remind you I didn't do."

"I never said you did!"

"You got me in big trouble."

"You got yourself in big trouble."

She was coming back, inch by inch. "Well, Schaeffer is the guy who knows this so-called universe. He was the one who told me about it even being out there, otherwise I probably wouldn't know anything about it because nobody reads that shit."

"*Every*body reads that shit."

"They read it, and they know it's junk," he said. "No one cares, Alison."

"If no one cared, they wouldn't have done it," she told him. "And I worked so hard for them. I showed up on time. I was nice to the crew. I was polite. I never made a fuss when I got the shittiest trailer, or when they kept fucking with my costumes, or when they were *mean* to me, I was never rude back—no matter how much shit they threw at me, I was *good*. I was *grateful*. I always knew my lines. I flirted with everyone, yes, because you're *supposed* to, if I didn't flirt with everybody, you know what they would say about me? She's *cold*. She's *stuck up*. And I don't care—I *don't*—but what are they so mad at *me* for? I was *good*. Like a good person, good." The breath of something deeper, a profound disappointment, had entered the room. "And I'm not saying I'm perfect. I've done bad things. I have, I'm not . . ." She shook her head, trying to get out from something from the past. He wondered what it was she was trying to forget. "But that wasn't true here. It wasn't. And even if people don't believe what they said, in that stupid article? They'll believe I did something *bad*, something that made them hate me. But what was it?"

She had a point. Sadly, not much of one. "Alison, people just do this shit," he told her. "They don't care if it's true or not. They just do it and it makes them feel good and then they go and do other shitty things and that's the world," he said.

"That's not the world," she said. "You think that? You think *that's* the world?" Behind her, the phone rang.

"Yeah, I do," he admitted. "You can't answer the phone—Alison—"

"It's my sister Megan."

"Family are the worst," he warned. "They'll want to talk about it. They'll want to try and make you feel better, but it will end up making you feel worse."

"So, like, the only thing I can do for the next three days is hide in my apartment and drink water," she noted. "That's great. Five years of starvation and acting like a Barbie doll and and and being nice to the stupid *reporters* following me everywhere and wearing all those tight dresses and not acting, none of any of that was real acting, and and and now, now nothing. The only thing I can do is nothing. Because it doesn't matter that I didn't do anything wrong. I just I just—fuck it. Fuck all of it. I mean seriously, cheers. Cheers, it's so much fun being a movie star, seriously, it's a fucking *blast*." She picked up her plain little glass of water and toasted him.

On the side table, her cell started buzzing.

"Don't answer it," he warned.

"It's my *sister Megan*," she sighed. "It's fine. I'm just going to get this over with."

twenty-five

MOM WAS SICK. Dad was out of town, off fishing somewhere in Alaska of all places; all the kids had chipped in and given him this stupid fishing trip for his seventieth birthday. So they were still trying to get ahold of Dad. And Mom was sick. They were operating.

Alison couldn't tell *how* sick Mom was—she was only sixty-eight, her health had always been excellent—but the story that Megan told was not so great.

"It's something in her colon."

"Something like what kind of something? Like cancer?"

"No, it's not cancer. It's, the whole colon shut down."

"What do you mean, *shut down*?"

"I don't know, Alison, it apparently shut down. She was having like a bad stomachache, and she called last night and we took her to the hospital and they did a bunch of tests and then they said they had to operate because there was a blockage."

"A blockage is cancer."

"The surgeon said it *wasn't* cancer."

"Who's the surgeon?"

"Dr. Webster. Weathers. Wiggans. I'm sorry. I've been up for thirty-six hours." You couldn't get mad at Megan; she sounded exhausted and there was some baby screaming in the background. At a time like this, you couldn't get mad.

"I'm coming home."

"I'm not sure that's, the doctor said she came through the operation pretty good and they think she'll come off the respirator today—"

"She's on a *respirator*? Sorry sorry I'm not yelling, sorry."

"It's okay. I don't know if you have the money? But if you want to come home for a few days, that would be good."

"Who's at the hospital now?"

"Well—no one," Megan admitted. "But she's anaesthetized. They said they'd call when she wakes up."

Of course there were more specifics than that, but they didn't seem relevant. Alison took a cab out to LaGuardia and got herself on the first plane home.

It was six in the morning. The flight was fluid, effortless, and before she knew it the air around her dinged and the two tired attendants started to sweep the plane for empty water bottles. Alison was so used to the five- and six-hour flights between New York and Los Angeles, it was startling to hear that they were making their descent after little more than an hour in the air. It was nothing, really, to fly to Cincinnati. By the time she climbed into the rental car she found herself focused and increasingly secure. The highways were open, featureless, easy to drive. Thirty minutes later as she turned into the virtually empty hospital parking lot her brain started to unfreeze. Megan hadn't really been all that upset on the phone, and no one else seemed to think this situation was serious. It was good that somebody came home to help out until Dad was back, but Mom was surely going to be fine.

Her completely fabricated self-confidence hit a roadblock at the front desk, where hospital ambiance hit her like a ton of bricks. It was like a third-rate casting office—the furniture was lousy, the light a horrible shade of green, the assistants peculiarly unhelpful. Rose had come in with Megan to the emergency room, and then gone to surgery, after which she was admitted to the hospital proper. Now, apparently, no one knew where she was. The name of her doctor was also not clear. There was a surgeon and an anesthesiologist, but one was off site and the other was making his rounds and was unavailable for consultation. Alison felt a kind of sick panic rise up in her. After months and years of playing the role of a Hollywood starlet, she knew how to smile her way through bullshit and pretend it was all fine. Smile and gush. Smile and be humble. Smile and listen. But the cruel dismissal of a studio exec who thinks you're nothing and wants you to make sure you know that you're nothing paled next to this automaton who didn't seem to care that her mother was lost somewhere in this grimy fluorescent hospital.

The answer to the mystery was finally solved by a call to Megan.

"She's in the ICU," Megan announced. "Tell them she's in the ICU."

"She's in the ICU," Alison told her nemesis, a severe Indian woman in teal scrubs.

"Ohhh, the IC*Uuuuuuuu*." The nurse—for that is clearly what she was, a middle-aged nurse just doing her best in fatal circumstances—resumed typing. "She is in room B-two, that is on the seventh floor of the Leugers Pavilion."

The shock of finding your mother alone on a respirator in the intensive care unit of an understaffed Midwest hospital would be significant no matter who you are or what your history with your mother might be.

And now Alison was fried. It had taken her twenty minutes to find the room, because the Leugers Pavilion, as it turned out, was inaccessible from the elevators in the main building; you had to take the elevator down the hallway from the front desk to the fourth floor and then walk down another hallway, take a left, and then enter a second elevator bank on the right. The whole complex had clearly been constructed by some sociopath with a complete axe to grind on sick people and their pathetic relatives. Finally she located the ICU on the seventh floor after going down the hallway to the *left* of the elevator bank and then taking the first right, where you went through multiple sets of doors and found yourself in a giant room with little pods of people full of mysterious and dire purposes, pushing giant machines around.

Rose was indeed on a respirator; she was hooked up to several machines that were beeping and flickering peacefully over the rasp of the machine that was breathing into her. Her hair was matted and her face so distorted around the mouthpiece of the ventilator that there was a terrible moment when Alison wasn't sure that this was her mom after all. But on approaching the bed, she saw Rose's hand, the tiny gold engagement ring and wedding ring she had let her children play with so often, never taking it off no matter how many times they begged, but letting them twirl it around her slender fingers. *You'll have one of your own one day*, she had promised her daughters. That dream had evaporated for Alison by the time she was ten and had already been so fully identified as the family's rebel. *Rebels don't get married. They turn into spinsters, or Hollywood starlets.* It didn't matter. Her mother's hand was shriveled and claw-like, clutching at the institutional bedsheets, without thought or consciousness or even memory. Where was Dad? Did he even know yet, that Mom was here?

Something was going on. Rose started to move, her body contorting and kicking. Alison, now at the bedside, could see that her mother's arms were held down by restraints.

"Mom, I'm here. It's Alison. Do you need something? What do you need, Mom?" Asking Rose anything whatsoever was of course absurd, as she could hardly be expected to speak with a huge ventilator shoved in her mouth. "You want me to call the nurse, Mom?" Rose's struggling body became angular and unpredictable. The too-thin hospital gown which had been tossed over her bare limbs had ridden up one hip and for a moment Alison could see her mother's exposed pudenda, white, flaccid, old. She covered her quickly and looked around the bed, desperately trying to figure out where the stupid button was to call the nurse. She had only been there thirty seconds and already she was failing. "Nurse! I need a nurse!" she finally yelled. It was what they did on hospital shows; eventually everyone just started shouting.

And of course no nurse came. Alison had to run out to the nurses' station, where there were the people pods and the machines, and then it took her forever to find someone to help. The one unoccupied nurse she finally located was named Patricia. Patricia was sort of both young and middle-aged, impossible to tell how old she was, actually, a little stocky, with a bouffant hairdo—an actual bouffant, in a hospital!—and she wore a white uniform, as opposed to the colorful scrubs everyone else had on. But her attitude was exactly the same as the Indian nurse at the front desk. That was another way actual hospitals were different from the ones on television. On television, everyone raced around and tried to help. In a real hospital, none of the nurses got all that jacked up about anything at all.

Patricia was nice enough, but she wasn't giving out any extra information. She messed with Rose's machines until she stopped thrashing about, and then talked to her like she was six years old. "What are you fussing about, Mrs. Moore? You're being a bad girl now, if you manage to tear your sutures I'm going to be very upset with you."

"What is the matter with her?" Alison asked.

"She just had major surgery, for one."

"I'm her daughter," Alison announced. Nurse Patricia glanced up at that one but again didn't have a comment. "I just flew in, my sister was here with her yesterday during the surgery but she had to go home to be with her kids, so I'm really catching up here. I just I don't know anything about the surgery or or or—I don't know really anything."

"Her doctor will be by in about twenty minutes," Nurse Patricia told her. The machine breathing into Rose reasserted its mechanical rhythm as the unconscious woman's distress eased itself. The nurse checked her watch to make sure, then nodded: Twenty minutes, that's how long it would be before the doctor showed up. "He can fill you in."

"Can't you fill me in?"

"He'll have more facts." And with that she was gone. Alison assumed that Nurse Patricia had adjusted Rose's pain meds, and it was that which had calmed her mother down. But she didn't know for sure.

When the doctor didn't show up after twenty minutes, and then thirty, Alison called Megan.

"The doctor hasn't shown up yet," she told her.

"I think they're pretty understaffed there."

"Yeah, but I've been here an hour and I haven't spoken to *anyone* about what happened."

"I know, it's frustrating. You should have been there when I brought her in, she was really a mess and no one would even *look* at her for four hours and then they were all like, rush her to surgery, it was so scary."

"She doesn't look good, Megan." This news fell like bricks tumbling out into the universe. The significance and weight of it floated away as soon as the words were uttered.

Megan sighed. "Well, what do the nurses say?"

"They don't seem to want to tell me anything."

"Did you ask?"

"I did, but—"

"You have to ask them really nicely. They're not supposed to tell you things, but if you are super friendly and polite, usually one or two will let you know a few things, they know a lot."

"Okay, I'll try, but—"

"They think that because you're so young and you're a girl they don't have to tell you, they actually think that. When Dad gets home, he'll be in a better position to take care of things," Megan promised.

"Have you talked to Dad?"

"They told me they were getting a message to him, up at that fishing lodge, but he hasn't called yet."

"Megan, I'm here in the ICU and it doesn't look good. She looks bad. I think people should come."

"What people?"

"Everybody," Alison said. "Jeff and Andrew and, everybody. This is serious."

Megan was an innate skeptic. Plus, she was exhausted.

"But you haven't talked to the doctor yet."

"I can't find the doctor!"

"Just sit tight. Don't go to the bathroom. If you miss them, it's hours before they show up again."

"YOU CAN'T USE YOUR CELL PHONE IN THE ICU!" Nurse Patricia suddenly and mysteriously appeared in the door behind her, and she was finally worked up.

"I got to go," Alison muttered, and tapped the phone off.

"You cannot make phone calls in here." Nurse Patricia was staring at her as if she expected Alison to leave. Alison stared back.

"Yeah, okay, I won't make any phone calls in here," she said. She held the phone up and then dropped it into her purse. Pissed, Nurse Patricia went back and checked her mother's vitals. Alison stepped forward, tentative. "How's she doing?" she asked. "Is the doctor coming?" Now proving a point, Nurse Patricia silently continued her procedures, checked her watch, and left the room.

I wonder why it's so easy for me to piss people off, Alison thought. She sat in the chair next to her mom, and reached up and held her hand. Her skin was so fragile, her hand clawed, the knuckles prominent. It was the hand of an old woman.

She had missed seeing her mother growing old. When she started insisting that she couldn't come to Cincinnati anymore—*I don't have the money, Mom, I have an audition this weekend, I have to be in LA*—Rose had done her best to fill in the blanks. She called every week, whether or not Alison called her back. She sent birthday presents, packages full of cookies Alison couldn't eat and old-fashioned photos of all her kids and grandkids, the ones who actually did make it back to Ohio for Christmas. And Alison had just blocked it all out, let the rift establish itself. *Movie stars don't have families from the Midwest.* For a moment Alison had the urge to climb up in that bed and wrap her arms around her mother's tortured body, give her a hug, hold her, tell her stories, apologize. But she knew that she'd just wreck everything. Nurse Patricia would come in and yell at her. Megan would hear about it and roll her eyes. Besides which, she probably would just yank out Rose's IVs and kill her. So that was a bad idea. Better just wait for the doctor.

Who, when he did show up, was not reassuring or even clarifying. Young, bespectacled, and Jewish—he wore a yarmulke—he managed to be both serious and evasive.

"How are we doing in here?" he asked semiconsciously. He was looking at a clipboard in his hand. "How are we doing, Rose?" This a little more loudly, as if the unconscious woman on a respirator in the hospital bed hadn't immediately answered the first time because she was hard of hearing.

"Well, you tell us," Alison began. "I'm her daughter, I just flew in this morning. My sister was here with her all day yesterday and a lot of last night."

"Yeah, we had a little bit of an emergency, didn't we?" *Why did they all sound like they thought everybody was in kindergarten?*

"A little bit, yeah." Alison offered up a sardonic laugh, trying to put them back on equal footing. The doctor ignored her. There was a black metal box on a pole right by Rose's head, with lots of blinking lights and numbers, which the doctor seemed to think was a little worrisome. Or maybe that was the look that was always on his face when he was thinking.

"Are you Doctor Wiggans?" she finally asked. He glanced over at this with a distant surprise.

"Oh no, Doctor Wiggans is your mother's surgeon. I'm Doctor Frankel, I'm the attending," he said.

"I'm sorry, what does that mean?" Alison asked. "I'm a little confused."

"These are confusing situations," Frankel admitted. "Your mother came in yesterday with a blockage in her small intestine, which Doctor Wiggans felt needed to come out immediately."

"What kind of a blockage?"

"A tumor."

"What kind of tumor?"

"I don't have the epidemiology in front of me."

"Is it cancer?"

"As I said, we don't have the epidemiology. When Doctor Wiggans makes his rounds, he can fill you in on the status of the cultures."

"My sister said, when she called me this morning, she said that they told her it *wasn't* cancer."

"That is probably true, then. I don't know why the surgeon would tell her that, without the follow-up from the lab, but doubtless he has other information that I'm sure he'll be happy to share with you."

"So how is she doing? How long does she have to stay on this respirator?"

"Well, her system has been through a shock and her blood oxygen levels are not great."

"They just came in and gave her some painkiller."

"Yes, that's here on the chart," he acknowledged. "We'll know more in a couple hours."

"More what?"

"We'll just have more details." He looked at her with a sudden, earnest concern, and took a step forward. He paused, as if considering whether or not he should just tell her the truth. "Are you on television?" he finally asked.

"I was—yes," she admitted, surprised. "Sometimes. Yes."

"I thought I recognized you," he said. "My daughter watches your show."

"I'm not on that anymore," she told him. It surprised her how embarrassing this felt, and she tumbled on like an idiot. "I still do guest spots on different things and I was in a movie that just came out a little while ago, *Last Stop*, it's called *Last Stop*." *It's not like he's a casting agent. You don't have to feed him your résumé.*

The doctor was charmed. He beamed at her with a stupefying appreciation for her achievements. "What's your name again?"

"Alison Moore."

"Alison Moore. Alison Moore! She is going to be so excited to hear that I met you. Alison Moore," he repeated, so as to be sure that he didn't forget it.

The surgeon, when he finally showed up, was little better. He was tall and slender, a silver fox. He didn't say much, but he also didn't mince words.

"Your mother had a blood clot," he said. "It was lodged in the second quadrant of the small intestine, where it gathered a mass of cells around it. Unfortunately, there was also a series of perforations, she's probably been suffering from undiagnosed diverticulitis for a number of years, and peritonitis is acute."

"Diverticulitis?"

"Has she had a colonoscopy, ever?"

"Has my mother ever had a colonoscopy? I have no idea."

"Well, there's significant infection. We need to get that under control before we can take her off the respirator."

"I don't understand why she hasn't woken up yet."

"When patients come out of the anesthesia, they generally try to rip that respirator right off, so we've got to keep her sedated for a little while. As soon as her system indicates that it can transition into breathing on its own, we'll take it off."

Having spent the last five years in show business, Alison was more or less used to people talking at you without really saying anything. But the things directors and producers and studio execs and agents said were often lies, and these nurses and doctors were clearly not lying. They were obfuscating, but without a purpose that Alison could intuit. She couldn't even tell, from the things they said, if her mother was all that sick. *She's on a respirator, and she hasn't regained consciousness*, her brain reminded her. *She's sick.*

But then why won't anyone admit that? The other, more pathetically hopeful side of her brain was clutching at straws.

What do you want them to admit?

Megan said she's fine.

Megan's not here.

Nobody's here—it's clearly not serious, or wouldn't they be here?

If it's not serious, why don't the doctors tell you that?

If it is *serious, why don't they tell me* that?

This went on for hours. Alison continued to update Megan, and get her own updates—they finally got through to Dad and he would be on a flight from Anchorage tomorrow, it was going to take at least eighteen hours to fly him from his fishing lodge, which was out in the middle of nowhere. Reinforcements were on the way, but Megan herself couldn't get there before five, maybe not even that soon, she still hadn't landed a babysitter. Lianne was driving down from Chicago sometime tomorrow. The possibilities of even one other sibling showing up any sooner were dicey; everyone was too far away; there were kids, and planes, and problems. Alison spent a lot of time holding Rose's hand and whispering nice things, *it's okay, Mom, Dad's on his way back, I love you, you're doing great, the doctors say you're fine, it was nothing, undiagnosed diverticulitis! You'll wake up pretty soon.* She kissed her head and stroked her hair. The nurses came and went without report.

At one point, Rose squeezed Alison's hand. It was not much of a squeeze, but it was real; she didn't imagine it. She squeezed her mother's hand back with both of her own, delighted there was finally a sign.

"Hi, Mom. Hey, hey!" she said, cheerful. "I'm here. It's Alison. Wow, you have so put us through it, hey!" Rose's eyes were half open, the pupils skittering under delicate lids. Alison felt a rush of adrenaline. Rose was coming back. She reached over and banged the call button for the nurses, which she had finally figured out how to use. "Okay, I'm not going anywhere. I'm not going anywhere. We'll just get someone in here right now, to take care of you. You're fine! You're going to be fine."

Another ten minutes, but Nurse Patricia did manage to make a pretense that she had hurried over.

"Something going on with our girl?" she inquired.

"She squeezed my hand!" Alison told her. She fucking hated Nurse Patricia by now but she was also desperate to tell anyone good news. "And her eyes are open. She knows I'm here. I think she's waking up." Nurse Patricia was predictably unimpressed by this but she went to Rose's bedside and looked her in the face. "Rose?" she asked, loudly. "Can you see me, Rose? Can you squeeze my hand, Rose?" Having taken Alison's place at Rose's bedside, she somehow made the possibility that Rose was actually in there a more distant reality. "Give me a squeeze, Rose," she ordered. "I really need you to give me a squeeze."

After a whole thirty seconds of this kind of encouragement Nurse Nightmare stepped back and considered Rose where she lay, the respirator pumping away. "You should ask the doctor when the ischemia set in, and what caused it," she announced. "It's usually the sign of something bigger going on." She started to leave. Alison felt her chest constrict, as if an elephant had decided it was time to finally squash her completely. Nothing in her insanely fucked-up career had ever felt as truthfully bad as what that nurse just said, but at the same time, it felt real, like there were terrible things happening here, but they were *real* terrible things, that she was responsible and she had to do the best she could.

"Please don't—please, sorry," she said. "Sorry. We don't, my father is out of town and I don't know even, isn't there someone we can talk to, about what is going on here?"

"Does she have a GP?" Nurse Patricia asked. "Do you know anybody on staff here? Sometimes it helps to have a doctor with a personal relationship, just to get things sorted." She didn't look at her, but Alison got the message. *Who do you have on the inside? You better have someone, or we're just going to let your mother die.*

Who knows if that was what was being said? Alison was out of her depth. She made the only phone call that was available to her.

Van picked up.

"Hi—yes, hi, uh, Van? This is Alison Moore, Kyle's friend?"

A surreal silence bloomed on the line.

"Sure, Alison, I remember you," Van said. Just as poised and appropriate as ever. Even cheerful. "How have you been? Are you in town?"

That was vastly better than anything Alison could have hoped, aside from Kyle picking up the phone himself. "Yes, I am. My mother's ill," she explained.

"Oh, I'm sorry to hear that."

"Could I speak with Kyle? I tried him at his office and they told me he had already left for the day. And I, it's very complicated here at the hospital, I really don't know how to get any of these doctors to just tell me what's going on. And I thought, maybe Kyle, I'm sure he knows someone on staff over here, or at least, because he's a doctor one of them might talk to him."

"What hospital is it?"

"Jewish."

"I don't think he knows anyone there."

"Could I just talk to him?"

"He's busy with the baby."

"I really need to talk to him." Alison knew she was reaching for straws. But this runaround with the hospital just couldn't continue, and she needed help, and she also knew enough about the way the world worked. When you're getting a runaround, you need an insider. She just needed Kyle to get on the phone with one of these nurses, for two minutes. It might help. It had to help.

"Well, I'll tell him you called," Van said.

Alison willed herself not to panic. "I just need him for a second, Van. My mom is really in trouble and there's no one here to help us, I just need to even ask him just a few questions. She's really sick."

"Awwwww," said Van. "I'm sure they're giving her great care there."

"Well, they're not—they're not—I just thought—"

"I'll have Kyle call you right back," Van promised.

And then she hung up the phone.

twenty-six

VAN SLIPPED the phone back into its cradle in the kitchen. She turned back to the lovely granite countertop and wiped off the leafy remains of a head of cauliflower she had just finished dismembering. The idea that Alison Moore would call their home and ask for help from Kyle was laughable, aside from the fact that it completely laid bare all of Kyle's insistent lies about his relationship with her. Alison just *happened* to come into town because her mother *happened* to be sick, and she *happened* to need a doctor? It was a ludicrous story, particularly when you factored in that Kyle didn't work at that hospital and that oh by the way he's a *pediatrician. Your mother is sick in the hospital, so you decided you needed to call in your local pediatrician?* That was hilarious, really. This whole situation was hilarious.

Van's bitterness had settled into a permanent distortion. She knew she could not stand in it forever, but her wound was fresh, and exceptionally deep. The hopes she had nurtured for a life with a man who adored her were less than nothing now. She was humiliated by the fact that she had ever hoped anything. Why Kyle had refused to grant her an annulment, no one honestly could say. He insisted it was a lie that he would not tell to his God, but lying relentlessly about his feelings for this other woman seemed to be something he was fine with. He insisted that it would be bad for the girls, to be raised by someone who wasn't their own father, but he didn't seem to think that it was a problem for *him* to raise someone else's child. In fact, he made quite a show of doting on that baby. It was unseemly, frankly, given the fact that the boy wasn't his. Another lie he felt okay about perpetrating. It's okay to tell the world that the baby is your baby, but it's not okay to say, hey, we made a mistake, we should get an annulment? People got divorced all the time; who cared what you called it? If the Catholics wanted to call it an annulment, what was the big deal?

The light in the kitchen was shifting, settling into stronger angles; the sun was starting its descent. It was all too late anyway. Martin was gone. Not gone from Cincinnati, but gone from her life; as the days ticked by, he had become more and more frustrated with the way Kyle was dragging his feet. And then he was gone, and she was stuck. She could have gone to see him at his law office, she could have created a scene, embarrassed him, embarrassed herself. But the whole idea seemed disgusting to her. *I'm carrying your child. I betrayed my husband. I have put my whole family through months of torture and you're tired. So sorry you found this tiring.* She did not send him an announcement when the baby was born.

Kyle never asked about her lover. After their one hissing argument the night he finally figured a few things out, he had been silent, and she resented his impassivity even more than she had the months and years before this crisis. Why was everything so hidden with him? Over time she had found in his silence betrayal, then judgment, then punishment, then cruelty. There may have been love in there at some point, but who could tell? It was a stunning change of course to have him insist on going into couple's counseling, where apparently all anyone did *ever* was try to communicate, in ever more grueling detail. Up to this moment in time, she would have said that communicating was the last thing Kyle wanted to do, with anyone.

He had ruined everything for her. If he had just agreed to the annulment when she asked for it, this whole thing would have been over before the baby was born. She and the girls would have moved on; everyone would have moved on. He wouldn't have even had to pay alimony. But Kyle's insistence that they talk through every exhausting detail of their non-marriage doomed her plans for escape more completely than anyone could have predicted. He seemed so reasonable. And Martin's infatuation with the idea of claiming Van and her two adorable girls began to look—to Martin himself—tawdry.

Or was it Kyle's seeming forgiveness that made their affair look tawdry? When that idea flitted across Van's consciousness, it really pissed her off; Kyle was in no position to stand in judgment of her. She didn't fully believe that he had been sneaking off to New York for passionate weekends with his old girlfriend, but you couldn't tell her that he didn't lust after Alison in his heart. And Van had sat through enough of those boring Catholic Masses to know that *that* was a sin too.

She pulled the spray attachment out of its dock at the edge of the sink and rinsed the cauliflower one last time before tossing it into a buttered glass casserole dish and shoving it into the oven. It was so hard to get the girls to eat any vegetables. After years of serving them nothing but whole organic anything, they still complained and whined; all they wanted was pasta, peanut butter, pizza, hot dogs. In the few months of her fleeting happiness, she had let her lover occasionally spoil the girls with these treats—it was so important that they all like each other—and now they were in a constant sı it that they couldn't have that junk all the time. Maggie was already getting a little chunky, although Kyle the pediatrician insisted that she was right where she should be in terms of height and weight. After years of ignoring both girls, Kyle now seemed to think he was the expert on everything.

Speak of the devil. There he was, in the doorway, holding the swaddled baby and looking completely besotted, even though Gabe was as usual colicky and screaming. Kyle didn't seem to mind; he was more in love with that boy than he had ever been with his own daughters. It was infuriating. Her lover had just evaporated, and she and Kyle had never once spoken of her broken heart, her disappointed dreams. This whole public charade, that the baby was Kyle's, that was another thing that just happened without any discussion. Even when you're forced to sit through nobody can even count how many hours of couple's counseling, the important things never make it to the table. Bouncing the fussy baby on his shoulder, Kyle looked at Van, curious.

"Who was on the phone?" he asked.

"Just some wrong number," she said. "Oh, give him to me." She took the baby into the next room to feed him.

After some four days of casual consideration, Van decided to pass along the message. If Alison wanted to come along and cry on her old boyfriend's shoulder because her mom was in the hospital, why should she care? The whisper of guilt which hovered in the back of her head had begun to bother her. She had no reason to feel guilty. She in fact refused to feel guilty. In regard to Alison she remained blameless. The bitterness of her heart informed her that Alison could not say the same. But her own sense of moral certainty finally insisted that she do the right thing.

"I meant to tell you, your friend Alison called." This was tossed over her shoulder as Van fetched dinner plates from the kitchen cabinets.

"Alison called?" Kyle's voice took on a quiver, the slightest of strains. *I knew it*, Van thought. The girls, at the table, were coloring wildly. They didn't even look up.

"She's in town, her mom is in the hospital, she was having some problem. I'm not sure . . . Maggie, come on, sweetie, we're setting the table now."

"What did she say?" Kyle asked steadily. "Did she want me to call her?"

Honestly, he was trying so hard to be cool.

"I think she did."

For the next three hours everyone pretended that everything was normal. Kyle helped feed the girls, then he and Van had dinner, then the baby woke up, and while Van fed him, Kyle did the dishes, and then he took the girls upstairs and gave them a bath, and then he changed the baby and rocked him while Van put the girls to bed. And then, while she took the baby back for his nine o'clock feeding, she looked up at Kyle and smiled with a friendly, helpful encouragement.

"Aren't you going to call Alison?" she asked. "She sounded like she really needed to talk to you, about her mom. I think she said she was ill."

"Are you okay with that?"

"Of course! Kyle. I think that you should be allowed to talk to your ex-girlfriend on the phone." She smiled at him, as if he were being silly. How she was pulling this off, she didn't know, but it felt good, even virtuous.

"Did she leave a number?"

"Actually, she didn't," Van acknowledged. "You probably should try her parents' house."

Kyle nodded and reached for the phone by the side of the bed. *Yes, okay, you're going to do it in front of me so you can prove that you don't have anything to hide*, Van thought. *But you still know the phone number by heart.*

Kyle waited patiently, listening to the burr of the phone ring across town. His wife was sitting on the bed, breastfeeding their baby; his daughters were sleeping down the hall. Alison had called him. He could call her back.

"Hello," she said. In high school, in that household of millions, she always had seemed to be the one to pick up the phone.

"Alison, yes, hello," he said. "Hi, it's Kyle."

"Kyle," she said. "Hello, Kyle."

They could still say hello to each other. The past and the present started to merge.

"I heard you called, that your mother was ill?" he said. "How is she doing?"

"She died," said Alison.

twenty-seven

YOU COULDN'T BLAME KYLE. He was such a relentlessly decent guy, he had come to the funeral. There he was, at the back of the church, braving his way all the way up to the side of the coffin to say good-bye, expressing his condolences to her thousands of relatives. She managed to avoid talking to him at the visitation and the Mass—there was a lot going on, after all—but when he showed up at the graveside, she knew she wasn't going to get out of this. And she wanted to get out of it. She didn't want to talk to him, she really didn't; having a talk with Kyle at this point in time wasn't going to help anybody. But there he was.

He was still so good looking. And sad. Why would a successful doctor with three beautiful children look so sad? Well, it was a funeral, so everyone looked pretty sad. Except for Alison, who was just pissed off. They had all somehow managed to move through the shock of Rose's sudden illness and death with courage and humility, but Alison was the one who had been there, that long horrible day, and she still hadn't released the terrible sense that more could have been done, that people weren't paying attention, mistakes were being made not because those doctors and nurses were incompetent, but because they didn't understand that Rose was *young*, it wasn't time for her to die.

Of course by now her death was inevitable, that was all that anyone could see. You couldn't go back in time and say, put her on a different antibiotic, that infection should have been brought under control faster. Or, the surgery didn't have to be done on an emergency basis, it released too much bacteria into the body from the cutting, which is why the sepsis set in, if they had waited they could have prepared her, made sure her intestines were empty. Or, maybe they could have been more cautious in how much of the intestine they took out. There was too little prep time and yes of course the doctor didn't want to leave dead tissue in there but taking out as much as he did undermined her whole system. If they had just waited a day.

That last bit she couldn't say out loud because Megan had been there, she was the one who had told Rose she should go ahead with this. It wasn't Megan's fault, there was no way she could have known that there were other ways to approach this situation and Mom might not be *dead* now. And no one of course would even whisper that Alison hadn't been proactive enough, she should have gotten more attention faster from the hospital staff and maybe she could have stopped Mom's whole system from going into arrest. No one would ever *ever* suggest the hospital had been incompetent and Alison hadn't done enough. People would do that in New York. In Cincinnati it would be rude, to accuse a hospital of laziness or ineptitude or anything, those people worked hard, death is a part of life, you accept that and don't blame anybody. But Alison felt the full weight of it. Her mother was dead, and nobody had really done anything to stop it. It was her fault. She couldn't get them to save her. And now there they were, on a cool wet day, standing around a hole in the ground, listening to yet another priest read exhausted verses out of the Bible, reassuring them that Rose's spirit had drifted upward and crossed some sea and now was sitting at the right hand of God.

"It's not your fault," Megan informed her.

"I know," Alison said.

"Nobody thinks it's your fault."

"She's dead, though, she died and now she's dead and I didn't stop it."

"Alison." Everybody knew she thought it was her fault and it gave them an excuse, for once, to stop teasing her and to just take care of her. Jeff, back from Hong Kong with a Chinese wife, cornered her in the kitchen and explained in no uncertain terms that the hospital did what it could but that Rose's colon had been compromised far too thoroughly and far too quickly, even before Alison arrived. Andrew hugged her in passing and handed her a beer. Lianne ignored her, which was as close as she could get to asking how she was doing. Paul smiled at her sadly and asked if she wanted to ride to the funeral in his car.

And now here they were, a sea of Moores, everywhere the eye could see. Dad up front, looking completely lost. "I don't know what he's going to do without her." Megan sighed.

"I could never tell what he did *with* her," Alison observed. "Even when he was retired he was never there."

"Well, he's going to miss her now," Megan said.

"We all will," said Alison, the tears starting up again. It had been a terrible, long week. "I can't stop crying," she muttered. "I feel like I've been crying for a week."

"It's okay, Alison, at least you were there," said Megan. "Maybe you have to cry for all of us."

Maybe that's what artists did; maybe they cried for everybody who couldn't. Certainly the rest of her family had fallen into a sort of dull sobriety. Her father up front, unable to move. Paul endlessly making sure that everyone had a ride. Jeff almost single-mindedly focused on his Chinese wife. And now, in the middle of this, there was Kyle.

"Don't you think you should talk to him?" Megan said. "It's nice that he came."

Was it nice that Kyle came? Alison wasn't so sure. But she really didn't need much of a push. She corralled her grief, and drifted through the mourners who were now drifting away. He looked up. He knew she was there.

"Hey, Kyle."

"Hey," he said. His greeting was husky, heartfelt and simple, and tragically, you could see he was better looking than ever, once you were within five or six feet of him. His hair had gotten darker, which made those gray eyes even more startling.

"I'm sorry," he said. She knew he was talking about her mother, but for a moment she allowed the sentiment to float over her. *Sorry we never got it together, sorry I let you go so easily, sorry sorry.*

"Yeah, it's kind of a big shock," she said. "She wasn't even sick, so nobody, you know. Nobody thought this could happen."

"I wish there was something I could have done," he said. This was actually so aggravating it was better. Better to be on antagonistic footing. It made more sense, honestly, to just stick with the facts, and to express some of what she had been feeling for five days, while everyone mourned the fact that there was "nothing to be done."

"I wish that too. When I called you I was really in the soup. Those stupid hospitals, they act like everybody's just going to die anyway, so what's the point. I could have used some help, because she didn't, actually. She didn't have to die. She didn't." Okay, crying had not been in her plan, but what are you going to do. Her mother was dead.

"It was her time."

Did he actually say that? "It *wasn't* her time," she informed him. "It, there were a lot of things that were—that's why I *called* you, because I couldn't get anyone at the hospital to help me. I tried, but I, and no one would help me." Her face was a mess now, she knew it. She had really been careful with her makeup, too; she wanted to look beautiful for Mom, so she had also gone out and bought the chicest black dress she could find in Cincinnati. And now her makeup was running all over and as far as she could tell, there was snot dripping down her face, and of course not a Kleenex in sight. Her utter failure to be a good daughter to Rose hung over her like a curse.

Kyle fortunately had a handkerchief, which he handed over silently while she sobbed. She blew her nose like a ten-year-old, and tried to use the corners to blot the mascara carefully but without a mirror it was impossible to tell if this operation was even remotely successful.

The funeral party was nearly gone and all that was left was a bewildered little wave of people in black trudging to their cars. Kyle glanced behind her, taking note of the retreating mourners. She considered handing his handkerchief back to him, but that would surely be the end of the whole conversation and she didn't want to let him go yet. There he was, right in front of her. He was still there. She wanted to tell him everything that had happened, the strangeness of her journey, the years of floating in the demimonde, the hurtling upward to a place where she was no one, and what it felt like to be no one, to be a no one who everyone could see, the collapse of the dreams that she had never dreamed for herself, the recognition that she had betrayed herself more than anyone, the hunger to be whole and at peace. She wanted to take his hand and go to his car with him, drive back to Mom and Dad's, sit around the family room with Andrew and Megan and Jeff and even Lianne, snuggle under his shoulder, feel the earth firm under her feet.

"But by the time you called, she was gone," Kyle said.

It was so incongruous and strange it took her a moment; she didn't know what he was talking about. He continued, an urgency growing in his explanation. "I called you back as soon as I got your call. Well, a couple hours, it did take me a few hours." She could see that those few hours smote him—he had probably needed those few hours to get up the nerve to call her, and he felt bad about it. But what he was saying other than that didn't make sense. "I should have called back immediately, I'm sorry about that," he said, "but Van didn't tell me there was any urgency. And your mother was already gone, wasn't she? She must have been gone, even, when you called."

"I called—I called—" Alison started. The words were on her lips *I called five days ago. I actually did call when you could have done something. I told your wife. You never called back. My mother was dying, and your wife didn't give you the message.*

The puzzlement in his face stopped her. And then something else, a breath of understanding, as he figured it out for himself. He flushed. And she rushed in to save him.

"I'm just upset," she said. "I didn't mean anything. I know you did what you could."

"When did you call?"

"It doesn't matter."

He was struggling, she could see, to put that genie back in the bottle. "I'm just upset, Kyle, seriously. Sorry. I didn't mean anything. I really didn't."

He nodded, looked away. After a moment, there was nothing else to do but plunge ahead. "You think they made mistakes, at the hospital?" he asked.

"I really don't want to talk about it, Kyle. It won't bring her back."

"I would hate to think that." He sounded so lonely; he always had. It was so easy for him to fall into himself; she'd always had to work so hard to get him to stay in the world. He hid in his head, and it wasn't good for him, he was always so much happier when she would coax him out of there. *He still has a beautiful soul*, she thought, *there's so much light in him.* She wondered if the two of them would have been less lonely together.

"I heard you had another baby! Congratulations."

"Yes, a boy," he said. "Gabe."

"Gabe. That's a great name," she said. A flush of pride passed over his face. It was charming, a whisper of youth and vulnerability. She remembered the moment she first saw him, in a parking lot of some dumb football game.

"I heard you were in a big movie, some Hollywood blockbuster," he offered.

"Oh, the movie kind of fizzled. I mean, I did it, it was cool, it was kind of a nightmare—but parts of it were cool," she admitted.

"Are you going to do any more Chekhov? Maybe Shakespeare?" He smiled at her, remembering their last fight. She remembered the hours she spent practicing scenes for high school plays, lying in his arms, memorizing the lines. Beatrice in *Much Ado.* Helena in *Midsummer*, those were her parts, the feisty funny ones. Her resolve started to flag. *Don't fall in love with the past*, she thought. *You don't live there. Now is when you live.*

"I don't know."

"You're a brilliant actress."

Being brilliant doesn't matter, she thought. What she said was, "How's the baby business?"

"Fine, fine," he said.

"You'll start that clinic someday," she said. "Maybe when your kids are bigger."

"Maybe."

Another silence. Perhaps they were finished, finally. She looked down, took a breath, thinking about saying good-bye.

"Are you happy?" Kyle asked. He seemed to really want to know the answer to that one. He seemed to hope that she was.

"Well," she said. And then, "My mother just died."

"She's with God now," he told her, as a comfort.

"Yeah, that's what the priest said, at the funeral."

"Do you not—believe that?"

"It's what she believed, so I guess I will believe it for her," Alison replied, careful.

"I will too."

"Thanks." She smiled at him for a moment. "You know what, Kyle?" she said. "I'm glad about you."

He blinked. Appeared before her. Not so lost that she couldn't still find him in there.

"I'm glad about you too," he said.

"I'll see you, okay?" she added, although she knew that she would not. She reached up and kissed him on the cheek, and felt grateful that he still felt like himself. As he turned and walked away from her, she dreamed for him a journey to South America, mountain villages, people in need. She dreamed of the lives he would save, and the gratitude of a simpler tribe who might call forth his best self. She dreamed children who would jump up and down with glee upon his return from his adventures, and a son who would grow into a partner for him, someone he could teach to be a good man, and in so doing become the better man he had always dreamed of being.

She dreamed for herself a play in a small theater, something dark and original, which would call upon her forgotten talents and demand that she make them real. She dreamed a Shakespearean stage, plain and promising, a heroine of wit and courage, someone who demanded height.

Rosalind, she thought. *I wonder if Ryan knows anybody who would see me for Rosalind.* She dreamed of constructing entire worlds out of thin air, planets where girls were allowed to eat, and men weren't driven by power.

When she looked up, Kyle was gone. There were a few workmen hovering nearby waiting for her to finish her prayers, or her farewells. They were already bored with how long this was taking. She really needed to go. There would be a giant feast back at Mom and Dad's, lots of food with mayonnaise in it, brothers and sisters who were worn down and punchy in their grief, others too, good-natured neighbors and relatives who would express their sorrow and then try to pump her for stories about show business. She would be nice to them all, and diplomatic; she wouldn't tell the whole story, which no one would believe anyway. And then she would sneak off into one of the back bedrooms, call Ryan and let him know that in a few days she would be back, available for auditions by the end of next week. Maybe she'd call Seth and make him have a drink with her; they could drive out to Montauk and howl at the moon. Make out in his backseat. Life had to be more fun than being a movie star made it out to be.

How old am I? she wondered. For a moment, she couldn't quite remember. The last time she'd talked to Ryan, there was some discussion of shaving a few years off. You turn thirty, no one wants to know about it. What did it matter? Surely starting over was something that life would insist on, one time or another. She dug into her bag for the keys to her rental car. In spite of everything, the world was still new.

acknowledgments

For the support of my wonderful agent Loretta Barrett, I thank the stars. This novel could not have been written without her unfailing confidence in it and me. When she succumbed to cancer, Nick Mullendore, her second in command, stepped forward and his wisdom and coolheaded nerve have informed all aspects of this book. Thanks to him and also to Laura Van Wormer for reminding me not to give up five minutes before the miracle.

I have had singular luck with my editors, although that too was an odyssey. Shaye Arehardt quite literally called this book into being. When I came to Putnam, it was under the guidance of the great Amy Einhorn, then Liz Stein steered the ship. I thank them all. My fourth editor, Tara Singh Carlson, has been a startling reminder why we don't, in fact, give up five minutes before the miracle. It is because someone like Tara might actually just show up.

The edgy intelligence of Theodore Blumberg, lawyer and literary adviser, stands, as always, behind me. Marisa Smith likewise stands behind me in so many ways I can't even figure them all out. John Weidman consistently refuses to let me throw my brain out the window. Eric Holmes lived through so much of the murky background of this book, his DNA is everywhere in it. It is a privilege to know them all, and I cannot live without any of them.

I thank Louise Krakower for her insights into the Navajo language. I thank my parents for raising me well. I thank my many siblings for their idiosyncrasies and their tribal wit. I thank my husband, Jess Lynn, my son, Cooper Lynn, and my daughter, Cleo Lynn, for being my family. Living with a writer is a peculiar task. They never fail at it.

In 2011, Theresa Rebeck was named one of the 150 Fearless Women in the World by *Newsweek*. She has had more than a dozen plays produced in New York, including *Omnium Gatherum* (co-writer), for which she was a Pulitzer Prize finalist, and the *New York Times* has referred to Rebeck as "one of her generation's major talents." She was the creator of the NBC drama *Smash* and has a long history of producing and writing for major television and film successes. She is the author of *Three Girls and Their Brother* and *Twelve Rooms with a View*. She has taught at Brandeis and Columbia and lives in Brooklyn with her family.